Magical Mayhem

Carol R. Ward

Brazen Snake Books
Billings Montana

Magical Mayhem

*This book is dedicated to Jennie Madeline Sleep
who wasn't able to stick around to see how it ends.*

Prologue

Howard Ruskin stared at the object resting dead center on his work table. It looked like an adder stone, or hag stone, one of those stones with a natural hole in it. They were supposed to have magical properties and when he was a teenager, he spent days scouring the rocky beaches for one.

He'd awoken to the sound of a thunderclap and the vision of this very object hovering over his bed. As he sat up and his eyes focused, it floated slowly out of the room. He'd followed it, and only when it settled gently on his work table did he realize he wasn't dreaming.

"Howard..." a disembodied voice said. "Activate your scrying bowl."

A few months ago, Howard would have been horrified at objects floating around his apartment and disembodied voices talking to him. In fact, he would have thought seriously about getting some psychiatric help.

But that was before he'd learned that real magic was possible. Before he learned how to use it himself. Before he'd accidentally sent his best friend, Jessica, into a magical realm in another dimension. Before he'd begun talking with wizards from this other realm by way of the scrying bowl.

With a yawn he went over to the book case and pulled down a

heavy ceramic bowl, glazed in black. Using his sleeve, he wiped the dust out of it - it had been a while since the bowl had seen any use. His friend Jessica preferred using a mirror to communicate, while Paranithel, the wizard teaching him magic, was in the midst of administering the Trials - the final examinations for the senior students at his school of wizardry.

He pulled a plastic jug of oil off a different shelf and poured it into the bowl. Fingering the moonstone pendant hanging around his neck, he waited for the oil to settle. Originally the pendant had been in two parts – he had one part and Jessica the other. They'd used them to communicate, but her half had been lost somewhere in the magical realm.

Jessica, it turned out, was not a native of earth, but of the magical realm. She'd been sent to earth as a baby for her own safety and had grown up not knowing she was adopted nor of her magical heritage. When Howard used Jessica in a teleportation experiment to prove magic was real, her father and grandfather cast a spell at the same time to bring her back to her own universe.

The combination of spells worked a little too well and she overshot the wizards' mark. Instead of landing in the southern lands close to Thackery and Paran's magic school, she ended up in the Kingdom of Ghren where she met up with the dastardly Prince Ewan.

She escaped his clutches with the help of the bard Sebastian, and was making her way southward when she accidentally turned a thief into a dog and had to figure out how to change him back. It turned out that Dominic, the thief, was an old friend of Sebastian's, but before they could continue their journey, Jessica was kidnapped and ended up back in Ghren.

Dominic also turned out to be Ewan's older brother, who had, thanks to Ewan, disappeared many years before. With the help of some ghosts from the past, Jessica was able to stop Ewan once and for all, and since Dominic didn't want the job, a new king of Ghren was installed.

The last Howard had seen of them, Jessica and Dominic had been getting quite cozy. As for Jessica's father and grandfather... now that Howard was no longer needed to act as a go-between with Jessica he rarely saw her father, Thackery. But Paranithel, her grandfather, kept the promise he'd made to teach Howard the rudiments of magic that would make the most of what little power he had access to.

The oil in the bowl churned and then cleared to show the face of a beautiful woman with brilliant blue eyes, silver hair, and slender, pointed ears.

"Aracelia!" Howard said in surprise, then added, "Ma'am."

The Lady Aracelia was Jessica's fairy grandmother, or to be more precise, her elven grandmother.

"Howard, you are looking well, my friend."

"Uh, thank you. You're looking well too. How may I help you?" he asked.

"Paran has told me what a promising student of magic you are, but he finds your world's lack of magic most frustrating."

"As do I," Howard admitted. Truthfully, he found it far more than just frustrating.

"I have sent you a talisman imbued with elven magic that should aid you in your lessons. It should last for several months, at which point you have only to contact me and I will re-energize it for you."

"I don't know what to say," Howard said, a little surprised.

From what he'd learned, the elves guarded their magics closely. "Your generosity humbles me."

She smiled gently. "You have been a good friend to my granddaughter and I feel somewhat responsible for the loss of your connection to her. Have you heard aught from my granddaughter lately?"

"Sorry to say, I think Jessica and Dominic are still in the honeymoon phase of their relationship," Howard said with a sigh. "I don't think I'll be holding my breath while I wait."

"Honeymoon phase?" Aracelia asked with amusement.

Howard searched for the proper words to explain. "It's that period of time in any new relationship when two people are pretty much so wrapped up in each other they're oblivious to anything else."

Aracelia laughed, the sound like bells. "A most interesting expression to be sure. Yes, I can see that it does indeed apply to my granddaughter. Holding your breath while you wait would be most unwise indeed."

"Have you thought of making contact with her yourself?"

The elf shook her head. "I promised Thackery I would not. Not until she has been told of her parentage."

"He doesn't trust you to keep his secret."

"No, he does not. And he is probably right in doing so. I do not believe it is wise to keep the truth from her."

"I don't believe it either," Howard agreed. "He doesn't know Jess like I do. She's not going to be happy at all when she finds out what's going on. And she's going to like it even less when she finds out everyone around her knew the truth and never told her."

"And someone with her power..." Aracelia's voice trailed off and she shook her head. "But I gave my word and I cannot go back on it."

Howard hesitated a moment then blurted out the question that had been on his mind lately, "This enemy of Thackery's ... this whole secrecy thing is because Thackery is afraid of Anakaron finding out about Jessica before she's able to defend herself. Do you think this is something we need to worry about?"

Anakaron was the powerful blood mage who'd killed Jessica's mother, and the reason she had been sent to the earthly realm to be raised.

"Yes," Aracelia agreed without hesitation. "It is my hope that Dominic will find a way to broach the subject with her."

"Good luck to him," Howard muttered. "Just how much danger is Jessica in?"

Aracelia sighed unhappily. "In truth, I do not know. She has Dominic and the bard with her, and as long as she keeps her magic under control– "

"Which she won't see the need for unless she's warned of the danger she's in," Howard pointed out.

"Indeed. When our seers look to the future it is clouded, like a storm is brewing. There is a feeling of great unease amongst the magical beings of this land."

"That doesn't mean it's Anakaron though, does it? Couldn't it just as easily be something else?"

Aracelia shook her head. "I do not even wish to imagine something worse than Anakaron loose upon the land once more. Even the fall of Mythago did not provoke such unease."

"And Anakaron was responsible for that, wasn't he?"

The elf nodded. "After the fall of Mythago, Anakaron

disappeared. Some believed he had burned his power out or even died, others that he fled to the waste lands of the icy north to lick his wounds."

"What do you believe?"

"I believe he cloaked himself in what magic he had remaining and sank into a restorative sleep. I also believe he has awakened, but he must gather power before aught else."

"Well that doesn't sound good, gather his power how?"

She looked at him soberly. "As a blood mage he draws his magic from the sacrifice of living creatures – their life essence fuels him."

Howard couldn't suppress a shudder at that. "Jessica might have been better off if she'd stayed in the Elven Realm and let her father come to her."

Aracelia frowned, an expression that looked out of place on her face. "Perhaps, perhaps not. Our borders are being tested, to be sure, and we know not by what or whom."

"I wish there was something I could do to help," Howard said sincerely.

She smiled at him. "Were you on our world your help would be greatly appreciated. Paranithel believes you will make a skilled sorcerer."

He smiled wistfully. "Instead I'm stuck here where magic is almost non-existent."

"I believe you are safer where you are. But perhaps someday Jessica will bring you to visit."

"If she's still talking to me," he said with humorless laugh. "Once she finds out I was keeping secrets from her..."

"As you say, you will have to cross that bridge when you come to it. Indeed, we all will. In the meantime, you have my charm to aid you in your studies."

"I'll be sure to make very good use of your gift," Howard told her.

"I know you will," she said with a smile. "Good eve to you, friend Howard."

"Good eve to you," he said to her image as it disappeared.

With a sigh he waved his hand over the bowl to end the spell. You'd think attaining his lifelong dream of proving magic was real would make him happy, but it didn't. All the guilty feelings he harbored over being the one responsible for Jessica's current predicament came surging forward.

Taking the bowl to the kitchen he dumped the oil and cleaned the bowl thoroughly, and put the kettle on to make himself a cup of tea. While he waited for the kettle to boil he took the bowl back into his work room to replace it on the shelf and looked at the adder stone on the table. On the surface it seemed rather nondescript - a stone such as could be found on any of the rocky beaches bordering Georgian Bay.

As he stared at it, its surface rippled as a light wave appeared to pass over it. He didn't need to reach out and touch it to realize the extraordinary power it possessed. Shaking his head, he went back out into the kitchen to finish making his tea. The last of the chamomile went into his mug and he was reminded he'd no longer be able to just go downstairs and cadge some more from Jessica.

He missed her terribly. Taking his tea with him, he went back into the work room and sat on the stool, staring at the adder stone. It was mind boggling that something so small and innocuous looking could hold enough magical energy to fuel several months' worth of the spells he and Paran had been working on. A sudden thought occurred to him, making him sit up straight.

Enough magic for a series of small spells, or maybe enough for one very large spell . . .

Chapter One

Jessica savored the taste of the ale as she sipped from her wooden mug. She wasn't normally over-fond of beer or ale, but this brew, the house specialty of the Laughing Goat Inn, tasted particularly smooth. Of course, anything other than stale water from a water skin would probably taste just as good at this point.

With her long auburn hair, and dressed as she was, in what was normally considered men's clothing, she attracted more than just a passing glance. But any thought other than a glance died in the making at the sight of her two companions – the tall, dark-haired man with the look of a warrior about him and the wiry, but no less tall, man with his sandy-colored hair pulled back in a queue.

"What's wrong?" Dominic, the fiercer of her two companions, asked. Really, he was more than just a companion, but they hadn't really had enough time alone together to figure out just what their relationship status was yet.

"You realize," she mused, after another, larger, sip. "That this is the furthest south I've been since I got here? I mean, considering that's all I've been trying to do, go south that is."

"I believe Eglion is actually further south than the port of Grenin," Sebastian, the bard, pointed out, "However it also lies further to the west."

She shivered at the mention of the name. Eglion was the border town where she'd been taken by the witch guard as she lay recovering from backlash illness.

In the beginning she had been trying to get to the south to a pair of wizards powerful enough to send her home again. But now she was going there because she *needed* to meet them. It turned out one of those wizards was her father and the other her grandfather and they played no small part in her being here, but though her friends all knew, no one knew *she* knew. She really should come clean about it but the opportunity just never seemed to arise.

"And while we're on the subject," she said suddenly, derailing her own train of thought, "Why didn't you suggest taking the river the first time I headed south? It would have shaved weeks off the trip."

"Ah, but then we would have never met," Dominic said with a cheeky grin. "Just think of all the fun would you would have missed."

"Fun? Fun? You call getting lost in the woods, rescuing you from the dog fights, losing my moonstone, and being taken by the witch guard fun?"

"Well at least you weren't bored."

"Back to the matter at hand," Sebastian said quickly to forestall another of the arguments that were becoming a habit with these two. "What has you so pensive? I thought you couldn't wait to get onto dry land again."

"What? Oh." Jessica switched mental gears once more. "Nothing, really. It's just..."

"Just what?" Catching her mood, Dominic shifted his chair a

little closer.

Jessica sighed. "I just can't help thinking the other shoe is about to drop."

Both men looked at her a little blankly. She shook her head with a chuckle. "Sorry. What I mean is, every time I think things are looking up, something bad happens. Things have been going really well lately, so I can't help feeling we're due for... I don't know – something."

As if on cue there was a disturbance in the air above their table. A tiny winged creature appeared and dropped what looked like a short straw in front of Sebastian.

"What was that?" Jessica asked, wide eyed.

"It was a wind imp," Sebastian said absently, unrolling what turned out to be a message.

"If you're rich enough to afford the services of an elemental wizard you can have them send messages by imp," Dominic told her.

"It's from the Guildmaster in Camser. There's some trouble with my mother."

"Trouble, what kind of trouble? I thought your mother was a weaver?" Jessica said.

"She is, she is a master weaver. He does not say what kind of trouble, just that my presence is required. I must go to her at once."

"We'll come with you," Dominic said. "We– "

Sebastian shook his head as he rose to his feet. "I will travel swifter alone."

"But..." Jessica bit her lower lip, knowing when he talked about being able to travel swifter alone he meant she was the one who'd slow him down. "Why don't you at least take Dominic with you, just in case?"

"I thank you for your kind offer," Sebastian said, smiling down at her. "But I'm sure it's nothing."

"I mislike the timing of this," Dominic said. "Perhaps– "

"The fact that it is the Guildmaster, not my mother herself who has sent the message tells me that it is not as dire as he believes. But still, it is worrisome."

"And it *is* your mother," Jessica said. "We'll miss you. If you can, let us know what's going on."

"Do not think to be rid of me this easily," Sebastian assured them. "We can meet up again in..." he closed his eyes for a second to think. "Claverton."

"Claverton it is," Dominic agreed, nodding.

"How does he do that?" Jessica asked as Sebastian headed up the stairs to gather his things.

"Do what?"

"Keep track of all those towns and villages. It's like he's got a GPS in his head."

"A what?"

"GP– it's like a whole series of interconnected maps that let you instantly plot the quickest route to wherever you want to go."

Dominic shrugged. "It's a bard thing. I wouldn't let it worry you, he knows where he's going."

"I wasn't worried, just curious I guess." But nevertheless, Jessica resolved to keep her mouth shut the next time she had a feeling of impending doom.

Dominic sat brooding as Jessica said her goodbyes to

Sebastian. He understood the bard's need for haste and that having him and Jessica along would only slow him down. And with Jessica's talent for getting into trouble there was no question of her being left behind by herself. But he'd been counting on his friend's counsel and perhaps aid. He cared far more for Jessica than was wise, and that could be a problem.

He sighed, idly running an index finger through the spill of ale on the table.

"Well, he's off," Jessica announced, plopping down in her seat. "And he seemed pretty certain that he could travel faster without you along too, something about secret bard ways. Is this true?"

Dominic shrugged. "Probably. There are some things bards do not share with even the closest of friends. That they could have secret paths of their own would not surprise me in the least."

"Huh." Jessica sat back in her chair and took a sip of her ale. "Every time I just think I'm getting the hang of this...world...I learn something new."

He peered more closely at her. "I sometimes forget that you are not from this land, and that our purpose for travelling south is to send you home again." And that was another reason not to get too attached. Most of her time here was spent trying to get back to her own world. As much as she seemed to enjoy his company, would there be a place for him in her life once she achieved her goal?

"To be honest? Sometimes I forget too," she admitted.

Dominic felt a stab of guilt. Lies, secrets, and an uncertain future. That seemed to be all he had to offer her. Though he did not initiate the lies that hid her true heritage, continuing to keep it secret did not sit well with him. Further, though she knew he was a former prince there were other, less savory, things in his past which she knew nothing about. Royal blood or not, he was not a worthy mate for her.

At first it had not mattered, he was no longer the man he'd been, and the world she came from was so very different from this one. From what he could glean it was all but utopian in comparison. Certainly it was far more civilized. But the closer they became, the more he felt she deserved to know the truth.

He had said as much to Sebastian one night.

"So tell her," the bard advised.

"I would, but I fear to see the affection in her eyes turn to distaste."

"I think you do her a disservice, underestimating her so." Sebastian looked at him shrewdly. "It is not like you to worry over past deeds. Your feelings must run deep indeed."

"No! She– I– " He heaved a sigh. "I do not know how it happened, but she is like a piece of me I did not know was missing. How is this possible?"

Sebastian had merely smiled that damnable enigmatic smile of his and went back to tuning his lute.

"Were I in your place," Dominic told her now, "I doubt I would fare nearly as well."

"Oh, I don't know," she said, cocking her head as she looked at him. "You seem to be pretty adept at landing on your feet."

You don't know the half of it, he thought morosely. In an effort to lighten the mood, he asked, "How *do* you feel about being in this land now?"

"I don't really know," she said with a sigh. "A lot of the time it almost seems kind of fun, more dream than reality." She shot him a mischievous grin. "You know, like when I'm not running for my life or healing anyone from a life-threatening injury." Shaking her head, her expression sobered. "But other times I miss the conveniences of being home."

"Like what?" he asked, curious.

"I don't know, like phones with GPS, public transit, movie theatres, and pizza. I'd kill for a pizza." She looked at him and gave a laugh. "And you have no idea what I'm talking about." Reaching over, she patted his hand. "That's okay. I miss that stuff less and less all the time, and for all its conveniences, I wasn't really living when I was there, you know what I mean? I was just going through the motions."

Her hand lingered on his and his thoughts immediately went to the room they had paid for upstairs in the tavern, the room with the nice, soft bed. Since they'd first started this journey, private time together had been something of an issue and they made the most of what stolen moments they could find.

He should have been happy that Sebastian had been called away, now they would have nothing but time alone together. But until he found the courage to confess his sins, he needed to keep Jessica at a distance; for her own protection. Given the secrets between them, taking her upstairs was a bad idea, a really bad idea.

Suddenly, he had a much better one. Well, perhaps not better, but more practical.

"I've been thinking," Dominic said slowly. "We have not yet purchased our horses, and you seem to enjoy the speed of river travel, we could take a boat downriver to Turksin and from there go overland to Claverton."

"Get back on a boat?" Jessica asked.

He could see she was surprised by the suggestion as he warmed to the idea. "It will only take us a little out of the way, and the speed of our travel will more than make up for any time lost on our journey to Claverton."

"But– " Jessica looked at him searchingly but he would not meet her eyes. Giving a slight shrug, she said, "If that's what you want."

"It's said the horse market in Turksin is the best in the land," Dominic said. "And the route from here to Claverton would not take us near it."

"Well then," Jessica said after a moment of silence. "Here's to the horse market." She raised her flagon and drained it.

Dominic hadn't thought he could feel any worse, but he was wrong. He was deathly afraid he was making a muddle of things with Jessica. He'd come to know her well, and her cheerful acceptance was belied by the hurt in her eyes. The last thing he wanted was to hurt her, but she needed to hear the truth about his past.

Chapter Two

Far to the south, in the stone citadel-come-magic school, there were indications that all was not well in the realm of magic.

"Try again, Horace," Paranithel encouraged gently.

Dutifully Horace scooped up the stones and placed them back in the velvet bag. Paran was pleased to note the boy remembered the cleansing spell, to alleviate any negative energy, before he started again.

"Remember to focus on the question you wish answered."

"Maybe you should focus on whether or not you'll pass this class," one of the other boys snickered.

Paranithel rapped his cane sharply on the ground. "That will be quite enough of that!" His voice gentled as he gave Horace an encouraging nod. "Go ahead."

Face fierce with concentration, Horace slowly dipped his hand into the bag and stirred. He pulled five stones out at random and cast them onto the table in front of him. All five fell with the symbol marking them facing down towards the table.

There were murmurs from the boys and tears filled Horace's eyes. "I focused, I really did!"

"I'm sure you did, boy." Paranithel patted his shoulder. "These things happen when the stones have no answer to give. Garnet, why don't you have a try?"

A little nervously, Garnet approached the table. She took the bag of stones Horace offered her, smiling slightly in thanks. Taking a deep breath, she cast the cleansing spell and then focused on her question. Dipping into the bag, she pulled out five stones and cast them on the table. One again they all landed face down.

"Most curious," Paranithel murmured, looking over her shoulder. Rather than have Garnet try again he nodded to the next student. "Warner, you give a try."

Warner swaggered up to the table and took the bag from Garnet. "Let me show you how it's done," he boasted. He made an elaborate show of the cleansing spell, shaking the bag and casting the spell again for good measure. Finally he reached in and cast his stones. For all his theatrics, his also fell face down.

Paranithel had to bite back a chuckle at the boy's crestfallen face. Warner was one of those students who sometimes needed to be taken down a peg or two.

"Maybe the stones need to be re-energized," one of the students suggested.

"That's not how the stones work, as you should know by now," Paranithel said. "But it is plain we'll get no answers from them today. Class dismissed."

Murmuring amongst themselves, the students picked up their notebooks and filed out of the room. When the last student was gone, Paranithel reached into his pocket and pulled out the small box with his Tarot cards in it.

Lifting them from their silk wrapping, he did his own cleansing spell and began to shuffle. While the cards were capable of being more specific than the stones, he focused on the general future and what it held. Done shuffling, he laid the cards out in a spread.

For a long moment he stared at the cards in front of him. Too many reversals, too many swords, all leading to an uncertain future. With a sigh he gathered them up again. He needed to talk to Thackery. But before he did that, perhaps he would have a chat with Aracelia to see if the elves were experiencing the same problems.

Though he could scry anywhere in the castle, he preferred the relative isolation of the tower, even though it meant climbing all those damnable stairs. But there were strict rules in the school about using magic for one's own convenience. On the other hand, there was no one to witness it if he used a teleportation spell, just this once.

"Paran!" Aracelia said in pleased surprise. "This is indeed a pleasure."

"Would that it was pleasure I had to speak of." At one time that's all they did talk of, pleasurable things, but that was many years ago.

"What has happened?"

She knew him too well. He told her what passed during the morning's magic lesson and by the time he was finished there was a frown on her face.

"Most unusual."

"Indeed. I believe there is something in the offing, and I do not believe it bodes well for either human or elf."

"What have your cards told you?"

"They show only darkness, an uncertain future."

"What does Kiranthus have to say on the matter?"

"Thackery," he corrected automatically. "You know he changed his name many years ago."

"A foolish conceit," Aracelia muttered.

"You also know he has never put much stock in signs or portents."

"As ever, he is short-sighted," she said.

Paran leaned closer to the scrying bowl to study her. "There is something you're not telling me. What is it?"

She hesitated a fraction, then said quietly, "Elves have been disappearing."

He pulled back, shock etched on his face. "Disappearing? How is this possible?"

"I do not know. But we are no longer able to communicate with the Wild Woods Realm."

"The realm closest to the Shadow Mountains," Paran murmured. The Shadow Mountains, where it was believed Anakaron fled to after his defeat in Mythago. "You believe that Anakaron has something to do with it?" This was not good. This was not good at all.

"Who else would have the audacity to risk a war with the elves?"

"Or the power to do so."

"There have been rumors of other magical races ... it is not clear whether they have gone into hiding or simply vanished as well."

The more they talked, the larger the feeling of unease grew within him.

"How close will Jessica's route take her to the Wild Woods Realm?" He knew that though Aracelia had given Jessica a charm to prevent her from being spied upon through the art of scrying, she was still able to track her movements.

"It is possible she will not even know it is there. You know we do not go out of our way to invite company."

"But...?"

"But she also carries a safe-conduct with her should she wish to visit any of the elven realms. And Wild Woods would take her but a handful of days out of her way."

Paran blew out a sigh that rippled the oil he was looking down into. "Then let us hope she does not learn of it."

"Agreed."

After a slight hesitation, he added, "And perhaps, at least for now, it would be wise to keep this information to ourselves."

"You do not wish Thackery to know?"

"I– "

"You do not wish Thackery to know what?" a voice behind him interrupted.

Paran gave a guilty start and cursed under his breath, but as he turned from the scrying bowl he straightened up. "You scoff at my cards and stone casting, but this morning's foretelling class went amiss. And I am not the only one seeing the signs of impending darkness."

"You would be a fool indeed to dismiss so lightly what others have seen," Aracelia added, her voice slightly chiding.

For a moment Paran thought Thackery was going to argue with her, he'd been so temperamental lately, but then the wind seemed to go out of his sails.

"You're right," he admitted. "We have always suspected Anakaron was but laying low, gathering his power, but even I, sequestered here in the south, have sensed him stirring."

"And you said nothing?"

Thackery shrugged. "It was just a feeling, I wished to cause no alarm without proof. For aught I knew it was merely the pricking of my conscience that I am no longer able to aid my daughter."

The glance Paran and Aracelia shared was just a quick one, but Thackery caught it anyway.

"What is it? Is there news of Jesseminathus?"

"Jessica," Paran and Aracelia said at the same time.

He scowled and opened his mouth to speak, but Paran beat him to it.

"If you wish to keep up the ridiculous pretense of an assumed name, you must respect your daughter's wish to do the same. And in any case, Jessica is the name she grew up with."

Still scowling, Thackery agreed. "Fine. But what news of my daughter?"

"She and her companions have taken to travelling by boat, down the river Ells," Aracelia said smoothly.

"Good, they'll make better time that way. What else?"

Again, Paran and Aracelia exchanged a look. "What makes you think there is anything else? Isn't it enough that they're making progress in the right direction?"

"No, it isn't. You two are keeping something from me."

"There has been a marked drop in magic users of late," Aracelia told him. And then repeated what she'd told Paran about Wild Woods Realm and the lack of magical creatures.

"Many old friends are missing," Paran added reluctantly. "Some are laying low, but some are missing. I've told the others there is always room in the south for more magic workers."

"Missing, you say? I don't like this. I don't like it at all," Thackery said.

"Nor do I, but– "

"Enough of this waiting, I will make arrangements at once to go to Jessim– Jessica and bring her to safety.

"No!" both Paranithel and Aracelia said at the same time.

"It is too dangerous for her," Paran insisted.

"She is my daughter, I– "

"You sent her away for a reason, did you not?" Aracelia asked sharply.

"To keep Anakaron from learning of her presence," he admitted.

"Then do not hand her to him now. She wears the medallion of protection, it guards against others sensing her power. Your own power is not so protected."

"As risky as her current position is," Paranithel put in, striving to sound reasonable, "It would be far more risky were you to join her."

"Anakaron must not know the daughter of Farenalyssia lives," Aracelia added. "I shudder to think of the ways in which he would use her."

"Then what am I to do?" Thackery asked helplessly.

Paran opened his mouth to speak, but once again Aracelia beat him to it.

"I will keep a close eye on her," Aracelia assured him. "And should I see she is in need of assistance, I will take the Fae Road to come to her aid."

Thackery's brows rose in surprise and even Paran could not hold back a small gasp. "I did not realize the elves still used them so," he said. "Were they not outlawed as far too dangerous?"

"They mostly do not," she said. "But I am willing to make an exception when it comes to my granddaughter."

23

Chapter Three

Tears pricked in Jessica's eyes as she packed up her belongings in the room she'd arranged for them upstairs in the tavern but she blinked them back. Just when she thought she'd found Mr. Right, he turned into a...a...dog, figuratively speaking this time.

As much as she loved Sebastian like a brother, she'd been getting a little tired of him being their chaperone, no matter how unintentional. She'd thought Dominic had felt the same way, but obviously she was wrong.

When they landed here in Grenin the first thing she'd done was get them rooms at the tavern. Two rooms – one for her and Dominic and one for Sebastian. She couldn't wait to drag Dominic up here for a little afternoon delight. Sebastian going off on his own to see his mother was like a gift from heaven. But now Dominic couldn't wait to get back on a boat again where they'd have zero privacy.

Plunking down on the bed, she let out a sigh. Where had things gone wrong? He'd been so attentive when she had backlash sickness and he and Sebastian hadn't hesitated when it came to rescuing her from the witch guards. She'd even risked her own life to restore his hands when his brother Ewan chopped them off, for crying out loud.

Maybe that was it. Maybe he was uncomfortable with the amount of magical power she had. Well, he wasn't the only one. Being able to work magic scared the crap out of her and the sooner she had help figuring out how to control it, the better. You'd think Dominic, of all people, would have understood that. He had magical abilities of his own, although he had only just started learning how to use them when he'd been shanghaied by his brother.

Or maybe the problem was that he was a prince and she was just a commoner. Oh, sure, he *said* he didn't want to rule, but seriously, how cool would it be to be king? Was he only escorting her to the south out of duty? And she while she hadn't exactly killed his brother in cold blood, she had been partly responsible for his death.

Again the tears pricked, and this time one escaped to roll down her cheek. It was so unfair! Dominic was everything she'd ever imagined in a boyfriend – tall, dark, and handsome, and man was he buff! But it went beyond looks. She'd felt a spark the first time she laid eyes on him and she was sure he felt something too.

"Get a grip girl," she admonished herself, swiping at her face with her sleeve. "This isn't the first time you thought you were in love, and it probably won't be the last."

But that didn't make it hurt any less. At least with all her other break ups she and the guy were able to go their separate ways. This time they were going to be stuck together for who knows how long.

Although...was this really a break up? Were they even a real couple? They'd been thrown together by circumstance and apparently made the best of it. As much as she didn't like the idea, they were both young and healthy and maybe what she was mistaking for love was actually just convenience.

"Well sex is definitely off the table," she decided. "And there's no point becoming emotionally invested if he's just going to cut me loose at the end of the road."

The end of the road. That nebulous place where she was going to meet her father and grandfather. The question was, was it really the end of the road, the gateway back to her old life, or was it the beginning of a whole new life?

"I wonder what he'll think when he finds out that Thackery is my father?"

Thackery had been Dominic's mentor when he was growing up in Ghren and from what she understood the two had been very close.

"Maybe I should have told him about Thackery," she mused. Of course, then she'd have to explain about meeting the ghost of her dead mother, and why she hadn't told him before.

With a sigh she got to her feet and checked her reflection in the small hand mirror she used to scry with.

"Mirror, mirror in my hand, tell me, is my love-life damned?" There was no answer, but then she didn't really expect one.

More than anything, Dominic wished he could just enjoy his time with Jessica, however much of it they had left. But no, he had all these feelings churning around inside him now and he didn't like it. Not one bit.

While Jessica was at the tavern packing up her things in the room he'd been looking forward to sharing with her, he was on his way to the docks to secure passage on a boat to take them further south. It was still early enough in the day that with any luck he could find one ready to set sail sooner rather than later.

A kaleidoscope of pictures ran through his mind of the time they'd spent together. Jessica smiling, Jessica laughing, Jessica looking pale as death when she had backlash illness. She had the most compassion and the biggest heart of anyone he'd ever known, and luck! For certain she had been born under a lucky star to have survived in such a foreign land. Was it fate that brought them together, or more of that luck?

How had this happened to him? Did he fall in love with her after Ewan cut off his hands and she restored them? Or was it when she restored him to human form after turning him into a dog? Or maybe it was when he was in his dog form and she rescued him from the fighting ring, tending his wounds with such care.

He sighed deeply. Or maybe it started when he snuck into her camp that night, intending to steal her amulet and she turned him into a dog, and instead of abandoning him took him with her until she could change him back.

And the worst part of it all? Though they'd never spoken of it, he knew she returned his feelings. Or at least she was developing feelings for him. But though she knew some of his story, she didn't know it all, and it was the missing part that was bound to change her mind about him.

"Eh, mate. Step to the side or move along."

Dominic gave a start. Without realizing it he had paced his way along the edge of the waterfront to where goods were being off loaded to the market. He obligingly stepped to the side so the porters could go about their business.

Jessica would love this, was his first thought. Then he sighed again. Sebastian was right, he needed to tell her the entire truth, the sooner the better. Not just for her sake, but for his as well. The longer they were together, the deeper his feelings would grow, making it that much worse when she returned to her own world.

That she would happily leave him behind when they got to the end of their journey he had no doubt, but it was still the right thing to do. With that in mind, he turned his attention to the port and a boat to take them southwards.

At some point in its history, some enthusiastic port master had divided the docks into sections – fishing, merchant, travel. Dominic found what he sought in the merchant section. The low-lying barge was laden with cargo but for a nominal fee accepted passengers as well. It was not that Dominic was trying to save money, but there were no cabins for the passengers, they had to make do with what space was available on the deck. This would solve the problem of any expectations Jessica might have of him while on the water, and if he found the courage to tell her the truth before landfall, the rest would take care of itself.

Chapter Four

Ellen Chang, Jessica's former roommate, cursed under her breath as she took the stairs two at a time. It was just like her father to decide without warning to change from working with the *shinai*, the split bamboo practice sword, to the *bokken*, the solid white oak wooden sword, for her kendo lessons. While she should be pleased that he'd finally decided she was making progress, it was less pleasing that he thought she should be a mind reader and have brought her *bokken* with her. Normally she left her practice weapons at the dojo, but she'd brought the *bokken* home to give it a good oiling.

If only Jessica could see her now! Jessica knew Ellen had been studying the art of *kendo*, the way of the sword, but she'd had no chance to tell her that she'd progressed to *kenjutsu*, the art of the sword. Her brothers, three of whom were also studying with their father, had taken to calling her their little samurai, while her youngest brother, who'd made the mistake of challenging her to a match, called her a blood thirsty little ninja.

She missed Jessica terribly. They were more than just friends, they were sisters of the heart, as corny as that sounded. Even after all this time she still hated coming home to an empty apartment.

Jiggling the recalcitrant lock, she got the door open and

grabbed for the envelope that had been wedged between the edge of the door and the frame. Taking it with her, she made a beeline for her room. Taking the *bokken* from its stand on her dresser, she slipped it into its carry case and slung it over her shoulder. As she started back out, she looked at the envelope she was still holding and stopped with a frown.

It was a heavy, buff colored paper and all it bore on it was her name. Still frowning, she slit it open with a long fingernail and read the note that was inside. She read the note a second time.

"What the hell?"

It was a note from Howard, giving her his power of attorney over the building they lived in. He said he'd be going away for a while and didn't know when he'd be back. She really didn't have time for this, but it sounded like he was going to go do something stupid – as stupid as when he accidentally sent Jessica into the magical realm.

She stood indecisively in the doorway for a minute, and then decided her father could wait, this was more important. It was just a few stairs upwards to Howard's apartment. Not bothering to knock, she tried the door knob and it turned easily in her hand.

There was no sign of him in the main room of his apartment. As she glanced quickly around her stomach sank – it was unnaturally neat and tidy. What was he up to?

Cocking her head, she thought she heard noises coming from his work room. Thank God, he was still here. Crossing the room, she pushed the door to the work room open and winced at the light emanating from the object Howard was holding in his hand.

Ellen had the hand holding the letter extended towards him

but before she could say anything Howard caught sight of her. His eyes widened in horror and she faintly caught the sound of him saying, "Ellen, no!" before whatever it was he was holding seemed to explode into a million shards of light.

After a secondary, brilliant flash, everything went black.

Howard woke with a groan. It took a few seconds for his memory to catch up and when it did he sat up too quickly.

"Ow, ow, ow!" He held his head as it threatened to explode with pain. "Jesus! Why didn't anyone warn me about side effects?"

The pain receded slightly and the spots that had been dancing in front of his eyes lessened. It was at that point he realized he wasn't alone. He was surrounded by a ring of heavily armed elves, all dressed in some kind of dark grey uniform, all with drawn swords pointed at him.

"On your feet, human," the one with extra decorations on his tunic ordered.

"Okay, okay. Just give me a minute to catch my breath." The pain in his head seemed to recede a bit as he took several deep breaths.

This was not how he pictured arriving in the magical realm, although he was grateful that it appeared to be where his transferal spell had landed him. A quick glance around showed that he landed in someone's formal garden. In fact, he was fortunate that he landed on the path and not in one of the flower beds with their ornate statuary or worse, in the fountain.

The soldiers, he couldn't think of them as anything else, showed signs of impatience so with a supreme effort he got to his feet. Another quick glance around had him expelling a quiet sigh of relief. There was no sign of Ellen, thank God she hadn't been close enough to get caught up in his spell - he'd have never heard the end of it. Of course, he was also going to be in for it from her for leaving her behind, but he'd cross that bridge when he returned. If he was able to return.

"I don't suppose one of you kind gentlemen could tell me exactly where I am?" he asked, a puzzled frown on his face. While he hadn't expected to land at Jessica's feet, he had hoped to be in her general vicinity. When he last spoke with her, she and Dominic had been well off of Ghren lands, taking a boat on a river or something. This looked to be a town or city of some kind.

"Silence. You will come with us."

As much as Howard would have liked to protest, he had a feeling it wouldn't do him any good. The pain in his head receded to bad hangover strength and he was feeling slightly dizzy, so at first he focused entirely on staying on his feet. Gradually the dizziness passed and he began to look at the passing scenery with interest.

The path through the garden was made from something like flagstone, only this was no dull grey slate but a white, marble like stone. On either side of the path were flowering shrubs and exotic blossoms, slender trees that bore unfamiliar fruit. They came to a finely wrought gate that appeared to be carved from the same stone as the shimmering white walls surrounding the garden.

There were two elves guarding the gate who stared at them impassively as the company passed through. With an ominous clang the gate shut behind them. Howard couldn't help gawking a bit as they walked. This had to be an elven city, or at the very least a town, something he'd always dreamed of but never imagined could be real.

The street was a smooth cobblestone, not quite as fine as the path through the garden, but still not ordinary stone. The buildings looked like they'd be right at home along the shores of the Mediterranean - no more than two or three stories, made of white stone with low walled gardens separating them from the road. He caught glimpses of carvings and embellishments on the walls and wished he could stop to examine them more closely.

There was a profusion of flowers everywhere, clinging to the walls and climbing up the staircases that led to upper stories. Though he couldn't see them, Howard could hear a medley of bird song, hauntingly beautiful sounds. The sun was shining high overhead, from which he deduced it was close to noon, but there were no other people – elves – around.

The reflection of the sunlight on all that white was making his headache worse. Howard stumbled along with his guards, only vaguely aware of numerous twists and turns in their path. After what seemed like forever, they halted in front of a squat, unadorned building and he was led inside.

The elven equivalent of a jail, he deduced. It reminded him of the jails from old western movies. The room was large and scrupulously clean, the walls and floor made of the same stone as the other buildings he'd seen. There was a desk made of pale wood, polished to a shine, to one side of the door with a mirror hanging on the wall behind it. A row of carved wooden chairs of the same wood as the desk were lined up along the opposite wall, and the back had been divided into two cells with sturdy looking bars.

"In here," he was told, the elf in charge indicating the cell closest to them.

"Hang on a minute. I've been nothing but co-operative, so I'd like– "

"In here," the elf repeated, hand on the hilt of his sword.

Howard huffed out a breath but did as he was told. The elf locked the cell door behind him. "Someone will be in to question you shortly."

The cell was actually very genteel when compared to an old west hoosegow. There was a cot along the outside wall, neatly made up. A washstand was placed against the wall between the bed and the bars dividing the two cells, with a pitcher and wash basin on it and a folded towel beside them. On a whim he checked under the cot. Sure enough, there was a covered chamber pot. The elves may be low tech, but they were nothing if not civilized.

He sat down on the narrow cot and sighed. This was *definitely* not the way he'd anticipated making an entrance into the magical realm. But as bad as things looked, he couldn't help the grin that spread over his face. He'd done it; he'd actually teleported himself to the magical realm. Now all he had to do was find Jessica.

One of the elves who'd accompanied him took a seat at the desk and pretty much ignored him. Poor guy probably drew the short straw and was stuck on guard duty, Howard thought. Though he tried not to stare, he couldn't seem to help himself. The elf was beautiful, and Howard's head filled with all kinds of delicious thoughts.

Time passed slowly. Other than the elf, there wasn't much to look at. The only windows were on either side of the door, too far away to really see anything through. After what seemed like hours, another elf entered the jail bearing a large, cloth covered tray.

Howard sat up straight on the cot where he'd been slouching, his heart working double time. Were they going to torture him for information he didn't possess? They'd certainly never believe the truth.

The elf whisked the cloth away and he relaxed again. It was nothing more ominous than lunch. One plate was left on the desk for his guard, the other was slid through a gap in the bottom of the door to his cell. This elf was even cuter than the one sitting at the desk.

Smiling his most charming smile, Howard said, "Thank you, that's very kind of you. It looks delicious."

The elf looked somewhat surprised, but smiled faintly in return. He looked like he was about to say something, but after shooting a glance at the guard, who was scowling, he hastened to leave.

None of the food was familiar looking, but the smell of it made Howard's mouth water. He hadn't realized until that moment how hungry he was, and no wonder. How many times had he scolded Jessica for not refueling after working with magic?

The food tasted even better than it looked, and he was a little surprised to find the small, corked bottle that accompanied it contained one of the smoothest tasting wines to ever hit his pallet. If this was how prisoners were treated, how much better would it be once he had the chance to prove to them he was a friend?

After lunch there was another rather long wait, but finally the door to the jail opened and an older elf entered. The one behind the desk was startled out of a doze and stood at attention. "Nothing to report," he said crisply.

"It would be more surprising if there was," the other replied dryly.

Howard got slowly to his feet as the elf eyed him up and down. "I think there's been some– "

"It would be best if you refrained from speaking unless it is to answer my questions," the elf told him.

Reminding himself that he was pretty much at their mercy, Howard didn't argue.

"How were you able to open a portal in the formal garden of the council?"

"Is that where I was? I do apologize, I– "

"For what purpose did you breech the wards of the barrier to this enclave?"

"I didn't exactly mean to breech any wards, my spell sort of went awry and– "

"We require that you produce the spell that enabled you to do so."

"Well here's the thing," Howard said, a little sheepishly. "I kind of combined a couple of different spells."

The elf eyed him dispassionately.

"You will be given writing materials to reproduce these spells. Once we have determined their intent, we will have further speech."

The elf turned to leave.

"Fine," Howard said. "But I'd appreciate it if you could get word to an elf by the name of Aracelia and let her know I'm here."

The elf gave no indication that he recognized the name, just closed the door behind him.

Chapter Five

Jessica leaned on the ship's railing, the breeze pushing the hair off of her face. She wasn't sure if she liked being on one of these over-crowded boats that sat so low in the water, but she had to admit it was a much quicker way to travel.

Shifting her position slightly, she turned her head and looked towards the group of men gathered around a large barrel. They were playing some kind of dicing game and of course Dominic was right in the thick of things. As though he could feel her eyes upon him, he looked up, eyes seeking hers. He grinned and she couldn't help but smile back – he really was almost too good to be true.

She wasn't one to believe in love at first sight but from the moment she'd seen him dozing in the chair beside her sick bed, she'd felt a connection to him. There was just something about him that drew her like a moth to a flame. And she was so sure he'd felt the same way.

In some ways nothing had changed, he was still affectionate and attentive and made no bones about them being a couple. But at the same time he was holding back, as if there was an invisible line he was afraid of crossing. Before Sebastian had left she could envision a future with Dominic. Now she was just ... confused.

There was a sudden cheer from some of the men, groans from others, and the group broke up to drift away to other things. Dominic made his way over to stand beside her at the rail.

"So, how'd you do?"

"Do you have to ask?" he said with a grin, holding up a small pouch. "Now what were you thinking about so hard over here? I swear I could all but see your thoughts scurrying about."

Jessica sighed and stepped a little closer so she could lean up against his warmth. Dominic obligingly put his arm around her waist, pulling her a little closer.

"I was thinking that other than a lack of cabin space, this isn't a bad way to travel. At least we don't have to saddle and unsaddle a boat."

Dominic was silent for so long that she turned her head to look at him. There was a distant expression on his face.

"What's wrong?"

He gave himself a bit of a shake and then led her over to the corner they'd staked out as theirs. The boat was more of a barge, designed to carry goods downriver. It wasn't really intended for passengers, which meant there were no cabins for sleeping.

"Dominic?" Jessica felt a little shiver of nervousness. He just looked so...grim.

"I have a tale to tell," he said, sitting down beside her but not touching her. In fact, he couldn't even seem to bring himself to look at her.

Jessica couldn't help the shiver of apprehensive that travelled up her spine. Of course he noticed, because he was considerate like that. The big jerk.

"Are you cold?" He pulled a blanket out of his pack and

wrapped it around her shoulders. "Tis only a few more days to Turksin and then I promise you a hot dinner and a soft bed."

That made her feel slightly better. He wouldn't be promising her things in the future if he was planning on dumping her and her problems once they reached the dock. But if he didn't spit out what his problem was she wasn't going to be held responsible for her actions.

"Tell me what's wrong," she said bluntly. "You've been pretty serious ever since we left Grenin."

He turned his head so he was looking out over the water instead of at her. "We have learned much of each other over these last weeks but there is something I have not shared and it weighs heavy on my mind."

Jessica started worrying all over again. "What is it?" She slipped her hand into his when he continued to hesitate. "Whatever it is, I'm sure we can handle it." Unless it was something like a wife in another port he'd failed to mention, or some other kind of commitment.

"It is about the time between when I left Ghren and when I returned."

"Oh." She blinked in confusion. "I thought Ewan arranged for your disappearance?"

"He did. He paid two former guards to do the deed. They'd been caught asleep at their post and were dismissed without receiving what was owed them, so they had no love for Raynor, or his heir, despite the fact I had no power of my own."

His voice was curiously devoid of inflection and that alone told Jessica how serious the situation was.

"At any rate, Ewan drugged me and paid them to take me to the port of Wickerton. There they were to kill me and make it look as though I'd been set upon by ruffians."

"That's pretty harsh," Jessica said, in spite of herself. She knew first-hand what Ewan was capable of. After all, he'd murdered his own father and then tried to put the blame on her. "What happened," she asked. "Obviously they didn't go through with it."

"No, they were too superstitious to murder me, but what they did might be worse. They sold me into slavery."

"Oh, Dominic." She wanted to put her arms around him but his body language warned her off.

"Because we were at a seaport, it was easy for them to sell me as a galley slave. Most of the ships who use galley slaves aren't picky about where the bodies come from, just so long as they can hold an oar."

"And you were young and strong – perfect for them I bet."

He gave her a faint smile. "Sad to say I wasn't the only noble on that ship, not that we received any special consideration except maybe an extra lash or two when the rowing master was doling them out."

Jessica's heart went out to the young man he had been. "I can't imagine how you were able to survive."

"Many was the time I thought I would not," he said sadly. "We'd pull at the oars 'til our muscles screamed, and then we'd pull until we dropped from exhaustion. We were fed the cheapest and most foul of food – gruel that was watered down, rotting vegetables, we learned quickly not to eat any meat we were given because it was tainted. There was no mercy for anyone taken ill, you'd be forced to row in your own filth until you either recovered enough to clean up your own mess, or you died."

Jessica had tears in her eyes. Things like this only happened in the movies, not in real life. "How long before you escaped? And how did you escape?"

He shrugged. "I have no way of knowing. We were somewhere on the Mythric Ocean when we were set upon by pirates."

"Pirates? You met real pirates?" she asked, unable to help herself. She'd always had a thing for pirates – she had the whole set of the Pirates of the Caribbean movies on DVD and drove Ellen crazy, watching them so often.

A hint of a smile crooked at the corner at his mouth at her enthusiasm. "I was one of the lucky ones. Those too weak to be of any use had their throats slit and were tossed overboard. The rest of us were conscripted into service."

"Holy Saint Christopher!" Her romantic vision popped like a soap bubble.

"I swabbed the decks and climbed the rigging with the best of them. And when they stuck a sword in my hand, I killed innocent seafarers right alongside them."

Jessica was silent for a moment as she digested his words.

"So if you'd rather not be associated with the likes of someone like me– "

"Wait. What? Where is this coming from?"

"Did you not hear a word I've said? I've been a slave and a pirate. This does things to a man. When we met I was little more than a thief."

"You did what you had to, to survive," she protested. "If it bothers you so much, why didn't you say something sooner?"

He hung his head and if she didn't know better she'd think he was ashamed. "Because I never thought I'd come to love for you as much as I have, and you deserved to know the truth. No respectable woman– "

"Hold on a minute. You love me?"

"Of course I do," he said, a little irritably.

She smiled broadly. "That's good. Because I love you too."

He stared at her in disbelief. "Did you not hear a word I've said?"

"You've been through some terrible ordeals," she said. "But it's made you into the man you are today and it's a man I've come to love."

"I was a *slave*," he said, emphasizing the word. "There is nothing lower than being a slave."

"You were a victim of circumstance," Jessica said firmly.

"What about my being a murdering pirate?"

"Stockholm syndrome," she said smugly.

"What?"

"It's where the victim of a kidnapping begins to identify with their kidnapper. It's a form of survival instinct."

He shook his head as though to clear it. "You're saying my past does not bother you?"

"Not a bit. Is this why you've been acting like you have a bee up your butt for the last few weeks?"

Dominic grabbed her and pulled her in for a hard kiss.

"What was that for?" Jessica asked breathlessly when he released her.

"I don't deserve you," he said gruffly.

"Probably not," she agreed. "But I definitely deserve you. Now kiss me again."

He was only too happy to comply.

Chapter Six

Ellen could feel the sun's warmth beating down on her, which was very strange because she couldn't remember going outside. But she must have at some point; she could hear birds chirping and the rustling of leaves somewhere above her. Taking a deep breath, the scent of woods and growing things filled her. She really needed to open her eyes to check things out, but there was a big part of her that was afraid she knew what had happened and she didn't want confirmation.

"Please let Howard have blown the roof off the house," she muttered, then screwed up her courage to open her eyes and sit up. "Holy freaking crap!"

She appeared to be lying in a small glade surrounded by tall, leafy trees. The scent of flowers wafted up to her and she realized the glade was carpeted in an abundance of wildflowers, none of which were familiar to her. Climbing to her feet she turned in a circle but all there was to see were trees, the flowers, and a few bushes. There was no road, no path, no indication of civilization.

"I don't freaking believe this!"

What had Howard done this time? There was no question in her mind that he was the one responsible for this. And where was he, anyway?

"Howard?" she called out. "Where are you?"

She took a few steps towards where the trees seemed slightly less dense. "Are you hurt Howard? Or just hiding from me?"

Rustling sounds came from behind her and she whirled, wishing she was armed with something more than just a *bokken*. She didn't see anything but to be on the safe side she slid the weapons bag from her shoulder and pulled the *bokken* free. Even a wooden sword could cause some serious damage if used correctly. At least that's what her father always told her.

"Howard? Is that you?"

The sound wasn't repeated but she kept the wooden sword in her hand anyway. A flock of birds took to wing, startling her. As she was searching the sky to see where they were going, several silent figures slipped from the forest and before Ellen knew what was happening, she was surrounded.

"Holy freaking crap," she whispered.

It was like falling down a rabbit hole but ending up in Middle Earth instead of Wonderland. The eight men were all tall and lean with long hair and slender, pointed ears. They were dressed in homespun tunics and trousers in various shades of green, all armed with bows though a couple of them were wearing sword belts as well. And they were, each and every one of them, drop dead gorgeous, despite the fact they had drawn bows trained on her.

"You trespass on elven lands. What business have you here?" The one asking had a thread of silver running through his hair and the coldness in his voice sent a shiver through her.

"Holy freaking crap," she repeated.

"Perhaps she is addled," the elf on his left suggested, the point of his arrow lowering slightly.

"Her manner of dress is most strange," the one on his right said.

"And she thinks to threaten us with a wooden sword," another one observed with obvious amusement.

Ellen stiffened in anger. "It's easy to talk big when you have me surrounded. Try taking me on one-on-one and we'll see who the threat is," she said.

"Enough!" the leader barked. "We have an outpost nearby; you will accompany us there for further questioning."

Knowing she had no other choice, Ellen gave a sharp nod and stowed her *bokken* back in its case.

If this was nearby, Ellen thought later, she'd hate to see what far away looked like. They walked for what seemed like hours, following no trail that she could discern. The elves moved silently, with incredible grace, making her feel like a clumsy child. There were two in front of her and two behind her but the rest seem to have melted back into the forest. If they were with them then she had no idea where.

She had to give them credit though, the leader adjusted his stride so that she had no trouble keeping up with them and they stopped twice for a rest. Both times she was offered food and water. The water she accepted, but the food she refused. Hadn't she read somewhere that if you ate the food from Faery land you could never leave?

Okay, so these guys were elves, not Faeries. But same thing, right?

At last they reached a small handful of picturesque, thatched cottages in a clearing beside a small river.

"You can wait in here," the leader said, gesturing to the cottage in the center of the cluster, one with a dour faced guard already standing by the door. "Food and drink will be brought to you."

Ellen opened her mouth to protest, but he was already gone. The guard held the door open for her and really, having no other choice, she went inside.

To her surprise, there was already someone seated at the table in the center of the one room cottage. "Hey!" she started to protest, but the guard had already shut the door behind her.

"Holy freaking crap! Did I end up in the land of giants or what?"

The man at the table had risen to his feet and he was just as tall, if not taller, than the elves who had brought her here. His lips twitched into a grin at her words.

"Alas, I can do nothing to alter my stature, but I assure you that you have nothing to fear from me, my lady," he said.

"Maybe not from you," she said, after a quick glance showed he was unarmed, "But what about them?" She nodded towards the door.

"Ah. That remains to be seen," he said with a shrug.

"Could you please sit down again?" she said, taking a step closer. "You're giving me a crick in the neck."

"As you wish, my lady," he replied with a full out grin. "Will you join me?"

She eyed him a little more carefully. Though tall, he was somewhat slender, though not as slender as the elves who'd detained her. In some ways he reminded her of Howard, though he was blond where Howard was dark haired. There was something familiar about him but she couldn't put her finger on it.

Sliding into the chair opposite his, she asked, "Do you know if they've brought anyone else in? I seem to have misplaced my friend."

He arched an eyebrow. "Indeed? I regret to tell you that you are the first non-elf I have seen since I was brought here this morn."

"Damn."

"But if your friend went missing in the elven realm, then rest assured they will find him or her."

Ellen sighed. "It was a him. And I don't even know for sure that he got lost in this 'elven realm'. God only knows where he might have ended up."

The door to the hut rattled and then opened as an elf brought in a large tray laden with food and drink. Without a word to them he set it on the table and then left again.

Ellen, who hadn't had anything to eat since a bagel for breakfast, practically salivated at the smell wafting upwards from the bowls of stew.

"After you, my lady," the man said politely.

"Are you sure it's safe?" she asked.

"Why wouldn't it be?" he asked, genuinely puzzled. "Had they wished us harm, they would not be keeping us here, nor feeding us in the first place."

"You have a point," she said, and without further prompting, dug into the bowl of stew closest to her. When her companion held up the bottle of wine, she nodded and he filled the two wooden goblets, setting one of them in front of her.

They polished off the stew, a loaf of home baked bread, and a chunk of a mild white cheese in record time. Apparently her cell mate was just as hungry as she was. He offered her the last of the bread and she shook her head.

"You go ahead and finish it. I'm stuffed."

As he ate, Ellen took a look around the cottage. There was a large fireplace, with wood already laid out for a fire. A window with a deep ledge was in the wall opposite the fireplace and there was a cot on either side of it. One of the cots had a pile of gear on it, presumably belonging to her companion.

"So, what did they get you for?" she asked.

"I am almost ashamed to admit my folly," he said with a rueful sigh. "I was taken in by a pretty face."

Ellen grinned. "Same old story."

"In this case, the pretty face was that of a bay mare. I had thought to travel in style and purchased her from a trader of less than stellar reputation."

"Let me guess, she wasn't as sound as she looked?"

"Nay, she was sound enough. I know enough of horse flesh to know that much, it was her temper that was uncertain. The varlet had given her a potion to keep her tranquil, but once he was miles behind us and the potion wore off, she became a changed horse. She shied at every noise and resisted going in the direction of my choosing. There was a howl from a wolf and she bolted. Next thing I know I'm in the elven realm, flat on my back and without my horse."

"The elves must have caught her - aren't those your belongings?" she pointed at the cot.

He heaved a sigh. "I do not know how it was possible, but the misbegotten creature managed to divest herself of all my gear. It was found several yards from where I was."

"Oh, my." Ellen tried to stifle her laughter.

"Might I inquire as to your name, my lady?"

"It's Ellen, Ellen Chang. And you are?"

"A pleasure to meet you, milady Ellen. I am Sebastian– "

"Sebastian Descartes!"

A frown furrowed his brow. "Forgive me, mistress Ellen. Have we perchance met elsewhere?"

"No, but I certainly know you. We have a mutual friend."

He shook his head, clearly puzzled.

"Jessica. I'm Jessica's friend Ellen."

"But– but how came you to be here?"

"Extreme bad luck and Howard Ruskin," Ellen said with a heartfelt sigh.

Chapter Seven

Aracelia was taking tea in her garden when a guard interrupted her.

"Forgive me, Lady, but there is an incident that requires your attention."

She set her tea cup back in its saucer and dabbed daintily at her mouth with a napkin made of silk. "What incident could possibly require you to disturb me at my tea?"

"A portal was opened in the formal gardens of the council– "

"A portal?" Aracelia sat up straight in her chair. "There was no such activity authorized for today. Why was it not stopped at the barrier?"

"We do not know, Lady, but there is more. When we went to investigate we found a human had passed through the portal– "

"A human?"

"Yes, Lady. And he asked for you by name."

"For me?" Aracelia was astonished, to say the least. "Where is this human now?"

"He is being held in the detention house."

"Then I suppose I had best see who this human is and what he wants with me, hadn't I?"

"Yes, Lady."

"And more importantly, I need to find out how he was able to breach our defenses."

"Yes, Lady," the guard said unhappily.

Just as she'd risen to her feet, another guard came hurrying up. "Forgive me, Lady, but I have a matter of great concern."

"Another one?" Aracelia asked with a frown. "Don't tell me another portal has opened up in the town?"

"I do not know, Lady. I have received word from the River Run Outpost, they have detained two human intruders."

"And did they appear from portals as well?"

"I– I do not know, Lady."

Aracelia sighed. "I mislike the coincidence of all these humans appearing simultaneously in our realm. You had best have them brought here for questioning as well."

"Yes, Lady." The elf bowed and then departed as swiftly as he'd arrived.

"I know you from some place," she said to the elf escorting her to the detention center. "Pray, what is your name?"

"It's Kaelan, Lady."

"Ah, yes. Kaelan. Son of Sioned and Carwyn the Silversmith. We met near the Field of Sorrows when I was there with my grand– " she hastily corrected herself, "my companion Jessica."

It had been quite the adventure for her, not only meeting her granddaughter whom she had seen only once as a baby, but testing her in her magical abilities.

"Yes, Lady," he said with a smile. "How fares the lovely Jessica?"

Aracelia smiled as well. In the short time he'd been with them at the camp near the Field of Sorrows, he'd developed a bit of a crush on Jessica. "She fares well."

"That is good to hear, Lady."

They reached the detention center and he held the door open for her and then took up a post outside. Aracelia nodded her thanks and went inside. The guard at the desk rose to attention and nodded towards the occupied cell.

"He's in there, Lady," he said, a little unnecessarily.

The occupant appeared to be sleeping. She approached quietly and studied him for a moment. "Howard!" she gasped in shock when she recognized him.

He woke with a start and sat up quickly. Struggling to his feet he ran a hand through his disheveled hair and smiled a little sheepishly.

"Hello, Aracelia. It's great to meet you in person at last."

"But what are you *doing* here?" This was certainly not what Paran had intended. Or was it? She must have infused more power in the stone than she realized. "No, never mind that. Guard, let him out. I will take responsibility for this human."

The last thing she needed was to have rumors flying around regarding her gifting humans with sources of magic. She needed to hear Howard's story on her own before sharing it with the council.

"I'm sorry, I didn't mean to cause you any trouble," Howard said in a small voice.

"The captain will need to know you have taken charge of him," the guardsman warned as he unlocked the cell.

"That's fine, tell him this human is known to me."

"Very well, Lady. But I must insist that you have protection."

"All right, I'll take Kaelan with me. Will he suffice?"

"Very well, Lady," the guard said, but he was clearly unhappy.

She startled Kaelan as she swiftly left the detention center, the human with her, and motioned him to follow. He had to practically run to keep up with the pace she set. Howard lagged behind, head turning this way and that as he tried to take in the scenery. Aracelia hustled him back to her house and inside, away from prying eyes. Once the door was shut behind them, she was able to breathe easier.

"Forgive me, my friend," she said. "But these are perilous times we live in, and I fear this is just the beginning. But first, how, pray, did you come to be here in the Darkwood Elven Realm?"

"Well...I...ah," he shot a look at the Kaelan standing guard just inside the door.

Aracelia sighed. "You had best sit down, both of you. Kaelan... the things you are about to learn are not to be shared except with the beings involved. And Howard is just one of them."

Kaelan hesitantly sat down on the edge of one of the pillow laden sofas, Howard following suit after a moment.

"What do you mean, these are perilous times?" Howard asked. "Did something happen to Jessica?"

"You know the fair Jessica?" Kaelan asked.

"The *fair* Jessica?" Howard repeated with a snort. "I've known her most of my life. I can tell you stories that would curl your hair and they have nothing to do with her being fair. In fact, she cheats. Especially at poker."

Kaelan looked at Aracelia who smiled faintly at him. "Howard is a close friend of Jessica's. Now, first to fill you in on a few details of Jessica and Howard and where they come from."

Aracelia gave Kaelan an abbreviated version of how Jessica was sent to the earthly realm as an infant and grew up there, and how Howard accidentally, with the help of Jessica's true father and grandfather, sent her back to the world of her birth.

After a brief hesitation, knowing if she was going to enlist his help he'd need to know everything, she admitted to being Jessica's grandmother.

Chapter Eight

"Forgive me, Lady," Kaelan said when she came to the end of her story. "I am most honored that you would share this with me, but– "

"I am not yet finished," she chided gently. "There is– "

A chime interrupted.

"Who could that– drat!" Aracelia rose to her feet. "I'd forgotten I requested the other humans be brought here. This will just take a moment to deal with."

Leaving Howard and Kaelan in her sitting room, she swept towards the entrance of her home. "Forgive me, I had forgotten you were coming. I am afraid I will have to ask– " The words stuck in her throat as she caught sight of the two weary humans standing with the guards.

"Aracelia?" the woman asked uncertainly.

"Oh, my!" Aracelia's looked at them with astonishment.

"You know these humans?" the guard with them asked, dubiously.

"The lady is Ellen, a friend from a far-off land. I'm afraid I am unacquainted with the gentleman." Although she felt like she should know him.

"Sebastian Descarte, at your service, ma'am," he said, sweeping her a courtly bow.

"The bard, of course. My grand– the Lady Jessica has mentioned you."

"My Lady?" the guard prompted.

"I will take responsibility of these two humans," she told him. "Upon my authority you may surrender them to me."

"As you will, Lady."

"Stop in at the Grey Swan before you leave to refresh yourselves – tell them I will see to the payment."

"Thank you, Lady!" The guard bowed and he and his fellows left.

"There are forces beyond my ken at work here," Aracelia said, still not quite able to wrap her mind around the appearance of these two so hard on the heels of Howard. Ellen, yes, but the bard as well? "And for the life of me I do not know whether it bodes good or ill."

"I have to admit it's nice to see a friendly face," Ellen said. "I still can't even believe I'm really here."

"I'm having trouble believing it as well," Aracelia said with a short laugh. "Perhaps you both should join us in my sitting room and we can talk."

She led the way back to where Howard and Kaelan were waiting. Howard stood when he saw Ellen, mouth open in surprise.

"Ellen? Damn, I thought you were far enough away when I cast my spell– "

Ellen stormed up to Howard and punched him right in the jaw. "Did you really think you were going to sneak away without telling me? Get up!"

"No," Howard said from where he was lying on the floor, holding his jaw. "You'll just hit me again."

"Damned right I will!" she stood over him with her fists clenched. "You were just going to teleport yourself to the magical realm and have a grand old time and leave me behind to deal with all your crap? Get up!"

Sebastian held her back as she tried to kick the prostrate man.

"I didn't know if I even had enough power to get me over, let alone two of us, and I didn't want to get your hopes up."

The situation was fast spiraling out of control. Aracelia opened her mouth to speak as Kaelan helped Howard to his feet but the tiny human beat her to it.

"I'll show you getting my freaking hopes up!" Ellen snarled. She twisted free from the Bard's grip.

Howard ducked behind Kaelan for protection.

"Out of my way!"

"Forgive me," Kaelan said, adopting a protective stance in front of Howard. "But I don't– "

Ellen surprised him with a flurry of unfamiliar moves. She wrenched his arm around and almost slipped past him. Clearly she'd had training in the art of combat. It was all he could do to counter her moves and get his arms around her, pinning her arms to her sides.

"Enough!" Aracelia's voice rang out. "Ellen, I understand that you might bear Howard some ill will, but nothing will be solved by beating him to a pulp, no matter how satisfying it may be."

Ellen stopped struggling in Kaelan's arms.

"Now, I think perhaps explanations are in order. Why don't we sit down? Kaelan, I think it is safe to let go now."

The tips of Kaelan's ears reddened as he loosened his hold on Ellen.

"Ellen, perhaps you would like to sit here?" Aracelia indicated the chair furthest away from Howard.

Ellen grudgingly sat in the chair the elf pointed out to her, glaring daggers at Howard. Once everyone was seated, Aracelia began.

"Howard, perhaps you should start."

But Howard's attention was on the Bard, who seemed to be equally mesmerized. Without breaking eye contact, Sebastian sat on the sofa beside him. "I had hoped that we might meet one day…"

"So did I," Howard said.

"Oh, for the love of– " Ellen began, a scowl on her face.

"Gentlemen!" Aracelia said sharply to get their attention.

They both started. Howard flushed slightly, but Sebastian had a decided twinkle in his eye.

"Sorry," Howard said.

"Howard, the talisman you were sent did not contain enough magical energy to open a portal to this realm. However did you accomplish such a feat?"

"You know I've spent the better part of my life doing research on magic," he said.

Aracelia nodded.

"Earth wasn't always devoid of magic. There are ancient texts…scrolls that are barely decipherable…one of these scrolls had what looked like an amplification spell." He shrugged. "I took a chance that it would amplify the magic in the talisman. What I don't understand is why we ended up in the Elven Realm instead of wherever Jessica is."

"That is a question easily answered." Aracelia nodded towards the pendant that had become untucked from his shirt. "The moonstone is of elven origin, as was the magic in the talisman. Both would have been drawn to this realm."

"Drawing us along with it."

"I should have known you were up to something," Ellen said, arms crossed over her chest. "You've been too freaking quiet these last few days."

"I'm sorry, really," he said, sounding sincere. "But I wasn't sure the spell I'd found would amplify magic, it might have amplified something else. Something...bad. It was okay to risk my own life, but I couldn't risk yours too."

"You still could have told me. What if something bad *had* happened?"

"That's why I left you my power of– why are you dressed like an extra from the Karate Kid?"

Ellen rolled her eyes. "I came home in the middle of *kenjutsu* practice to get my *bokken* and I found your note. I didn't expect to get pulled into another universe with you or I would have changed into something more practical."

"I quite like what you're wearing," Kaelan put in. Ellen opened her mouth for a quick retort, but then she looked over at him and a faint flush suffused her face instead.

"I am getting too old for this," Aracelia muttered under her breath. Humans were so ... volatile in their emotions, so chaotic. She took charge of the conversation once more.

"Perhaps it is just as well that you stumbled in upon Howard as he was casting the spell. With the power he generated, who knows where he might have ended up? You both know what happened when Thackery and Paranithel interfered. Your presence helped use up the excess of energy."

"So Ellen's presence here is both a good and a bad thing,"

Sebastian hazarded. When everyone turned to look at him, he continued. "It's good because it used up magic that might have sent Howard someplace dangerous, but it's bad because now she's trapped here as well."

"I wouldn't say trapped," Aracelia said. "Either Thackery or Paranithel will be able to create a portal back to the earthly realm. Jessica as well, once she has been properly trained." She, of course, also had the ability to send them back, but she had her own reasons why it was not feasible at this time.

"What about Howard?" Sebastian asked.

Howard looked at him blankly.

"You have studied wizardry your whole life. While Jessica held the moonstone amulet you were able to assist her in her magical endeavors. Do you mean to tell me you have not once tried out your own magic since arriving here?" Sebastian said with some amusement.

"I– I– " Howard seemed to have trouble finding his tongue. "I never thought of it," he admitted.

Aracelia's lips twitched at his chagrined expression. "Never fear, friend Howard, there is plenty of time for magic now that you are here."

"But– "

She shook her head. "Later, if you wish, I can test your abilities, but first we must make plans. As I've said, these are perilous times and growing more so each day." In fact, the timing couldn't be worse for these friends of Jessica's to arrive from the other realm. "There have been...disappearances."

"Disappearances?" Ellen asked, half rising from her seat. "What kind of disappearances? Is Jessica all right?"

"Be at ease, Jessica is fine, as far as I know, but there have been reports of others, creatures imbued with magic, vanishing."

The bard, Sebastian, was nodding in agreement. "I've heard rumors of such things – sylphs and nymphs abandoning their glades, trolls disappearing from their bridges, springs becoming fouled with no unicorns to purify them, and a darkness building in the west."

Aracelia nodded. "Yes, and even we elves have not remained untouched. At first it was just any who strayed beyond our barriers, but then an entire company was sent on an undertaking to the Wild Woods Realm and never reached their destination. Now communication with Wild Woods remains silent."

There was a gasp from Kaelan.

"You must forgive me," Aracelia said. "We have been keeping the news to ourselves so as not to alarm the populace."

"My mother's people come from Wild Woods," he said quietly.

"I am sorry, I did not know." She reached out and touched the back of his hand, then looked at the three humans.

"I'm not trying to sound unsympathetic or anything," Ellen put in, "But if magical beings are being targeted by something nasty, isn't Jessica in danger? I mean, she's got magic coming out the whazoo."

"She is in possession of a talisman that masks her magical abilities, and it is to be hoped that she is judicious in her use of magic."

Howard and Ellen exchanged a look.

"Fortunately, she's with Dominic and he well knows the dangers of drawing the wrong kind of attention," Sebastian assured them. "We are to meet in three weeks' time in the town of Claverton," he added.

"Claverton," Aracelia mused. "That would be several leagues west of the Inland Sea, is it not?" This was most fortuitous – perhaps there really were other forces at work here, benign forces at that.

"Safety in numbers," Ellen said. "We'll be okay if we travel together, right? I mean, that is the plan, right? We hook up with Jessica and head south to find her dear old dad?"

"Of course," Aracelia assured her. "But I would beg a boon of you. The Elven Realm of Wild Woods is not far from the town of Claverton. I ask only that you go there and see what has happened to my people. In return I will provide you with horses and supplies for the journey, as well as safe conducts should the elves within the realm be hostile. I would ask also that you go with them Kaelan, to bring back word."

The humans looked at each other. "I think it's the least we can do," Howard said firmly. "After all, we did kind of drop in on you unexpectedly."

"That you did," she said with a chuckle, feeling a small part of her burden of worry lift.

Chapter Nine

The hour was growing late and they moved to Aracelia's formal dining room. There was no question that they would stay the night as Aracelia's guests and start off in the morning. While Howard and Aracelia chatted amiably about magic, Ellen remained quiet at dinner. Without her anger to sustain her, she was finally feeling the impact of what had happened.

"You are troubled," Kaelan observed.

"I was just thinking that my parents must be going out of their minds with worry," she said, picking at her food. "I didn't exactly have time to let them know I'd be going away."

"I'm sorry," Howard said, looking a little guilty. "I should have told you what I was up to."

She waved him off. "What's done is done."

"Perhaps I could get a message to them," Aracelia said thoughtfully. "I am sure I would be able to open a portal small enough for a wind imp to slip through."

"A wind imp?" Ellen asked.

"Each of the elements have creatures linked to them. A wind imp is the most useful of the air elemental beings."

She sent one of the servants for a quill and paper.

"This is so cool!" Ellen said, dipping the quill into the small bottle of ink. She wrote a deliberately vague message to her parents about a sick friend who desperately needed her help, apologizing for the short notice and asking them to let the boutique where she worked know that she'd need a leave of absence.

When it was dry Aracelia folded it carefully and summoned the wind imp. It was smaller than the letter the elf gave it to carry, invisible but for an indistinct outline of its body. "Hold the image of your parents' home in your mind," she told Ellen.

Ellen did as she was told and Aracelia muttered a guttural sounding incantation under her breath. A small hole opened up in the air in front of her and the wind imp, carrying the letter, slipped through.

Ellen couldn't hold back a smirk.

"What?" Howard asked her.

"Gives a whole new meaning to the term, 'air mail', doesn't it?"

The pair of them laughed while the others at the table remained mystified as to what was so funny.

"I believe there would be time enough to perform a rudimentary testing, should you wish it," Aracelia told Howard.

His whole face lit up. "Really?"

"Perhaps we should adjourn to the garden for this," she suggested, with a smile for his eagerness.

She led the way, Howard and Sebastian following and Kaelan and Ellen bringing up the rear. Ellen couldn't help but notice that Kaelan didn't quite tower over her the way everyone else did. But he was as slender as the other elves she'd seen, and he moved with the sinuous grace of a cat. She'd always liked cats.

As though he was aware of her scrutiny, Kaelan turned his

head and smiled at her, then quickly reached out and steadied her when she stumbled. Ellen's face flushed as she stammered a thank you, then looked away.

His eyes were more green than blue and she wondered if they changed color to suit his mood. Not that it mattered to her. Nope, not one little bit.

They reached the center of Aracelia's garden, which was bare and flat with what appeared to be a fire pit in the center. Howard was filled with a nervous anticipation.

"We already know you are quite talented in Conjuring," Aracelia told him, "And Paranithel believes you show promise in Alchemy as well. These are the two most powerful Thoughts of Magic. Have you ever had visions or been able to predict the future?"

"No, never." He shook his head.

"Hmm. Probably not predisposed to Mind Magic then. Do you have a way with animals?"

"I haven't been around many," he confessed. "But dogs seem to like me."

"So does old lady Krantz's cat," Ellen offered. "And that cat hates everybody."

"So, some talent as an Animagus perhaps. Now, let's see how you do with the elements." She pointed to a flowerbed that looked somewhat neglected when compared to the rest of the garden. "See if you can coax one of those plants into growing."

Howard took a few uncertain steps towards the flower bed the elf indicated. He hadn't expected to be tested in magic so quickly – it would have been nice to have some time to prepare.

And he really wished he could do this without an audience – especially Sebastian. It would be just too embarrassing if he failed.

Pushing such thoughts from his mind, Howard concentrated on the task at hand, reaching inside himself for the magic spark, just as he had once instructed Jessica to do. Like her, at first he just let his inner self bathe in the magical flame. Then, resolutely, he focused harder until he could see the separate strands of color that made it up. There didn't seem to be any healing green but there was a dark green strand, twisted with strands of blue, white, and scarlet.

He envisioned ghostly fingers working the green strand free, and aimed it towards the small flowerbed. In his mind he pictured the flowers being revitalized, growing and blooming.

"That will do," Aracelia told him.

He opened his eyes, unaware that he had closed them. It was not just one plant that was blooming, the tiny patch was a riot of blossoms. His mouth dropped open and then curved into a silly smile. This was even better than the transportation spell!

"That was so cool!" Ellen said. "Like one of those time-lapse films."

"Obviously you have an affinity for earth. Let us try water. Focus on the birdbath in the center of the flowerbed and see if you are able to draw water to it. I warn you, this may be more difficult as we have been undergoing a dry spell."

Like he'd done with the earth, Howard went into himself seeking the strands of magic. This time he touched on the blue strand, focusing on the bird bath. He could see the bird bath in his mind's eye and when it was filled, he stopped the flow of magic towards it and opened his eyes. Water filled the bird bath without spilling over.

"Excellent! Now, see if you can send a breeze to unfurl the flag on top of that pole." She pointed towards a pennant hanging limply from a pole in the center of another small flowerbed.

Howard took a deep breath and then searched out the white thread from among the others. Picturing a cartoon cloud in his mind, he aimed it towards the flag and had it gently blow.

"Well done," Aracelia told him. "And finally, we have fire." She placed a large, fat candle in the center of the fire pit. "You need simply to light this candle."

Again, Howard went inside himself. Each time he tried it became easier and he had no trouble at all separating the scarlet thread from the others. Gently he directed it towards the candle's wick. It flared to life, but quickly settled down to a steady flame.

"Your control is most impressive Howard. With the right training you could easily become a Master of Elemental Magic."

"Really? You think so?"

"Oh, indeed I do. To have an affinity for one or two of the elements is not unheard of in most magic workers. I, myself, am partial to Earth and Air. But you wield all four with ease. To light a candle takes far more control than lighting a fire in a fireplace." She waved a hand and a puff of air blew the candle out again.

"It felt so natural," Howard said, filled with wonder at what he'd done.

"It is not unheard of for a mage to have a natural talent for one or more areas of magic," Aracelia told him, leading them back inside again. "Yours could very well be the elements. With the proper training, I believe you could retain mastery over them even in your own realm."

"Who do I see about training?"

She laughed at his eagerness. "Alas, though many have an affinity for the elements, few have the mastery over them. I know of only one or two qualified to teach you but they are quite distant from here. But perhaps Thackery or Paranithel know of someone."

Howard couldn't wait to meet them face to face. They owed him big time for keeping their secrets from Jessica, and he knew just how they could pay him back.

Chapter Ten

Aracelia didn't know whether to feel hopeful or filled with misgivings at the breakfast table the next morning. Her guests all seemed a little tired. The bard and Howard kept shooting meaningful glances at each other when they thought no one was looking, which she found almost amusing. Kaelan had a troubled look on his face, thinking on his kin at Wild Woods no doubt, while Ellen – she found it difficult to read the human.

Was she doing the right thing, sending these four to Wild Woods? On the one hand, she needed to know what was happening there, and there was no one else to send. But on the other hand, Jessica would be most distraught should any ill befall her friends. What right had she to put them in danger?

The bard's gear had been sent along with him, so he was dressed in his travelling clothes. Kaelan had opted for hunting gear, rather than his uniform, which was most sensible of him. It would be far more comfortable for travelling, and a uniform might cause problems with any humans they might encounter as well the elves of the enclave.

The clothing Howard was wearing seemed durable enough, however he had not thought to bring any more with him. This was easily rectified as she sent Kaelan to the open market for what clothing and other gear he deemed necessary for the journey. The boy had a good eye for sizes and returned with an admirable selection: boots, packs, and foul weather gear.

Though the clothing Ellen had been wearing when she arrived may have been suitable for her combat practice, it was not the best choice for the kind of travelling they would be doing, nor should it be the only thing she had to wear. Aracelia had seen to her outfitting herself, and picked out an assortment of tunics, trousers, and vests, all of which had to be altered magically.

All in all, the group was nothing if not well dressed for their journey. Though Aracelia had misgivings about the dynamics of the group - a single guardsman, a human female warrior of unknown ability, an untried human wizard, and a bard – she convinced herself they would be fine. If Jessica could travel the Darkwood Forest alone, these four could easily reach the Wild Winds Realm and more importantly, send word back.

Once everyone had eaten their fill, Aracelia rose gracefully and everyone focused their attention on her.

"I wish I was going with you," she admitted, "if only to see my granddaughter again."

"Why don't you?" Howard asked impulsively. "I'm sure she'd love to see you too."

She smiled, even as she shook her head. "Alas, I am needed here. As I said before, these are troubled times we live in. In any case, I am grateful Kaelan need not make the journey to the Wild Winds Realm alone."

"We're happy to help," Ellen assured her. "I'm sure Jessica would be the first to agree."

"Speaking of the lady Jessica, what are we going to tell her?"

As all eyes focused on him, Sebastian shrugged. "Do we perpetuate the lie of who she really is, or..." He spread his hands wide.

"We do not," Ellen said firmly. "The first order of business is to come clean with her."

"I have to agree," Howard admitted. He looked at Aracelia. "You know I was coerced into keeping Thackery's secret– "

"Blackmailed, more like," Ellen muttered.

"Blackmailed," he agreed. "But now that we're here..."

"Now that you're here, things have changed," Aracelia finished. "I agree," she said, surprising them.

"It is to be hoped that her joy at seeing her friends will offset her anger at being deceived for so long," Sebastian said, with a wry smile.

Deftly changing the subject, Aracelia unrolled the map she'd had made. "Now, as to the best route to your destinations. You said you were to meet Jessica and Dominic in Claverton?"

"That's right." Sebastian got up and moved to stand beside her. "It looks to be a little further on than the enclave, and more to the south. I would make the most sense for us to journey first to Wild Winds and if all is well we can continue on to Claverton."

"And if all is not well?" Aracelia hated to be a pessimist, but it was unheard of for an enclave to be silent for so long.

They looked at each other. Finally, Howard spoke up. "Would...would I be able to use a wind imp to send you a message? I think it would be a little impractical to cart around a bowl and containers of oil for scrying."

"An excellent idea!" Aracelia beamed at him. "But as you are so new to your magics you will need a spell to do so."

"Oh." He seemed rather crestfallen.

She motioned him closer. "This is the one I used," she said, and touched the center of his forehead.

"Oh!" His eyes widened in surprise. "It's so simple!"

"Now, I believe you have everything you will need for your journey. It is not a well-travelled path but I do not foresee you running into any difficulties. What is it?" she asked Ellen, who was looking slightly uncomfortable.

"You've already done so much for us..." Ellen hesitated, then plunged ahead. "I was on my way to *kenjutsu* practice," she said, emphasizing the word practice. "While I can do a significant amount of damage with my *bokken*, when all's said and done it's still a wooden sword."

"Say no more," Aracelia said, nodding in understanding. "I presume you would prefer a weapon similar to the one you are familiar with?"

Ellen gave her a half smile. "I doubt very much that you will find a *katana* at your local blacksmith. As long as I can have something similar in weight and length, I should be all right."

"May I see your practice weapon, the *bokken* you called it?"

Ellen got up and went over to her personal gear, pulled out the *bokken* and brought it over to Aracelia. Unsheathing the wooden sword, she handed it to her.

"An interesting design." Aracelia took it from her and turned it this way and that. "And blade would be the same?"

"More or less."

"Not at all," Howard broke in. "The metal used in the forging of a *katana* is folded, to remove the impurities. And after it's forged it goes through a hardening process called the differential hardening, which creates the *hamon* that gives the

73

blade its curved edge. That makes it hard along the cutting age and softer along the non-cutting edge. What?" he asked when he caught Ellen staring at him.

"How on earth do you know so much about the forging of a *katana*?"

Howard blushed and shot a glance at Sebastian. "I, uh, dated a blacksmith at one time and he was commissioned to make a *katana*. I helped him do all kinds of research, but in the end he decided it wasn't worth his time or trouble."

"Excellent! Then perhaps you and I can work in tandem to create Ellen's weapon," Aracelia said. Holding the *bokken*, she turned to Howard. "Come stand beside me."

He did as she requested and she laid the *bokken* on the table in front of them. Taking one of Howard's hands in hers, she rested her free hand on the *bokken*. "Place your hand on the weapon as well," she said. When he'd done so, she instructed. "I want you to think of the forging process for the weapon we wish to create. I will pull the images from your mind and together we shall craft it."

"Like a 3-D printer," Ellen murmured.

They ignored her and focused on the task at hand. For long moments nothing happened. There was a pressure in the air, like an impending thunderstorm. It started to build. The *bokken* on the table quivered, and then was suffused in a silver glow. The glow intensified to an almost blinding light. When it disappeared, it left behind a sword unlike any Aracelia had ever seen before.

"Holy freaking crap!" said Ellen.

"Try it out," Aracelia said with some amusement.

Ellen reached out tentatively, as though afraid if she touched the sword it would disappear. Wrapping her hand firmly around the grip, she raised it to eye level.

"This is amazing," she said breathlessly. She turned it one way, then the other. It was the perfect weight, the perfect size for her. Stepping back, she performed a basic kata with the sword.

"Freaking amazing," she said. "How can I ever thank you?"

"Use it well," Aracelia said with a smile.

"I guess there's nothing left but for us to be on our way," Sebastian said.

Grabbing their personal gear, they followed Aracelia as she led the way to the courtyard where their mounts were waiting.

"Holy– " Howard stopped in his tracks.

"What?" Ellen asked, almost running into him. She peered around him. "Wow, now that's what I call a horse!"

"Those aren't just horses," Sebastian said, a note of wonder in his voice. "Those are *estrada!*"

Ellen was not one of those girly-girls who had a thing for horses, but even she had to admit the animals were magnificent. They were as tall as draft horses, but not as heavily set. They had long, thick manes and tails and there was an unexpected intelligence in their eyes.

"They look like Friesians, only...better," Howard said. There were two dappled grey, two black, and two glossy chestnuts that were outfitted as pack animals. He went up to one of the greys and stroked its nose. "Hello beautiful."

Ellen looked at him with a mixture of amusement and surprise. "I never knew you were into horses," she said.

"I took riding lessons as a kid - mother thought it would make a man of me - and ever since I've always wanted a horse of my own," Howard replied, still stroking the velvety nose.

Ellen eyed them as well, although not quite as appreciatively. "So, do these things come with a step ladder?"

Sebastian and Kaelan turned to look at her, barely suppressing smiles at the comparison of the diminutive human standing beside the huge animals. Howard was still fixated on his own mount.

"Allow me," Kaelan said, moving quickly in front of Sebastian who was about to make the same offer.

He put his hands on Ellen's waist and lifted her effortlessly into the saddle.

"Thank you," she said a little breathlessly.

"You're welcome," he said, smiling up at her.

"I feel like a kid at the pony ride," she admitted. "I'm not exactly experienced when it comes to riding and it's a long way down if I fall off."

"Do not fear, you will be fine. The *estrada* has the smoothest gait of all horses."

"If you two are quite done?" Aracelia said, with a trace of laughter.

Ellen looked over to see Howard and Sebastian both seated on the dapple greys, leaving the other black for Kaelan. He swung up into the saddle of his *estrada* a with a grace no man should be allowed to possess. But then he wasn't a man. He was an elf. She would do well to keep reminding herself of that.

Chapter Eleven

Filled with second thoughts and misgivings, Aracelia sent a servant for a tall stool which she had placed in front of the large, silver mirror. Seating herself upon it, she whispered an incantation and waved her hand in front of the mirror, frowning when it failed to activate.

She stood, repeating the incantation in a louder voice and used both hands to gesture with. The glass cleared almost immediately to show a surprised Paranithel looking back at her.

"Aracelia! I was just preparing to contact you." He shoved his hat further back on his head as it dipped towards the bowl of oil he was peering down into.

"How fortuitous that we are in such accord."

Before she could say anything else, he continued. "It was the strangest thing. I was first attempting to contact Howard, but was unsuccessful. It was almost like he was– "

"Not where you expected him to be?" she asked dryly.

"Why yes, however did you– oh, no! What has happened?"

She gave him a brief rundown of the recent events and it was to his credit that he allowed her to finish without jumping in with questions. "Oh, dear. I never expected him to try anything so foolish."

"He didn't just try, he succeeded," she said with a faint smile.

"He does credit to his teacher."

"Yes, well, be that as it may," he said, preening just a little. "Thackery is not going to like this. No, not one bit."

"Whether Kir-Thackery likes it or not, the deed was done," Aracelia said mildly.

"And just what is it that Thackery isn't going to like this time?" a voice from behind Paranithel asked.

The old man gave a long-suffering sigh.

There was a scowl on the handsome face that appeared next to Paran's in the mirror. Aracelia was tempted to break the spell, but that wouldn't have been fair to Paranithel.

"Howard has used a magical talisman to replicate the spell that sent Jessica to our world."

Shock replaced the scowl briefly, but then it was back again, fiercer than ever. "And just where did he obtain a talisman capable of this feat?"

She drew herself up proudly. "I sent it to him. After infusing it with elven magic."

"Why would you send him such a thing?" he asked, a muscle in his cheek twitching as he clenched his jaw.

"It was meant to aid him in his magical studies, lessons that were promised him." She felt it prudent to remind Thackery of the bribe he had dangled in front of the young man.

Thackery opened his mouth and snapped it shut again on whatever he was about to say.

"We had no idea he would find a way not only to amplify its power, but to transport himself to this realm," Paran hastily added.

"Not just him," Aracelia clarified, "but Jessica's friend Ellen as well."

"Of all the stupid– where are they now?"

"I have sent them to join Jessica and Dominic."

"Alone? Those two cannot possibly– "

"Of course they're not alone!" Aracelia snapped. She was getting a little fed up with his attitude. "The bard, Sebastian, is with them, as is one of my elven guards."

"I suppose it could be worse," he admitted grudgingly. "Where are they to meet up?"

"I believe Claverton," Aracelia said. She saw no need to mention Wild Woods at this time. Braced for an explosion, given Claverton's proximity to the Shadow Mountains where it was believed Anakaron had fled to, she was almost disappointed when it didn't come. Instead Thackery sighed.

"This is going to add weeks to Jessica's journey while she waits for them."

"Not exactly," Aracelia admitted. "They're riding *estrada*, with an extra two for Jessica and Dominic."

Thackery's eyebrows shot up. "That's very generous of you."

"I fear there is a darkness building, and I would have my granddaughter away from these lands as quickly as possible."

"At least we agree on something," Thackery grumbled. "I am surprised you did not join them yourself."

"It was a tempting thought."

"How bad is it?" Paranithel asked.

Aracelia hesitated. "There is a...wrongness that is spreading. Even those without magic are uneasy, and those with magic are stealing away in the night."

Paranithel nodded. "I have heard many say the same."

Thackery paced away from scrying bowl but Aracelia could still hear his heavy footsteps.

"I would you had sent a whole squadron of warriors to accompany them."

"Yes, I daresay you would."

"What's that supposed to mean?" His face appeared in her mirror again, the scowl back in place.

"Four, or even six, travelling in a group would not be an uncommon sight. A squadron of elves, or even a squadron of elves accompanying other elves would not be amiss. But a group of humans travelling with a squadron of elves? What would you believe should you see such a thing?"

Thackery sighed. "That whoever was being protected by all those guards was someone of importance. You are right, of course."

"And because the guards were elves, whoever they were protecting must wield a great deal of magic," Paranithel added.

"I believe the point has been made," Thackery snapped.

"Peace!" Aracelia raised her hands. "It serves no purpose in arguing with each other – we work towards a common goal, namely to see that Jessica and her friends reach the southlands safely."

"And from there we can send her back from whence she came."

Aracelia caught Paranithel's eye and he gave a minute shake of his head. He knew her too well. She kept silent instead of pointing out that it may be what Thackery wanted, but Jessica might have other ideas on the matter.

"You tried to warn me, both of you," Thackery said. "I ignored your concerns, just as I ignored the signs and portents that Anakaron's presence was manifesting once more."

"I don't think any of us– "

Thackery made a sharp gesture with his hand, effectively cutting off what Paranithel was about to say.

"Even had Howard's spell not amplified my own she would have been at risk, no matter where she ended up. What was I thinking?"

"You cannot– "

"I was utterly selfish. I wished to see my daughter and gave no thought to the risks."

"At the time the risks– "

"If anything happens to her," Thackery said darkly, "It will be all my fault.

"Are you quite finished?" Aracelia asked dryly.

Thackery's mouth snapped shut as he glowered at her.

"Far be it for me to pierce your bubble of self-flagellation," she said. "But it ill suits you and it serves no purpose. You would be better served to turn your attention to the bigger issue at hand."

"And what would that be?"

"How we are to deal with Anakaron."

Both men stared at her.

She frowned in return. "It is not just Jessica who is in danger, it is all of us. Anakaron must be stopped, preferably before he comes into his full power."

"She is right," Paranithel said before Thackery could speak. "We have let our fears for Jessica cloud our reasoning. We need to be thinking ahead, formulating strategies, preparing for the eventual confrontation with Anakaron."

"In my head I know you speak truly," Thackery said heavily. "But in my heart I do not know how much use I will be for anything until she is safe."

Chapter Twelve

The elven city was hours behind them and although Kaelan would have liked to have push as quickly as possible towards Wild Winds, he had his companions to consider. While the bard was well-travelled the other two were obviously unused to being in the saddle.

He paid more attention to the passing landscape, searching for the travelers' markers indicating a rest stop. Nudging his *estrada* slightly, he led the group to one such spot and stopped. Ellen's mount drew up beside his and stopped as well.

"Is something wrong," she asked.

"We have been on the trail for several hours, I thought it best to have a brief stop to eat."

"Wow, I must have been really lost in thought. Either that or I fell asleep without realizing it. In which case I'm just glad I didn't embarrass myself by falling off."

She swung her leg over and, keeping a hold of the saddle, slid off the *estrada* to the ground. Her legs were like rubber and she grabbed for the stirrup to keep her balance. "I guess we were in the saddle longer than I thought."

Kaelan's brow furrowed. "How long has it been since you last rode?"

"Let's see, I was about nine, so that would make it about

seventeen years."

Sebastian had already unpacked one of the food sacks and he and Howard joined them. "But how do you travel if not by horse?"

"This might take some explaining," Howard said. "Why don't we sit down first?"

Kaelan led the way to a cleared area that had several logs for seating. He and Ellen seated themselves on one log while Sebastian and Howard sat on the one next to them so they could share out the food easier.

"I'm surprised Jessica hasn't told you all about our world already," Ellen said to Sebastian.

He shrugged. "I never thought to ask. Although to be fair, a lot of the time we've spent together thus far had more to do with rescuing her."

They all laughed.

"Well, this might shock you both," Ellen told them, "But where we come from people don't use horses for getting from one place to another. In fact, not many people even own horses. Those that do use them mostly for pleasure riding, or sporting events like racing, or equestrian jumping."

"Some places they use them for hunting with," Howard put in.

"Do you not travel then?" Kaelan asked, brow furrowed.

"Oh, don't get me wrong, we travel. Some people travel great distances. But we use machines - cars, trains, plane..."

"These are all unfamiliar terms," Sebastian admitted.

"Okay, well a car is a machine like a ... do you people ever use carriages?"

"The elven folk do not, although the old or infirm are

sometimes transported by cart," Kaelan said. "I do know what a carriage is though."

"Only the very well off can afford a carriage," Sebastian added.

"Okay, well a car is like a carriage, only it has a motor to move it instead of horses. All the controls are on the inside - speed, direction, lights for when it gets dark - it's probably the most common form of transportation."

"It sounds very strange," Kaelan said.

"You have no idea. They come in all kinds of shapes and sizes - some only have enough room for two people inside, others have room for six or seven."

"And the really big ones, called buses, can have thirty or forty people travelling in them," Howard added.

"Surely this is but a tall tale," Sebastian said. "Such a thing could not be possible."

"If you have a hard time believing in cars, you'd never believe in planes," Ellen said with a laugh.

"Very well, what is a plane?" Sebastian asked.

She and Howard looked at each other.

"Be my guest," she said.

"Thanks," he muttered. "Okay, a plane is a large, bird shaped machine that uses these huge engines that make it move fast enough that it flies through the air, just like a bird. And like the cars, the passengers sit on the inside. And there are different sizes of them as well. Some small planes only carry a few people, but the really large ones...I haven't a clue how many people a large one can carry. Probably two or three hundred."

Kaelan and Sebastian stared at him.

"Were it anyone but you telling me this," Sebastian told him,

"I would call him a liar. But even so, I find this difficult to comprehend."

"Oh, it's true all right. Jessica and I took a plane to Cuba last fall for a vacation. The most amazing thing about a plane is it travels hundreds of miles in just a few hours," Ellen said.

"I promise you," Howard said at almost the same time. "We're telling the truth. I just wish there was some way I could show you."

Kaelan thought about it for a moment.

"What is it?" Ellen asked.

"Though we are to refrain from seeking out people through scrying," he said, "I do not see the harm in calling up a place."

"Yes, but I don't have the proper equipment," said Howard.

Shrugging, Kaelan said, "The Lady Aracelia prefers to use a mirror. But many use water with which to scry. There is a pond close to where we will stop for the night. If you wish, you could try to scry with it."

Howard stared at him a moment and then laughed. "I keep forgetting that I'm surrounded by magic here. I can't guarantee the results, but I'd love to give it a try."

They gathered up the remains of their lunch, deciding to push on until it was time to stop for the night. Kaelan noticed Ellen glancing around the clearing, and it occurred to him she was looking for a stump large enough to use as a mounting block. Before he could offer his assistance, Howard figured out what she was doing too and went over to her.

"Let me try something," he said. He went up to the head of the animal and stroked its neck. When it lowered its head he began whispering in its ear. It shook its head in a negative reply to whatever Howard was saying, but he whispered some more and finally it bobbed its head in agreement.

With a very human-like sigh, the *estrada* slowly knelt on the ground beside Ellen. From this position she was able to climb into the saddle without assistance.

"That's amazing Howard, thank you!"

He shrugged. "Don't thank me, thank your *estrada*. I only made a couple of suggestions, she's the one who agreed to it."

"Thank you," Ellen said, reaching down and stroking its neck. "That was really nice of you– hey, Howard. Did she tell you her name?"

"I'm not Dr. Dolittle," he said, a little irritably.

"Though the *estrada are* incredibly intelligent," Kaelan told them, "They have not the power of speech, though they understand our language well enough. To truly communicate with them takes an Animagus."

"That's too bad. I think it's a little disrespectful to just call her "steed". Do you think she'd mind if I picked a name out for her?"

Kaelan smiled at her. "Why don't you ask her yourself?"

"Oh, sorry! I'm new at all this," she said seriously. "How about it? Would you mind if I picked out a name for you? I promise to keep trying until I hit on one we can both agree on."

The *estrada* bobbed her head.

"Let's see...you being an *estrada* and all, it can't be anything ordinary. Maybe something Irish, or Celtic." She thought about it for a few minutes. "How about Epona?"

"Epona?" Howard asked. "Where'd that come from?"

"Epona is the name of the Celtic horse goddess. And she truly is a goddess amongst horses."

Kaelan's mount snorted, shaking his head, but Epona bobbed her head up and down in agreement.

"Then Epona it is," Ellen said, sitting back in the saddle. "And I really have to thank you for putting up with me, Epona. As I'm sure you've guessed, I'm not much of a rider."

Epona whickered in response.

"Our next halt will be for the night," Kaelan told them. "The rest spot is just inside the barrier surrounding the elven-realm."

"Barrier?" Howard and Ellen asked in unison.

"There is nothing to fear. You will experience a slight... tingling sensation as you pass through it but it will not harm you. It is only when entering an elven realm that you need worry. The barriers can sense intentions. Anyone intending harm to the elves are discouraged from entering. And if they do, an alarm is sent out and the barrier will hold the intruder fast."

"Do you think someone found a way around the barrier at the Wild Woods enclave?" Sebastian asked.

"I do not know," Kaelan said. It was a troubling thought. "Being unable to communicate with an enclave is unheard of. Not even Lady Aracelia's silver mirror can see into it."

They travelled in silence after that, even Howard and Sebastian were quiet. Other than a slight breeze rustling the leaves, the woodland they were traversing was also silent - no birds or animals, just the soft footfalls of the *estrada*.

Reaching a fork in the trail they were following, Kaelan led them to the right. They only had to travel a short distance to reach the small, cleared area that had obviously been used as a camp ground in the past. Once they halted, Epona turned her head to look at Ellen.

"That's okay, Epona," she said, patting her on the neck. "It's only the mounting up I have trouble with. Getting down is as easy as falling off a horse." She giggled as the horse snorted and shook her head at her. Throwing her leg over the saddle, she slid to the ground, ending up on her butt in the dirt.

Kaelan hurried over to offer her a hand up, which she took with a sigh. "That would have been much more impressive if my legs weren't made out of rubber."

"It will get better as you become used to riding," he promised.

"If you think this is bad, just wait until tomorrow when your muscles have all stiffened up," Howard called over. He and Sebastian were already busy unsaddling their mounts.

"I'm starting to think I should have waited back at Aracelia's house," Ellen said ruefully. She studied the arrangement of straps holding the saddle in place.

"What is wrong?" Kaelan asked

"I'm just trying to figure out how to remove it without doing any damage to either the saddle or Epona."

"I would be honored if you'd allow me to take care of your steed," he offered.

"Normally I would insist on doing my fair share," she said. Turning, she gave him an apologetic smile. "But between the height difference and the fact I haven't got a clue what I'm doing, I would be happy to accept your kind offer. But only if you allow me to cook supper."

Kaelan brightened at her words. "I think that is more than a fair bargain. In fact, I think it is a bargain we will all enjoy. I fear cooking is not one of my accomplishments."

"Mine either," Howard put in. "I eat a lot of take out."

"What is 'take out'?" Sebastian asked.

"It's where you phone your favorite restaurant, tell them what you'd like to eat, and they not only prepare it for you, they deliver it to your door."

"I think I would enjoy this 'take out' very much," the bard said. "I, myself, prefer eating at an inn or as a guest at someone's table. What I am able to prepare is edible, but it is lacking in variety."

"Then you guys are in luck," Ellen said. "Not only can I cook, my family used to go camping a lot so I can cook over an open fire."

Sebastian pulled the saddle bags from the pack animals while Howard collected wood for a small fire. By the time Kaelan unsaddled his and Ellen's mounts, and fed the animals, the fire was burning brightly and Ellen had a pot suspended over it.

There was an impressive variety of food in the paniers on the pack mounts. Bags held root vegetables, and there was both dried and fresh fruit. There was a small amount of smoked meat – which she figured she was better off not knowing what it came from – and a substantial quantity of strips like jerky, which she presumed was for emergencies.

A basket held a half dozen loaves of dark bread, and another several cloth-wrapped rounds that she guessed was cheese.

Despite being unfamiliar with most of the ingredients, she managed to prepare a simple, but savory stew. This was accompanied by the fresh bread, with some of the fresh fruit for dessert.

"Okay everyone," Ellen said. "Supper's ready."

The men were vociferous with their praise, and Ellen basked in their compliments.

"You should see what I can do with a stove," she said.

"You must think us backwards indeed if you believe we are not familiar with something as simple as a stove," Sebastian said.

"Ah, but the stoves you know burn wood to make heat, right?" Ellen asked.

"What else would it burn?"

"Nothing. But the stoves I'm familiar with run on electricity. Electricity is used for just about everything - cooking, heating..."

"Entertainment, lights..." Howard put in.

"Electricity must be a most powerful magic," Kaelan said, trying to wrap his mind around these wonders.

"Not magic, technology."

"Explain this technology," Sebastian asked.

Howard looked at him helplessly. "I wouldn't know where to start."

"Where's Wikipedia when you need it," Ellen said with a wry smile. She held up her hand to stave off any questions when it looked like both Sebastian and Kaelan were going to ask. "Wikipedia is an information source that people can access, but it's not one hundred per cent reliable."

"Like an oracle," Kaelan suggested.

Ellen looked at Howard, who shrugged. "I guess."

"Your world sounds like it is filled with wonders," Sebastian said. "I would very much like to see it some day."

"And I would very much like to show it to you," Howard said. "If it's at all possible."

They fell to staring at each other. Ellen rolled her eyes and Kaelan smothered a grin.

"I think, perhaps, we should get some sleep. Tomorrow will be a long day. We will be leaving the protection of the Elven Realm," Kaelan told them. And then their adventure would truly begin.

Chapter Thirteen

Kiranthus slowly climbed the stairs to the room he used for meditation. Oh, he could change his name and insist everyone call him Thackery, but the truth was, in his heart of hearts he would always be Kiranthus, youngest wizard to ever sit on the council of Mythago, beloved of Farenalysia, mortal enemy of the blood mage Anakaron.

Though he had no reason to feel so, in some ways he felt responsible for the path Anakaron had taken. At one time they'd been friends, a very long time ago perhaps, but true nonetheless.

They had started at the Conservatory of Magic in Mythago at the same time, on the same day even. Anakaron had been fresh off the boat from the Mythric Islands, while Kiranthus had arrived fresh off the farm from the hills of Sonara. Both boys had been often ostracized by the more cosmopolitan scholars making up their year group – Anakaron for being nothing more than a blood thirsty island savage, Kiranthus nothing more than a hayseed. Later, when they individually proved to have more power than the rest put together, they were more fully accepted, although there were still a few who were jealous enough to shun them.

They'd shared a room, and no few adventures, and most of all they'd shared a love for the beautiful Farenalysia, daughter of one of the most prestigious houses in the city.

To be fair, almost every lad at the conservatory was in love with her. Not only was she beautiful, she was intelligent, quick-witted, fearless, kind, and generous. Her father was a well-respected wizard of some note, the only wizard to ever refuse a seat on the council, while her mother was rumored to be an elfin princess.

Kiranthus and Anakaron agreed that there was no point putting themselves out to impress her, given their backgrounds it was unlikely they'd succeed anyway. They were not the only ones surprised when, by the end of her first year of classes the three had become fast friends.

Farenalysia was blunt when she told them she was not interested in romance, but she would appreciate friends. She favored neither one of them over the other and the three remained close friends throughout their time at the conservatory.

And yet, it was not their feelings for the young sorceress that drove a wedge through the two young men. In their fifth and final year, the students were given their own quarters. These rooms were high in the towers. Kiranthus chose a bright room with a view of the harbor and the Mythric Ocean beyond, while Anakaron chose the east side where the Shadow Mountains blocked the sun. The year was to be spent in research and study, practicing the skills they'd acquired and learning to tap into the Wells of Power for their final testing.

Anakaron had taken to spending long hours wandering the hills outside of Mythago. He started carrying a crystal topped staff, a fey look in his eyes as he explained how he'd found it in a cave during one of his rambles. He would allow no one to touch the staff, nor was anyone allowed in his chambers. An acrid smell clung to his robes and his temper grew short.

Disturbing reports began coming in, reports of the bodies of animals who'd died under mysterious circumstances being found. This was followed by word of shadow creatures being seen in the hills. When a group of young magic students was set upon by a wraith-like creature one night, and one of the youngsters killed, the council met with the senior wizards from the conservatory and came to the unpleasant conclusion that there was a blood mage amongst them, a practitioner of the dark magics that had been outlawed ages past.

Still, Kiranthus had no reason to suspect his friend. Not until "accidents" began befalling anyone who crossed Anakaron. The student who jostled him in his rush to get to class tripped on the stairs and broke his leg. The serving wench who spilled the ale on their table during one of the rare occasions Kiranthus was able to pry him from his room somehow caught her apron on fire and was burned horribly before the fire could be put out. A dog that growled at them as they passed by choked on a bone and died.

Kiranthus was troubled by these events, but wasn't sure how to broach the subject with his friend. He and Farenalysia had become much closer during this time and so he confided in her.

"There is a darkness in Anakaron," she said in a troubled voice. "And the staff he carries troubles me. But for him to have turned to blood sorcery..."

"I know. It does not bear thinking of. And yet..."

She nodded. "And yet it is hard to dismiss." She sighed. "Maybe if we both spoke with him. We could take him to dinner, perhaps an opportunity will present itself."

And so, they persuaded Anakaron to leave his studies for the night and join them at a tavern near the harbor for dinner. Kiranthus thought perhaps the view of the sea would help his friend recall where he had come from and how far he had progressed. The dinner was a pleasant one, so much so that Kiranthus was ready to dismiss their fears as groundless. But then on the way back to the conservatory, as they crossed a busy avenue, they were almost run down by a farmer's cart.

"My apologies!" the farmer called out. "It has been a long journey and the beast is over eager for his dinner."

"No apologies necessary," Kiranthus called out. They were as much at fault for not paying better attention.

At the same time, the donkey stumbled, and then fell its traces, sides heaving as it labored for breath.

"And now the beast can have eternal rest," Anakaron murmured. A quick glance at him showed a slight smile on his face.

"Not if I can help it," Farenalysia said grimly, pushing between them.

She knelt by the fallen animal and put one hand on its neck, one on its nose. Using his inner eye, Kiranthus could see the green healing magic flowing from her into the beast. Farenalysia was strong in the healing magics.

But then he saw the green fading, as though it was being pulled away. Farenalysia swayed slightly, redoubling her efforts. Kiranthus glanced towards Anakaron who wore a look of intense concentration, the crystal topping his staff glowing.

Kiranthus stepped in front of him. "Stop this," he said.

Anakaron did not look at him but said, "No. I would have my

vengeance."

"And what of Farenalysia? Would you have your vengeance even at the cost of her life? She would heal the beast and even now is pouring her personal energy into it."

That startled Anakaron enough that he glanced towards Farenalysia, and then had the grace to look slightly ashamed.

Once the energy stopped draining away she was able to complete the healing. She stroked the donkey's neck and urged him to his feet. The farmer was beside himself with joy.

"I thank you from the bottom of my heart, lady," he said. "I do not know what I would have told my daughter had I come home without him. He's something of a pet of hers; I only used him today because the horse came up lame."

"I'm glad I was able to help," Farenalysia assured him.

"Blessings on you, lady. Blessings."

The farmer continued on his way, leading the donkey by his own hand rather than climbing back up on the cart. The three friends stood for a long moment at the side of the road, Farenalysia leaning on Kiranthus for support.

"I suppose you'll be reporting this to the conservatory," Anakaron said, a slight sneer on his face.

Farenalysia said quietly, "If you continue upon this dark path we will not need to."

"Bah!" Anakaron spun on his heel and stalked off in the opposite direction.

The following morning, Anakaron's room was found empty. No one knew when or where he had gone, but there was not a trace of him left in those dark chambers.

By mutual consent, Farena and Kiranthus could no longer keep their suspicions to themselves. They did not believe he was the blood mage causing so much misery, but they did believe him to be in league with him – an apprentice, still learning the dark arts.

They went to Paranathel, who in turn passed their suspicions to the council. The council was already aware of Anakaron's fondness for the darker magics, and a full investigation was launched.

But Anakaron had disappeared. Some believed he went back to the islands from whence he came, others believed he was hiding in the hills. Kiranthus and Farenalysia knew he was not far, because bad things were still happening.

Still, life went on. Kiranthus and Farena become closer and the time of testing was soon upon them. Kiranthus and his year mates were summoned to the council chamber that had been built around a Well of Power for the testing. Though Kiranthus was saddened that his former friend was not with them, he could not let it distract him.

One by one the students were called upon. There were eleven sorcerers who sat on the council – one for each of the Seven Thoughts of Magic, and one for each of the four directions. Each had a part to play in the testing.

The testing went smoothly until the final student. Hagan and Anakaron had never gotten along, and privately Kiranthus thought it was just as well he wasn't here now to see how well his rival was doing.

As Hagan began drawing power from the well, a darkness fell on the chamber. There was a blood curdling scream, one of soul-searing agony. By the time anyone was able to produce enough light by which to see, it was too late. Hagan's smoking corpse lay where he had stood, and there was a "wrongness" to the well.

"It was as though all the power of the Well fed through the poor boy and then back into it somehow and the passage left the magic...tainted," Paranithel told them later.

"I've never heard of such a spell," Farena said, shaking her head.

"I have," Kiranthus said. "It was one of the forbidden spells locked up in the reference section of the conservatory library." He shrugged and held his hands wide as the other two stared at him. "We were new to the conservatory and were having trouble making friends. We spent a lot of time in the library."

Farena shuddered. "I do not like to think Anakaron is capable of such a deed."

"That is because you wish to see the good in everyone, daughter," Paranithel said. "What is it?" he asked Kiranthus.

"How could we have missed seeing the darkness in him?" Kiranthus asked. "We were friends – how could I have missed it?"

Paranithel sighed and shook his head. "It is the nature of darkness to stay hidden. And now that he has revealed his true nature, I fear what he may be capable of."

It was more than a year before the taint could be cleared from the Well. A unicorn was summoned, but the taint was beyond its ken. There was too great a difference between cleansing a pool of water and cleansing a well of magic.

Farenalysia prevailed upon her mother, the elven princess, who came accompanied by two other elven sorcerers. They, in turn, summoned a blessing of unicorns and working alongside the human wizards, were able to successfully clear the taint. It was to everyone's sorrow that one of the unicorns died during the process. Her body was returned to the well.

For a time, it seemed like that was the end of the trouble in Mythago. Farenalysia and Kiranthus married (to no one's surprise), and as a newly fledged master sorcerer he was invited to stay on at the conservatory to teach.

But then a great sea creature decimated the fishing fleet. The few survivors described it as a creature of smoke and shadow with no substance to fight. The council stood upon the seawall to keep it from entering the city and it took their combined power to repel it. Two of their members did not survive the encounter and Kiranthus was invited to take the place of the eastern representative.

A search was mounted for Anakaron's lair, there being no doubt in anyone's mind who was responsible, but no trace of him could be found. People stayed as close to their homes as possible, many made plans to leave. But it was far too late.

Anakaron's shadow creatures were swift and brutal, cutting a swath of destruction through the city and beyond before the citizens were even fully aware of the danger they were in. The council, and indeed, every able-bodied magic worker, stood on the wall against them. Few escaped with their lives.

Thackery sighed. How many times had he chided students for dwelling on past mistakes instead possible future triumphs? There was no point in looking to the past, even if there had been something he could have done he could not go back and change things. All he could do was hope Jessica reached him before Anakaron learned of her.

Chapter Fourteen

The ground was no harder than the ground she'd slept on while camping with her family, but Ellen did not get a good night's rest. Sore muscles aside, she'd been plagued by uncomfortable dreams.

It was finally starting to sink in that this wasn't just one of Howard's games, this was real. It was a little unnerving, looking around the clearing and being unable to identify the trees and plant life. This was not her home. Not her world. She didn't belong here.

She wasn't even sure she had a place in this little expedition. If it wasn't for the fact that they were going to meet up with Jessica, she'd have opted to stay with Aracelia. Howard had his magic, Sebastian was an experienced traveler, and Kaelan, from all accounts, was a fierce warrior. And what was she, in her borrowed clothes and magicked up katana? A wanna be designer who worked as a clerk in a clothing store. She couldn't even mount or dismount her freaking horse. What use was she? Camp cook? Mascot?

Before she could sink too far into her wallow of self-pity it was time to pack up and be on their way. Kaelan had already saddled Epona for her and placed the saddlebags with her personal items behind the saddle. Even with Epona kneeling down for her it was a stretch to get into the saddle, and she hung on tightly as the mare straightened again.

"Are you feeling well?" Kaelan asked her solicitously. He'd noticed that she was moving rather stiffly throughout the meal preparation that morning.

She gave him a grimace of a smile. "It's going to get better, right? I mean, I'm not going to feel like my muscles are on fire this whole trip?"

He just barely succeeded in hiding his grin at her description. "I promise, as you get used to being in the saddle it will affect you less and less. Before you know it, your muscles will loosen up and it will feel completely natural."

"I doubt that," she muttered. "But I'm going to hold you to that feeling better promise." She smiled down at him but her smile faded as she noted his expression had turned serious. "What is it?"

"I hope you will not take what I say amiss, but as you are not an experienced rider I am wondering if you would not like a few tips to make things easier on both you and your mount."

"Why do I get the feeling we won't be walking our mounts once we're out of the elven realm?" Ellen asked.

"For the most part we will not need to go above a walk, even at a walk the *estrada* are far superior to horses. Their stride is longer and they do not tire easily."

"But...?"

He shrugged. "But there may be times that will require speed. The land outside of the enclave is riddled with bandits and thieves. I would not like for you to become unseated at such a time."

"So you're offering a crash course in riding, eh?" she asked.

"Crash course?" he repeated with a frown.

"Sorry. Yes, of course I would appreciate any tips you have to make this easier."

"I think we could all benefit from a few pointers," Sebastian pointed out. "I am a seasoned traveler, but I have never had the pleasure of riding an *estrada* before. The evenness of their gait is not the only thing that is different about them."

Kaelan launched into a long-winded explanation of the differences between the *estrada* and horses, to which Ellen only listened to with half an ear. It was kind of like when her brothers were discussing the finer points of their favorite cars. But when he segued into the tips on making the riding experience more comfortable, she was all ears.

By the time he finished his lecture on the finer points of riding an *estrada*, they had reached the barrier for the Elven Realm.

"You will feel a slight disorientation as we pass through," he told them, "But it will only be a momentary discomfort."

"Wait a minute," Howard said as they prepared to pass through the barrier. They turned to look at him. "Even though I have magical abilities here, I'm not used to them yet. I just wanted to know how safe it will be for me to use them once we're past the barrier. Paranithel and Thackery were pretty adamant that Jessica use hers as little as possible for fear Anakaron might target her."

Kaelan hesitated before replying. "It is to my great shame that I had not considered that. Nor, I think, did the Lady Aracelia, else she would have tested you more fully. She tested your potential for the different Thoughts of magic, not the amount of power you wield."

"Thoughts?" Ellen asked.

"Yes, there are seven Thoughts of Magic as set out by the wizard's council of Mythago: Alchemy, creating potions and elixirs or transmuting matter; Animagus, the ability to influence or communicate with animals; Conjuring, using incantations for spell-casting; Elemental, having mastery over one or more of the elements; Healing, from curing an illness to regenerating a limb; Mind magic, which includes the gift of prophecy and being able to manipulate energies solely with the mind; and Necromancy, being able to communicate with and sometimes even raise the dead."

"What about blood magic?" Howard asked, having heard the term in reference to Anakaron.

Kaelan looked at him seriously. "Blood magic is an anathema to all right-thinking beings. A blood sorcerer is able to pull the life essence from living beings to use to fuel their spells."

Ellen shivered at his tone of voice. "This guy who's after Jessica's family, Anakaron. He's a blood sorcerer, isn't he?"

"From what I understand, yes."

"So...it would probably be best if I used as little magic outside the enclaves as possible," Howard said, half-hoping the elf would tell him otherwise.

"Small magics would not draw undue attention, nor would defensive magics - fear tends to amplify power - but I would advise against a major conjuring."

"To be honest, I never thought of defensive magics," Howard said. "I figured I'd just use a sword like the rest of you."

"Not a chance!" Ellen told him. "You may have forgotten what happened when Jessica tried to teach you to use a sword, but I haven't."

They had just come from a Lord of the Rings marathon at the Cineplex, all three movies and all the popcorn you could eat for a donation to the local historical society to fund their yearly Renaissance Faire. Howard badgered Jessica until she agreed to teach him how to use a sword.

The lesson took place in the dojo belonging to Ellen's family, it being the only indoor space they had access to that was big enough for their purpose. Howard had not only proved he was not inclined to be a swordsman, he was equally inept fighting with a knife. In the process he managed to sprain his wrist and drop the sword, hilt first fortunately, on his foot, breaking a couple of his toes. The sword may have been wooden, but the hilt was solid metal to give it some weight.

"Jessica used fireballs to defend herself," Sebastian put in, "When she remembered she had magic to use."

Howard held out his hand and concentrated. A flame sprang to life, but after a few seconds he shook his hand and it went out. "Ow!"

He looked around sheepishly. "This might take a bit of practice."

"It is a shame you had not the time to learn elemental magics," Kaelan said with regret. "The elements can be truly powerful when used as a defense. Have you no weapons skill at all?"

Howard shook his head, feeling more embarrassed than he'd ever been in his life. "We have a lot of laws in place where I come from to keep people safe. And people who break these laws are dealt with by law enforcement agencies."

Kaelan looked puzzled. "And yet you carry a sword and it is to be presumed you know how to use it," he said to Ellen.

"My father is a master in the martial arts," she replied. "I guess it's only natural that all of his children showed interest in it too. I'm just as good at hand-to-hand combat as I am with the sword," she said without a boast. "But though I'm trained in both, I've never used either outside of competition."

"And you?" he asked Sebastian. "What of your abilities?"

"Normally being a bard is enough to keep the ruffians at bay," Sebastian said with an easy grin. "But I'm a fair shot with the bow and I can defend myself with both sword and knife. Though I didn't have the intensive training Dominick received as a lad, he passed on his knowledge to me and we'd spar often enough."

Sitting back in his saddle, Kaelan looked at the group he was shepherding. One small, untried female, one bard who was better suited to the tap room than a battlefield, and one magic worker with little experience of magic. What had he gotten himself into?

Chapter Fifteen

Once again Jessica was standing at the rail of the boat, but this time she was in a much better frame of mind. Things between her and Dominic were good – well, barring the lack of privacy – and they'd be in Turksin in just a couple of days. She was smiling as she let the breeze blow the hair back from her face, the sun warming her.

Then her smile turned to a frown.

"What was that?" she asked Dominic as he came up beside her.

"What was what?"

She pointed to a dark shape in the water that seemed to be following alongside the boat. "That."

His indulgent smile also turned to a frown as he looked to where she was pointing. "Damn!"

Turning quickly, he cupped his hands around his mouth and bellowed, "Snake! There's a snake in the river!"

Even as he gave warning there was a bump, hard enough to rock the boat, and one of the merchants crowding the bow fell overboard with a yell.

Jessica griped Dominic's arm. "Isn't anyone going to try and help him? Throw him a line or something?"

Dominic shook his head. "It's too late for him, love."

Even as he spoke there was the sound of rushing water and the snake's head rose out of the water, the merchant's body clasped in its jaws. The man wasn't moving.

"Holy Saint Christopher," Jessica whispered, her hold on Dominic's arm tightening.

The snake continued to rise, towering a good twenty feet over the barge. It tossed the merchant's body up in the air and caught it so that it slid head first into its mouth and straight down its throat.

Jessica's stomach spasmed as she closed her eyes and turned away. Dominic pulled her into the shelter of his arms.

"What will we do if it attacks?" she asked with a shiver of apprehension.

He hesitated a second, then admitted, "Hopefully the merchant will be enough to keep his appetite satiated until we're out of his territory."

She shivered again.

"Man the oars!" the shipmaster called.

Jessica's eyes widened. "Oars?" she asked. "This isn't– "

"Be at ease," Dominic told her. "These oars are used only for racing against another barge. But in this case the ship master wants to put as much distance between us and the snake as possible – the sail just isn't enough."

Jessica glanced up at the large, square sail. "I'll bet I could– "

"Don't even think about it," he warned, stripping off his shirt.

"What are you doing?"

"Helping." He dropped a kiss on the top of her head and handed her his shirt. "Hold this for me, would you?"

Several other passengers, as well as most of the crew, stripped off their shirts and were heading to the hold of the ship, presumably where the oars were shipped. As the last of them disappeared through the hatch, Jessica turned to look over the side of the boat, holding tight to the rail. The group of merchants seemed to be squabbling over their fallen comrade's belongings.

Almost in unison, the oars slid through the slots in the hull. Some kind of chanting drone began and the oars began to move. The barge shot forward and she was glad she had the rail to hold onto.

She had no idea how long, or how far, they travelled at this accelerated speed, but at last the captain called up to the lookout, "Any sign of the beastie?"

"No sign, capt'n. Looks like we be in the clear."

To Jessica's surprise, only every other oar disappeared back into the barge. When the oarsmen returned above deck, it was obvious only the passengers that volunteered had been released from duty.

"What's going on?" Jessica asked Dominic when he returned to her side. "Are we still in danger?"

"Probably not," he said, shrugging into his shirt again. "But then we never should have been in danger in the first place."

"What do you mean?"

"That was a sea snake. You might find them at the mouth of the river, but never this far south."

Jessica mulled that over for a moment. "Kind of makes you wonder what's at the mouth of the river that made it come this far."

"Aye, that it does."

Thanks to the use of the oars, they arrived at Turksin well ahead of schedule. Being a cargo barge the unloading of cargo took precedence over the disembarking of passengers, who were told to stand against the rail and stay out of the way.

From what Jessica could see, Turksin didn't seem all that different from any of the other port towns they'd been in, although it did seem cleaner than most. The docks were a hive of activity, the cargo being carried off or loaded onto wagons and then carted off. Several women, some with children, waited patiently, and several others, standing well apart from the wives, waited to ply their trade.

"Where's he going in such a hurry?" Jessica asked, spying the captain pushing his way through the crowd on the dock.

"Probably to the harbor master to report the presence of the snake," Dominic told her. "They'll need to send out a warning. We were lucky. The barge was big enough to discourage an attack but a smaller boat may not be as lucky."

Jessica shivered. "I never did like snakes much."

It was just as well she didn't know about the fire wyrms of the southern deserts that made the sea snake look small in comparison.

At last the barge was empty of its cargo and the passengers were allowed to leave. The merchants, in particular, seemed to be in a hurry to leave, muttering and complaining the whole time.

"I think the first thing we should see to is about getting a room for the night," Dominic said. "It's too late to visit the horse market today, but we can settle in and seek it out in the morning."

Nodding in agreement, Jessica let him lead her away from the small cluster of men around the harbor master and towards one of the side streets.

"How do you know where to go?" she asked. "Have you been here before?"

"No, but I trust the merchants to lead us to the street the decent inns are on," he replied, nodding towards the group ahead of them.

Jessica recognized a couple of them from the barge and wondered if they were taking news of the one who'd been eaten by the snake to his next of kin.

The merchants stopped at an inn that resembled a small fortress, but Dominic led her down a quiet side street to one of the smaller establishments. While Dominic dickered over the price of a room, Jessica looked around. Like the town itself, the inn was pretty much like all the other inns they'd stayed in – a tap room and bar on the main floor with rooms up above. There was a clear spot in the corner opposite the fireplace and she wondered if that meant there was entertainment at night.

At last they were able to make their way upstairs. Jessica dropped her pack by the door and flopped down on the bed with a sigh. "The water may be a faster way to travel, but I'll take a soft bed on dry land any time."

"And thanks to the water snake, we have an extra day to enjoy it," Dominic told her, sitting down at the small table for two near the window.

"Really?" Her eyes lit up.

"Really. But first, come here. We need to talk."

Chapter Sixteen

Jessica eyed Dominic apprehensively. "Talk about what? In my experience when someone asks you to sit down to talk it's never good." Things had started going good for them again. Maybe this was where he confessed about having a wife and kids in some distant port. If he did, she'd turn him into a snake for jerking her around.

"You come over here," she suggested, swinging her legs around to give him room on the bed. She turned slightly sideways so she was facing him. "Now, how bad is it?"

"It's nothing bad. Well, it is bad, but not in the way you're thinking. Probably not, anyway."

"Just spit it out Dominic," she said. "Honestly, you can be as bad as Howard sometimes. And that's saying something because he is a champion at beating around the bush."

"Did you not wonder why I stopped you from offering to call up a wind to fill the sails when we were fleeing from the snake?"

"Well, I just assumed it was because you were afraid I'd overdo it and call up a hurricane or something."

"That was a small part of it, yes," he admitted. "But the other reason is that it takes a great deal of power to conjure up a wind, unless you can control an elemental, and too much power can attract the wrong kind of attention."

"I thought we didn't need to worry about the witch guard or anyone like that now. We're well off of Ghren lands."

He sighed and ran his hand through his hair and she stifled the urge to reach over and smooth it out again. "Have you noticed that although magic is available, magic workers do not flaunt their abilities?"

Jessica frowned. "Now that you mention it…. In Ghren it kind of made sense, given that the king had a hate on for all things magical, but even in Grenin the only dealers in magical items were tucked away down the back streets. Why is that?"

"The reasons are twofold," he said, shifting slightly. "Firstly, there are many who are jealous of those with magical abilities and it is prudent for those with even minor power to exercise caution."

"Okay, I get that."

"Secondly…" Here Dominic paused, as though unsure how to go on. "You recall the mention of the destruction of the city of Mythago?"

"Yes, but I got the impression that was a long time ago."

"Though the deed was done long ago, the dark lord who caused it still exists."

"And?"

"Though he disappeared for a time, Thackery believed he would return. There are signs he has done so, but he is not alone. He has acquired …." He hesitated, searching for the right word.

"Goons? Minions? Agents?"

"Let us call them lackeys. They're spread throughout the northern continent and their sole purpose is to seek out objects of power or anyone who shows an excess of magical ability."

"Okay, but I'm kinda new to the game. Who's to say these lackeys will even look twice at someone like me?"

"Me," he admitted glumly.

When he didn't continue right away, Jessica elbowed him in the ribs.

"Ow! Hellfires woman, you have sharp elbows."

"Talk, dog boy. How do you know I'm in danger?"

"Careful, witch. This dog has a bite." To prove his point he nipped her lower lip and then kissed her thoroughly.

He almost forgot what he wanted to talk to her about but Jessica resolutely pushed him away. "You're the one who wanted to talk, so talk. We can finish this later."

Dominic heaved a sigh. "Fine. Things have been happening so fast that we never got a chance to talk about what I was doing in your camp the night you turned me into a dog."

Frowning, Jessica said, "I thought it was pretty obvious. You were there to rob me."

"Not exactly. I was hired by a wizard named Braxton– "

"Braxton. Where do I know that name from?"

"I don't know. Anyway, Braxton hired me to steal a specific item from you. It– "

"Braxton! He was the wizard that set the spell over Castle Ghren that chased everybody out and kept them out with that army of illusions."

"He– I thought no one knew who set the spell?"

Jessica looked at him a little guiltily. "Well, we couldn't really tell anyone the truth without having to explain Wendel's part in it– "

"Wendel's that little hedge wizard that ended up with your lady's maid, right?"

"Right. Braxton tricked Wendel into being in the castle once the spell was set so that he'd take the blame if anyone was able to break the spell."

"So that's how he knew about it," Dominic mused.

"Knew about what?"

"Your amulet."

"Let me get this straight," Jessica said. "This Braxton hired you to steal my moonstone amulet because he thought it was the source of my power?" She leaned away to better see his face.

"He actually had me convinced that you'd stolen it from him and you were using it to harm innocent people."

"Hmm."

"We were on Ghren lands and ... I know it's no excuse– "

"But you were trying to protect the innocent citizens of Ghren," Jessica finished for him.

"Something like that," he admitted, a little shamefaced.

He hung his head with a sigh and was startled when he felt her hands on his face. She moved closer, framing his face with her hands so she could kiss him.

"Are you sure you don't want to be king?" she whispered against his lips.

"Very sure. I like my freedom too much. I'd much rather be your valiant protector."

She smiled. "Like a super hero with a secret identity. I've always had a thing for super heroes."

Before he could ask what a super hero was, she was kissing him again. He thoroughly enjoyed himself for a few minutes before gently pushing her away.

"There's more," he said reluctantly.

"More? What more could there be?"

Unable to face her, he got to his feet and began pacing as he talked.

"I made myself a promise that I would never lie to you, and it's put me in somewhat of an ethical dilemma."

"I think that's ad– wait. What kind of ethical dilemma?" The smile that had begun to blossom on her face died in the making at his serious expression.

"While I have not lied to you, I am guilty of perpetuating a lie of someone else's making."

"Stop that and sit down," she said when he paced close enough for her to reach out and grab his arm. She pulled him down beside her. "That's better. Now who's been lying to me?"

His mouth opened and closed a couple of times before he was able to speak. "Pretty much everyone," he said quietly.

"What?"

"I guess it started with Howard."

"Howard?"

"To be fair, he didn't know what was going on at first, and by the time he did there was no good way to tell you, and then he kept getting himself in deeper and deeper– "

"Holy Saint Christopher!" she exploded. "Will you get to the point?"

"Thackery isn't just some random wizard, he's your father. And he and your grandfather are the reason you're in this world in the first place."

"Oh."

Dominic waited for the explosion that never came. "That's it? Just 'oh'?"

It was Jessica's turned to look uncomfortable. "I've been meaning to tell you..."

"Tell me what?" he asked with growing irritation. He'd been agonizing over telling her the truth for weeks, he just hadn't been able to find the right words.

"Do you remember when I was lost on the Fae Road?"

"Yes." He would never, ever forget. He'd almost lost her forever, just when he'd found her.

"I ended up somewhere called the space between worlds where I met my mother."

"What?"

"Well, I guess it was more like the spirit of my mother, but she seemed real enough. Anyway, she kind of told me what was going on."

She slanted a look in his direction but he could only stare back blankly. All this time and she'd known the truth.

"She's also the one who gave me the incantation I used on Ewan," she added helpfully.

"Why didn't you say anything before?"

"Things happened so fast, it just never seemed to be the right time to tell you," she said in a small voice.

Dominic's annoyance ran from him like water. He sighed and pulled her back into his arms. "Well, I'm glad you know, and that neither of us need keep secrets from the other."

"No more secrets," Jessica said, and leaned up for a kiss.

"No more secrets," he agreed. "I think that's enough talking for tonight."

Chapter Seventeen

Kaelan led the way and they watched the shimmer as it passed over him. Ellen couldn't suppress a shiver, but Epona never hesitated, just walked steadily through the barrier. It tingled, like a mild electrical shock. Howard and Sebastian followed close behind.

The world outside the barrier was dull and dreary. For Ellen it was more shocking than the sensation of the barrier passing over her. "How can you bear to leave the Elven Realm behind?" she asked.

Kaelan looked at her curiously. "To be honest, I see very little difference between the two. I have often heard, however, that to humans the Elven Realms are of a much more vivid appearance. We elves do not see it thusly."

"I wonder why that is?" Ellen mused. "Maybe it has something to do with your natural elven magic."

"Perhaps," he conceded. "Or perhaps it is because we are so used to it the intensity of it has faded in our view."

"Kaelan, are we still on the right path? I can't see it anymore," Howard said.

"If you look behind us, the path has faded from there as well. Its purpose was to guide us out of the Elven Realm. Now that we are free of it, it will vanish and only reappear if we were to pass through the barrier again."

"Would that be true no matter where we passed through?" Sebastian asked.

"Yes, however it would not necessarily take us back the way we came, it would lead us to the nearest settlement."

"Is that part of the elven magic as well?" Ellen couldn't resist asking.

"But of course!" He flashed her a grin.

As they continued onward, they soon got used to the appearance of the more normal looking landscape. They could have been on a trail ride at a nearby ranch back home, thought Ellen. Save for the size of the animals they were riding, the clothes they were wearing, and the oh-so-handsome elf leading the way.

"It's like going from HD to regular TV," she said, not realizing she was speaking aloud.

"I wouldn't know," Howard told her a little smugly. "I don't own a television."

"What's a television?" Kaelan and Sebastian asked in unison.

"It's, uh, it's ... a little help here?" Howard asked Ellen.

"You said that Aracelia had a mirror she uses for scrying?" she asked Kaelan.

"Yes, a large silver one."

"Okay, picture a large, square mirror that you can see moving pictures in, but it doesn't require any magic to operate it. You can just change the channel to watch something else. But the big difference is, you can only look at what someone else is doing, like Howard was doing with Jessica, you can't send messages through it."

"But then what is it used for?" Kaelan asked, bewildered.

"Mostly it's used for entertainment. Think of it as a play you can watch through a scrying bowl or mirror. There are all kinds of weird and wonderful things you can watch on television - from stories that people are acting out, to live coverage of sporting events, to real-life events that are unfolding even as you watch."

"And is this television run on electricity as well?" Sebastian asked.

"Of course," Howard said with a grin. His grin broadened.

"What?" Ellen asked.

"I was just thinking of Sebastian's reaction to a radio," he said. "A radio is similar to a television, only there's no picture. Just sound."

"As you used the moonstone pendant to communicate with Jessica?" Sebastian hazarded a guess.

"Sort of," Howard said. "You can't speak through a radio, only listen to it. And mostly what you listen to is music."

"All different kinds of music," Ellen put in. "Jazz, rock and roll, classical, country and western..."

Sebastian looked puzzled. "But where are the musicians? How are they compensated?"

"Oh, they're compensated all right," Howard said. "There's nothing in our world that's free. A large amount of music is recorded by a device that allows you to hear it over and over again. As many times as you wish. People buy these recordings and pay large sums of money to hear their favorite music makers perform at live concerts."

Shaking his head, Sebastian said, "I truly do not know if this is a good thing or a bad thing, this radio and the recording of the music. Your world is a most confusing place!"

"You're telling me," Howard said with a laugh.

They continued travelling in a more or less straight line, the rest of them trusting in Kaelan to know where he was going. He assured them that the road that would lead to Claverton, passing close to the Wild Woods Realm, was not too distant. And it turned out he was correct.

The road was hard packed dirt and the trees began to thin out considerably by the time they reached it. It twisted and turned, winding through the ever-diminishing trees and up and down several small hills. But at least the scenery was more interesting than it had been.

"So how far is it to the Wild Woods Realm?" Ellen asked eventually. Stiff muscles aside, she was actually enjoying travelling by horseback, but she was unused to such long periods of silence. What she wouldn't give for her iPod!

"Wild Woods is actually the closest enclave to the Darkwood Forest Realm," Kaelan responded. But before Ellen could get her hopes up, he added, "It should take no more than a week to reach it using the elven mounts."

Ellen sighed. She was pretty sure the novelty of riding and camping out would completely wear off well before the week was out.

Chapter Eighteen

Jessica and Dominic spent two days and two blissful nights in Turksin and on the morning of the third day visited the much-vaunted horse market. Though Dominic was quite impressed with the animals offered, quite frankly one horse looked pretty much like another to Jessica. She still missed her old mare and hoped whoever it'd been sold to treated her well.

"You're thinking about your mare again, aren't you?" Dominic asked as she sighed heavily.

"I can't help it. She and I went through a lot together, and she was a pretty good sport considering how inept a rider I was."

"I'm sure in time you'll form just as close a bond with your gelding."

"Well, I will admit he's prettier," she said, reaching down and patting the horse on its neck.

"See?"

"But pretty is as pretty does," she added ominously. "He might be short on stamina, or have a touchy stomach, or any number of things wrong with him that might crop up later."

Dominic bit back a sigh and barely refrained from rolling his eyes at her. They were less than a day out of Turksin and if he thought it would do any good he'd turn them around and find her a different mount. But he knew that it wouldn't so all that was left was to press on and hope she grew content with her current horse.

The sun was starting to lower in the sky and with resignation he began to keep an eye out for a good place to make camp. Jessica was not going to like this. The man who'd sold them the mounts had assured them that there were a number of towns and villages on the route they were taking to Claverton but they'd yet to see any sign of them. Just when he was about to stop them, he saw a traveler's marker.

"Are we stopping for the night?" Jessica asked in a tired voice when he turned off the trail.

She seemed so at home in the saddle that he often forgot she was not born to this way of life. "We're in luck, there's a travelers hut just ahead. Hopefully it's intact enough to shelter us from the elements."

This was not a busy trail so they had the shelter, such as it was, to themselves. Dominic took their packs inside and left Jessica to start a fire in the big, stone fireplace and cobble together dinner while he took care of the horses.

"What's wrong?" he asked when he came back inside. He'd found a second bucket in the lean-to for the horses and pumped it full of water so they could wash up inside.

Jessica was sitting beside the fireplace with a frown on her face. As with most shelters, this one was just that – shelter from the elements. It was a single room with a large, stone fireplace at one end and wooden planks covering the floor. She'd spread a cloth on the floor and had laid out their supper on it, but her attention was focused on something in her hand.

"I was trying to get in touch with Howard but I'm not having much luck."

"Are you sure you're using the right incantation?" he asked.

She turned to him in surprise. "There's more than one?"

"Of course, just as there are many different ways to scry." He sat down next to her. "Surely you learned that much from Thackery's spell book."

Jessica looked a little chagrined.

"You forgot you even had it, didn't you?" he said, a grin teasing the edges of his mouth. "And after Gareth was kind enough to send for all the gear we left behind in Eglion."

"Okay, I admit it. I did forget I had it. Not that I've had a lot of time to sit around to read it. And I'm still mad at that innkeeper for selling my horse. But back to this scrying business. Watch me to see if I'm doing this right."

Using the sleeve of her shirt she wiped the face of the silver mirror clean then spoke the incantation that would seek her friend out in the earthly realm. Her hand passed over the mirror, close to the surface but not touching it, to activate the spell. There was a shimmer of a pale, gold glow, but the mirror stayed dark.

"What am I doing wrong?" she asked in frustration.

"Nothing that I can see," he said with a frown. "You see the glow at the edge of the mirror? Perhaps Howard does not wish to be disturbed at this time and has a block in place."

"But why...oh. Well. Good for him. But the same thing happens when I focus on Ellen, and she's not able to block me out."

The beauty of the spell that let her speak with the friends she'd left behind was that she could use it for either of them. The spell was directed to the realm itself, all she had to do was focus on which friend she wanted to talk to.

"Here, you try," she said, passing the mirror over.

Dominic sighed. "You know scrying is not one of my better talents."

"All the more reason for you to practice," Jessica said with a smirk.

Grumbling under his breath, Dominic took the mirror from her. She watched intently as he grounded himself, then muttered the spell. When he passed his hand above the surface of the mirror, gold sparkles appeared around the edges, but the mirror itself stayed dark.

"Maybe the mirror's defective," Jessica suggested. "All this travelling around...maybe I jostled it and– I don't know, maybe the magical properties leaked out."

Dominic shot her an exasperated glance. "You know it doesn't work that way."

"Well, you explain it then."

He was quiet for a moment. "I can't."

Jessica's stomach chose that moment to give a loud rumble. He laughed outright as her face reddened. "Maybe we should worry about it after we've eaten."

"Maybe you're right," she agreed sheepishly.

They ate in a thoughtful silence and after they cleaned up, Jessica pulled the heavy spellbook from the bottom of her pack and began to leaf through it, looking for a different scrying spell. Dominic shook out their bedrolls and made himself comfortable in front of the fire.

"In the Forest of the Heart grow trees unlike any ever seen before," Jessica read aloud. "Giant, like the mountains, but filled with story and song. Firm, like the ironwood, but filled with a puckish sense of humor. Twisted, like a breeding ball of snakes, but with great peace and beauty. Walk amongst them and enter a world of tranquility."

She shut the book, a thoughtful look on her face.

"Sounds like the afterlife to me," Dominic said. "Or one of them at any rate."

She turned to look at him. "You think there's more than one?"

"I think there are as many as there are religions to believe in them."

"Well I hope that's not the afterlife I'm headed for," she said, joining him on the pallet. "I'm fast reaching my limit of trees, thank you very much."

Chapter Nineteen

Kaelan called a halt at midday, more for the sake of the humans than their mounts. Since this was just a rest stop there was no need for a fire, and Ellen threw together a quick meal of bread, cheese, and the last of the fresh fruit.

"I've been thinking, Howard ..." she began.

"Uh, oh. This can't be good," he said with a smirk.

"Ha, ha. No, seriously. I know that an edged weapon is out as far as you're concerned, but what about a staff?"

"A staff?"

"Yeah, like Gandalf in Lord of the Rings. Don't all wizards carry staffs?"

"Gandalf's staff was magic, I don't think it works that way here."

"I was thinking more about you carrying a staff to defend yourself with."

"You really think a wooden staff would be any use against a sword?" Howard asked dubiously.

"One of my brothers was part of an exchange program with a student from Japan. Akiro was really good with the *bo* – a staff used for fighting in the martial arts – and he taught us all to use one. And Jack, my oldest brother, picked up some pointers when he was in Japan. During a sparring match between my father and Akiro, Akiro was able to disarm my father using his *bo*. You should have seen my father's face." It was one of her fondest memories.

"Do you really think you could teach me?" Howard asked hopefully.

"I can try. We can practice during our breaks." She grinned suddenly. "At the very least, it'll keep our muscles limber."

"Could you teach me as well?" Sebastian asked suddenly.

They looked at him, surprised.

He shrugged. "Sometimes I find myself in situations where a weapon is needed, but a sword is a little..."

"Overkill?" Howard suggested.

"Exactly. At times it needs only a show of strength to ward off an attack. With a sharp sword a person can become injured for no good reason. I have seen staffs being used for defense in the west. In some cases they're even used for attack. I've just never had the time to learn. Or anyone to teach me."

"I don't see why not. And it might be easier for Howard to have someone his own size to spar with," Ellen said with another grin.

"Where are we to acquire these staffs with which to fight?" Kaelan asked.

Sebastian pointed to a spot downstream from where they were gathered. "There is a stand of ironwood trees just over there."

"Unfortunately, we have no axe," Kaelan pointed out. "And the ironwood would greatly damage the edge of a sword."

Ellen looked thoughtfully towards the grove of trees.

"You have an idea?" Kaelan asked.

She nodded. "Maybe we don't need to cut them. Howard,

come with me."

Mystified, he followed behind as she led the way to the grove. The trees were perfect for their needs. The trunks were squat and thick with a cluster of long, straight branches at the top, capped with a burst of leaves. They wouldn't even need to trim away excess branches, just trim the leaves off.

"Okay, do your thing, Howard."

"What thing?" he asked, completely baffled.

"Your magic thing. Use your earth magic to ask the trees nicely if we could have three of their straightest limbs - about six feet long."

He looked at her dubiously. "I think you've been out in the fresh air too long. All this oxygen is affecting your brain."

"There's no harm in trying," she insisted.

"Your success in Lady Aracelia's garden does suggest you have talent with the earth magic," Kaelan pointed out.

Howard looked helplessly over at Sebastian. "This is crazy, right?"

Sebastian grinned at him. "It's only crazy if it doesn't work."

Huffing a heartfelt sigh, Howard walked into the grove. When he reached the center he stopped. Closing his eyes, he reached inside for his magic spark, separating out the dark green thread. It was much easier this time. Feeling foolish, he began to speak.

"Uh, I don't know if you can understand me, but I need a favor. If three of you ironwood trees would graciously allow me to have one of your straightest branches - about as long as I am - I would greatly appreciate it. And in return, I'll give each of you a drink of my earth magic."

For a long moment, during which Howard projected peaceful

intentions towards the trees, nothing happened. Then there was a sound like branches rattling together, like a shiver went through the grove. There was a gasp behind him. Howard opened his eyes and just about gasped himself.

Lying on the ground, where there had been nothing before, were three long limbs. "Those are perfect!" Ellen exclaimed.

"I, um, thank you," Howard stuttered. He went to each of the three trees that had shed a limb and placed his palm on their trunks, concentrating on transferring some of his energy to each of them in turn. After the last one, he staggered slightly. "Whoa!"

Sebastian hurried over to steady him. "After all those times you berated Jessica for over-extending herself, here you do the same thing," he scolded. He helped Howard back to where they'd sat for their lunch.

"Sorry," Howard said. He looked up at the concerned faces surrounding him. "Really, I'll be okay in a minute or two."

Kaelan went over to the supply steed and returned with a water skin and a handful of dried fruit. "Here, these will help."

"Thanks," Howard said. Although his stomach turned at the thought of eating anything, he knew the elf was right. His blood sugar was probably dangerously low. He nibbled on the fruit, alternating it with sips of the water.

"This wood is amazing," Ellen said, holding one of the limbs in her hands. "It's the perfect weight for fighting - not too light, not too heavy. And it's so unbelievably dense!"

"It's ironwood," Sebastian said by way of explanation. "It's not particularly rare, but it's exceedingly difficult to work with which makes items made of it fetch incredible prices. It is said that only earth elementals are able to create designs in ironwood."

Howard brightened at that. "That will be my first goal in learning elemental magic – embellishing our staffs." To his surprise he'd finished off the fruit and was feeling much better. "I guess I've held us up long enough. I'm feeling okay."

"We will have to push ourselves if we are to reach the river before dark," Kaelan said.

Sebastian tucked the staffs in the pannier one of the pack mounts was carrying. They stuck up a little too far, but he secured them so that they wouldn't fall or move around too much. Joining the others, he mounted up so they could continue their journey.

Chapter Twenty

Ellen could hear Howard and Sebastian murmuring to each other, but they were lagging too far behind for her to make out what they were saying. Maybe it was just as well, she thought with a fleeting smile.

She studied the elf riding in front of her. Damn, he looked just as good from behind. He'd been nothing but courteous to her, but the air seemed to sizzle between them every time they got too close. She wished Jessica was here. Of course she knew what Jessica would say. Jessica would tell her to stop being such a wuss and go for it.

Normally she wouldn't hesitate. She'd had a number of boyfriends but things never got overly serious with any of them. But Kaelan...there was something different about him, and it wasn't just because he was an elf. She could very well lose her heart to him, and that scared her more than anything. Because it could only lead to heartbreak. She couldn't stay here, and he wouldn't want to come to her world. Would he? There was only one way to find out.

Stretching upwards, she whispered to Epona, "Do you think you could move up beside Kaelan please?"

Epona's ear twitched and she whickered, but her stride lengthened.

"Thank you," Ellen whispered.

Kaelan looked over at her in surprise. "Is anything wrong?"

"No," Ellen said, trying to control her blush response. "I was just curious about the Wild Woods Realm. Is it like the Darkwood Forest Realm?"

"No," he shook his head. "For one thing it is much smaller and there is no city as there is in Darkwood, just a handful of villages and a town in the center. Truthfully, it has been a long time since I have been there. My mother's family was not happy she chose to leave Wild Winds with my father and raise us in Darkwood."

"You don't visit your extended family in Wild Winds?"

"The visits became fewer as I became older. There never seemed to be time."

Ellen was trying to picture Kaelan as a child. She'd bet he was just as cute as a little kid. Elf. Whatever.

"Didn't your mother's family ever visit you in Darkwood?"

"My mother's family did not wish her to marry my father, despite the fact he would be able to provide well for her. To marry meant she would leave them."

"But love won out," Ellen guessed.

He glanced over at her. "It did indeed. They have been very happy and my mother never regretted her decision to follow her heart." Smiling, he faced forward again. "My father says they met when he was delivering a set of silver gauntlets to the lord of the Wild Woods Realm. There was a festival and he was invited to stay over for it. Mother was with a group of young women who kept fawning over him, supposedly because he was from outside the realm. Mother was the worst of the lot and wouldn't leave him alone until he danced with her. After that she was determined to make him hers and chased off every other woman who approached. Apparently the magic was strong in her blood. By the end of the evening he truly was hers, heart and soul."

Ellen laughed. "And what does your mother say?"

"Ah. Mother claims this cheeky apprentice silversmith noticed the setting up for the festival and wheedled an invitation from the lord of the realm, who gave it to him only because he was so impressed by the quality of his work. He was making such a nuisance of himself, pestering all the young women for dances, that she took pity on her friends and made the supreme sacrifice of dancing with him herself. By the end of the festival he proved his way with silver also included a silver tongue, because he sweet-talked her into running away with him."

"And which story do you believe to be true?"

"The one that my grandmother tells, that my mother noticed my father lurking on the fringes of the merry-makers and, feeling sorry for him, went over to see if she could convince him to join in. From the moment their eyes met they were lost to each other, and my grandmother knew she had lost her daughter, but gained a son."

"I think I like your grandmother's version best," Ellen said with a smile.

"And your parents?" Kaelan asked, genuinely interested. "You said they were from very different cultures, how did they meet?"

"Now that's a story in itself," she said. "They were friends growing up – their parents lived next door to each other."

Kaelan nodded. "Ah. So they knew from the beginning they were meant to be together."

"Actually, no. My father spent his senior year in Japan, studying the martial arts with one of his uncles. My mother went off to university where she became involved with one of her professors. She was very young, and far away from home, and he swept her off her feet. They had an affair and when she ended up pregnant, he married her."

"Your father is not your mother's husband?"

"He is, but it happened later." Ellen had to smile at his confused look. "Mom finished school right before she gave birth to twin boys. There was a lot of friction between her and George, her first husband. He wanted her to stay home and look after the boys, she wanted to put her degree to good use. Before she could find a job in her field – art restoration – she found out she was pregnant again."

"How many siblings do you have?" he asked in surprise.

"Four – two sets of twin brothers."

He shook his head in disbelief. "Elves bear only one child at a time, and we are not a prolific race. My mother is considered a wonder for having three children."

"I don't think mom was really happy having the boys so close together. In fact, from what I can gather it wasn't a happy marriage at all. But it didn't last long. She was still pregnant with the second set of twins when her husband died unexpectedly. She ended up moving back home with her parents – who were thrilled to have a houseful of children."

"Children are a blessing," Kaelan murmured, "no matter the circumstances."

"That's exactly what my grandparents believed," she said with a smile. "My father returned from Japan just after the second set of twins were born, fell in love with her all over again, and they were married a year later."

"He must be quite the man, to take on four children not his own."

"He is," she said proudly. She couldn't help but wonder what he'd think if he could see her now. Would he be proud? Or appalled?

Chapter Twenty-One

Because they were following a proper road, the *estrada* made good time and they reached the river just as the sun was beginning to set. Sebastian had just enough time to try his skill at fishing, which seemed to consist of him standing motionless in the river and then suddenly swooping downwards to fling a fish up onto the shore. More than willing to do his part, Howard would then kill and clean them.

What Sabastian lacked in technique he more than made up for in success. Before long he'd caught four large, fat, fish.

"Leave the skins on," Ellen told Howard. "It'll protect them so we can bake them."

She'd had him build a fire as soon as they reached a spot beside the river to camp, and by the time the fish were caught and cleaned it had burned down low enough that she was able to bake them in the hot coals. She'd placed a selection of the dried fruit inside for flavor, and added an assortment of the tubers to the coals.

"Now," she said, just as Sebastian and Howard were making themselves comfortable. "Why don't I give you your first lesson in fighting with a staff while our supper is cooking?"

The two men looked at each other with resignation.

"C'mon, on your feet." She prodded them with one of the

staffs, the other two she held in her other hand.

They grudgingly climbed to their feet and each took one of the staffs.

"Okay, then. You hold the staff in thirds, like this," she showed them. "This way when you hold it horizontally in front, the right palm is facing away from the body and the left hand is facing toward the body. This allows you to rotate your staff like this." She demonstrated and they awkwardly followed suit.

Because he had no previous weapons training to overcome, Howard actually did better than Sebastian at this.

"The power is generated by the back hand pulling the staff, while the front hand guides it." She showed them what she meant by slowly going through the motion. "When you're striking, the wrist is twisted, just like you were turning your hand over when punching."

Again she demonstrated slowly so they could see what she meant. Together they repeated the motion and once she was sure they had it, she began to speed up.

"That's great, guys. Now, there's a wide variety of blocks, strikes, and sweeps I could show you, but to start I'm just going to show you a couple of simple ones. Once you have them down, I'll let you have a go at each other."

Kaelan had been watching the proceedings with interest. "Forgive me for doubting you," he said. "To be honest I had not thought a stick would be much of a defense against a sword, but an ironwood staff, wielded such as you have been instructing, could make for quite an effective defense."

"A staff made out of this ironwood could make an effective offensive weapon against a sword as well," Ellen said smugly.

When Kaelan looked at her doubtfully, she said," Don't believe me? All right, why don't we give it a try to find out?"

He was already shaking his head no. "I cannot take advantage of a..."

"What? An opponent who's shorter than you are?" She poked him in the chest with her staff. "A woman?" She poked him again.

Sebastian and Howard stood using their staffs to lean on for support to watch.

Something flashed in Kaelan's eyes. "I do not wish to take advantage of a comrade."

"What's the matter, chicken?" she asked, poking at him again.

This time he backed out of her way, and drew his sword. "Very well, but do not say that you were not warned."

"Right back at you," Ellen said with a grin.

She spun the staff in her hands and Kaelan suddenly found himself back pedaling to keep out of its reach. He immediately found the first disadvantage of staff versus sword. The staff had twice the reach that his sword did. Twice he only just barely managed to turn the end of the staff away from doing him serious damage.

Finally, he saw his opportunity and slashed downwards, his sword connecting with the ironwood with an ominous clang that reverberated up his sword arm. The end of the staff was touching the ground and he was close enough to Ellen that he was able to tell her, "I yield!"

Ellen grinned. "Me too."

They straightened up and he told her, "If you are half as good with the sword as you are with the staff, I fear for any ruffian who dares approach us."

She shook her head. "I think that will be a wait and see

scenario. It's one thing to spar in a dojo, or even have a match with a friend, but you never know how someone will react in a life-or-death situation until they're actually in it."

"Don't sell yourself short, El," Howard said, coming up behind her and slinging a friendly arm over her shoulders. "You'll go all Terminator on their asses, wait and see."

"Hopefully we won't have the opportunity to find out," she said dryly. "Now let's have our supper. I've really worked up an appetite."

Supper was pulled from among the coals and loaded onto the wooden plates. It was declared another success.

"I've cooked fish in this fashion before," Sebastian admitted, "But I've never thought to stuff it with fruit."

"One of Jessica's former boyfriends was a chef in training. We both learned a lot from him. He was very inventive when it came to cooking."

"Too bad he was such a dud when it came to other things," Howard said. "What?" he added when they all looked at him. "That was the reason she gave me for them breaking up."

"You know," Ellen said, "There's no reason why you two can't get a little extra sparring in."

"It is especially important for you, Howard, if you are to use this as your primary means of defense, to practice every chance you get."

With a sigh Howard got to his feet, turning to give Sebastian a hand up as well.

"Isn't it a little dark for sparring?" Howard asked.

"The fire's giving off plenty of light," Ellen assured him. "And I want to see how much you both retained from your lessons earlier."

"As loathe as I am to admit it," Sebastian added, "We will not always have perfect fighting conditions should someone choose to attack. It is wise to learn to adapt to as many different circumstances as possible."

"Figures you'd take her side," Howard said with a grimace. "Okay, then," he held his staff upright. "En guard!"

Ellen rolled her eyes. "That's for fencing, you nit. And you're not holding your staff properly."

She corrected his grip and then Sebastian's, then stood back with a critical eye. "All right, begin."

Howard took the offensive, the staffs meeting with an ominous crack. Sebastian dropped his and shook his fingers.

"Way to go Howard!" Ellen exclaimed.

But Howard was standing there looking stricken. "Sebastian! I'm so sorry!" He dropped his own staff and cradled the bard's hand in his own. "Are you all right? Did I break anything?"

"Calm yourself, Howard," Sebastian said, torn between amusement and bewilderment at the other man's extreme reaction. "I will be fine."

"Will be?" Howard's voice rose. "I did damage your hand! I'll never forgive myself if you can't play anymore."

"Ah!" Sebastian said, understanding dawning. Giving in to impulse, he hugged the other man to him. "It's fine, Howard. A rap on the knuckles will not keep me from my music. I've taken worse damage in a tavern brawl."

Howard pulled back just a little. "What were you doing brawling in a tavern," he asked with a frown. "Are you sure you're all right?"

Sebastian sighed and disengaged himself from Howard. "I will prove it to you. Let me get my lute and I'll play a tune or two."

"I can't believe you fell for that," Ellen said to Sebastian.

"Fell for what?"

"Howard's been dying to hear you play since we got to this world. He was just too chicken to ask."

Sebastian grinned. "Is this true?"

Howard reddened and ducked his head. "Maybe. Just a little. I *have* heard you play, just never in person."

The bard went over to the pile of gear and returned with his lute. Sitting down again, he plucked a few notes, gave a couple of the tuning pegs a turn, and turned to the three expectant faces.

"If you've travelled much in the human realms," he said to Kaelan, "You will perhaps be familiar with this song. It is popular in the taverns, especially at festival time."

The song was like an Irish reel - fast-paced and spritely. It lifted their spirits just to hear it and they had to suppress the urge to get up and dance. It was quite infectious and left them all smiling when he finished.

He segued into another and then a third before he took a break.

"Wow, you really can play," Ellen teased.

"You play beautifully," Howard added.

"Do you sing as well," Ellen asked. "Or do bards only play?"

Sebastian smiled. "I have some small talent with my voice as well," he said, with a wink towards Howard. "What would you have, a ballad? a dirge?"

"Do you know 'The Price of a Kiss?'" Kaelan asked suddenly. His glance slid involuntarily towards Ellen before he caught himself.

The bard's smile widened. "Indeed, a most fitting song before we retire for the night."

From the opening cords he held them spellbound. The song was the story of a lord who had been separated from his hunting party and came upon a fair maid who was bathing in a secluded pond. Her beauty was so great he was instantly smitten. She showed no fear when she turned to leave the water and saw him standing on the bank. He questioned the wisdom of her bathing alone in such a secluded place and she questioned his morals in spying on defenseless women. He gallantly turned his back while she dressed, but suggested he be rewarded with a kiss. There was no answer from her and when he turned again she was gone.

He searched for her but could find no trace. His friends, when he told them of her, told him that he'd fallen asleep by the pond and she was but a dream. Either that or a ghost. But he knew in his heart she was real, and he was determined to make her his bride. He haunted the area around the pond, offering rewards for any information of her. Finally, an old woman came to him and told him he had seen the Lady of the Forest. When he asked her where he could find this lady, he was told he could not. She would have to come to him.

He began bringing gifts to the pond - fine silks and jewelry, wines and offerings of exotic food - and always they would disappear when his back was turned. And the day came that he came to the pond, his hands empty. He told her he had one last gift to give, a song he had composed himself. Closing his eyes, he sang of his great love for her, of his regret for offending her with earthly possessions, and how although his heart would be forever hers, he would leave her in peace. When he opened his eyes, she was standing before him.

But before they could tell each other what was in their hearts, they were attacked by a band of ruffians. Telling the maid to flee, the lord faced them with his sword in hand. He fought valiantly, but although he drove them off, he was sorely wounded. As he lay near the pond, close to death, his lady came to him. She held him and cleansed his wounds with her tears, telling him she loved him as well but she'd been afraid of having to leave her forest behind. And she told him she would regret to her dying day that she had not paid him the price of a kiss.

There were tears on Ellen's face as Sebastian finished the song, and even Howard was dabbing at the corner of his eyes.

"That was so beautiful, but so sad!" Ellen said.

"It is based on a tale my grandmother used to tell me," Kaelan told them. "Only in the end, the lady finally kissed her lord's cold lips and he was brought back to life. She went gladly with him to his kingdom where they spent the rest of their days together as man and wife, raising seven children to carry on their legacy of true love."

"I think I'd like your grandmother," Ellen said. "I definitely like the way she ends stories."

Kaelan laughed. "I hope that you will have the chance to meet her in the Wild Woods Realm," he said. "My thanks, master bard. Though I have heard the song many times, I have never heard it so well done as by you."

"It was my pleasure," Sebastian answered. "But enough music for tonight. The sun rises all too early and I suggest we get some rest before task-mistress Ellen has Howard and I practicing some more."

Chapter Twenty-Two

No more than fifty miles to the southwest, Dominic set a leisurely pace for the journey to Claverton. Jessica was surprised to find the trip almost enjoyable at times. Her old life was starting to seem more and more like a distant memory and she had no idea whether that was a good or a bad thing.

"Have you noticed anything about the land we've been travelling through?" she asked.

"Trees, rocks, hills, streams...looks much like the lands we've journeyed through before the river, save for the Darkwood Forest."

"I meant the people we've seen." Not that there'd been an abundance of them.

"What about them?"

"They seem...happier, I guess."

"Happier?" he asked in amusement.

"Well, for sure they're friendlier. Like that farmer who restocked our supplies when we stopped to help him with his cart stuck in the mud."

"He was just naturally grateful – and it took both our horses and his mule to pull that cart free."

"Okay, but what about the fields we passed where the workers were singing?"

"They're having a good harvest, why wouldn't they be happy?"

"Dominic!"

"All right," he chuckled. "Yes, I have noticed that as we travel further southwards the people seem less oppressed."

"But I'm still not seeing much in the way of magic," she mused.

"Nor should you expect to."

"But why not? You'd think magic would make everything easier– "

"Jessica," he said firmly.

She turned to look at him.

"Not everyone is as blessed as you are with magical abilities."

"But still..."

"Most can work small magics only, as your friend the hedge wizard Wendel. And even small magics can cause fear and distrust in people."

"But it shouldn't be that way," Jessica grumbled. "Just think of all the good someone with magic could do."

"And think of the price that would be demanded for that good. Even were the price not demanded in gold, there would be a price to pay. Not everyone is as generous in spirit as you."

"I guess you have a point," she conceded.

"And what if that person did not wish to be helped with magic?"

"But..." Jessica thought it over for a moment. "Okay, you have another point."

"It may surprise you to learn that most villages have a wizard or some kind of magic worker that those who wish to may consult. The larger towns and cities often have a wizard's guild."

"Really? Then why haven't we– "

"Because we do not wish anyone to know of your true power."

"Oh, right."

They rode in silence for a time, but it didn't last long.

"So what kind of magical power do you have?"

Dominic sighed. "Therein lies a question that has thus far remained unanswered. At one time I harbored a secret desire to become a wizard. I had been all but ready to beg Thackery to allow me to become his apprentice, even though we would have had to flee Ghren for that to come to pass."

"But before you could arrange it, Ewan had you kidnapped," Jessica guessed.

"Exactly so," he nodded.

"Well, that sucks," she said succinctly.

"I was just coming into my power, and as such it was not yet predictable. I could scry, after a fashion, and had some control over fire and earth, but Thackery had not yet been able to test my abilities fully."

"So you might be more powerful than you realize," Jessica said.

He shrugged. "Perhaps."

Jessica glanced at his profile and let the question she was about to ask die unborn on her tongue. He seemed so nonchalant about it, but she got the feeling it mattered a great deal to him. She thought about the life he'd led as a prince, the way his father treated him, and realized what a godsend Thackery would have seemed to him. And then to have had all that taken away by his own brother...

Still...she was like a dog with a bone. "So if I just stopped doing magic, eventually my power would all just go away?"

"No."

"So then yours didn't either," she said, a little smugly.

"Your point?" he asked in a weary voice.

"My point is that maybe all you need is practice to juice up your magical mojo and then Thackery can test you properly when we see him."

"Jessica." Dominic stopped his horse and turned to face her. "We are trying not to draw attention to ourselves. Especially not the attention of anyone searching for magic workers."

"But I thought this Anakaron guy was in the northern mountains. The further south we travel the safer we should be, right?"

"No one knows for certain where he is, and I, for one, am not willing to take the chance that his reach does not extend this far. Nor, might I remind you, is your father. Isn't that why we're seeking him out?"

"Okay," she conceded. "But if it's so dangerous, why was he letting Howard teach me how to use my magic when I first entered the Darkwood Forest?"

Dominic ran a hand through his hair and started his horse forward again. "I don't know. If I were to hazard a guess, it would be that he was unaware that the danger was so close."

There was a thoughtful look on her face as she rode beside him. "I have to wonder if he still would have brought me over if he'd known how much power I have inside me. I mean, did he know the danger I was going to be in?"

He glanced at her. "I– " Mulling it over, he said, "I am sure had he known of your potential he would have waited until a safer time. Although perhaps Howard's spell precipitated events."

"I guess we won't know until we reach the end of our

journey," she said with a sigh.

Jessica's words about his magic not going away stayed with him, and that evening after they'd secured a room in a shabby but clean inn in the small village they'd stopped at, he tried out one of the lessons Thackery had taught him.

"That is so cool," Jessica said, watching the bed bugs, fleas, and other assorted vermin vacate the room.

"Would that I had been able to use that spell back when I was a pirate," Dominic said with a grin.

Jessica looked at him searchingly. "Can I ask you something?"

"You can ask me anything," he told her, still looking rather pleased with himself that his spell had worked. "But I make no promises as to the answer, nor whether you will like it."

"It's just...I was wondering..."

He turned to look at her, raising one eyebrow.

Jessica took a deep breath. "I know that you were rescued from the slavers by the pirates, I just wondered how you got away from the pirates."

"Oh." He turned away again. "Let's just say I had a little help in my escape."

"You had help? What kind of help?"

"It was nothing, really. Repayment for a good deed," he said evasively.

She eyed him speculatively. He was acting very strangely. "What kind of good deed?"

"I helped one of their captives escape, and they in turn helped me."

"A captive? What kind of captive?" she asked suspiciously. "A female captive?"

"Well, in a manner of speaking," he said uncomfortably.

"Dominic!"

"All right, all right. 'Twas a mermaid. We'd put into shore at one of the Mythric Islands and some of the crew stumbled upon a crowd of mermaids sunning themselves on some rocks. They all got away but one. Several of the worst of the lot were going to make sport with her but I set her free."

"A mermaid?" she asked in wonder.

"Yes, a mermaid. And I was found to be a traitor amongst pirates for it and thrown overboard for my troubles."

"You were thrown overboard?" Her voice had risen to a squeak. "But she found you and rescued you?"

"You needn't make it out to be so romantic. The merfolk can be a vicious lot, especially when crossed. I was lucky to have escaped with my life."

As much as Jessica would have liked to hear the whole story, just one look at Dominic's face told her this was a part of his past he would rather stay in the past. She wasn't sure if he was embarrassed or just uncomfortable, but she knew enough to let the subject drop.

Chapter Twenty-Three

Ellen wondered how far they'd come as the landscape changed to one of a vast grassland. The road cut a more or less straight swath through tall, waving grass the dried out green color of late summer, disappearing into the horizon. Lines of trees marked the waterways in the area, few and far between.

Whenever they stopped to rest, she would have Sebastian and Howard drilling with the ironwood staffs. After breakfast and at the break for the noon meal she would have them practice the moves she taught them in unison, but while dinner was cooking at night she'd have them spar. Sometimes one or the other against her while the other looked on, but mostly against each other.

Howard, surprisingly enough, took to the staff like he was born to it. Sebastian, although able to wield the weapon with some dexterity, kept trying to use it like a sword.

The weather held until the fifth day, when they were awakened by a downpour. Fortunately, they had found a way station the night before, so they were safely inside when the rain started. But even so, they had to go out into it eventually. With resignation, they unpacked the wet weather gear.

"There is a village, Glanerco, close to the Wild Woods Realm,"

Kaelan told them. "It is by no means a large village, but it has both an inn where we can pass the night and a large market where we can replenish our supplies."

"An inn?" Ellen said with longing. "With real beds?"

"They may not be the softest of resting places, but I daresay they will be more comfortable than the ground," he said with a smile.

"Lead on!"

The grasslands gave way to gently rolling hills and the rain had stopped by late afternoon. They left their long rain capes on to give them a chance to dry out before packing them away again. The shadows were growing long as they reached the gates to Glanerco, and it was a weary group indeed that entered the stable yard of the inn.

Ellen slid off of Epona's back and for once managed to stay upright.

"Why don't you three see to securing us rooms and I'll see to our gear," Kaelan suggested.

"Are you sure you don't want some help?" Sebastian offered.

"I'm sure I can manage on my own," the elf told him, "But I do have a favor to ask."

He whispered something in Sebastian's ear and then handed him a few coins. "This should take care of the cost of the rooms with plenty left over for a hearty dinner." He turned to Ellen. "As much as I enjoy your cooking, we are much limited on what we can take with us for you to cook."

She waved a hand at him. "No problem. I'm just as happy not to have to cook for a change. I guess we'll see you inside then?"

He nodded and, with the help of two stable boys, led their mounts into the stable. The others picked up their saddle bags/packs and went around to the door of the inn. A scullery boy was just finishing lighting the lamps hanging from the heavy beams around the room.

"Boy," Sebastian said in an authoritative voice. "Go fetch your master."

Without a word, the boy scurried off and returned several minutes later with a rather heavyset man with thick black hair tied back in a queue and a neatly trimmed matching beard. He was wiping his hands on a white apron.

"I be Bennet and this here is my place. We don't open to the public for dinner for another hour," he said. "Overnight guests be served first."

"We'd like to rent some rooms for the night," Sebastian said.

The inn keeper eyed the lute sticking out of Sebastian's pack. "You be a songster?"

"That I be," Sebastian agreed.

"I can give you a discount should you like to sing a tune or two."

The two fell to dickering and Howard and Ellen wandered around the room. The furniture was somewhat crude - heavy benches and tables made of thick, dark wood. The wood was heavily scarred, and there were stains on the table-tops. There was a large fireplace at one end of the room and a staircase leading upwards on the left side of it. The bar where Sebastian and the inn keeper were negotiating ran along the opposite side and the wood of it was equally weathered.

"Done!" the two men at the bar agreed.

"I'll see to getting the rooms ready," Bennet said, and turned just as Kaelan entered.

The inn keeper hesitated but Sebastian said, "It's all right, he's the fourth member of our party."

Bennet nodded and continued on.

"Everything okay in the stable?" Howard asked.

"It is a well taken care of stable. The mounts are even now enjoying a good feeding."

Howard's stomach chose that moment to rumble. His face reddened.

Sebastian laughed. "Apparently the *estrada* are not the only ones in need of a good feeding."

Kaelan caught his eye and he nodded slightly.

After less than thirty minutes, Bennet returned. "Your rooms are at the top of the stairs to the right. The lady's is the one with the bath."

"Bath?" Ellen repeated, eyes widening. "Did he say bath?"

"It was Kaelan's idea," Sebastian said with a grin.

"Thank you!" She went over and hugged Kaelan. "That was so thoughtful of you!"

Releasing him, she grabbed up her packs and started up the stairs. "Why don't we meet down here after I'm done?" Without waiting for an answer, she disappeared up the stairs.

"She's probably going to need these," Sebastian said, handing a towel and a bar of scented soap to Kaelan, who was still looking a little bemused after Ellen's enthusiastic hug.

The elf looked from the towel to the stairs and back again, his mouth opening and closing a couple of times before a smile spread across his face. "Thank you!"

Shouldering his pack, he took the stairs two at a time.

"Her room is the second on the right, yours is the third,"

Sebastian called after him.

"You know," Howard said, picking up his own pack. "If your voice ever went and you could no longer play, you have a promising career in match making."

Sebastian laughed, picking up his own pack. "I could if every couple were as easy as those two. I've never seen two people more perfect for each other."

"You're just a big romantic," Howard teased.

"That's what makes me so popular as a bard." He led the way up the stairs.

Kaelan rapped gently on Ellen's door, and pushed it open when she called for whoever it was to come in. Her room was pretty standard for a village inn. Most of the space was taken up by a bedstead set against one wall. Ellen's pack was on the floor beside it and her cape hung on a hook in the wall beside the door. There was a chair on one side of it and a washstand on the other. A large fireplace with the fire already lit was at the opposite end of the room. There was a rag rug in front of the fireplace and centered on the rug was a metal tub.

"What is it?" she asked at the sound of footsteps. She didn't even bother to turn around, she was too busy staring hungrily at the small, copper tub with the steam wafting upwards.

Two maids were hard on Kaelan's heels, yokes across their shoulders with pails of water suspended from them. They poured the water into the tub, bringing the water level up to three quarters.

"If you be needing anything else, miss, you've only to ask."

"This is just wonderful," Ellen told them. "Thank you."

Kaelan couldn't help the grin that slid across his face. "Sebastian thought you might be in need of these." He held out the soap and towel.

At the sound of his voice she turned and smiled. Her eyes lit up when she saw what he was holding.

"This just keeps getting better and better!"

"Enjoy your bath," he told her. "I will see you downstairs."

"Thank you, Kaelan." she said.

He smiled in response and pulled the door firmly shut behind him. Howard and Sebastian were in the hallway, just entering the room on the left, so he took his things to the room on the right of hers. It was almost identical, save there was no tub. Stripping off his clothing, he washed up as well as he was able using the pitcher of tepid water on the wash stand. Though he liked being clean, he was not a slave to the bath as one of his brothers was. Still, had Ellen asked him to join him he wouldn't have refused.

He brushed the worst of the dust off his leather trousers, then rooted around in his pack until he found a tunic that wasn't too badly wrinkled. Since they had nowhere to go tonight, he found his house slippers for his feet.

When he went back down to the tap room he hesitated only slightly when he came to Ellen's door, visions of her in that copper tub filling his mind. Shaking his head ruefully, he continued onwards. Sebastian and Howard had taken a corner table near the fireplace and they motioned him over when they saw him. There were only two other tables occupied and they were further back in the dimly lit room.

Kaelan took the seat that allowed him a good view of the stairs and his back to the wall. The lone barmaid hurried over to take their order. She leaned further down than necessary to wipe their already clean table, to allow them a better look down her loosely tied blouse.

They ordered ale all around and were informed that the choice for dinner was mutton or guinea fowl. They chose the fowl, ordering for Ellen as well. They had just received their second round of drinks and were told their dinner would be along presently when Ellen appeared at the bottom of the stairs.

Kaelan couldn't help but stare. She was breathtaking. Her beautiful black hair was twisted up onto her head, held in place by a pair of long, thin sticks. Her clothes were elvish in design, but she had a way of wearing them that made them seem extraordinary. She'd chosen a long skirt and tunic of deep forest green, and over them a tabard in a lighter green, embroidered with gold, blue, and grey.

"Looking good, El," Howard told her as she approached their table.

"Thanks, Howie."

"Beautiful," Kaelan said under his breath.

"What was that?" she asked, having not caught what he said.

"I said, allow me," he responded, practically leaping to his feet to pull out her chair for her.

"Why thank you, kind sir," she said, beaming at him.

The barmaid brought their dinners over and her only outward reaction to there being a woman at the table now was using a little more force than necessary to set Ellen's dinner down in front of her.

"Pardon," Kaelan said, as she made to turn and leave them. "I believe the lady would like a drink."

With a long-suffering sigh, the barmaid cocked an eyebrow at

Ellen. "What'll ya have?"

"A mug of very hot water will be sufficient," Ellen said smiling sweetly. "And could you have someone sent up to my room to get rid of the tub?"

Tossing her head, the barmaid flounced away.

"Was it something I said?" Ellen asked, a little bewildered at the other woman's response to her.

Howard was snickering into his mug of ale.

Sebastian was grinning as well, but Kaelan looked a little uncomfortable.

"C'mon guys, what is it?" She looked from one to the other.

"I believe that just by your very appearance you have dashed yon barmaid's plans for the evening," Sebastian told her.

"What plans?"

"I think she was looking for a threesome, or maybe a foursome, but then you showed up all clean and well dressed..." Howard added.

"Thank the lords!" Kaelan said fervently.

"Oh, my," Ellen said. "But you know, if you guys are looking to experiment I can always move to another table. Or have my supper brought up to my room."

"No!" all three of them chorused.

Ellen laughed at the appalled expressions on their faces. "All right, all right. I'll stay. Now let's eat. I'm starving."

The meal was surprisingly good. The guinea fowl had been roasted, and it was served with a selection of boiled vegetables. There was also fresh bread and a smooth tasting white cheese to go with it.

The barmaid brought Ellen's mug of hot water, slapping it down on the table in front of her. Ellen just smiled her thanks, then reached into her pocket and pulled out a small pouch of leaves.

"Tea," she explained at Kaelan's curious look. "I usually carry some with me and Aracelia was kind enough to give me some of her own special blend."

The travelers were hungry and made short work of their meal. During the time they were eating, the tap room of the inn had begun filling up. A few of the tables at the back were removed so more benches could be brought in.

"I think the word of your appearance tonight has gotten out," Howard said to Sebastian.

The bard nodded. "'Tis no more than I expected. Bennet probably sent one of his lads off to make the announcement when he went to see to our rooms. These are simple folk, for the most part, and have little in the way of entertainment."

There was no stage, but Bennet had cleared a space on the other side of the fireplace and set a single chair in it. Sebastian picked up his lute and made his way over to the chair. As soon as he sat down an expectant hush fell over the room.

The songs he performed for the crowded tap room were very different than the ones he'd played around the camp fire. For one thing they were shorter. To save his voice he alternated singing them with just playing. And twice he brought out a flute like instrument. After several songs he took a brief break, during which the barmaid came over to him with a mug of ale to refresh himself, and then he took requests from the audience.

All told he probably played for close to three hours. Then, pleading fatigue, he put away his instruments. The applause was deafening and coins were tossed in his direction. One of the stable boys swept them up and brought them over to him.

Sebastian thanked him and tousled his hair, then gave him a couple of coins for his trouble.

"Well, I don't know about you guys, but I think I'm going to turn in," Ellen said, rising to her feet. "There's a real live bed upstairs and it's calling my name."

Kaelan rose with her. "I believe I will take my leave of this fine company as well," he said. "May I escort you to your room?"

"You may," Ellen said, taking the arm he offered. "Good night, boys. Don't stay up too late."

"We won't, mom," Howard called after her.

Kaelan was very solemn as he escorted her to her room.

"If it does not offend, I would like to say you looked most beautiful tonight," Kaelan told her.

"It most definitely does not offend."

"That is not to say I do not find you beautiful the rest of the time, it is just that tonight you were...more so."

"Thank you," she said, a little amused at his babbling. "I think you're very beautiful as well."

"I think I have had too much to drink," he said with a frown. "My thoughts keep escaping through my mouth."

Ellen couldn't help smiling at him. "Maybe you should go to bed and sleep it off."

"Maybe I should," he nodded in agreement

"Pleasant dreams, Kaelan."

"One more thing," he said, pausing in the act of turning towards his room.

"What's that?"

"This." He pulled her into his arms and kissed her. After a second of surprise, Ellen threw caution to the winds and kissed him back.

Ellen and Kaelan slowly pulled apart and stood looking at each other.

"I cannot apologize for doing that, because I am not sorry," he said.

"I'm not sorry either," she told him. "But I am tired, and you've had too much to drink. So good night, Kaelan."

"Dream of me," he told her as she slipped inside her door.

"I don't have any other choice." The words drifted back to him.

Chapter Twenty-Four

The next morning Ellen was not at all surprised that she was the first one down stairs. Sebastian had arranged for breakfast to be included in the price of their rooms.

"Would you be wanting your food now or would you be waiting for the gentlemen?" Bennet asked her as she sat at the table they'd occupied the night before.

Ellen laughed. "I may starve to death if I waited for those three. That ale they were drinking last night must have been pretty strong."

He flashed her a grin. "Aye, that it is. Make it myself, I do."

"Then if it's not too much trouble, I'd like my breakfast now," she replied. "There's no telling when they'll roust themselves."

Breakfast consisted of some kind of grain mixture stewed with fruit. There was also apples, bread, and cheese to go with it. Bennet offered her a mug of fresh milk to wash it down with, but Ellen requested hot water instead. Kaelan appeared at the foot of the stairs as she did so. He had his pack with him, which he left on the floor by the fireplace.

He seemed a little tentative in his approach to the table, as though afraid of her reaction. He wouldn't meet her eyes as he slid into a seat. Bennet appeared with Ellen's water, as well as a bowl of the stewed grain for Kaelan. Kaelan looked like he wanted to say something but didn't quite know how to say it.

"I hope you're not going to use your inebriated state last night to apologize for that kiss," she said, after Bennet left again.

"I – no, I am not."

She looked up at him. "Are you sorry you did it?"

"I –" His inner struggle was written all over his face. "No, I am not sorry," he told her, almost defiantly.

Ellen smiled. "Good," she said, and went back to eating. "Because I'm not either."

Before Kaelan could form a reply, they were joined by Howard and Sebastian. They piled their packs with Kaelan's and sat down with dual sighs. Howard looked dubiously at their meal.

"I'm not sure if I can handle food," he said.

"Serves you right," Ellen said primly. "But you need to eat something, and this tastes way better than it looks."

Finishing the last sip of her tea, she got to her feet. "Guess I'll go pack up my stuff. It'll just take me a couple of minutes while you guys finish up."

True to her word, she was back a few minutes later, dropping her pack with Kaelan's. She'd confined her hair neatly in a braid down her back and was dressed in a dull green tunic and matching trousers embellished with more of the same color in a leaf design embroidered around the edges of the tunic and around the throat. The tunic was cinched in at the waist by a black leather belt and her sheathed sword was stuck through the belt.

"Are you expecting trouble?" Sebastian asked.

"No, I'm just having trouble figuring out how to carry my katana. I know the original samurais carried the sheath through their belts, but I can't seem to get the angle right. This wasn't exactly something we covered in my lessons."

"Why not just stick it on your back?" Howard suggested. "That way you could carry it easier when you're riding."

"I'm not sure my reach is long enough to be able to draw it properly." She looked at Kaelan. "What do you think?"

Cocking his head to one side he looked at her, then the length of her sword. "I think it would work with a different sheath, but the style of the one you carry might cause difficulties."

Ellen sighed. "This isn't even a regulation length katana. My father had the *bokken* custom made for me to adjust for my height." She stood back a few paces and smoothly unsheathed it. "See? It's just that it makes it a little awkward for walking."

"There is sure to be a sword smith at the market," Kaelan said, rising to his feet. "Perhaps he can be of assistance."

Ellen brightened immediately. "That would be great! And we can pick up some fresh supplies while we're at it."

"We'll stay here and get the gear loaded up," Sebastian said. "It might take us a while to finish eating."

"Okay," Ellen said agreeably. "We'll be back in a bit."

Instead of feeling silly, as she expected to, dressed as she was, Ellen felt a strange sort of confidence as they made their way towards the open-air market. There was something about carrying a sword that made her more sure of herself.

Though most of the other women they saw were dressed in skirts, there were a few dressed in trousers, but none were dressed as finely as she was. It gave her ego just that much more of a boost when a few admiring glances were cast her way.

The smithy was easy to find, they could see the smoke from the forge behind his shop, while in front there was a table under a canopy that displayed his wares.

Ellen was admiring a set of throwing knives when the sword smith came out of the shop to greet them. He was a tiny, wizened old man, even smaller than she was. His long white hair was confined in a leather-bound tail and his hands were gnarled and scarred from a lifetime of working with edged weapons.

"The lady has a fine eye. These knives were crafted on the Isle of T'nji."

"Truly?" Kaelan asked, picking one up with interest. "The craftsmen from the Isle of T'nji are famous for the trueness of their blades," he explained to Ellen.

Reluctantly she set the blade she was examining down again. "These are beautiful, really, but unfortunately I'm not in the market for knives today." She cast one last, longing look at them and then turned resolutely away.

"I actually have a blade," she told him, "What I'm in need of is a sheath so I can carry it on my back, but still allows me to draw it with ease. Can you help me?"

"I'll be needing to see your weapon."

"Oh, right." She pulled the sheathed katana from her belt and passed it over to him. "As you can see, this sheath is made to go through a belt rather than be attached to it."

"Hmm." The sword smith turned the whole thing over in his hands. "Most unusual design," he said. "May I?"

Ellen nodded and he unsheathed the katana. His eyes widened slightly in surprise.

"Most unusual indeed." He looked up at her sharply. "May I

ask where you acquired such a blade?"

"The far east," Ellen said promptly. "My people have carried such blades for centuries."

"Impressive," he said. He held the blade so close to his face it almost touched his nose. "This metal..."

"Has been folded," she acknowledged. "That's where it gets its strength, from the number of times it's been folded."

"Astonishing!" He looked up at her. "I don't suppose...."

She shook her head. "I'm sorry, I couldn't possibly part with it."

He shrugged, as though expecting such an answer, and cracked a smile at her. "No harm in asking. I believe I can construct a harness for you to wear the sword across your back and still allow you to draw it with ease, but it will take some time."

"Unfortunately, we do not have a great deal of time," Kaelan told him. He passed him a small pouch of coins. "Perhaps this might help?"

The sword smith hefted the weight of the bag. "Indeed it will. Perhaps if you would be willing to leave the weapon with me while you peruse the market?"

Ellen looked at Kaelan who gave a slight nod. "We do have some supplies to pick up. When should we return?"

"Say ... an hour?"

"An hour it is."

Before they left the smith measured the length of Ellen's arms, her back, and her waist, all the while asking questions about whether she used one hand or two to wield the sword and which hand would be more comfortable for drawing with. Muttering to himself, he took up the katana and disappeared into his shop. A few seconds later an apprentice appeared to look after the table.

"Are you sure we can trust him?" Ellen asked as Kaelan took her by the elbow and steered her away towards the market proper.

"He would not dare to risk his reputation by stealing from a customer," Kaelan assured her. "Now, what should we buy first? And remember that Aracelia was quite generous in her funding of this journey."

"First stop is the spice merchant," Ellen told him. As she recalled from her history lessons, spices were rare and therefore quite expensive, but she was finding cooking without them rather bland. Of course this wasn't a matter of going back in time, so maybe things would be different here. She wasn't as big a history buff as Howard, or even Jessica for that matter, and this world was more like being caught up in a story, rather than in the past.

She quite enjoyed the variety of foodstuffs available, choosing mostly dried or preserved fruits and vegetables, hesitating over dried and smoked meats before shrugging and choosing a large selection of them as well, and of course her spices. There was a tea seller's stall where she could have easily spent the day sniffing different teas, but she limited herself to several of the more appealing ones. It was a little harder to resist the rounds of several different cheeses, and she had to ask Kaelan's advice when it came to adding grains to their stores. He left her at one point while he procured a sack of grain for the *estrada*, and she tucked a couple of bottles of wine into their provision bags. For a special occasion.

They could have easily passed the entire day wandering

amongst the stalls, but after their hour was up they reluctantly turned back towards the sword smith's shop. He was there waiting for them, and an arrangement of straps had been added to the wooden sheath.

"I had thought to replace the wood with leather," he told them, "But the sharpness of this blade prevents it. However, I believe I have created a harness that will allow for both the ease of movement when carrying the blade and for drawing it."

He showed Ellen the arrangement of straps and explained how they worked. She put it on and was surprised at how light the sword felt across her back. "This is perfect! Thank you," she said.

"If you ever wish to part with your blade . . ."

"I'll keep you in mind," she promised.

He bowed and they took their leave.

"It's too bad Howard didn't come with us, he could have gone over the whole forging process with him."

Kaelan chuckled.

"What's so funny?"

"Do you really think it took him a whole hour to attach a few leather straps to a wooden sheath? He probably memorized every detail of your sword and even now is in the process of trying to recreate it."

"Really? I– " She stopped suddenly as three men with stout clubs blocked their path.

Kaelan, loaded down as he was with supplies, had a bad feeling about this. These men were not interested in going to the market. And the few people that were on the street disappeared.

"Excuse me," Ellen said, striving to stay polite in the face of such blatant rudeness. "But you're blocking our path. Would you mind stepping to one side?"

"Ellen, why don't we just go another way?" It didn't happen often, but he'd faced such prejudice before. The best way to handle it was to walk away.

"But the path to the inn is that way," Ellen said. Turning back to the men blocking their path, she said, "Look, I've asked you politely. Now stand aside and let us pass."

"We don't want the likes of him in our town," the leader said. He spat into the dust. "The only good elf is a dead elf."

The others nodded in agreement.

"Let's just go, Ellen," Kaelan said. It served him right for not bringing his sword. While he wasn't afraid of having to fight these ruffians off, even though he was outnumbered, he didn't want Ellen caught up in what was an age-old prejudice.

"You ain't going nowhere, elf-boy. Not until we teach you a lesson."

"If there's anyone in need of a lesson here," Ellen said, "it's you."

Dropping the bags she was carrying, she drew her katana and sliced upwards, all in one smooth motion. Half of the leader's club lay on the ground and the point of her sword pricked his chin.

"The next cut goes through your wrist," she said in a calm, no nonsense voice. "Now, if you want to keep all your fingers and other assorted body parts then you will let us pass."

The three men disappeared even swifter than they had appeared. Ellen sheathed her sword again and picked up her bags.

"Well, at least we know the harness holding the katana to my back works," she said, leading the way onward.

"Ellen, I– " Embarrassment warred with admiration and Kaelan wasn't exactly sure which he was feeling more of.

"Does that happen often?" she asked. "People treating you like that because you're an elf?"

"Often enough," he said with a sigh. "There are many places where differences are not well tolerated."

She frowned. "I would have thought this close to an elven realm... "

"In some places close proximity creates friends. In other places... it does not. This is one of the reasons we tend to avoid towns and cities when we are travelling."

"And I probably didn't help matters by attacking that man," she said. "I'm sorry."

"Do not be!" he said. "It is to be hoped that they will think twice before confronting someone in that manner again."

"It is to be hoped, but I wouldn't count on it," Ellen said, shaking her head. "I've known bullies like that in the past. I would have had to do him serious bodily harm before he'd learn any kind of lesson, and it probably would have just added fuel to the fire."

"Just so," he nodded in agreement.

They reached the inn and Howard and Sebastian were waiting in the courtyard with the *estrada*. The animals were saddled and the packs in place.

"What is that you're wearing?" Howard asked Ellen.

She turned around so he could have a better look. "The sword smith made it for me. It's very comfortable, and it allows me to carry my sword on my back and still be able to draw it if we're attacked."

"Bennet told us there's a band of raiders somewhere between here and the enclave and he warned us to keep an eye out."

"Well, I'm doubly glad we took the time to have this harness made," Ellen said.

Kaelan finished stowing away the last of the food stuffs. By unspoken agreement, neither of them mentioned the altercation with the bullies on their way back to the inn.

"If that's everything, we should be on our way. It's still two days' ride to Wild Woods and we'll need plenty of luck for the weather to hold. I'd like us to reach the way station before night fall, so we'll be picking up the pace."

The others groaned good-naturedly at Kaelan's pronouncement and mounted.

Chapter Twenty-five

Jessica could hear the birds fluttering and chirping in the trees and could feel both the warmth of sun and cool from shade on her face. They must be in the trees with the sun filtering down, but she could see nothing through the blindfold Dominic had tied over her eyes.

"Where are you taking me?" she asked with a laugh.

The land they were currently passing through was nothing if not picturesque. Dominic's horse had picked up a stone in its shoe and since they had plenty of time before they had to be in Claverton they decided to spend an extra day camped out to give the horses a bit of a rest.

"Have patience, you'll see soon enough," he told her. "Watch your step here, there's a tree root."

Even with his warning she stubbed the toe of her boot on the root, stumbling on the path.

"Sorry," he said, steadying her.

"This better be worth it," she muttered.

"Just a little further," he assured her.

The hard packed earth beneath her feet turned to something spongier. Jessica frowned, trying to figure out what she was walking on.

"Is that running water I hear?" she asked suddenly. It

sounded like a fast moving creek, or maybe a waterfall.

"All right, we're here," Dominic announced, stopping. He whisked the blindfold off her face and she blinked in the sudden light.

"Oh!" The word came out on a sigh as Jessica stared around them, turning her head this way and that. The woods opened up to a small glade. There was a tumble of rocks from which a small waterfall cascaded into a clear pool before flowing away through the trees lining a creek. Bullrushes and other water plants lined the edges of the pond, while the softness underfoot was a thick carpet of dark green moss.

"This is beautiful!" she exclaimed. "How on earth did you know it was here?"

Dominic shrugged, but she could tell he was pleased by her reaction. "I didn't. I stumbled across it when I was looking for firewood."

"Do you think the water is safe for swimming?" she asked, a note of longing in her voice. Swimming was the next best thing to having a bath.

"Probably, but I thought maybe we could have a nap first."

"A nap?" she turned to see he'd already spread a blanket over the moss and divested himself of his swordbelt and boots. "Oh, you mean a *nap*."

Jessica dropped her sword belt on top of his and sat down to remove her own boots. She was still struggling with the left one when he tackled her the rest of the way to the ground, his arms around her keeping her from hitting her head.

"Hey!"

"You were taking too long," he grumbled. He pulled the boot the rest of the way off and tossed it to the side.

"So, Mr. Pirate, is this the part where you ravage me?" she asked a little breathlessly.

"As milady wishes," he said with a leering grin.

They had barely gotten started when she went very still.

"Wait, what's that noise?" Jessica asked, pushing at his shoulder.

"I don't hear anything but birds," Dominic said, intent on the task at hand, namely divesting her of her tunic.

"No, seriously." She sat up, pushing him away. "I think– "

Before she could finish her thought a dark figure rose up from the pool beside them.

"How sssssweet," it hissed. "Young thingsss rutting in the grasssss."

"Holy Saint Christopher!" Jessica said. "What is that thing?"

"Water hag," Dominic returned grimly, eyeing the swords that lay just out of reach.

The creature rose and rose, towering over them, water sluicing off its scaly skin.

"You trespasssss," it said, swaying in place like a cobra.

From the waist up it appeared female – thin pointed features on a face framed by dreadlocks that seemed to move of their own accord, flaccid breasts on the scaly chest – but the rest of her was a cross between a snake and an octopus – long broad torso with tentacles undulating from it.

"Um, sorry about that," Jessica said, getting to her feet. "We didn't know. Our apologies. We'll just be on our way now."

Dominic got to his feet as well, trying to put Jessica behind him.

"Thosssse who disturb my ressstmusssst pay a priccce," the water hag hissed, leaning closer so that the water coming off of her dripped onto them.

"Sure thing," Jessica said with more bravado than she was feeling. "Just let me go get my wallet."

She put a hand on Dominic's arm to drag him backwards with her and one of the hag's tentacles shot out and wrapped itself around his other arm. He let out a yell as his flesh sizzled from the contact.

"Hey! Let go of my boyfriend!" Jessica didn't even have to think twice before she let loose a fireball at the creature. It struck the hag square in the chest and she drew back with a shriek.

"Murderer! Assassssin! Wass only looking for a bit of sssport!"

The tentacle released Dominic so fast he fell backwards onto his butt. A smell of rotting fish filled the air as the creature continued to burn. With a wail the hag slithered into the water just enough to douse the flames, then rose partway out again.

"I'm sorry," Jessica stuttered. "I can heal you if you need it..."

"Are you crazy?" Dominic whispered fiercely. He'd gotten back to his feet and grabbed her by the arm as she started forward.

"I didn't mean to hurt her so badly; I was just trying to get her to back off."

She snuck a glance at the creature but it was keeping its distance, although its attention seemed to be caught by the amulet around Jessica's neck. "You are more than what you sssseem," it hissed.

"I don't– "

"You sssseek to join the othersss in the sssouth," the hag said.

"What others?" the two humans chorused.

"Thossse who answser the calling," she answered, swaying slightly in place. "Thossse who gather to fight the great evil in the north."

"Then I guess yes, we are," Dominic said. His glanced flickered towards the swords and then back at the creature. "I don't want to have to fight you, but we can't let you take us to the dark lord."

"No. No fight," the creature hissed. "No love for the dark one."

"But aren't you a creature of darkness?"

"Yesss."

"And you're just going to let us go?"

"My darknessss preysss on the light, 'tisss true. But his darknessss consssumesss the light. He will leave nothing in his wake – no good, no evil; no light, no dark. Nothing will remain."

"There can be no darkness without light, nor light without darkness," Jessica murmured. "They are two sides of the same coin."

"Jussst so."

Jessica eyed her thoughtfully. "Are there others who feel as you do?"

"Many othersssss."

"Then why don't you come with us?"

"Jessica, what are you doing?"

She ignored Dominic. "You could help us in the fight against this dark lord. Together we could– "

"No. No fight. We ssstay."

"Then perhaps we should be on our way to this gathering," Dominic said.

He turned to lead Jessica away and froze.

"Wait, I want to hear more about– Dominic?" His lack of

movement suddenly registered with Jessica. "Dominic? What's going on? Why aren't you moving?"

"Be at eassse," the water hag told her. "A sssmall harmless ssspell. I would ssspeak privately with you."

"Okay," Jessica said cautiously. "What about?"

The creature undulated a little closer. "I am a sssseeresss for my kind. I have sssseen you."

"Seen me," Jessica said. "Seen me what?"

"The darknesss isss yoursss to battle."

"Me?" Jessica's eyes widened. "Why me? How can you be sure?"

"You wear the amulet. It massssksss your power."

Jessica's hand went to the disk around her neck. "Granny Warrick, the gypsy, gave this to me."

"Yesss."

"She knew about this?"

"Yesss."

"What if I don't want to battle this dark lord?"

The water hag shrugged. "Then the light diesss."

"The light dies? What's that supposed to mean?" Jessica asked, anger lacing her tone. "You can't put this all on me, I wasn't even raised on this world."

The water hag said nothing, just watched her pace back and forth.

"I didn't ask for this!" She spun on her heel to face the hag. "What am I supposed to do, lead some magical army?"

"Alone," the water hag said.

"What?"

"You will facsssse him alone."

"Well this just keeps getting better and better." Jessica moved back beside Dominic and looked over at the water hag. "I don't suppose you saw how, exactly, I'm supposed to defeat this dark lord?"

The water hag swayed in place. "Magic."

"You mean the magic I have no idea how to use?"

"You mussst learn."

"I must learn, in secret, because I can't tell anyone about this because even if they believed me, they sure aren't going to support me. They'd probably lock me up and throw away the key. For my own safety of course."

Jessica glanced at Dominic. "He's not going to like this."

There was no comment from the water hag and she looked back at her. "I don't know if I'm grateful you told me this or not, but I'll thank you anyway. Now, if you could please unfreeze my companion here, we should be on our way. Apparently, I have a destiny to fulfill."

Chapter Twenty-Six

While Jessica and Dominick continued to Claverton, her friends continued to the elven realm. As promised, they reached Wild Woods in two days. The land around them became rockier, and the trees thicker. When they came to a land mark Kaelan recognized they left the road entirely, following what looked like a game trail. They were forced to ride single file between shadowy cliffs before the trail crossed a stream and opened up again.

They were all uneasy, but could not have told why. Just before they came to the enclave barrier, Kaelan called a halt.

"What's the matter?" Ellen asked, riding up beside him.

"Something is not right," he said, looking all around them. "We should have been challenged by a sentry at the pass, but there is no one."

"Is it possible they're having a celebration of some kind?" Howard asked, realizing how unlikely that was as soon as the words left his mouth.

"At times of celebration it is even more imperative to have a guard at the pass. Nor do I understand what is happening with the barrier." He nodded towards the trees in front of them.

"That barrier?" Ellen asked.

"Precisely. We should not be able to see it easily from here."

Howard squinted at the trees. "I can see something...it's not a shimmer like the barrier at the Darkwood Forest Enclave, more like a pale mist or fog."

They nudged their mounts a little closer. Ellen's mount snorted and shook her head.

"Epona doesn't like it," she said, hand on the mare's neck.

"Nor do I," Kaelan said unhappily. "But if we seek to know what lies beyond we have no choice." Taking a deep breath, he nudged his steed forward.

Squaring her shoulders, Ellen followed. And after the briefest of hesitations, so did Howard and Sebastian.

Instead of the tingle of electricity, this was more like a whisper of breath across their skin as they passed through the barrier. It seemed alien and unclean somehow. Once everyone was inside, they stopped again.

"Even I can tell this isn't right," Ellen said.

Where the Darkwood Forest Realm was clearer, brighter, more vivid, the Wild Woods Realm was just the opposite. It was ... diminished somehow. There was no breeze rustling the trees, no birds calling. It was as though everything was in hiding.

"I've got a bad feeling about this," Sebastian said.

"As do I, my friend," Kaelan said, glancing around uneasily.

"What do you want to do?" Howard said.

"Had the Lady Aracelia known things were so ... grave here she would never have asked you to accompany me. I must continue onward, but you three, you should continue on to meet Jessica and Dominic as planned. But I thank you for your company thus far."

Howard and Ellen looked at each other.

"Yeah, I don't think so Kaelan," Howard said. "We started this together and we're going to finish this together." He moved his steed up beside the elf's. "Let me tell you the story of the Three Musketeers while we ride."

Ellen grinned as she dropped back beside Sebastian.

"Why are you smiling?"

"The Three Musketeers is a story and Howard tends to get his stories mixed up. I guarantee poor Kaelan is going to be completely confused before Howard gets to the point."

"And the point would be?"

"The point would be the Musketeer motto: one for all and all for one. Which is basically Howard's way of telling Kaelan that we're sticking together - no matter what."

Sebastian laughed. "He is a good man, Howard is."

"Yes, he is," she agreed.

The bard glanced at her. "You appear to have something on your mind. Would you care to share it?"

"Howard *is* a good man," she repeated. "I haven't known him as long as Jessica has, and to be honest I've always thought he was a bit of a flake, but he's a *good* flake."

"And you're telling me this because ..."

"It would take a blind man not to see what's going on between you two and I just don't want to see anyone get hurt."

"You mean you don't want to see Howard get hurt."

She turned to look at him. "No, I mean either of you. For all Howard's big talk, he's pretty innocent in the ways of the world."

"And you think I'll try and take advantage of him?"

"No." She shook her head. "That's not what I mean at all." She sighed. "I'm not sure I know how to explain this to you."

Glancing towards Howard and Kaelan, she gave it a try. "Do you play any games? You know, for entertainment or to pass the time?"

Clearly puzzled as to the change in topic, Sebastian shrugged. "I've been known to indulge in the odd game of chance."

"Where we're from, games are a very popular form of entertainment. You wouldn't believe me if I told you just how many different kinds there are, but Howard's favorite are the RPGs - role playing games. Specifically, fantasy role playing games. The players assume the identity of a character in a fictional setting. The moves they make in the game are restricted to what the character they are portraying is capable of."

"It sounds complicated."

"It can be. Howard usually plays his games on his computer, but about once a month he gets together with a group of people who also like to play these games, and they'll sit around a table, pretending to be someone else. And then, twice a year, he'll go off for a weekend at someone's farm where they play a live-action-role-playing game. They dress up in costumes and pretend to be the character they're portraying. Then they go out in the woods fight evil or save the princess or whatever scenario the leader, called a game master, comes up with."

Ellen hesitated. "I'm not trying to make it sound like they're obsessed with the games they play. They're mostly just ordinary people like you or me. But a few of them, just a few, take their games way too seriously."

"But you believe Howard may see what we're doing as just part of some game?" Sebastian asked slowly.

"I just think he has a little bit of trouble separating fantasy from reality."

"And what about me," he asked. "Do you think he sees me as

just part of the fantasy?"

"Oh, no," she said with a wide smile. "I'm pretty sure he knows you're all too real. I just wanted to make sure you keep an eye on him."

"I thank you most kindly for your advice. I will indeed keep an eye on Howard. Perhaps even both eyes," he added with a grin.

Ellen laughed.

"What's so funny?" Howard asked, rejoining them.

"I was telling Sebastian about the time the bat got into your apartment and you slept on our couch for a week."

"That wasn't funny!" Howard protested. "Bats carry diseases and– and– they're just really creepy."

"You thought it was a vampire bat and it was going to turn you into a vampire."

"What's a vampire?" Sebastian asked.

"It's a fictional creature that lives on blood - usually human blood. They're also supposed to be able to turn into bats."

"You don't know they're just fictional," Howard muttered. "They might be real."

"Jessica finally chased it outside with a broom," Ellen said with a grin. "She even repaired the screen in the bathroom window where it got in."

"I think I hear Kaelan calling you," Howard said pointedly.

Still laughing, she urged Epona forward until she drew up level with Kaelan.

"So, was Howard able to explain the Three Musketeers to you?"

"I believe so, yes. However, I am puzzled about one thing."

"What's that?"

"What exactly is a musketeer?"

Ellen opened her mouth to answer him when there was a rustling in the trees above them. She looked up in time to see a large net dropping down over Kaelan. Without even thinking about it, Ellen stood up in her stirrups, drew her sword and slashed at the net. The katana sliced through it like butter and Kaelan was able to free himself and his sword.

Sebastian had his bow drawn and was looking around them for the source of the net. Howard had managed to conjure up a fireball without hurting himself. Without being told, the two brought their mounts up so they were together in a group, facing outwards.

Laughter rang out through the forest.

"Diarmad," Kaelan said in disgust. His sword slammed down into its sheath. "What are you doing here? And more importantly, how long have you been tracking us?"

A tall, dark-haired elf dressed in muted colors swung down out of the trees. Doing a flip that would have made a gymnast proud, he landed lightly on his feet in front of them.

"Don't worry, little brother," Diarmad said. "It's only been since you entered the Enclave. You should work on your stealthiness. You were embarrassingly easy to follow."

"This man is your brother?" Ellen asked in surprise.

"Diarmad, at your service," he said, sweeping her a bow. "And you would be?"

"Ellen," she said in return.

"Ellen, a beautiful name to suit a beautiful woman." He took her hand in his, kissing the back of it before she snatched it back.

"What are you doing here, Diarmad?" Kaelan asked irritably, nudging his steed so that it moved between his brother and

Ellen. Diarmad's eyes lit up, as though accepting a challenge.

"The same as you, I expect, brother dear," he said, stroking the nose of Kaelan's steed. "Trying to figure out why we have been lacking in communication with the Wild Woods Realm."

He slipped his fingers through the steed's bridle. "My camp is not far. Why don't we go there and discuss this further in more comfortable circumstances."

Without waiting for permission, he began leading Kaelan's steed away.

Looking back over his shoulder, Kaelan said, "Apparently we're going to my brother's camp."

Ellen glanced back at Howard and Sebastian, who shrugged. Shaking her head, she urged Epona on after the two elves.

Diarmad was camped in the lee of a rocky outcrop. His own *estrada* was picketed off to the side. There was a fire pit in a cleared space in front of the rocks with a bed roll beside it.

"Make yourselves at home," he said, arm sweeping out in a gesture that encompassed the entire clearing.

Ellen made sure Howard's mount was between her and Kaelan's brother before dismounting. Although as Kaelan had promised she was more used to riding and her legs were no longer like rubber, she was still far from graceful when it came to dismounting.

Leading Epona to the picket line, she tied her to the end. Epona lowered her head so Ellen could slip the bit from her mouth, and Ellen in turn slipped her the apple she'd pocketed at the mid-day stop.

"You must be special indeed. *Estrada* do not often take to humans," said a quiet voice behind her.

Ellen jumped in surprise. Turning, she asked, "What about

elves?"

Diarmad flashed a smile at her. "Some elves are very fond of humans." He held out his arm. "Shall we join the others? I'm sure Kaelan will be more than happy to take care of the mounts."

Ellen glanced towards Kaelan who was standing off to the side. His face was expressionless and he did not meet her eyes.

A few seconds more of hesitation and then Ellen rested her hand lightly on Diarmad's arm. Giving him a half smile, she said, "As long as Kaelan has no objections."

Still not looking at her, he shrugged. "It's fine," he told her. "And anyway, our arrangement still stands."

Ellen allowed Diarmad to escort her to the fire. There was something off-putting about Kaelan's older brother. He was a little too sure of himself. He was also arrogant and she didn't like the way he treated Kaelan.

There was already a pot of stew on the fire, and Howard and Sebastian were sitting on the far side of it. Diarmad led Ellen to a seat on a log he'd dragged into the fire light, and then turned to stir the stew.

"Which one of you guys started supper?" she asked the two humans.

"Neither," Howard said with a rueful grin. "It was all Diarmad. Did I get the name right?"

"Indeed you did, my friend." Diarmad flashed a smile.

"He had the whole thing lit and the pot started before we even finished unsaddling our mounts," Sebastian added.

"It takes but a flicker of power to light a fire," Diarmad said modestly. "Well, for most elves at any rate." His glanced flicked off to the side and Ellen realized Kaelan was standing there. She also realized Diarmad's words had been a deliberate jibe aimed at his brother.

Though he didn't say anything, a muscle in Kaelan's jaw twitched. Ellen didn't understand why his brother was being such an ass hat, but she didn't like it. Not one bit. Diarmad quickly sat down beside Ellen on her log, leaving no space for Kaelan. Howard motioned for him to sit with him and Sebastian.

"Now that we're all here," she said, deliberately including Kaelan. "Perhaps Diarmad can tell us why he's here. Were you sent by someone in the Darkwood Forest Enclave or did you just wander in here on your own?"

"Actually, I was sent her by our mother," Diarmad said, with a nod towards Kaelan. "Her sister is close to giving birth and she grew worried when she didn't hear from her." This he said directly to Ellen.

"And what has happened?" Kaelan asked.

"I know not. I only just arrived before you all did. You know, for a warrior/hunter you make an unconscionable amount of noise. It is a wonder you have survived so long, brother."

"We had no reason to suspect there would be a need for stealth," Kaelan countered, finally coming to his own defense.

"You did pass through the barrier, did you not?" Diarmad said, with a greater show of surprise than the question warranted. "Or at least what passes for the barrier? And have you not noticed the lack of a road?"

Kaelan's jaw clenched again. At this rate he was likely to break a tooth or two, Ellen thought.

"What road?" Howard asked.

"Whenever a non-elf enters one of the enclaves, a road will appear to take them to the nearest outpost. Brother," he said, turning to Kaelan again. "How remiss of you not to tell them this."

"Actually," Ellen said. "He did, back in the Darkwood Forest Realm." She glared at Howard.

"Guess I wasn't paying attention," he said sheepishly.

"I think your stew might be ready," Sebastian pointed out, sensing an argument brewing.

"Why don't you serve it up?" Diarmad said to Kaelan. "There's a good boy."

It was Ellen's turn to grind her teeth as Kaelan said nothing, just did as he was told. Obviously being treated like this was normal for him. Well she didn't like it. Not one bit. And if it was the last thing she did, she was going to see that that pompous ass of a brother of his was put in his place.

All she had to do was bide her time. She'd been around enough men like Diarmad to know that all she needed to do was let him blather on until an opportunity presented itself. And then he'd better watch out.

She smiled sincerely at Kaelan when he passed her a bowl of stew. Diarmad passed around a wineskin filled with a very mellow elven wine, and managed to boast of his accomplishments throughout dinner without appearing to do so. Howard and Sebastian chatted with him amiably, but Ellen could tell that Howard, at least, wasn't completely buying into the elf's act.

When they were finished, Kaelan began collecting the eating utensils, despite the fact Howard and Sebastian usually took care of the clean-up.

"There's a stream just a short distance that way," Diarmad said helpfully, gesturing to a path near the picket-line.

Even Howard and Sebastian were a little taken aback when Kaelan said nothing, just departed for the stream.

Ellen started to rise. "Maybe I should go help him."

"Nonsense," Diarmad said, taking her hand to stop her. "He'll be fine on his own. While I, on the other hand, would be desolate at your loss."

"You don't even know me," she said, amused in spite of herself. He really was pulling out all the stops.

"Ah, but that can be easily mended. You have only to tell me about yourself, beautiful Ellen. What brings you to the Wild Woods Realm in the company in such a poor guard as my brother?"

Ellen shot a glance towards Howard and Sebastian. The bard shook his head slightly at her. Right. Charismatic as Diarmad was, he was still an unknown.

"We're here as a favor to a friend, and Kaelan came highly recommended."

He offered her the wine skin again but she shook her head.

"And what do you do, when you're not roaming around in ghostly elven realms playing pranks on your brother?"

Diarmad threw back his head and laughed. "You have to admit, he is an easy target. His lack of magic makes it so simple. Like my little brother, I'm a guard. But I'm one of the king's guards, something he can never be."

"Why is that," Howard asked.

"Why his lack of magic, of course. The most he can ever aspire to is a common guard or foot soldier."

"He mentioned he has more than one sibling," Sebastian said quickly. "Are all of you guards or soldiers?"

"Not at all," Diaramad said. "Our brother Aodhfin is a trader, while Eoghan and Brogan follow in father's trade. Something else poor Kaelan lacks talent for."

Ellen was sure that last comment was tacked on for Kaelan's benefit. He'd just returned to the clearing and was hovering on the edge. It broke her heart, but she wasn't sure what she could say that wouldn't make things worse for him.

"I'm pretty sure Kaelan mentioned a sister as well," Howard said, having not noticed Kaelan standing in the shadows. "What does she do?"

"Iana?" Diarmad gave a dismissive shrug. "She need do nothing. She will be wed soon to an elf lord and has many servants to prepare for her wedding."

Something of what Ellen was thinking must have shown on her face, because Diarmad quickly changed the topic.

"Wild Woods is considered one of the most beautiful of all the elven realms," he told her. "The full moon is very bright tonight, perfect for a stroll along the water."

Ellen smiled. "I believe you're right, Diarmad," she said. "A walk would be perfect. Kaelan, would you care to join me?" She rose gracefully and held out her hand.

"But–" Diarmad seemed a little pole-axed.

Kaelan's smile was slow, but one hundred percent sincere. "It would be my pleasure to be your escort."

He took her hand and together they disappeared down the path to the stream.

"But–"

Sebastian handed Diarmad the wine skin. "There's no divining a woman's mind," he said. "Might as well have a drink."

Chapter Twenty-Seven

Kaelan and Ellen were quiet as they followed the path to the stream, but Kaelan did not stop there. He led her along the bank until the stream widened into a waterfall fed pond. The waterfall itself was only a few feet high, the source lost in a rocky outcrop. A handful of night blooming water lilies bobbed gently around the edges of the pond while the moonlight sparkled on the water.

"This is so beautiful!" Ellen exclaimed.

"My grandmother used to bring me here for picnics when I was young," Kaelan said. He led her over to a stone bench that was half-hidden by ferns.

Once they were seated, Ellen said, "Your brother is really something, isn't he?"

Kaelan's expressive face grew still as he shrugged carelessly. "Yes, many are drawn to him."

She turned to look at him. "That wasn't meant to be a compliment."

"I don't understand."

"Was he born that big of a jerk, or does he have to work at it?"

He looked back at her, eyes wide.

"Kaelan, are you so used to the way he treats you that you don't even notice it anymore?"

"I– I– "

She took his hand, cradling it in hers. "I hate to tell you this, but your brother is a pompous ass and the way he likes to belittle you makes me want to thump him with one of our ironwood staffs."

Kaelan looked searchingly into her eyes for a moment, and then leaned in and kissed her. He'd only meant it to be a light, friendly kiss, but at the first touch of her lips under his, all his good intentions evaporated.

Ellen melted into his arms. It just felt so right. Her hands seemed to have a mind of their own as they slid up his arms, across his shoulders, and buried themselves in his hair.

When they finally broke apart, they did not loosen their hold on each other.

"I did not intend for this to happen, but I cannot seem to help myself when I am alone with you."

"This really isn't the time or place for something like this," Ellen said. "Well, actually it's the perfect place and time, but you know what I mean."

"Yes, I do," he agreed, and began kissing her again.

"Can I ask you something?" she asked when they stopped for a breath.

"You may ask me anything."

"Diarmad said your lack of magic held you back. What did he mean? I thought all elves were magic."

"Ah." He moved slightly away from her.

"Hey." She put a hand on his arm. "I'm not trying to insult you, I was just curious. If you'd rather not talk about it– "

He placed his hand over hers. "No, with you I do not mind." Taking a deep breath, he continued. "Yes, all elves are magic, but in varying degrees. The amount of magic one possesses plays a large part in one's status. Unfortunately, I was born with very little magic."

"So when he made that crack about the king's guard?"

"Only those with the highest level of magic can be a kings guard." That he could say this without any bitterness was points in his favor.

"And following in your father's footsteps? He's a silversmith, isn't he? What's stopping you from working with silver, or any other metal?"

"To do so would require more magic than I possess," he said.

"That's ridiculous!" Ellen sputtered.

"I do not understand."

"We don't have magic where I come from, but you should see some of the art people are able to create – painting, sculpting, even metal work."

He simply looked at her, silent for a moment. "I wish I could see your world," he said softly.

"I would love to be able to show it to you."

When they returned to the camp they were both a little disheveled looking, much to Diarmad's irritation. The fire was burning low and it was decided that they should all turn in for the night.

As was her custom, Ellen made sure her sword was within easy reach.

"Are you so fearful of my brother's intentions that you need to sleep with your sword?" Diarmad asked with a bark of laughter.

Ellen raised an eyebrow as she gave him a quelling look. "How sad that you know so little about your own brother."

At least he had the grace to look abashed.

Bedroll arranged to her satisfaction, she lay down to sleep.

Morning came all too early, with the sound of the *estrada* neighing and pounding the ground with their hooves.

Kaelan and Ellen were first on their feet, swords in hand. Howard struggled to extricate himself from his bedroll, but he'd taken Ellen's advice and slept with his staff close to hand. Sebastian had his staff on the ground at his feet and his bared sword in hand. And Diarmad was still blinking the sleep out of his eyes when the attack came.

They appeared to be elves, but they had been altered somehow. Their features and their ears were elongated, giving them a somewhat sinister appearance. And their skin tone was a greyish brown.

Ellen was grateful that her father insisted her *bokken* be weighted down like a sword. It built up much needed muscle in her arms. Muscle that came in handy now, when it counted. Her katana practically sang as it sliced through the air and the intruders alike. There was some part of her that was horrified at what she was doing, but right now she was fighting for her life, for all their lives, so she shoved that squeamish part aside. She could throw up later.

Diarmad managed to get a hold of his sword and Ellen couldn't help but notice he was not the swordsman Kaelan was. He was stiff and his strikes lacked follow through. Though he seemed adequate when it came to defending himself, he was lacking in the aggression needed to drive these other elves back.

Kaelan, on the other hand, was poetry in motion. He used

twin swords, weaving a deadly pattern with them while his feet took him on a complicated and elaborate dance that cut a wide swath through their opponents. His face showed only the fierce concentration needed to keep two swords in play at once.

The attack may have lasted for minutes or hours. Afterwards they were never able to tell. All they knew was the attack ended as suddenly as it started. They stood in the clearing, breathing heavily, staring around at the carnage.

"Is everyone all right?" Kaelan asked, taking charge. "Ellen? Howard?"

"I'm fine," Ellen said, voice steadier than she felt. She was waiting to fall apart, surprised to feel unnaturally calm.

"Who were they?" Howard asked in a dazed voice. "And why did they attack us?"

"Dark elves," Kaelan said grimly.

"Dark elves?" Sebastian looked up sharply. "I thought they stayed on the other side of the Shadow Mountains?"

"They did," Diarmad said, for the first time all serious. "Until now."

"Diarmad, you need to go to the Darkwoods Realm, tell them what happened. They can send word out to the other realms."

Diarmad bristled slightly at being ordered around by his little brother. "And what about you four?"

Kaelan hesitated. "I am committed to finding out what happened here in Wild Woods. I need to stay to search for survivors. But Ellen ... you and Howard and Sebastian. It would be safer for you to go back with Diarmad, or onwards to Claverton to meet with Jessica."

"Safer, maybe," Ellen said. "But I for one am not leaving you here alone."

"All for one, man," Howard said, leaning on his staff. Sebastian stood beside him, hand on his shoulder. He nodded at Kaelan in agreement.

Diarmad shrugged. "I have to admire your loyalty," he said, turning away to saddle his steed. "No matter how misplaced it is," he muttered in a voice low enough that only Ellen heard.

"I guess the first thing we should do is get rid of the ..." Ellen looked around the clearing, face growing pale. "Where did the bodies go?"

"Dark elves never leave anyone behind, alive or dead. If the wounded cannot hold a sword, they are dispatched. The bodies are disposed of in magical fire."

"How ... efficient of them," Sebastian commented.

"Swift and safe passage to you," Kaelan told his brother.

"Stay safe, little brother," Diarmad said. He whispered in his steed's ear and the animal leaped into a gallop, disappearing down the trail in a blink of an eye.

"How long will it take him to reach the Darkwood Realm?" Ellen asked.

"Three days at most." At her look of surprise Kaelan gave her half a smile. "I did tell you that the *estrada* are fast."

"You did indeed. Well," she said, pulling a handkerchief from her pocket to clean the blade of her sword. "What do we do now?"

"I suggest we do as Diarmad advised and continue on to the outpost," Kaelan said. "I mislike being out in the open like this."

They were all in agreement over the last part, and quickly packed up their things. Kaelan's route took them through the stream and Ellen looked wistfully towards the place where it disappeared around a slight bend. Just beyond that was the pond and the waterfall. Last night seemed so very far away right now.

The outpost, when they reached it, was ominously quiet. Like the outpost Sebastian and Ellen had seen in the Darkwood Realm, it was mostly a cluster of fanciful cottages, with a large, low building used as a barracks off to the side. There was what appeared to be a stable off to the side, but there were no animals in the corral. Nor were there animals in any of the pens around the cottages. Like an accusing finger a single watch tower stood pointing up at the sky.

"Why don't you three check the buildings while I find out what there is to see up in the watch tower," Kaelan suggested.

They split up, Sebastian headed towards the stables and barracks, while Howard and Ellen took opposite sides of the cluster of cottages. Kaelan began climbing the ladder in the watch tower and Ellen paused for a few seconds to admire the fit of his leather pants.

"Hey, get to work you!" Howard called out to her. She gave him a wave and turned to the task at hand.

Ellen hesitated in front of the cottage closest to her. It looked well taken care of with flowers in window boxes under the windows on either side of the door, and what she took to be herbs growing in a small plot to the left.

Knocking on the door first, she tentatively pushed it open and let her eyes adjust to the dimmer light before stepping inside. It was a single room - bedstead tucked up neatly in one corner, fireplace at one end with a kitchen type area beside it, complete with a table and four chairs. The table was set for two, the remains of a meal lying undisturbed. There was a fine layer of dust over everything.

Quietly she backed out again and closed the door behind her. The next two cottages were much the same, signs of an interrupted meal and a fine layer of dust indicating no one had been around for days. There were no signs of struggle.

The next cottage was a little bigger, with a ladder leading to a loft. This time there were four places set at the table. A jar holding a bouquet of wilted flowers was sitting in the center. Lying on the seat of one of the chairs was a rag doll.

Ellen slowly reached out and picked it up. She smoothed down the doll's dress and stroked its lifelike hair, wondering where the doll's owner had disappeared to. It seemed to be a much-loved toy. Why would the child leave it behind?

Taking one last look around she left the cottage, closing the door firmly behind her. Not being able to face any more of the empty cottages, she made her way over to the grassy square that surrounded the watch tower and sat down.

When Kaelan descended the ladder, he found Ellen sitting there, turning the doll over and over in her hands. He sat down beside her and after a moment put his arm around her. She leaned her head on his shoulder.

Sebastian and Howard came and sat down crossed-legged in front of them. "There's no trace of anyone in the barracks or the stable," Sebastian told them.

"Whatever happened, it looks like they were in the middle of dinner when it occurred," Howard put in. "But they left quietly. There's no blood, no sign of a struggle - it's like everyone just suddenly got up and left."

Ellen raised her head. "How could this happen? Could it have been an illness or drugs...?"

"Might magic have done this?" Howard asked tentatively.

"Could someone have cast a spell that would ... I don't know, turn everyone into mindless zombies?"

Both Sebastian and Kaelan were shaking their heads. "Though I have heard of spells that can weaken a person's will, none I know of can drain the will completely," Kaelan said.

"And a spell that could encompass an entire village..." Sebastian looked a little ill. "It does not bear thinking, a sorcerer of such power."

"What about these dark elves?" Ellen asked. "Could they be responsible?"

"The dark elves live on the far side of the Shadow Mountains," Kaelan told them. "Until this morning, I did not even know they were real. I thought them belonging only to stories my grandmother used to tell."

"What did your grandmother say?"

"Many centuries ago, the elves were of one race – good and bad both, but in equal measure as most races are. There was a great argument, something to do with magic I think, or perhaps it was the superiority of one race over another. It was not one of my favorite stories."

"One of your grandmother's stories?" Ellen couldn't help asking.

Kaelan smiled faintly. "At any rate, there was a great rift which led to the division of our race into light and dark. The light elves set up enclaves and lived in harmony with the other races, and the dark elves were banished to the Shadow Mountains and have not been heard of since."

"Until now," Howard said.

"Until now," Kaelan agreed.

Chapter Twenty-Eight

The sun had been rising steadily while they searched the outpost, and was high in the sky when they were done. Despite missing breakfast none of them felt like eating. Howard passed a waterskin around.

"Any idea what the dark elves might want?" Sebastian asked.

Kaelan shrugged. "Their magics are dark and twisted, you saw what using them has done to them. Perhaps they have used up the resources in their own realms and seek to steal ours. But I do not understand what they would want with the elves themselves."

Sebastian looked distinctly uncomfortable.

"What?" Howard asked. "You look like you have something to say," he said when Sebastian turned to look at him.

Still Sebastian hesitated. Then he said, "This wizard, Anakaron, that Thackery and Paranithel are so concerned about. I've heard it said he's not just a blood mage but has a way of draining a creature's magic."

"You think he could drain magical energy from the elves?" Ellen asked with dawning horror. "What would happen to them if they lost their magic?"

"They would become hollow husks," Kaelan said slowly. "Without their magic, an elf could not live. Even I, though I am not able to wield magic for spells, am imbued with magic. It is part of our very nature."

"But would the dark elves be involved with something like that?" Howard asked.

"If the price were right," Kaelan said. He got to his feet, bringing Ellen with him. "I do not think it is wise to stay here. Come, there is a place we can go – the sanctuary."

They mounted up and he led the way out of the outpost.

"Aren't you worried that the dark elves might follow us?" Howard asked.

"The sanctuary would prevent such a thing," Kaelan said. "They are warded against dark beings."

"Like the enclave was warded by the barrier?" Ellen asked gently.

He glanced at her. "No this is different. The barrier detects ill intentions through emotions. The warding for the sanctuary detects creatures of evil nature and repels them."

Kaelan said no more until they reached another glade-like area. "We'll need to lead the mounts from here."

They dismounted and watched as he led his steed between two oak trees. His form seemed to shimmer, and then he disappeared. The three humans looked at each other, then Ellen shrugged and led Epona forward. The sensation that washed over her as she passed through the warding was more like the one passing through the barrier at the Darkwood Realm. Epona gave off a shiver as it passed over her.

Ellen's jaw dropped open and she gazed around in wonder. There were definitely caves, but they were openings in the rocky outcroppings that surrounded a circular meadow. Flowers grew in abundance and there was a waterfall at the far end of the meadow that fed a small pond before disappearing underground.

"All of the smaller enclaves have such places," Kaelan said absently, looking from side to side. "It is a haven should an enclave ever come under attack."

"You were hoping to find survivors here, weren't you?"

"Yes."

"I could use a little help here," Sebastian called.

They turned to see he'd dropped the reins to the *estrada* as he struggled to keep Howard upright. Howard seemed almost boneless in his arms.

"What happened?"

"We were just about to pass through the warding and he stumbled off the path. Something stabbed him in the leg."

"Let's get him into the nearest cave," Kaelan said. He and Sebastian managed to half-carry Howard into the nearest cave and eased him gently to the floor. Wood was already stacked, ready to be lit, in the fire pit in the center of the chamber, with more wood along one side.

Sebastian got out a flint and steel and got the fire lit while Kaelan used a belt knife to slice open Howard's trouser leg. Howard protested feebly.

"Ah, man. Those were leather!"

"They can be replaced, you can't," Ellen scolded. "How are you feeling?"

"Weak. Like my energy's being sucked away. And it hurts. My leg. Hot." He closed his eyes and began to shiver.

"It's elf's bane," Kaelan said grimly.

"Elf's bane? I've heard of that," Sebastian said. "But I thought it was eradicated."

"It was, and the last place I would expect to find it is in an elven realm."

"So ... this elf's bane. I take it it's poisonous, but why is it affecting Howard? Wouldn't it only be dangerous to elves?" Ellen asked.

"It causes elves ..." Kaelan stopped what he was about to say, eyes widening. "It saps the will."

"Ohmygod! That must be what was used on the elves of the enclave! But how could it have spread to everyone at once?"

"Never mind that now," Sebastian said. "I remember it's also said to be dangerous to humans. What exactly does it do?"

"It causes pain and a fever," Kaelan told him. "And in severe cases it will cause a drain in energy that makes the fever become more dangerous."

"So he's going to be weak and feverish, but then he'll get better, right?" Sebastian asked.

"In some cases this is true, but others ..."

"Isn't there a cure?" Ellen asked. "There's got to be a cure!"

"Howard didn't just touch an elf bane plant, one of the thorns pierced his leg. The poison is in his blood stream."

"What can we do?" Sebastian asked, an edge of frantic in his voice.

"It will take a powerful healer to rid him of the poison."

"Good thing I know a powerful healer," Sebastian said, getting to his feet.

"Wait! Where are you going?" Ellen scrambled to go after him.

"To Claverton, to bring back Jessica." He untied the pack horses from the back of his saddle.

"Wait!" Kaelan called to him from the mouth of the cave.

"Take the pack animals for the trip back. A regular horse won't be able to keep up with your *estrada*."

"Thank you!" Sebastian said with relief. He began pulling the supplies from the two elven mounts. Reattaching the leads to his saddle, he mounted up. "Take care of him for me until I get back."

"Be careful going through the elven realm," Ellen cautioned. "There may still be some of those dark elves around."

"I don't intend to go slow enough for them to see me," Sebastian said. Feeling he'd already wasted too much time talking, he dug his heels into his mount and they shot out through the ward.

Ellen brought the packs into the cave and then went back out for the supplies. Despite the fire beside him, Howard was shivering with the fever.

"How's he doing?" she asked, kneeling down beside Kaelan.

"Right now he's in a lot of pain and he has a high fever."

"I've heard of people bringing down high fevers with ice. We don't have any of that here, but I'll bet that pond is pretty cold. What if we stick him in there?"

Kaelan was already shaking his head. "No, he is better off beside the fire. The second stage of the illness is a cold fever. We want to delay that as long as possible."

"I've never heard of that before. What's a cold fever?"

"It will start with him feeling cold, a feeling that he will never be warm again. Then his body temperature will begin to drop, I have heard of extreme cases where the patient will actually begin to radiate cold."

Ellen looked down at Howard and brushed a strand of hair off his face. Howard's eyes flickered and opened, but she wasn't sure he recognized her until he spoke.

"Where's Sebastian?"

"He's gone to get Jessica," she told him.

"Oh." His eyes closed again. "But he'll be back soon, right?"

"He'll be back before you know it."

"Good ... something I forgot to tell him."

His voice trailed off and Ellen looked up at Kaelan in alarm.

"He will slip in and out of consciousness as the poison works itself through his system. Then he will quickly begin to lose sense of where he is or even who he is."

"What can I do to help?"

"If you could watch him for a short while ..."

"Of course!"

"There should be a storage cave close to hand. I will see if there are any supplies that can be of use."

Howard was still shivering and Ellen laid the back of her hand his head. He was burning up with fever and perspiring heavily. He moaned tossing his head from side to side.

"When we were little, my mother used to stick us in a bath with vinegar in it to bring down our fevers," Ellen said. She fished around in her pack for a cloth and then squirted water on it from the water skin. As gently as possible she wiped the sweat from Howard's face. "It's too bad I can't just run down to the corner store."

Seriously, how did people live like this? No doctors or hospitals, no cars or electricity. And having to constantly keep vigilant for danger when you were travelling .... She felt utterly spoiled by her old life, where her biggest concern had been what shoes to wear with what outfit.

Kaelan returned, arms laden down with blankets, a large

cooking pot, and what appeared to be a thin mattress.

"Nothing in the way of food," he told her, "But I found extra blankets and this pallet for when he enters stage two."

"Good idea," Ellen said. "Why don't we set the pallet on the other side of the fire, close to the wall. That way the wall can reflect some of the heat back at him and the pallet will insulate him from the cold of the floor."

As Kaelan moved to do her biding, Howard whispered something.

"I'm sorry, Howard," she said, leaning closer. "I didn't hear what you said."

"Willow bark," he whispered.

She straightened back up again. "Yes, you're right! Why didn't I think of that?"

"Think of what?" Kaelan asked.

"Willow bark. Once, when I was running a fever but couldn't afford to miss any work, Jessica brewed me a tea of willow bark. It worked wonders. Do you have a knife I could borrow?"

Without hesitated he pulled the knife from his belt and passed it to her. "What do you have in mind?"

"You're meant to be self-sufficient here. I'm betting that there's at least one or two willow trees down along the water by the waterfall. Hopefully one will be a white or even a black willow. I'll be right back. You put a pot of water on to boil."

As she hurried away Kaelan chastised himself for not think of willow bark himself. He remembered his mother making him drink it as a child when a sickness swept through their town. It was not only effective on fevers, it would help reduce Howard's pain as well.

By the time Ellen returned, he had a small pot of water

bubbling over the fire. She held the strips of bark she'd cut from the trees in a fold of her tunic, the material wet.

"I washed them in the pond," she said. "Unfortunately, I never paid attention to Jessica when she was making infusions, so I don't know how much to use. I know when you're using herbs you need less of dried herbs than you do of fresh ..."

"I would guess that we should use the same amount we would use to make tea," Kaelan said.

"Okay, here goes," Ellen said. She chose a medium length strip and sliced it into pieces, dropping them into the pot. "That looks about right for tea."

Kaelan, meanwhile, found some flat, squarish rocks that he pulled closer to the fire. "If you lay the rest of the strips out on these, we can dry them out to use later."

"Great idea!" Ellen did as he suggested. "I guess that's all we can do for now until the tea's ready."

Chapter Twenty-Nine

S ebastian lay practically flat over the *estrada's* back as they raced out of the sanctuary and down the trail again, the two former pack animals easily keeping pace. He was confident he'd have no trouble retracing their route, he had an eidetic memory - the ability to recall things with great precision. As they raced along the route past the outpost and towards the clearing they'd camped that first night, he kept expecting to run into more dark elves.

It was a relief when he didn't. But when he passed through the barrier it sent an unpleasant tingling sensation through him, not the mild sensation from before, nor even the energy charged one from the Darkwoods barrier. This one made him feel ... unclean.

But it was over in seconds and only minutes later he found the road that would take him to Claverton. He just prayed that nothing had delayed Jessica and Dominic and they would be there waiting for him.

Once on the road it became fully apparent to him the speed the *estrada* possessed. Running flat out, the scenery seemed to blur past him. He had to wonder though how long they could keep this up.

When the sun began lowering in the sky, he realized it would be too dangerous to keep going in the dark, so he reluctantly started slowing the *estrada's* pace. He took heart from the fact that though winded, the beasts seemed to have plenty left to give. Fortunately, just as the sun began to sink below the horizon, he found a way station close to the road.

It appeared to have been abandoned long ago, but it had three solid walls and a fireplace at one end. He'd had the foresight to bring some grain for the animals and there was a dented bucket in the corner that he filled from the well outside for them to drink from. It was with great reluctance that he pulled the saddle from the steed he'd been riding, but he rubbed him down gratefully, telling him what a fine animal he was, how strong and swift.

"I pledge that when this is over I shall compose a song for all three of you, to commemorate your part in the saving of Howard," he told them. "And to the Lady Aracelia as well, for her foresight in gifting us with your presence."

Not only were the *estrada* incredibly fast, they were far more intelligent than a normal horse. Though unable to communicate, they seemed to understand the bard's words, and empathize with his sense of urgency. The steed he'd come to think of his own butted him with his head.

Sebastian smiled, scratching between his ears. "Thank you my friend."

He had not had the foresight to bring food for himself and had to make do with some dried strips of meat he kept in his pouch for emergencies. Chewing on one of them gave the illusion of eating more however, and when he was done he wrapped himself in his cloak and lay down in front of the cold fireplace.

The first light of dawn had him up and back in the saddle. He had no idea how close he was to Claverton, but it couldn't be too far.

"Let us away, my friends," he said. "And let us hope that Jessica and Dominic are waiting for us."

Keeping to a gallop instead of a full out run, it was still early morning when they reached Claverton. Sebastian chaffed at the time it took to locate the Blue Bull, the inn where he was to meet Dominic and Jessica.

Dismounting in the yard he told the stable hand who came out to greet him, "Feed and water them, but don't bother unsaddling him, I won't be staying that long. But I'll need saddles to fit these other two, and if you can manage it, food for three people for two days and grain for our mounts." He flipped the man a gold coin.

" 'Twill be my great pleasure master," the stable hand told him.

"Mind you make sure it's good quality gear and food and you can keep what's left for yourself."

The stable hand's eyes widened and he took the reins from Sebastian. "The very best master!"

But he was talking to Sebastian's back as he disappeared inside the inn. It took a few precious seconds for his eyes to adjust to the dimness. The room was typical of most great rooms, save there was no one inside.

Sebastian slapped the bar, the sound making a resounding echo. "Hello, inn keeper!"

"Keep the noise down," grumbled a stout woman coming in from the direction of the kitchen, wiping her hands on her apron. "Me husband be still sleeping at this hour and trust me, ya don't be wantin' to wake him."

"I'm looking for two people who're supposed to meet me here," Sebastian told her, struggling to stay patient. "The man is tall with black hair, probably dressed in leather, and his companion is a woman, handsome of face and form, probably dressed in men's clothing."

"Aye, they be here." She eyed him suspiciously. "Wot you be wantin' of them?"

"They're friends of mine, truly. And it's very important I see them as quickly as possible." He produced another gold coin.

The woman's eyes lit up. "Third door on the left, top 'o the stairs," she said, taking the coin. "And mind you don't make a mess!" she called out to his back. "I don't want no blood stains on the wood."

Sebastian took the stairs two at a time. When he came to the third door on the left he pounded on the wood.

After a moment there was a faint sound of movement and a muffled voice said, "Go away. We're paid up until the end of the week."

He pounded again. "Dominic, open up. It's me!"

There was cursing, then more movement, then the door cracked open a fraction. "Glad you made it Sebastian, but why don't– "

Sebastian pushed past Dominic and into the room.

"Hey! What's the big idea!" This was from Jessica who was sitting up in bed, covers clutched to her neck.

"I'm sorry, but I need your help." He began throwing their things haphazardly into their packs. "Howard needs your help."

"Howard? But ... what are you doing?" Jessica asked, bewildered. In all the time she'd known Sebastian, she'd never known him to act so erratically.

"It'll take too long to explain, but I need you to come with me, now."

"Okay, okay, but you just packed all of my clothes and I'm not about to go anywhere wrapped in a bed sheet," she told him.

Sebastian stopped and stared down at what he was doing. "I'm sorry." He ran a hand through his hair. "I'm sorry, but time is short and we have to leave as quickly as possible. And I know I'm not making sense but you're the only person who can help, and– "

"It's all right," Dominic said, taking him by the shoulders. He'd never seen Sebastian so worked up either. "Whatever it is, you know you can count on us to help."

"Why don't you wait for us down in the tap room," Jessica suggested. "We'll get dressed and be right down."

"Fine. All right. But bring all your gear. We have to leave immediately."

Chapter Thirty

Dominic shut the door behind him and turned to Jessica. "What do you think that was all about?"

She reluctantly got out of bed and pulled her pack over to search for clean clothes. "I have no idea, other than something has him all upset. Did he mention Howard's name?"

"I guess we'll find out," Dominic said with a sigh, pulling on his own travelling leathers. He'd really hoped they'd be able to spend at least a few days in the inn before travelling onward. Apparently, it was not to be.

When they went down to the tap room it was to find Sebastian pacing back and forth. Although the inn keeper had assured them that they did not serve breakfast, apparently the bard had cajoled or bribed the cook to provide a couple of bowls of stewed grain and berries.

"Hurry up and eat," Sebastian told them. "I'll go make sure the steeds are ready."

Jessica's eyebrows rose. "Steeds? Getting a little formal, isn't he?"

Dominic shrugged. "What can you expect from a bard?"

They shared a grin and started to eat. They'd barely had enough time to finish when Sebastian was back to harry them out the door.

"What is the big rush?" Jessica asked, beginning to question the bard's sanity. "Holy Saint Christopher, what are those!"

The three of the most beautiful horses she'd ever seen stood saddled and bridled and ready to go. Sebastian slung their packs behind the saddles and picked up the reins of the dappled grey steed.

"They're *estrada*," he told them. "They were a gift from your grand– from Aracelia. And trust me when I say they are a most timely gift indeed."

Wide-eyed Jessica looked up at the mounts, then over at Dominic. He shrugged and mounted the steed closest to him. A wide grin split his face. "This is every horse-man's dream, to ride upon an *estrada*."

Jessica mounted up, feeling like a kid on a pony. "Can I at least ask where we're going?"

Sebastian was already moving off. "To the Wild Woods Elven Realm."

Dominic and Jessica had only the time it took to ride from the inn to the edge of the town to get used to riding the massive *estrada* before Sebastian's steed broke into a flat out run. Needing no guidance from their riders, the other two mounts followed suit. Jessica yelped and hung on for dear life.

There was no possibility of conversation with the break-neck speed Sebastian set. Though his friends had no idea what was happening, they caught something of his sense of urgency. Whatever was happening was obviously of the utmost importance to him.

Sebastian spared no thought on the comfort of his friends and kept up the grueling pace until the sun began to set. As though it could read his mind, the *estrada* began to slow and then turned off onto a barely discernible side trail which led to a well-used, but empty, camp site. The elven mounts were just starting to breathe heavily.

"Wow, that was ... that was..."

"Amazing," Dominic said, eyes glowing. "I've heard of *estrada* but never thought to have the pleasure of riding one. The experience was more incredible than I ever imagined."

He dismounted and stroked the sleek neck of his steed. "You are truly an amazing creature," he said.

"Would you two like to be alone?" Jessica asked waspishly, although she had to admit that she found their mounts every bit as enchanting.

Dominic chuckled and came over to help her dismount. She slid into his arms and he trapped her against her horse so he could steal a kiss.

"I'll water the horses if you want to put together something to eat," Sebastian said distractedly. He'd already pulled the gear from his steed and left it piled near the pit. "There's food in the provision bag." He began unsaddling their mounts as well.

With a sigh Dominic let go of Jessica as her stomach rumbled. She grinned up at him. "Better get to it, mister," she said. "You wouldn't want me to starve to death."

"Fine, why don't you start a fire." He gave her a smirk. "You could use the practice." Turning her towards the fire pit, he gave her a light swat on the rear.

"You're going to pay for that," she said, rubbing her butt.

He wriggled his eyebrows at her. "Promise?"

Laughing she turned to the task at hand.

When Sebastian returned from watering the horses at a nearby brook, the fire was burning brightly and Jessica had put together a dinner from the supplies the stable hand had packed for them - trail bread, fresh fruit (although she set aside three apples for the *estrada*), cheese, and some kind of meat filled pies. She found a flat rock and carefully placed it at the edge of the fire, placing the meat pies on it to heat them up. After a moment's thought, she put the remaining three apples on there as well.

"Okay," she said, once Sebastian had the mounts secure. "You wanna tell us what's going on?"

Sebastian dropped to the ground beside the fire and sighed. Running his hand through his already disheveled hair, he said, "I don't even know where to start."

Dominic jerked a thumb over his shoulder at the *estrada*. "Why don't we start with those? Where'd they come from?"

"You said something about them being a gift from Aracelia?" When he hesitated, she added, "It's all right, I know she's my grandmother." She shot a fond look at Dominic. "And I know who Thackery and Paranithel really are as well."

The breath Sebastian had drawn in left him in a whoosh. "Well, that makes this slightly easier. Aracelia was never happy with the decision to keep the truth from you, but it was out of her hands."

Jessica waved a hand at him. "It's okay, I'm not angry or anything. A little hurt maybe, but I can sort of understand why my father and grandfather were so worried about me learning the truth too soon."

"Howard was especially against keeping your parentage a secret, but he was afraid that Thackery and Paran would take away his ability to communicate with you if he said anything."

"Okay." Jessica drew out the word. "So ...?"

"You know, for a bard you seem to be having a great deal of trouble getting a simple story out," Dominic teased gently.

Sebastian ran a hand through his hair again. "It is, unfortunately, not so simple a story." Taking a deep breath, he sat back in his story-teller's pose.

"It goes thusly: Despite the loss of the moonstone pendant, and thus direct communication with Jesseminathus, the sorcerer, Paranithel, continued to teach the wizardling, Howard, magic. In an effort to aid this endeavor, the Lady Aracelia sent Howard an adder stone imbued with enough magic to last several months."

"What's an adder stone?" Jessica asked.

"Shh," Dominic told her. "Go on," he said to Sebastian.

"Unbeknownst to all, Howard had stumbled across a spell that increases magical power. It was his thought that he could use both the spell and the magical artefact to send himself the magical realm to beg forgiveness of his friend for his part in the deception perpetrated by her family."

Jessica was beginning to look faintly alarmed. "Oh my God, what has Howard done?"

"He put his affairs in order, leaving a note for the fair Ellen, giving her authority to act on his behalf. Unbeknownst to him, Ellen returned home earlier than expected, found the note, and desired speech with Howard to clarify its meaning. She arrived at his dwelling just as he was about to cast his transportation spell –"

"Holy Saint Christopher," Jessica whispered.

"– and was caught up by the portal as well. They both ended up in the Darkwood Elven Realm where they met with the bard Sebastian, who was, through an accident, without his horse, and all were taken to the Lady Aracelia."

"Howard and Ellen are here?" Jessica's voice rose several octaves, making the mounts shy on their picket line.

"The Lady Aracelia offered to furnish the humans with horses and supplies to accompany the bard to his rendezvous with her granddaughter Jesseminathus and her companion Prince Dominic. In return she begged only a small boon. That on their way past the Wild Woods Elven Realm they pause to determine why the other realms have heard nothing from Wild Woods recently. The elf Kaelan was to accompany them and return to Darkwood with news."

"Will you stop talking in the third person," Jessica said irritably. "What's happened to Howard and Ellen?"

"We reached Wild Woods in a timely fashion, but the barrier was ... diminished somehow."

"What do you mean diminished?" Dominic asked. "You think someone tampered with the barrier? Is that even possible?"

"All I know is, it distinctly lacked in strength. And within the barrier, things did not feel ... right. There was a heaviness in the air as though unseen phantoms lurked nearby."

"Creepy," Jessica said.

"Then we chanced upon Kaelan's brother– "

"Kaelan has a brother?" Jessica asked with interest.

"Three brothers and one sister, in fact," Sebastian told her. "We made camp with him that night and in the morning we were attacked by dark elves– "

"Dark elves?" Dominic repeated with a frown. "I thought they were only legend?"

"Indeed, so did we all. We managed to fight them off– "

"Wait a minute!" Jessica interrupted again. "You fought them off? I know Ellen's studied whatever the martial arts sword fighting is called, so I'll buy that she might have held her own, but Howard can't be trusted with a paring knife, let alone a sword."

"Perhaps not," Sebastian said with a sense of pride. "But he is a fair hand with a staff."

"A staff? A *staff*?"

"An ironwood staff," the bard confirmed. "We drove the dark elves off and Diarmad, Kaelan's brother, departed for Darkwood to tell them what had occurred, while we continued on to the outpost." Here he fell silent, staring into the fire.

"What did you find at the outpost?" Jessica asked gently.

"Nothing." He turned his head to look at them. "They were gone, all of them. The guards, the women, the children – all of them. There was no blood, no sign of a struggle, it was as though they suddenly got up in the middle of their meal and just … left."

They were quiet for a moment, and then Jessica had to ask, "What happened to Howard and Ellen?"

"We still wished to determine what happened to the inhabitants of the Wild Woods Realm. Kaelan suggested for safety's sake we retreat to the haven that lies within the heart of the realm, and as we were about to enter," here his voice faltered, "Howard was infected with elf bane."

Dominic sucked in a breath. "I thought elf bane was eradicated, by the elves themselves."

"So did we all," Sebastian said morosely.

"What's elf bane?" Jessica asked, looking from one to the other.

"A plant that is so highly poisonous that even to touch it will release the toxin," Dominic told her.

"How bad is it?"

"It's entered his blood stream."

"What does that mean?" Jessica asked, becoming more and more alarmed at the serious looks on the two men's faces.

"It means that only healing magic can save Howard," Dominic told her.

"Your healing magic," Sebastian said.

Jessica looked from one to the other. "Damn."

Chapter Thirty-One

Ellen and Kaelan took turns spooning warm willow bark tea down Howard's throat. Ellen wasn't sure how much it was helping his fever, but he didn't seem to be in as much pain. When his skin began to cool, they moved him over to the pallet between the fire and the wall, hoping the rock would reflect some of the heat.

When Ellen made the evening meal, she boiled a couple of strips of the dried meat with a few vegetables and strained the broth into a separate bowl. She coaxed half of it down Howard's throat and set the rest aside for later.

"The willow bark was a good idea," Kaelan said. "I've heard the pain from elf's bane can be excruciating."

"I feel so helpless," Ellen said.

Kaelan put a comforting arm around her and she rested her head on his shoulder. They were sitting together by the fire, near enough to Howard to act if he needed anything.

"If you were in your own world," Kaelan asked. "How would you have treated Howard?"

Ellen smiled. "I would have called an ambulance to take him to the hospital."

"Ah."

She turned her head slightly so she could see his face. "You have no idea what I'm talking about, do you?"

"I am sorry, but no."

"That's all right." Snuggling back against his shoulder, she explained. "A hospital is a place of healing - a really big place of healing. And an ambulance is a special vehicle that transports sick or injured people to the hospital."

"This ambulance, it is a vehicle like the car you described?"

"That's right. And once Howard was in the hospital he'd have many doctors - healers - to help him."

"They'd be able to cure him without magic?"

"I don't know," Ellen admitted. "But maybe."

"Truly your world must be a wondrous place."

"It has its moments," she said with a contented sigh.

Her head slipped a little further and Kaelan realized she'd fallen asleep. Carefully he eased her down until she was lying beside the fire, and covered her with a blanket. He checked on Howard, who seemed to be resting peacefully although his temperature was still dropping. Even the air around him was growing chill.

Kaelan threw several more logs onto the fire and picked up his own blanket. It had grown noticeably chilly in the cave, thanks to Howard, and Ellen was shivering in her sleep. He watched her for a few moments, wondering if he should awaken her and suggest she move to a different cave where she would be warmer, but he was loathe to wake her.

There were no more blankets, they'd put the rest on Howard. Telling himself it was purely a matter of survival, he covered her with his blanket and then slipped underneath them both, spooning up to her back. She stirred slightly and sighed in her sleep, snuggling back into his warmth.

For once Jessica made no complaints about getting up early. They had a cold breakfast of bread, cheese, and fruit and were in the saddle as the sun made its appearance over the horizon.

"How much farther to the Wild Woods Realm?" she asked as they prepared to leave.

"I'm not sure," Sebastian said. "You've probably noticed that the *estrada* are much faster than a normal horse, it makes it hard to judge. But we're more than half-way there, we should be there by mid-afternoon at the latest."

"What about these dark elves?" Dominic wanted to know. "Should we expect any trouble from them?"

"I really don't know. I didn't see any on the way out, but that doesn't mean they weren't there. And I was travelling pretty fast."

"Well, we'll just have to keep our fingers crossed, won't we?" Jessica said. "Now let's get a move on."

The *estrada* were more than ready to go. They were built for speed, as well as intelligence, and they were relishing being able to run.

They kept up their mile eating pace until just outside the Wild Woods barrier. Without instruction from their riders, they slowed and stopped.

"What's the matter?" Jessica asked.

"It's the barrier," Sebastian said. "There's something wrong with it. It was weakened when we first crossed it, but when I went through it yesterday I could feel it changing. It's somehow becoming ... wrong."

"Oh, this is just great," Jessica said. "We don't have time for this."

She urged her steed forward. Where a normal horse might have balked, the *estrada* pushed through the barrier. A shiver went over the great beast's skin. Jessica felt a burning along hers that left her nauseous.

"Holy Saint Christopher, what was that?"

"Dark elf magic probably," Dominic said, looking a little pasty himself.

"Whatever it is, it's getting worse. I just hope we can get back out again," Sebastian said.

He took the lead and once more they were pounding along the trail. They saw no sign of the dark elves, but they had the distinct feeling of being watched. Sebastian didn't care. All he cared about was getting to Howard. Praying there was still time to save him.

As they approached the entrance to the sanctuary, he called back over his shoulder, "We're going too fast to dodge low branches. Lay as low as you can, or else you're going to get scraped off your steed's back."

They did as he directed, and felt the clean shimmer of the warding wash over them. There was no time to admire the haven. Sebastian led them right up to the cave before halting his steed, practically falling from his saddle in his haste to dismount. They hurried into the cave after him.

"It's freezing in here!" Jessica exclaimed. She could actually see her breath.

"What I wouldn't give for a down filled jacket right about now," a tired, but familiar voice said.

"Ellen!"

The two friends embraced, laughing and shedding tears at

the same time.

"What's with the temperature in here?" Jessica asked.

"Don't blame me, it's Howard's fault." Ellen gestured to the form lying beside the fire. Frost rimed the blankets covering him.

"Why don't you build a fire or something?"

"Because he keeps putting it out," said Kaelan, entering the cave. He was carrying something wrapped in a blanket. Going over to Howard, he carefully began depositing hot rocks around him. Once he was finished he placed the hot blanket over top of Howard and the rocks.

"It is good you are here, Jessica," he said.

"We had to build a fire in another cave to heat the rocks," Ellen said. "It was Kaelan's idea when we couldn't keep one going in here."

"Oh, Howard," Jessica said, going over and kneeling down beside him. "What have you done to yourself this time?" He was very still and white. Ice crystals had formed on his eyebrows and lashes. His chest barely moved as he breathed shallow breaths in and out.

Reaching out, she placed one hand on his forehead and one on his chest, nearly snatching them back as the cold burned them. She took a deep breath, then another. Closing her eyes she concentrated, going deep inside herself where the magic lay. The flame was larger than it had been the first time she'd found it, and she had no trouble at all separating out the healer green.

The healing magic raced down her arms and into Howard, burning away the cold poison infecting his system. It was elusive, almost like it had an intelligence of its own. But in the end she was able to eradicate every molecule of it.

When she was done, she was proud of the fact that though she was weak, she didn't collapse. "Now that's what I call an efficient use of magic," she said with satisfaction.

Howard's color was back to normal and the ice crystals were melting from his face. His breathing seemed normal as well.

Sebastian was on his knees beside her. "Thank you," he said simply. Howard chose that moment to begin to stir, and a great smile lit up the bard's face.

"Are you all right?" Dominic asked, helping Jessica to her feet.

"Nothing a decent meal and a nice long nap wouldn't fix."

Ellen cleared her throat. Jessica shot her an irritated look. "What?"

When she looked pointedly at Dominic, Jessica flushed slightly. "Oh. Right. Ellen and Kaelan, this is Dominic. Dominic, I'd like you to meet Ellen and Kaelan."

"I remember your name being Bandit, and in a slightly different form last time we met," Kaelan said.

Dominic grinned. "Just slightly?"

"Nice to finally meet you, Dominic," Ellen said with a shy smile. "Why don't I get started on the meal?" She went over to Jessica and gave her a great hug. "That was amazing. You rock!"

"How long before Howard's ready to travel?" Dominic asked.

"A day, maybe more," Kaelan said. "Even with healing magic he will not be himself again soon. The cold fever - I have never heard of it manifesting itself in this way before."

"Maybe it's tied into his elemental magic," Sebastian said.

"Yes, perhaps you are right," the elf agreed.

"Wait, what? What elemental magic?" Jessica asked.

"When we were with the Lady Aracelia she was able to do a

quick testing of Howard's magical abilities," Kaelan told her.

Jessica's eyes lit up. "He has magical powers here? That's so awesome. We wondered about that, but had no way of telling."

"He turned out to be strongest in the elemental powers," Sebastian put in. He was still sitting on the ground beside Howard. "Aracelia believes with the right training he could become a master of the elements."

"Way to go Howie!" Jessica said, looking down at him fondly.

"Furthermore," Kaelan added. "Once he has mastered the elements he could retain much of this power should he wish to return to your world. Elemental magics work differently from other magic."

Dominic stacked wood in the fire pit and got the fire started. Ellen brought in food from their stores and started putting together lunch for them.

"Why did you want to know about how soon Howard could be travelling?" Ellen asked Dominic.

"Something's happening to the barrier around the enclave," Dominic said. "Sebastian, you said it was very faint when you entered as a group?"

"Yes, I do not believe it would have stopped anyone of ill will."

"And when you came out it was stronger."

"That's right, but there was a ... wrongness to it."

"A wrongness," Kaelan said sharply. "What kind of wrongness?"

"Like I'd passed through something unclean."

"It was worse when the three of us came through, wasn't it?" Dominic persisted.

"Yes, even the *estrada* did not wish to pass through."

Kaelan glanced at Dominic, a look of complete understanding

passed between them.

"We have to leave. Now," Kaelan said.

"It may already be too late," Dominic warned.

"What are you guys talking about?" Jessica wanted to know.

"The barrier," Kaelan said. "The dark elves somehow breeched it. And now that they've gotten rid of all the elves from Wild Woods, they're changing the barrier so only their kind can pass through."

"Which means we'll be trapped inside here with them," Jessica said. "Shit!"

Howard groaned and opened his eyes.

"You're awake!" Sebastian exclaimed, unashamed of the tears in his eyes as he leaned over him.

"Why is it so cold in here?" Howard rasped.

Sebastian smiled. "It's a long story. How do you feel?"

"Like I got run over by a zamboni," he muttered.

Ellen and Jessica laughed. Kaelan and Dominic just looked at each other and shrugged.

"Do you think you can sit up?" Sebastian asked. "Ellen is preparing one of her feasts. And there is someone here for you to greet."

With Sebastian's help, Howard was able to struggle into a sitting position. He's eyes widened when he spotted Jessica. "Jess? How'd you get here? I thought we were supposed to find you in ... whatever place it was Sebastian was supposed to meet you?"

"Oh, Howard." She went over to him and gave him a big hug. "What the hell have you done this time?"

He looked at her a little guiltily. "It was just a little spell ..."

"Don't look so woebegone. I'm glad you're here. I've really

missed you. Both of you," she added, looking over at Ellen.

"What happened to me?" he wanted to know. "Why do I feel so crappy?" He pushed the blankets off himself, looking at the rocks that tumbled out of the folds in surprise. "Why were you guys throwing rocks at me?"

"We weren't throwing rocks at you, you nit," Ellen scolded, bringing over a bowl of thick soup. "We were trying to keep you from freezing to death."

Sebastian took the bowl from her. "Here, let me help you," he said to Howard.

"This is embarrassing," Howard said. "Why am I so weak?"

"You've been very sick," Ellen told him gently. "On your way into the haven you were stabbed by a poisonous plant. We were afraid we were going to lose you."

Howard was finding it too hard to split his focus between talking and eating. He allowed Sebastian to feed him a few more bites and then looked up. "And Jessica?"

"Sebastian went and got her," Ellen said with a grin. "He took the *estrada* with him so they could make better time on the return journey."

Sebastian flushed slightly. "I was in a hurry," he said defensively.

Howard smiled at him. "My hero."

Jessica snorted. "Hurry was putting it mildly. I'm surprised he let us get dressed first."

"I hate to break this up," Dominic interrupted. "But someone needs to go check the barrier."

"I'll go," Kaelan volunteered. "There's another hidden way out of the haven that's closer to the barrier."

"I'll go with you," Dominic said. "I don't think anyone should go outside of the haven alone."

"Don't be too long," Jessica, yelled after them. "We need to start making plans."

Chapter Thirty-Two

Kaelan led Dominic to the waterfall of the haven. Behind it was a passage through the rocky outcrop that widened into a cave at the other end. About two thirds of the way along the passage, they came to the sanctuary's barrier.

"We must be extra cautious from this point onward," Kaelan whispered. "Once past this warding we will lose the protection of the sanctuary."

Dominic nodded.

The mouth of the cave was hidden by thick brush and the two men paused to listen before pushing through, Kaelan first.

Using his heightened elven abilities he cast about, trying to sense the presence of the dark elves but could detect nothing. At his nod, Dominic joined him. As though they'd been working together for years, they moved through the foliage silently, keeping alert for any signs of the dark elves. Kaelan stopped suddenly, holding up two, then three fingers. Dominic nodded in understanding.

They hunkered down beneath the shelter of a broad-leafed shrub as three dark elves skulked by. They might have been on patrol, but judging by the weapons they were carrying they were hunting.

"Have the elves been fully purged?" one of them was asking.

"Yes, the last group is on its way to the mountain hold."

"And what of the humans you encountered?"

"We have found no trace of them. There was a disturbance in the barrier earlier, it is to be hoped they are gone."

"Hope is for humans and light elves," the apparent leader spat out. "I want more patrols to be certain ..."

The voices faded as they moved off. Kaelan and Dominic waited several moments before cautiously straightening up. The elf raised his eyebrows and gestured in the direction the dark elves had taken. Dominic shook his head and Kaelan nodded in understanding, then continued leading him towards the enclave's barrier.

Instead of a clean, rainbow shimmer, the barrier had a smoky grey cast to it. They could feel its malevolence seeping off it in waves. Dominic reached out to touch it but Kaelan caught his arm before he could make contact and shook his head. Motioning to the human to follow, the elf made his way back to the cave.

Once inside they didn't speak until they were safely through the haven's warding again. They both let out identical sighs of relief.

"I'm getting too old for this," Dominic said ruefully.

"Indeed. As am I," Kaelan said.

By tacit agreement, they refrained from speaking about what they saw until they reached the others.

"Here," Ellen passed a bowl of thick soup to Jessica. "You might as well have something to eat while you wait."

Jessica took the bowl with a sigh. "Thanks, El," she said,

sitting down beside the fire.

They ate in companionable silence for a bit, and then Jessica looked up with a grin.

"What is it?" Howard asked. He was having trouble keeping his eyes open.

"If you told me a year ago that I'd be here, now, doing what I've been doing, I'd have had you committed."

He chuckled. "You wouldn't have had to do it, I'd have committed myself."

"You've been very ill, you should try and get some rest," Sebastian chided.

"Okay, but before I do, I have something I need to get off my chest." Howard had been slouched in Sebastian's arms but now he struggled to sit up. "Jessica, there's a reason I cast that spell that brought me– " he shot a look at Ellen, "– us, here. I needed to tell you face to face what's really going on– "

"You mean how I was really born here and my father and grandfather more or less blackmailed you into keeping it secret so they could tell me themselves?"

He stared at her, mouth agape.

"You knew?" Ellen demanded. "You knew and you never said anything?"

"Well," Howard said, leaning back again. "So...how do you feel about all this?"

With a sigh, Jessica admitted, "To be honest, I don't think I've really had time to assimilate it all. I mean, I hadn't even come to terms with the possibility of being adopted before I got zapped here."

"And then to find out you have both magical powers *and* living family..." Ellen said quietly.

"It's just a little much to take in all at once."

"So does this mean I'm off the hook?" Howard asked sleepily.

She smiled fondly at him. "Yes, Howard. That means I no longer want to rip your head off. In fact, I should thank you for all the help you gave me in the beginning. You were a real lifeline."

"Wasn't all me," he said, eyes closing. "Had lots of help."

"We'll talk about it later," she said in amusement. "You might as well get some rest while you can. You too, Sebastian. You're probably exhausted too."

"I could use a bit of a rest," he admitted. Still holding onto Howard, he scooted them both down until they were lying together on the pallet. "Did I remember to thank you for saving him?"

Jessica smiled. "See? I told you he'd be perfect for you."

He smiled back and closed his eyes.

"So," she said to Ellen as the bard's breathing evened out.

"So," Ellen said back. "Look at us being all self-reliant and awesome."

"Sebastian said you met Aracelia. How did that go?"

Ellen went into detail about meeting with Aracelia and then agreeing to check out the Wild Woods realm for her.

"You should have seen Howard in her garden, working his elemental magic. The look on his face was priceless."

They looked over at his sleeping form.

"I'm so happy for him," Jessica said. "It's what he's always wanted."

"The magic or the bard?" Ellen asked.

They shared a laugh.

"I was on my way to *ken-jutsu* practice when I got caught up in his spell, so all I had with me was my *bokken*."

"I've seen what you can do with that thing," Jessica said. "It's a good thing the elves that found you didn't try any funny business."

"Yeah, well, the best part is that Aracelia and Howard joined together to work some alchemy." At Jessica's questioning look she pulled out her katana. "They turned my wooden sword into a real katana."

"Wow," Jessica said, taking the blade gingerly and examining it. "It looks authentic."

"Doesn't it though?"

"Your father would have kittens if he saw you with this thing." She handed it back.

"Wouldn't he just?" Ellen asked with no little sense of satisfaction. "Nothing would ever make him believe his little lotus blossom could be trusted with a live blade."

They shared a laugh.

"Now, what's this I hear about Howard helping fight off a band of dark elves?"

"You'll be so proud of him, Jess! He was feeling a little bummed because he was the only one who couldn't fight, and I remembered when we had that exchange student from Japan."

"Akiro? I remember him. He was pretty cute," Jessica said.

Ellen grinned in return. "Remember he taught us all how to fight with a *bo*?"

"I remember more about you having the hots for him."

Giving her a mock punch in the arm, Ellen continued. "Anyway. Howard talked a couple of trees into providing us with some staffs, and I taught him and Sebastian how to fight with them. He's pretty darn good too."

"Way to go Howie," Jessica said. After a bit, she said, "You've seen my father and grandfather, talked with them, even if it was just through a scrying bowl... what are they like?"

"Your grandfather, Paranithel, is a really sweet old man. Kind of a stereo-typical wizard - has long white hair and a beard, likes to wear long robes and a pointed hat. But he's got a kind face and I get the impression he has endless patience."

"And my father?"

"Thackery is tall, with a medium build. I think he'd be quite handsome if he wasn't always scowling. And any fool can see how much he worries about you. He really felt that by keeping himself and Paranithel secret from you he was doing the right thing to protect you."

"What do you think about all that?"

Ellen hesitated. "When I was on the other side, I was furious with them both. I thought keeping you in the dark was a mistake. You should have been told who you were and what you were doing here. But since I've been here myself... I can kind of understand why they did what they did."

"That still doesn't make it right," Jessica murmured.

"No, and it doesn't excuse the fact they more or less bribed Howard with magic to make him toe the line. But they really did have your best interests at heart. I think Thackery was a little afraid of what you might do if you knew the whole truth before he had a chance to prepare you."

"You mean he was afraid I might go after Anakaron on my own because he was the one who killed my mother?" She thought about what the water hag had told her but kept silent.

Ellen shrugged.

Jessica looked up and caught Ellen staring at her. "You keep staring at me. Do I have food between my teeth or something?"

Ellen looked at her rather sheepishly. "Actually, I was looking at your ears."

"My ears?"

"Well, you know, you're part elf. I was just trying to decide if your ears had the slightest point to them or not."

Jessica gaped at her and then had to laugh.

"You kind of look like her you know."

"Who?"

"Aracelia. Something in the facial features, especially around the eyes."

"I really enjoyed the time I spent with her," Jessica said wistfully. "I wish I'd known then that she was my grandmother."

"If it's any consolation, she came very close to spilling the beans many times. But she swore an oath to Paranithel before he arranged for her to meet you, and he in turn swore an oath to Thackery."

Jessica was silent for so long that Ellen was forced to ask, "What are you thinking? Are you still planning on going south to meet Thackery and Paranithel? Aracelia has offered to send you back to our world herself, if that's what you want."

Smiling slightly, Jessica shook her head. "No, I'm going to see this through. No matter what. I may not agree with their methods, but it's obvious those two down south care about me. I find I really want to meet them, to find out about where I come from."

"And to learn about your mother," Ellen added softly.

"That too. Plus there's the whole magic thing ..."

"How cool is that?" Ellen asked with a grin. "You and Howard both."

"Sometimes it's very, very cool," Jessica admitted. "But sometimes it's pretty damn scary. What about you? Any magical powers for you popping up?"

"No! And I'm quite happy to keep it that way. I'll stick to being Aragorn and you and Howard can duke it out to see who's Gandalf."

They shared a laugh.

"Now all we need is a Gimli and a couple of hobbits," Jessica said. At Ellen's confused look she added, "Well, we've already got a Legolas ..."

At Ellen's blush she began to chortle. "I knew it! Don't think I didn't catch how comfortable you and Kaelan were around each other. Spill!"

"There's nothing to spill," Ellen said defensively. "I mean, yes he's cute and sweet and you should see him fight with those swords of his, but that's all."

"That's all my butt, have you slept with him yet?"

"No!" At Jessica's raised brow she added, "We may have kissed a few times, but that's all there's been time for. Really." When Jessica continued to just stare at her with her eyebrows raised she said, "And I'm sure you've been a freaking nun this whole time."

"But of course!" She held a hand to her heart and adopted her most innocent expression. She managed to hold the pose for only a few seconds before dissolving into laughter. Ellen joined her.

Chapter Thirty-Three

We are in serious trouble," Dominic said when they returned to the cave where the others were waiting. "There are indeed dark elves making themselves at home in the Wild Woods realm."

"The barrier has been tainted with dark elf magic," Kaelan added. "Being an elf, I might be able to pass through with some difficulty, but the rest of you..."

"It'd probably be like touching elf's bane," Dominic finished for him. "And there are patrols everywhere."

"So where does that leave us?" Jessica asked.

"Stuck here for the time being, I guess," Sebastian suggested. He and Howard were both feeling better after their rest. "Do you think the protection will hold?" he asked Kaelan.

"The dark elves we encountered did not appear to realize such a sanctuary exists," he told her. "With luck it will be some time before they do, if at all."

"Okay, time out," Jessica said. "First of all, why wouldn't they be able to find us here? Where is here? Sebastian didn't exactly give us a grand tour on the way in. And second, you "encountered" dark elves?" She turned to Dominic who had dropped down beside her and punched him in the shoulder. "You never said anything about encountering dark elves."

"Ow!" he complained, rubbing the spot she'd hit. "We were getting to that. On the way to the barrier we almost ran into a dark elf hunting party. Fortunately there was a nice big bush for us to hide under."

"'Here is the sanctuary located in the heart of the realm," Kaelan put in. "It is meant to be used in dire emergencies. It is heavily spelled and warded against detection."

"Sebastian said the elves from Wild Woods are missing, if they're not in here, then where are they?" Jessica asked.

"Taken," Kaelan said soberly. "Somehow the entire population was ensorcelled and taken away. We suspect to a dark elf strong hold in the mountains."

"Crap!" Jessica said.

"Indeed.

"We need to get a message to Aracelia," Ellen said. "She needs to know what's going on, to warn the other elves."

"I have not enough magic to make this possible," Kaelan admitted. "Perhaps someone with more power…"

"No problem," Jessica said, turning to root around in her pack. "I can contact her with my mirror."

Once she had the mirror in her lap, however, she just sat there looking at it.

"What's the matter?" Dominic asked.

She looked over at him. "It's just…" she bit her lip as she hesitated. "This will be the first time I've spoken to her since our blood relationship has come to light."

"You nit," Howard chided her. "She's thrilled about you being her granddaughter. And we could tell she was really unhappy about keeping the truth from you."

"If you say so," Jessica said dubiously. Deciding it was best to just get it over with, she held the mirror a little more firmly and chanted the activation incantation, then waved her free hand in front of it.

She frowned when nothing happened and tried again.

"Shouldn't something be happening?" Ellen asked.

"Yes something should be happening, it just isn't," Jessica snapped. She tried a third time with no better luck. "Maybe I'm getting the incantation wrong. Here, you try." She thrust the mirror towards Dominic who snatched it out of her hand to avoid being jabbed in the midsection.

"What makes you think I'd have better luck than you?" he asked. "You're the one with all the power, I'm just the muscle."

"But you know more about magic than I do, and I just worked a major healing," she said, gesturing towards Howard.

Dominic sighed, but did as she asked, unsurprised when he had no better luck that she had.

"This can't be good," Ellen said. "Maybe it's broken."

"Or maybe something's interfering with its magic," Kaelan said slowly. "Perhaps the changes the dark elves have made to the barrier are blocking your magic."

"Like a jamming signal," Howard suggested. "It makes sense. If there were any stray light elves hiding out, the dark elves wouldn't want them to be able to tell anyone on the outside what's going on."

"Okay, so how do we get in touch with Aracelia?"

"You need to boost the signal," Ellen said. "Like on Star Trek."

Jessica rolled her eyes. "That is so not helpful. This isn't a T.V. show - I can't just tell Scottie to give me more power."

"What about this?" Howard asked, pulling the moonstone pendant from his shirt.

"What about it?"

"It was made by the elves, and it has ties to Aracelia. What if you used it with the mirror? I don't know, wrap it around the handle or something. Maybe it would help boost the signal."

Jessica looked at Dominic. "What do you think?"

He shrugged. "Couldn't hurt to try."

She took the chain from Howard and wrapped it around the handle of the mirror with the actual pendant resting on the back of it. Taking a deep breath, she tried the incantation again.

This time there was a ripple in the glass.

"Try again," Dominic urged.

Jessica kept a hold of the mirror and chanted the incantation one more time, this time a little louder and more firmly, making the appropriate gesture with her free hand.

This time the glass rippled and then cleared, this time showing a worried looking Aracelia. "Jessica? My dear girl, what – "

"No time for explanations," Jessica said tightly, brow furrowed in concentration. "I don't know how long I can hold this. We're at the Wildwoods sanctuary. The realm has been overrun by dark elves."

"Dark elves!" Aracelia hissed in surprise. The glass rippled, then cleared again. "What do you need?"

"I– " Jessica glanced at the others. "Nothing. We just wanted to warn you. They've done something to the barrier - we're going to try and break through before they realize we're here."

"When you do, head west to– " The rest of what she said was lost as the mirror shattered in Jessica's hand.

"Holy Saint Christopher!"

"Well that can't be good," Ellen said.

"I've never seen metal do that before," Sebastian said.

"Let me see your hands," Dominic said, gently taking Jessica's hands in his. He brushed shards of silver off and turned them over. Aside from a few minor cuts, her hands seemed fine. There also didn't seem to be any damage to the moonstone pendant, which had dropped to her lap.

"I think this would be better off with you," she said handing it to Howard. Her heart was still racing.

Hesitantly he took the pendant from her and looped it around his neck again. He didn't want to worry Jessica, but he had to ask, "Do you think Aracelia's mirror shattered as well?"

They looked at Kaelan, who shook his head. "I do not believe so. It was most likely the barrier that caused this."

"I'm guessing the barrier will prevent me from attracting a wind imp too," Howard said, disappointed he wouldn't be able to show off in front of Jessica.

"This doesn't bode well for us getting through the barrier, does it?" Ellen asked.

They stared at each other uneasily, none of them wanting to voice their thoughts out loud.

"At least they know about the dark elves," Sebastian said.

"What's to the west?" Jessica asked suddenly. "She told us something about heading west."

Dominic looked at Sebastian and they both looked at Kaelan, who shrugged. "I do not know."

"It's a good bet whichever way we go the dark elves will be after us," Jessica said. "Wouldn't it be better to head for some place more defensible, like the city of Claverton?"

Dominic and Kaelan both shook their heads. "Fighting bandits is one thing," Dominic said, "But a hoard of dark elves is something else entirely. I don't like the idea of drawing innocents into this."

"We have no idea how many dark elves there are here," Kaelan pointed out. "They swarm like locusts. Claverton would be stripped bare before its citizens even knew they were under attack."

"Sebastian, you're the one with the mental GPS, can you think of anything significant to the west of us?"

Sebastian looked at Jessica blankly. "I have a mental what?"

"The map thing – the way you can figure out the best route from point A to point B all in your head."

"It only works with places I've been," he said. "I fear I have not been further west than the Trembling Hills."

"Trembling Hills?" Howard put in. "That doesn't sound good."

"It is not. Beyond them lie the Sirani Sea and the Shrine of Dorian."

Jessica huffed a breath. "Anyone think of anything special about either of those?"

Dominic shrugged.

"I believe," Kaelan said slowly, "there is a Well at the heart of the shrine."

"That's it!" Ellen said excitedly. "Aracelia must think you guys," she indicated Jessica, Dominic, and Howard, "can team up for some kick ass spell casting and, you know, kick some dark elf ass."

"I guess it's possible," Jessica said slowly, not really believing her own words.

"But a shrine?" Sebastian questioned. "In my experience they're not exactly the most defensible of places."

"The Shrine of Dorian lies upon an island in the Sirani Sea,"

Kaelan said. "Dark elves will not cross water. Small streams and brooks, yes, but they will not cross a river nor will they venture onto a lake or ocean."

"Or an inland sea, I take it," Ellen said wryly. "But if this shrine is on an island, how do we get there?"

Kaelan shrugged. "There must be a way, the followers of Dorian would have needed to get to the shrine for their ceremonies."

"Let me get this straight," Howard said. "All we have to do is break through the dark elf barrier, cross the Trembling Hills, make it to the Sirani Sea, and somehow reach the Shrine of Dorian. Then what?"

"What do you mean?" Jessica asked.

"We'll be trapped on the island just as surely as we're trapped in here now," he said.

"Aracelia must have a good reason for sending us there," Ellen argued. "I vote we go. Jessica?"

"We don't know for certain that's where she was going to tell us to go. What do you think Kaelan?"

He shrugged. "I guess it's as good a goal as any."

"So it's decided then," Dominic said briskly. "We break through the barrier and head for the shrine of Dorian."

Chapter Thirty-Four

E ver since his time in Ghren, Thackery preferred to have his workroom at the top of a tower. Most wizards preferred the confinement of an underground chamber, but not him. Knowing there was open air and freedom just beyond the wall soothed him.

The work rooms for the students were on the main floor of the castle, although the two for working major spells were below ground. As Paranithel had pointed out, it was easier to keep a spell gone awry contained that way. And Paran's own work room was underground as well, on the other side of the castle. But Thackery had chosen the tower diagonal from the scrying tower for his space.

As it was at Ghren, his work room was in the top most space, warded to a fare-thee-well, while his living quarters were directly below. Sometimes he regretted this predilection, like now when he had to climb the spiraling stairs to his rooms at the end of the day. In a perfect world he would have dispensed with stairs altogether and anyone wishing to see him would have to have the ability to teleport, but they were trying to set a good example for their students, that magic should not be used frivolously. More's the pity.

He could only trust that Dominic was instilling these self-same values in Jessica, and while it was to be hoped the boy was keeping his hands to himself, realistically he knew that was too much to hope for. They were both young and had needs, and despite the fact they'd been thrown together by circumstance, Jessica could do worse than young Dominic.

Thackery almost cracked a smile. He still thought of him as young Dominic, even after all this time. The boy must be almost thirty or more. Not a boy at all, but a man. A man he still cared for like a son. He'd hate to have to turn him into a lizard if he hurt Jessica in any way.

He reached the landing outside his quarters and paused a moment to catch his breath. The staircase wasn't getting any shorter, and he most definitely wasn't getting any younger.

Looking out the high, narrow window, he watched the sun lowering in the sky. It was still a bit of a shock every time he glanced out a window and saw not the lush green forests he was used to, or the sea, or even the mountains, but mile upon mile of sand, broken up only by the rocky outcroppings of Jendarra's Necklace and the city of Ombra in the distance. If it were not for the magical dome, much like the barrier of an elven realm, shielding them, there would be a hot wind blowing inwards, instead of the cool breeze circulating.

Thackery moved on to his workroom but didn't stop there. Instead he continued climbing the remaining steps to the very top of his tower, to the small space he used for meditation. It was a single room, open on all sides. It was bare save for the small platform in the center with the thick red cushion on it– his one concession to age.

Shifting around on the cushion he found the most comfortable position he could. He had a feeling he'd be sitting for quite a while. This was something he'd been putting off for too long, and in all fairness to Paran and his portents, it was time.

Settling into a meditative trance, he opened his inner eye and began seeking out the magical energies of the land. Almost immediately he sensed a "wrongness" to them.

Close to the Well the energy was clean, but when he cast his senses further afield he was filled with an uneasy sensation. Drawing power from the Well, he sent his awareness arrowing towards the northern continent. Here the feeling of wrongness increased. There were bright spots - the Wells and what he believed to be the elven enclaves, but where were the magical groves? The springs cleansed by the unicorns? And what was that darkness to the west? By his calculations, that should be one of the elven groves, Wildwoods if he was not mistaken.

There was another, larger darkness to the northwest, centering in the Shadow Mountains. He focused his awareness on it and was immediately overcome by a sense of evil. Pure, unadulterated evil. It called to him, cajoling him to join it. It was almost a living thing, reaching out to him.

With a gasp Thackery pulled back, shocked out of his trance. He shuddered, wiping a hand across his dampened brow. What a complacent fool he'd been, running and hiding while Anakaron had been building his strength. He hoped it was not too late for them to stop him.

Safe in one of those bright spots in the north, Aracelia stared in the silver mirror but saw only her own reflection. She'd been receiving reports from the other enclaves and the news was not good. Before she could sink too far down in her thoughts, there was a ripple in the glass.

"Jessica? There is no time to waste– "

The glass cleared and she gave a little "oh" of surprise. Thackery's countenance looked grimmer than ever.

"It seems I must beg your forgiveness," he said without preamble.

"You have it," she said automatically. "Whatever for?"

"For the doubts I have had, my stubborn refusal to face the facts of what is happening around us."

Aracelia was shocked into silence.

"It is to my shame I have allowed my ego to dictate the truth."

"And what is the truth?"

"The truth is, that while I am sure Anakaron still desires my death, that is not his primary focus. He desires power, above all else, and nothing, not even his vendetta against me, will stop him from amassing it." He paced away from the scrying bowl and came back.

"I have "seen" the magical overlay, and wrongness to it," he admitted. "There are blank spots where there should be light, and a darkness originating in the Shadow Mountains."

She sucked in a breath. "I thought as much."

"There is a similar darkness where I believe the Wild Woods Realm to be. I thought you should be warned."

"I– I thank you for your warning, though it is not unexpected. We lost contact with Wildwoods days ago." It was on the tip of her tongue to tell him that Jessica's friends were in fact there now but it would serve no purpose other than to worry him further.

He looked at her earnestly. "We have not always been in

accord, you and I. But in the name of the one whom we both loved, I ask for your aid in keeping my daughter safe."

"Even if it means telling her the truth?" she asked, a tad more sharply than she meant to.

To give him credit, he never hesitated. "Even so."

She stared at him for a long moment, wondering what else he could have seen to bring about such a change. At last she nodded. "I swear by my daughter's soul I will do everything in my power to keep my granddaughter safe."

Chapter Thirty-Five

J essica stood at the cave entrance looking out over the valley. They'd passed as pleasant a night as one could expect sleeping in a cave, but now it was morning and they needed to leave the security of the sanctuary. Dominic joined her, wrapping his arms around her from behind.

"What's wrong?" he asked.

She gave a short laugh. "What's wrong? Everything! Howard just about dying, him and Ellen even being here for crying out loud, us having to fight our way past a hoard of dark elves..."

He pulled her over to the flat rocks at the mouth of the cave so they could sit side by side. "I think it goes deeper than that. Something's been bothering you long before Sebastian ran us down in Claverton."

They watched Sebastian and Kaelan fiddle with the gear on the *estrada*.

After considerable debate, it was decided that the best strategy would be to send the mounts to where they'd originally entered the Wild Woods Realm. The hope was the dark elves would be so distracted by the large disturbance in the barrier they'd pay little attention to the smaller disturbance the group's passage would make. The mounts would circle around and meet up with their riders, hopefully before the dark elves caught anyone.

Sebastian and Kaelan were arguing over what to leave and what to remove. While they didn't want to take the chance of a dark elf being able to capture one of the animals by grabbing onto anything trailing behind, they couldn't afford to be slowed down by carrying the riding gear as well as their packs.

"Talk to me," Dominic said.

Jessica sighed, resting her head on his shoulder. "Nothing in my old life in any way prepared me for this one. My life before was so very different - the world I grew up in is so very different."

"What do you miss most about it?"

Jessica thought about it for a minute. "That's part of the problem," she said at last. "Now that Ellen and Howard are here I don't really miss any of it."

"I don't see how that's a problem."

"I don't either," she admitted. "I guess I feel like I *should* miss it more. I mean, I kind of miss all the convenience, but at the same time there wasn't the satisfaction you get over simply surviving. Everything is so much harder here, but I feel more alive. I never realized how easy we had it back in the earth realm."

He gave her shoulder a reassuring squeeze. "Maybe there's part of you that recognizes that you belong here, that you're home."

"Maybe," she said doubtfully.

"Hey! Are you two coming? We're burning daylight here," Ellen yelled at them.

Jessica turned to yell back and her jaw dropped as she got a good look at her friend. "Holy Saint Christopher! You look like a ninja elf."

Ellen flushed. She was dressed in one of the elven outfits Aracelia had given her and had her sword strapped to her back.

"She's a totally bad ass ninja elf," Howard said with a grin, coming up to stand beside her.

Sebastian and Kaelan joined the little group. "We've finished with the *estrada*," Kaelan said. "We removed the bridles - they don't really need them anyway."

"*Estrada* don't really need saddles either," Sebastian added, "But we'll be more comfortable in them so we left them on, just tied the stirrups up so they don't dangle."

"You're sure they're going to be able to pass through the dark elf barrier?" Jessica asked. She hated the thought of the beautiful animals being harmed.

"They should be fine," Kaelan reassured her. "The barriers are designed to discourage people - elven or human - not other creatures. If that were so, elves would have nothing to hunt within the enclaves."

"Does this mean if Jessica turned us into say rabbits or something like that we could pass the barrier without harm?" Ellen asked

Kaelan looked at her askance. "I ... I do not know. I do not think it has ever been tried."

"I don't know about the dark elf barrier," Dominic said, "But when I was a dog I still felt it when I passed through the barrier at the Darkwood Realm."

Kaelan nodded. "That is because you still retained your human mind. You would have to become fully the animal - no trace of your human essence could remain."

"But if no trace of human essence remained," Sebastian said,

"What's stopping you from forgetting you weren't really a rabbit and just wandering off in search of greens to eat?"

"Or you'd just get eaten by a hungry fox or something," Ellen said with a shudder.

"Well it's a good thing I have no intention of transforming anyone into anything then, isn't it?" Jessica said.

"A very good thing," Dominic said with a grin.

Jessica just shook her head and got to her feet. "As Ellen said, daylight's burning. I think being surrounded by dark elf magic is having a detrimental effect on my mental health. The sooner we're out of here, the better."

Dominic ducked into the cave long enough to grab their packs and handed one to Jessica. She donned it with a slight grimace at the weight and then chuckled.

"What?" Dominic asked.

"You asked me before what I missed about the other world, right now I'd have to say Ellen's old clunker of a car. We could just throw all this stuff in the trunk and drive away."

"My car is not a clunker!" Ellen protested.

"Is too!" Jessica and Howard said together, then laughed.

"Dirt bikes would do better on this terrain," Howard pointed out.

"I always wanted to ride a motorcycle," Ellen admitted.

"If you three are finished?" Dominic said, a little irritably.

Jessica went over and stood on her tip toes to kiss him on the cheek. "Some day we're going to go to Earth together and then I can show you all these weird and wonderful devices we've been talking about."

"Promise?"

"Promise. But first we have to escape from Wildwoods. So if

everyone has everything, let's go."

They decided the best place to try and break through the barrier would be close the area Dominic and Kaelan had scouted out earlier. Jessica gave the pool at the base of the waterfall a wistful look as they ducked behind it and trailed along with the others as they followed the elf in single file. With any luck, the disturbance the *estrada* made escaping would pull any patrols away from the area and they could make their own escape just as quickly.

"I've always wanted to give spelunking a try," Howard said, looking around the cave behind the waterfall with interest.

"Really?" Jessica asked.

"Don't let this wiry body fool you," Howard told her. "Ever since Jason took me to Bruce Caves Conservation Area I've had the bug."

"Who's Jason?" Sebastian asked with a frown.

"Just an old high school chum," Howard said with a grin. "That wasn't a note of jealousy I heard, was it?"

Sebastian didn't answer, but his face was flushed as he hurried after Ellen.

"If this is supposed to be a sanctuary inside what technically already is a sanctuary," Jessica asked as they made their way down the passage at the back of the cave, "Then why is there a secret way out of it? Not that I'm complaining, mind you," she added hastily. "It just seems strange."

"I don't know," Kaelan said with a shrug. "I'm not altogether sure it was meant to be. I only know of it because I used to play in these caves with my cousins as a child."

"I'll bet you went skinny dipping in the pond, too," Jessica said mischievously.

"I don't remember," he said, but the red tips to his ears gave him away. "Once we've passed the wards surrounding the sanctuary, the dark elves will know we're here," he reminded them.

"Why didn't they sense you and Dominic?" Ellen asked.

Kaelan shrugged. "They may have. But two have less of an energy signature than six."

"Let's hope they stay distracted by the *estrada*," Ellen said.

"Enough talking," Dominic growled. "We're about to pass through the sanctuary wards. From here it's not that far to the barrier, but we don't want to alert any patrols that are out there before we have to."

Sebastian had been keeping a silent count down and spoke up. "The *estrada* should be at the barrier ... now."

"Let's go, everyone!"

"Wait!" Jessica felt a sudden panic rise in her as Dominic made to move forward. He turned, one eyebrow raised in question.

"What happens if I can't break through the barrier? It's not like I've been able to practice for this kind of thing."

"You'll do fine," he assured her.

They followed Kaelan past the wards and out of the cave towards the barrier. This was no near invisible wall of benign energy. This barrier was like dark smoke, seething and roiling. The energy it gave off was unwholesome.

Jessica's heart was in her throat. "I ... I don't know if I can do this."

Howard came and stood beside her. "Well you'd better, or we're all dead. And I didn't come all this way just to die."

As she looked at him in shock, an arrow whizzed by her ear,

imbedding itself in the tree trunk beside her.

"We've got incoming," Ellen called.

To Jessica's surprise, she had her sword out and was standing beside Kaelan like they were a team. Dominic also had his sword out while Sebastian had pulled out a bow.

"Ellen and Kaelan," Dominic called. "You two protect Jessica and Howard. We'll see what we can do about these elves."

It was only one patrol, but it was still nine dark elves to deal with. Sebastian's arrows picked off three of them as they rushed at the group.

"It's like smoke," Howard said as he and Jessica tried to ignore what was going on behind them. "What if we used wind?"

"Wind, right." Jessica focused on the barrier and tried to create a wind to dissipate the smoke. All that happened was the swirling grew faster.

"No, like this," Howard said impatiently. Using his newly available elemental magic, he created a small whirlwind in front of them. It grew in size and strength and when it was as big as he could make it, he lifted it, aiming the point of it towards the barrier.

"I don't have enough power," he gasped. "It's not strong enough."

He gave a start as Jessica slid her hand into his. "Use mine," she told him. "Take what you need."

It was like tapping into a river of energy. Some dim part of him wondered how she was able to keep it all contained. Feeding her energy into his whirlwind, he strengthened it, then hardened the air.

"You're doing it!" Jessica yelled over the sound of the wind.

"You're breaking through."

The hole grew larger. When it was large enough for a person to pass through, Jessica yelled at Kaelan and Ellen.

"You two first."

There were only three dark elves left at this point and their attention seemed to be focused on Dominic and Sebastian. Kaelan and Ellen jumped through the hole and stood ready on the other side. Dominic took care of one of the dark elves, Sebastian another. The third turned and fled.

"Hurry," Jessica urged. "I don't know how long we can keep this open."

They didn't argue, just followed Kaelan and Ellen.

"The opening is going to start collapsing as soon as we let go," Howard said.

"Then we go through together," Jessica told him.

"No room. You first. There'll still be a few seconds - I'll be right on your heels."

There was no time to argue. They moved as close to the barrier as they could. At Howard's nod, Jessica stepped through, dropping his hand at the last second. The hole immediately began to shrink. Howard dove through, landing in an ungraceful heap on the other side. His left boot was smoking where the barrier had begun to close on it.

"Are you alright?" Sebastian asked, kneeling down beside him.

"We did it," Howard said, a little dazed. "We really did it."

"You mean you did it," Jessica said with a grin.

"I couldn't have done it without you," Howard told her.

Ellen rolled her eyes. "Enough with the freaking mutual admiration society already. We need to get out of here."

"What about the *estrada*?" Jessica asked, not relishing the idea of walking all the way to the Sirani Sea.

"They'll find us," Kaelan said, with more assurance than he actually felt.

Chapter Thirty-Six

Were there any difficulties securing the elven realm?" Anakaron asked the dark elf framed in the large, obsidian mirror.

Only someone watching for it would have noticed the elf's hesitation before he answered. "Nothing we were not able to handle. The first batch of elves should reach the Shadow Mountains soon."

Anakaron's gaze narrowed slightly. "And what of the disturbance of magical energy I felt, the one that came from the barrier of the elven realm?"

The dark elf's face took on a greyish cast. "I did not witness the occurrence. I received only a secondary report."

Anakaron said nothing, merely raised an eyebrow. The dark elf swallowed hard.

"There was a small group of humans, insignificant, that somehow became trapped within the realm. The disturbance was caused by them breaking through the barrier."

When the dark lord still didn't say anything, the elf hastened to add, "The damage to the barrier was minimal. It resealed itself the moment they were through."

"And how is it a human was able to breach the barrier in the first place?"

"One of them may have had slight magical abilities, a young male."

"And you did not think a human powerful enough to break through the dark barrier was worth mentioning to me?"

If the dark elf had been capable of it, he would have been sweating at the tone of his master's voice. "He was protected by a group of skilled swordsmen – only one of the patrol survived the encounter. By the time he made his report and we were able to return the barrier had resealed itself and they were gone."

Anakaron's rage was almost a palpable thing. "And you sent no one to pursue them?"

"There-there was another incident, my lord. Several *estrada* also escaped through the barrier. We believe they were the humans' mounts."

At last Anakaron's icy calm was shaken. "Humans? On *estrada*? Unthinkable. Unless..." He seemed almost lost in thought for a moment, then focused his attention back on his hapless minion. "Find out where these humans have gone, and whether these *estrada* were indeed their mounts."

With that he broke the connection in the mirror, leaving the dark elf almost sagging in relief.

Anakaron turned away from the mirror and paced across the room to seat himself on the obsidian throne. Humans on *estrada*, it was unheard of. And yet ... if one of those humans had elven blood in them.... No, it was not possible. He would have known!

With a flick of his hand he conjured up an image of the only person he had ever cared for. The ghostly form of Farenalysia spun gently before him, so lifelike her hair moved with each rotation, a smile on her lips. His woman, the one stolen from him through trickery by that dog Kiranthus.

It was rumored that they'd had a child together. Was it possible? Could a child have survived the attack all those years ago? The attack was the only thing in his life he regretted, and only because it took the life of the woman he loved. He had not known she was at her father's estate when he sent the skarjen there.

He thought back to that time, setting aside the rage he'd felt. There had been something...even in his weakened state he'd still been attuned to the magical energies. There had been a ripple, a portal opening to another place, another world. At the time he'd thought it was Paranithel fleeing this world, but what if instead he fled with a child to hide it?

Anakaron sat up a little straighter. But he did not stay away, He left the child and returned, making his way south while Kiranthus ended up in Ghren before moving south as well. The disturbance he felt in the Darkwood Elven realm ... a surge of magic for just an instant. What if it was a portal allowing the child, now fully grown, to return?

"I must know," he said, not realizing he'd spoken aloud. Pushing himself to his feet, he left the throne behind and went back to the mirror. With a wave of his hand, it was activated.

"My lord! We– "

Anakaron cut the startled elf off in midsentence. "The survivor of the patrol, I would speak with him."

"Yes, my lord." The elf gestured to someone out of Anakaron's sight. Several long minutes passed before another elf joined the first. "I await your command, my lord."

"This human magic worker who broke through the barrier, describe him to me."

"Yes, my lord. He was tall and slender, much like an elf but with dark hair. He was dressed like an elf too, and had an amulet around his neck."

"Describe this amulet."

"Ah," the elf hesitated, clearly nervous. "I did not get a good look at it, but it was white, I believe it was carved from a moonstone, and there was a taint like elven magic to it – that's the only reason I noticed it at all."

Anakaron's eyes blazed. It was true! The child of Farenalysia and his enemy lived, and now was returned home. "You will follow these humans – I wish to know where they're going."

"Pardon, my lord, but if they are riding *estrada*, as we suspect, it may not be possible."

"Everything is possible when I will it to be," Anakaron stated. The tip of his staff glowed as he spoke in a guttural tone. The elf in the mirror let out a gasp that turned into a shriek as his form morphed into that of a hawk.

"With the hawk's speed and eyesight you should have no trouble keeping up. You will keep this form for seven days and nights, at which time I will be ready to receive your report."

The hawk screeched again as it winged away, but Anakaron had already turned from the mirror.

Chapter Thirty-Seven

Kaelan had taken the lead as they fled from the enclave, leading them through a series of low-lying hills that offered plenty of trees and rocks for cover. The shrine lay to the south west and he'd been slowly changing their direction from the east.

Now he raised a hand to halt them. "Rest," he said succinctly.

Packs were lowered to the ground amid good-natured groaning and he climbed up one of the well-foliaged trees to have a look around. He hadn't been at all sure the elven mounts would seek them out - as a lowly guard he didn't rate one as a mount, and while he was familiar with their intelligence they were, when all was said and done, just glorified horses to his mind and were just as likely to return home to their stable. So it was with equal measures of relief and chagrin his keen eyes picked out the approaching equine shapes.

Dominic was waiting for him when he came down again.

"Are you sure this is a good idea? I'd be happier if we put some more distance between us and the dark elves."

"As would I," Kaelan agreed. "But I do not know how much further we can push those two," he nodded towards where Ellen and Howard had pretty much just sat down where they stopped, "and Jessica needs to replenish the energy she expended from using her magic."

Dominic looked over at them, and frowned.

Kaelan shrugged. "They do well, but they are not used to this kind of life."

"You're right," Dominic said with a sigh.

They rejoined the others, and passed out bars of pressed dried fruit, saved aside for such a purpose. Most of the other supplies had been divvied up between the packs. Sebastian started passing around a waterskin.

"From my vantage point I was able to see the *estrada*," Kaelan said to the group, and was met with weary cheers. "They are close - we might as well wait for them here."

"What about dark elves," Ellen asked. "Any sign of them?"

"There are none that I can see."

"I'm not trying to borrow trouble," Jessica said, "But I can't help wonder why they aren't following us."

"This troubles me as well," Kaelan admitted.

"Maybe they're short-handed, what with taking over the enclave and us killing a bunch of them," Howard suggested.

Sebastian frowned. "I think it more likely they did not think us worth the effort. They have the enclave, what more do they need?"

"If they're working for Anakaron, or at least with him, wouldn't they be looking for anyone with magic too?" Ellen asked, playing devil's advocate.

"Maybe they just figure there's no rush because we're on foot," Jessica suggested.

"Or maybe it doesn't matter," Dominic said. "Perhaps we should count ourselves fortunate they are so lax and keep moving."

With perfect timing, the sound of hooves reached them. Howard gave an audible sigh of relief as the *estrada* came into view.

Rest time over, they loaded their packs onto the *estrada* and mounted up. Time to put some serious distance between them and the enclave.

Not one of them noticed the hawk wheeling high above them.

One day blended into the next as they travelled onward, the *estrada* covering great distances with their ground eating lope. They stopped briefly at midday for a break and just before sunset each night.

Despite there being no sign of pursuit, they decided to avoid any towns and villages along the way. Even Jessica, with her longing for a proper bed, had no wish to put innocent lives at risk. It was bad enough that her best friends had been drawn into this mess – she would never forgive herself if anything happened to them. The sooner they reached the wizards in the south the better. She wouldn't rest easy until they were safely back in the earthly realm.

After five days the *estrada* came to a halt at the edge of a wide, grassy plain.

"I thought you said the name of the place we're headed for was the Trembling Hills," Ellen said.

Kaelan nodded. "They lie just beyond the grass plain."

"That's a whole lot of empty," Jessica said. She caught Dominic and Kaelan looking at each other. "What?"

"It's not as empty as it looks." Kaelan admitted.

"Dominic?"

He sighed heavily. "Snakes and khang locusts."

"What's a khang locust?" Howard, Jessica, and Ellen chorused.

"It's a large, multi-legged insect with a poison tipped stinger and a liking for warm flesh."

Jessica and Ellen shuddered. "He had me at snakes," Howard said.

They stared out at the grassy plain with its innocently waving grass for a moment.

"So how do we cross the plain?" Jessica asked.

"As quickly as possible," Kaelan said succinctly.

"If I may make a suggestion," Sebastian ventured. Everyone turned to look at him. "Though it is somewhat early to break for the day, I suggest we remove ourselves to yon grove and make camp." He nodded towards a cluster of trees they'd passed only moments before. "Both we and the mounts would benefit from a good night's rest. Morning is soon enough to cross the plain."

"And the quicker the better," Jessica muttered.

Everyone else agreed and they headed back to the grove. In what seemed like no time at all a camp was set up and the *estrada* taken care of. Everyone had a task to do and did them quietly and efficiently.

Jessica finished first, then stood back and shook her head at the scene before her.

"What?" Ellen asked, looking up from where she was sorting through the provisions they had left.

"It's just...you, me– us, here like this together."

"It's weirder than snake shoes, isn't it?" Howard asked, looking up from where he was spreading out the bed rolls. "It's like the coolest, most realistic RPG ever."

"Howard– "

"Don't worry, Jess. I know it's not a game. I'm too saddle sore for there to be any confusion about that. It's just…when it's not scare-the-crap-out-of-you dangerous, it's just really cool is all."

Jessica stared at him for a moment and then laughed and shook her head. "What about you Ellen?"

"I'm not a gamer, like Howard is, but I get what he means. I keep expecting to break out in hysterics any second now. Or to wake up and find out it's all been a really vivid dream."

Ellen sat back on her heels and looked around thoughtfully. "It's kind of scary, really, how quickly I've gotten used to this."

Jessica nodded in agreement. "I think it's something in the air," she said sagely, sharing a laugh with her two friends.

"You're looking more sober than usual, my friend," Jessica said to Kaelan. "Is anything wrong? I mean, more wrong than us fleeing for our lives from a hoard of dark elves."

Kaelan cracked a half smile at her banter. "I was just wondering if Diarmad made it safely back to the Darkwood Realm."

"Diarmad struck me as the type to fall into a pile of manure and come out smelling like a rose," Ellen said, coming up and taking his hand. "C'mon. I'll show you how I make that flatbread you like."

Jessica gave a laugh as Ellen led him away.

"What has you so amused?" Dominic asked, snagging her around the waist with one arm.

"That is one smitten kitten," Jessica said, nodding towards Ellen.

"And that's a good thing?" he guessed.

"I don't know," she said, smile fading. "But I hope so."

Chapter Thirty-Eight

They spent a pleasant evening swapping stories and listening to Sebastian play his flute – his other instruments he'd left behind in caves of the sanctuary to be retrieved at a later date. The morning found them well rested and ready to tackle the vast grass plain.

"It's probably best if we spread out," Kaelan suggested. "I don't expect any trouble, but best to present as wide a target as possible."

"Any tips for the ride itself?" Ellen asked.

Sebastian spoke up before the elf could. "If it's anything like my ride to Claverton, my best advice is to keep your head down and hang on tight."

"What about gopher holes?" Jessica asked suddenly.

"Gopher holes?" Kaelan asked, his confusion plain.

"Yeah, you know, gophers – rodent like creatures who like to dig burrows in grassy plains. I've heard of horses stumbling in a gopher hole and snapping their leg."

He shook his head. "Nothing lives on the plain save for the khang locusts and snakes, perhaps a few other insects and insignificant rodents. The snakes do tend to live in holes, but the holes themselves will not bother the *estrada*."

"All righty then," Howard said, filled with determination.

"Let's get this show on the road."

They ranged themselves in a loose line, far enough back to give the *estrada* a running start. For a moment all they did was just sit there on the mounts, then Jessica let out a whoop.

"All right cow pokes, let's go!"

Her *estrada* shot forward, the others taking a few seconds before following suit. It was both exhilarating and terrifying. Jessica had once ridden a dirt bike on a track, but even that didn't compare to the speed of the *estrada*.

The beast seemed tireless, its long-legged stride eating up mile after mile of the plain. Jessica tried to see how the others were doing but the wind streaming by made it impossible. Sebastian was right, all she could do was hang on for dear life.

Hours passed, yet still the steed's pace did not slacken. Jessica was only just starting to understand the true value of Aracelia's gift. The stamina of the creature under her was amazing.

She couldn't be sure, but the sun seemed to be lowering in the skies before the steed began to slow, and finally came to a stop, sides heaving. Though winded, it didn't seem more so than a regular horse after a good run. Jessica reached down and stroked its neck.

"You were amazing," she said with complete admiration.

The *estrada* whickered and bobbed its head, and of its own accord turned and walked slowly over to join the others.

"What a rush!" Howard said excited. "What I wouldn't give to take one of these guys home with me."

Ellen rolled her eyes at him. "And wouldn't that be just so easy to explain."

Dominic dismounted and the others followed suit. "I have to admit, even I had my doubts about their abilities."

"I didn't," Sebastian said smugly. "They made it from Wildwoods to Claverton in a day and a half – that would have been a week's journey with a mortal horse."

"*Estrada* or not," Howard put in. "After a run like that they should still cool down. I say we walk until we come to some place to rest for the night."

Jessica looked back over the plain they'd just traversed, six lines through the waving grass to show their passage.

"What are you looking for?" Dominic asked, coming up beside her.

She started. "Nothing, I just can't believe we came so far so fast – and it still looks so innocent."

He didn't say anything, just turned and rooted through the pack on his steed and came up with one of the strips of dried meat he carried for emergencies. They were several yards from the edge of the waving grass and he walked over to just within throwing distance and tossed the dried meat beside the leading edge – quickly stepping back after he did so.

Nothing happened for several seconds, then the grass seemed to explode. The strip of meat was suddenly covered with shiny, gold/green creatures – the color of the grass beside them. They were a cross between a beetle and a scorpion with hard round bodies and tails curling up with what was obviously a stinger on the end. The instant the meat was gone they vanished again.

"Holy Saint Christopher," Jessica whispered.

"Let's get out of here," Howard suggested, leading the way.

The land sloped gently upwards and they walked until coming to a small plateau. Beyond the plateau the land rose more steeply in a series of rolling hills.

"Let me guess, the trembling hills?" Ellen asked.

"Just so," Kaelan nodded.

"I wonder why they're called that?" Jessica said. "They don't look so bad, nothing to tremble in fear over. Or are there more creepy crawlies like the ones from the plain?"

"I've heard it said that there was a great magical battle fought there," said Sebastian. "It's also said there is a vast amount magic that lingers."

Dominic had been looking around them. There wasn't much to see, just grass and rocks and dirt – the golden green plain below stretching to the horizon and the hills above them.

"I think this is as good a place as any to spend the night," he decided. "Daybreak is soon enough to tackle the unknown."

He got no argument from the rest, who busied themselves stripping the gear off their mounts.

"Jessica, could you come have a look at Epona? She was limping a little when we were walking."

"Sure, El." She was glad of any excuse to use her healing magic. Squatting down beside the animal, she ran her hand down its legs.

"I don't feel anything with my hands, but it looks like she might have been stung a couple of times."

It was easier for her to use the healing magic than any other and it only took a second to draw the poison out. Epona stayed stock still, tossing her head when Jessica was finished.

"You're welcome," she said with a grin. As a precaution she went over the rest of the animals as well. All had some degree of poison in them but none as bad as Epona.

"You'd make a great vet," Howard told her.

She smiled back at him. "I always saw myself as more of an herbalist," she said. "You know me with my plants. But I have to admit, it is kind of cool to be able to heal with magic."

Dominic looked at Jessica thoughtfully. "It is as I've told you before, you could easily make your way with your healing skills, even without magic."

"As I recall," she told him dryly, "At the time I thought I'd lost my magic and you were in the shape of a dog."

They laughed.

"Among my people, to be a healer is amongst the highest of callings," Kaelan told her soberly.

"Really?" Jessica asked, somewhat surprised. "I would have thought it would be something more magical."

"Elves are magic in and of themselves," Kaelan said. "But we are at heart a peaceful race – and few have the healing touch."

"Really?" Jessica asked in surprise. "But it comes so easily to me."

"The more you use a gift, the stronger it becomes," Sebastian pointed out.

"And you've done some pretty major healings." Howard reminded her. "Just think what you'll be able to accomplish once you get your proper training."

"Oh."

Jessica looked a little discomfited at being reminded of the amount of power she held. Ellen decided a change of topic was in order and called out, "Okay everyone, soup's on."

"Soup?" Kaelan asked. "How is this possible without a cauldron?"

"Sorry, it was a figure of speech. But you guys should know we are starting to get low on supplies."

The discussion of how best to replenish their supplies kept them going through supper and beyond. Dominic and Kaelan had never been this far to the southeast, and Sebastian had only a vague idea of the area.

"I think our first priority should be water," Ellen said. "Not only do the *estrada* need it, so do we. And where there's water there will hopefully be fish and other game. What?" she asked, thread of irritation in her tone was the four men looked at her in surprise.

"You were a Girl Scout, weren't you?" Howard asked.

"Damn skippy I was. Although I'm pretty sure they didn't have a merit badge for getting sucked into another universe."

"We're getting off track here," Dominic grumbled, as he always did when the talk turned to the earthly realm. "Ellen's idea of locating the nearest source of water is a good one, but in which direction?"

They looked at each other. "Anyone here know how to use a dowsing rod?" Jessica asked.

"What's that?" Sebastian asked.

"It's kind of like scrying, only you use a stick and you focus on finding water."

"I don't think scrying is a good idea after what happened to your mirror," Ellen pointed out.

"I think we're missing the obvious," Kaelan said. "Friend Howard is a budding elemental master. He should be able to sense nearby water."

The rest looked at him, then looked at Howard. Howard looked a little sheepish. "I keep forgetting I have powers."

"Well, how about it?" Jessica asked, slapping him on the back. "Wanna find us some water?"

Looking equal parts nervous and proud, Howard took a few steps away from the others and then stood with his eyes closed.

Reaching deep inside himself he sought the magic deep and separated out the blue strand. Using it as a focus he turned in a circle, trying to get a sense of where there might be water.

"There," he said, pointing. Eyes still closed he said, "Let me see if I can figure out how far away it is."

It was a heady feeling, being able to control one of the elements. He followed the sense of water with his mind to the source and back again, not realizing he was bringing the water back with him until Sebastian tapped him on the shoulder.

"I think that's enough," Sebastian said quietly.

Howard opened his eyes to find a small artesian well bubbling up at his feet. He quickly stepped to the side to keep from getting his boots wet.

"Well," Ellen said with a breathless laugh. "I guess that takes care of our water problem."

By mutual assent, they let the *estrada* drink their fill before filling their water skins.

"Um, I think you can turn off the water," Ellen said tentatively when it showed no signs of abating. By now it had filled a shallow depression and was slowly expanding.

"Um, I'm not sure I know how," Howard admitted. He looked at Jessica.

"Don't look at me," she said. "I've never done anything like this," she gestured towards the slowly expanding pond. "I didn't even know it was possible. Dominic?"

He shook his head. "The only elemental magic I know is how to start a fire. Don't forget, I had just barely started to learn before my training was interrupted."

"I would think," Sebastian said, taking a step away from the water creeping towards his feet. "Instead of attracting water to you, could you not ... repel it?"

"I guess it's worth a try," Howard said. Once again, he closed his eyes and centered himself. He "saw" the flow of water and pictured it as hose. Using invisible hands he took ahold of the hose and bent it in half, just as he would to stop the flow from a garden hose.

"Whatever you're doing, it's working," Jessica said quietly, so as not to break his concentration.

Howard was glad it was working, but he wasn't quite sure what to do now. If he let go, the water would just start flowing again. He needed to dam it up somehow.

Following the hose back to the source he reached for his earth magic to seal up the space the water was flowing from. Cautiously he loosened his hold on the water, breathing a sigh of relief as it stayed behind the barrier.

"Well done!" Sebastian slapped him on the back.

"I think I'm jealous," Jessica told him. "This comes so naturally to you."

Howard preened a little at her words, and he hoped with all his heart that Aracelia had been right, that he'd retain at least some of this power when he returned home.

Chapter Thirty-Nine

They moved to higher ground to make camp for the night. By morning the pool Howard had created was gone, soaked back into the ground.

"Are you all right?" Dominic asked Jessica quietly as they were loading up their gear. She smiled wanly at him. "You're going to think I'm crazy."

He grinned at her, "I already think you that. What more could there be?"

She slapped his shoulder, but without any real force. "It's nothing, really."

He looked at her and raised one eyebrow in question.

Jessica sighed. "It's just ... I'm not used to all this open space. It kind of gives me the heebie-jeebies."

"From the time we first met you've done nothing but complain about trees, and now you complain about the lack of them? You are crazy."

"Told you so."

"C'mon," he said, giving her rear end a swat. "If you're lucky maybe we can find a nice cave to sleep in tonight."

They mounted up and joined the others. Ellen was looking around uneasily.

"What is it?" Kaelan asked.

"I don't know," she said. "It's probably just my imagination but I just can't shake the feeling we're being watched."

"Paranoid much?" Howard asked. "I mean, take a look around. There are no trees, no other kind of cover – there's nothing around except that bird up there."

Ellen gave a slight smile and an embarrassed shrug. "I guess this place is finally getting to me. It's been go, go, go since we got here, I haven't really had time to deal with it properly."

Kaelan looked up at the bird high above them, a slight frown on his face, but he said nothing.

Because the land was beginning to slope upwards they kept the mounts to a walk. If the dark elves had been following them, they were sure to have been stopped by the grassy plain. For certain the race across the plain gave the travelers a lead of several days.

By midday they were high enough that when they stopped for a rest they were able to look back the way they'd come. The grass waved in the distance, stretching to the horizon.

"I still can't believe we were able to cross that in one go," Jessica said.

"Kind of boggles the mind, doesn't it?" Ellen agreed, coming to stand beside her.

"How are you doing, El?" Jessica asked. "We haven't had much of a chance to talk."

"We've been a little busy," Ellen admitted. "I guess I'm doing okay. I'm kind of getting used to being in the saddle – I might have to take up horseback riding when I get back." She paused for a second then added, "If I get back."

"You will." Jessica gave her a hug around the shoulders. "I promise. You and Howard both."

"What about you?" Ellen asked.

"What about me?"

"Will you be coming back too?"

Jessica glanced towards where Dominic was talking with the other men. "I don't know," she said. "Probably not."

"That's what I thought."

"It's not just him you know," Jessica said pensively.

"I know."

When Jessica glanced at her in surprise, Ellen shrugged. "No offense, but we've been friends a long time and you've always seemed like you're just a step out of time."

"But you never said anything."

Ellen spread her hands wide. "What was there to say? It didn't impact our friendship, and it wasn't anything I could put my finger on."

"I guess I always did feel a little different."

"And now we know why – you were just a wandering wizard."

They shared a laugh together.

The land continued to rise, the hills growing steeper. Dominic and Kaelan kept their eyes peeled for signs of game, twice they went off and came back with fresh meat for when they stopped for the night – once it was a brace of rabbits, the second it was a dark furred creature about the size of a pig.

"What is it?" Jessica asked.

"It's a sloughic. A little gamey tasting, but filling," Dominic told her.

Jessica wrinkled her nose at the creature's smell, but figured if she really was staying in this world she was going to have to get used to such things.

The prospect of making a life here no longer bothered her.

And as she told Ellen, it had nothing to do with Dominic. Sure, he was an added bonus, but she'd never felt so alive as she had since she arrived here, despite all the trouble she'd experienced.

Of course, where she lived might be moot if what the water hag had told her was true. Ever since she first learned of her magic, she couldn't shake the feeling she was given all this power for a reason, maybe facing Anakaron was it. It was frustrating to have all this power and not know how to use it. But she could learn, even if it meant learning on her own. Fortunately, her father's spellbook had a large section on combative magic.

"I can all but hear you thinking too hard," Dominic said. They were riding side by side, Ellen and Kaelan in front of them, Howard and Sebastian behind them.

"I can't help it," she told him. "Ellen and Howard told me about Aracelia's offer to send them home and I have to wonder if we really need to be heading south at all."

He considered her words for a moment before speaking. "While I don't agree with your father's need to stay mysterious, I truly believe he had good intentions."

"The road to hell is paved with good intentions," she quoted.

"Be that as it may, I think you would regret it if you did not at least meet with them and perhaps give them a chance to explain."

She sighed heavily. "You're right, of course. I guess things have just been so quiet lately I'm starting to borrow trouble."

No sooner had the words left her mouth than the ground beneath them began to shake.

"Holy Saint Christopher!"

Without being told the *estrada* halted, riding the rippling

278

ground as though it were a wave. The earthquake only lasted a few seconds before the ground settled again.

"Trembling Hills?" Ellen asked.

"More like Earthquake Escarpment," Howard said. He seemed to be more shaken than any of them. "Just how bad is this going to get? I mean, is it going to get worse the further in we go?"

They were looking to Kaelan to give them answers and he had none for them. "I do not know. I know only their name, not why they were named thus."

"I think we just figured that part out," Jessica said dryly.

"Is there any way around them?" Dominic asked.

Kaelan shrugged. "None that would not add weeks to our journey."

"This really sucks," Ellen said. They all turned to look at her. "We don't know how bad it's going to get, or how often they're going to "tremble" – we don't even know how far across they are."

"What do you suggest?" Kaelan asked.

"I don't know. Jess?"

"Going back isn't an option," Jessica replied. "And we have no idea how far out of our way going around would take us. Maybe this is as bad as it gets – they're called Trembling Hills, not Knock You Off Your Feet Hills. I vote we keep going in the direction we were headed. Dominic?"

"I agree."

Sebastian and Kaelan signaled their agreement as well.

"Howard?" He appeared to be studying the ground, and she asked him again, a little louder, "Howard?"

He jumped. "What?"

"What were you doing?"

"I..." he hesitated, then admitted, "I was trying to see if there was some kind of pattern to the earthquakes."

"And?"

"There doesn't appear to be – they seem totally random."

"It is too bad the Lady Aracelia was not able to instruct you in the use of your elemental magic," Kaelan said. "When trade caravans came this way it was always with an elemental master to smooth a path before them. Of course, that was before the grassland became infested with Khang locust."

Jessica cocked her head to one side. "Elemental magic isn't my strong suit, but maybe I– "

"No!" three masculine voices rang out as Dominic, Sebastian, and Howard all spoke at once.

"Seriously, Jess," Howard said. "Have you used any of the elemental magics for anything but making a fire?"

"Well, no. But– "

"Do you remember what happened the first few times you tried to make a fire?"

"Well, yes. But– "

"I, for one, do not wish to find myself in the bowels of the earth, even if it's by accident."

She huffed out a sigh. "Fine. You're right."

"Let's keep going," Dominic said.

They kept to a walk as they continued on, grateful to be riding *estrada*. Regular horses would have spooked at the first hint of an earth tremor.

There were several mild tremors throughout the day but only one slightly stronger than the first one they'd experienced. Unfortunately, they were still in the midst of the hills when the sun began to lower in the sky and made camp on the relatively flat top on one of the hills.

"Is anyone else as creeped out by the idea of sleeping on this ground as I am?" Jessica asked.

"I like the idea of continuing onward in the dark even less," said Dominic.

"Do we dare have a fire?" Ellen wanted to know. "As much as I'd like a hot meal, I wouldn't want for it to get out of control if a tremor hits."

No sooner were the words out of her mouth than the earth began to shake beneath them.

"I believe it would be safe enough for now," Kaelan said. "It's usually several candlemarks between tremors."

"Maybe just a cooking fire," Dominic suggested. "Once we're done eating we can snuff it out."

They did as Dominic advised and afterwards waited for the next tremor before settling down for the night. While none of them got a good night's sleep, they were at least rested enough to move on in the morning.

"I'd kill for an espresso," Howard muttered.

"Make mine a regular," Ellen agreed.

"While I've seen an impressive selection of tea here," Jessica put in, "It's just no substitute for a good cup of coffee."

"What's coffee?" Sebastian asked.

While Howard waxed poetic on the subject near and dear to his heart, the rest of them finished off breakfast and packed up to continue on.

Midway through the third day the tremors seemed to be further apart and milder in intensity. The hills were not quite so high as before. They all breathed a sigh of relief as the landscape became more trees and rocks and less steep hills, but they saved any discussion until they stopped for the night.

"How much farther do you think is to this shrine where Aracelia wanted us to go?" Jessica asked Kaelan as they sat around the evening fire.

He shrugged. "It could be several days, it could be more than a week. All I know with a certainty is that there are no other obstacles before us save for those any traveler must face."

"Well there's that at least," Ellen said with a smile for him.

"Just imagine how long the trip would have taken on regular horse," Dominic pointed out.

"Or on foot," Howard added with a shudder.

Chapter Forty

The hawk that was formerly a dark elf was grateful for two things: the strength of his wings and the keenness of his eyesight. At first, following the group of trespassers posed no problem, but the speed at which they crossed the grasslands left him far behind and he almost despaired at finding them again.

He drew on his own magical energy to increase his stamina, following the lines of passage through the grass and then continuing on in the same general direction. He encountered them again just as the wizardling enchanted the earth to give up its life-giving waters.

As he wheeled above them in the sky he could not but help wonder at their destination. It was as though they had no fear of the Dark Lord. They did not flee to the south as he would have, but they travelled in a more easterly direction. It made no sense.

If any of the others had magic, they did not show it. Not even that abomination of a light elf. He would enjoy plucking that one's eyeballs out and feasting upon them, did his lord give him permission to do so.

The light elves had cast his people out of the enclaves, and they were forced to eke out a meagre existence in the mountains. Food was scarce and magic was scarcer. Why should they be made to stay in the cold and shadow while the

283

others enjoyed the abundance of the sun? Their allegiance with the other magical creatures and the humans was a slur on the name elf.

Now that the Dark Lord had risen things would change for the dark elves. The world would soon see their power and once again the dark kin would flourish. The Dark Lord was a harsh master, but their world would have no place for weaklings.

As he circled unseen above the group, he couldn't help but wonder at the Dark Lord's interest in them. The wizardling's power was mediocre at best, and none of the other men appeared to have any power of note. And the women! The women bore swords as though they were fighters.

He scouted ahead of the group, trying to puzzle out where they were going. If they kept on their current path they would encounter the Trembling Hills. Beyond was nothing but more hills and valleys, rivers and forest, right up to the shore of the Sirani Sea.

Suddenly, the hawk/elf felt a tug, a pull he was unable to resist. Instinct had him fighting it until common sense over rode him. He was being summoned by the Dark Lord.

For two days and nights he flew without stopping – no rest, no food, no drink, his magic and the magic of the summons sustaining him until at last he reached the Carenkraka mountains and the Dark Lord's lair.

He swooped into the inner chamber and then fell tumbling to the floor as the magic released him and he was once more a dark elf.

"Report."

The word hit him like an arrow. The dark elf scrambled to his feet, chest heaving from the strain of the long flight and sudden transformation. It was not in him to beg for the mercy of time to recover. Quickly he went over to where the Dark Lord waited and bowed his head.

"I live to serve, my lord. The group I was following travels in a southeast direction. With the *estrada* they were able to cross the great grasslands unscathed and were starting across the Trembling Hills when I received the summons to return."

It was only through sheer will he was still on his feet. Without the magic to sustain him he felt as weak as a human.

"I see," Anakaron said. His robes swished as he paced back and forth in front of the dark elf, who dared not move a muscle. "And did they use no magic?"

"The one that broke through the barrier did, he used his magic to draw water to them. The others appear to be nulls." He used the derogatory term the dark elves gave to anyone without magic.

"Interesting," Anakaran said. "But I wish to know more."

Stepping up to the dark elf, he drew the fingers of his left hand together into a point and slid them into his forehead. The elf's mouth opened in a soundless scream as the information was ripped from him, along with his life essence.

"Clever boy, he used elemental magic, which is hard to trace," Anakaron murmured. "But why to the southeast, why not due south where his father is?"

Letting the dark elf slide lifelessly to the ground, he spun on his heel and went to consult his maps.

Spreading one of the rolled up maps out on the table, he secured it in place with his magic. One long finger came to rest on the spot marking the Wildwinds enclave and followed an invisible path east and south across the grasslands to the

Trembling Hills.

At first Anakaron frowned, seeing nothing of note in the Trembling Hills. The land beyond was ordinary enough until he came to the shore of the Sirani Sea.

"The Shrine of Dorian," he murmured. He tapped his finger thoughtfully on the spot. "But to what purpose?"

Leaving the map room, he returned to the throne room where he paced around the edge of the arcane circle on the floor. "Why the detour," he wondered. "Why not a direct route south?"

The shrine was on an island in the midst of the inland sea. The followers of Dorian had died out more than a handful ages ago and they had never had much in the way of power to begin with. However...

Anakaron stopped in his tracks. "The shrine has a Well!"

That's what the boy was seeking. He was looking to replenish his power before continuing southward.

"You there," he barked at one of the guards. "Find Urion and have him come to me at once."

The guard vanished out the door. Anakaron continued to pace as he waited. Generally he had little use for goblin-kind – they were not the brightest of tools – but the small, slimy creatures were resilient, able to squeeze into the smallest of spaces, and made excellent spies.

He was able to smell the dull grey goblin assassin even before he entered the room. Anakaron stopped pacing.

"I live to serve," the creature said, the deep grating voice at odds with his diminutive stature. "How may I be of assistance to the Great Lord Anakaron?"

"You are familiar with the harpies?"

The goblin's face twisted in distaste. "Untrusting creatures, the harpies. Too good for treaties or alliances."

"Indeed." It was interesting that Anakaron had also found them so. The harpy queen had rebuffed his offer of an alliance as well. "So you are no friend of theirs?"

"No!" The goblin spat and his spittle sizzled and smoked where it struck the floor. "The harpies are friend to no one."

"Then you would not be opposed to stealing something from Loreana, the harpy queen?"

The goblin's eyes lit up. "It would be my greatest pleasure to serve the Dark Lord so. What shall I take? Gold? Jewels?"

"The harpy queen has a daughter, has she not?"

The goblin nodded vigorously.

"I want you to bring the daughter here. Unharmed. Perhaps the queen would be more reasonable if her daughter was our guest."

Chapter Forty-One

The library in Aracelia's home did not usually see much use, but this night two candles guttered in their holders, the fire in the hearth had died to glowing embers, and the glowing ball hovering above the desk was starting to lose its brightness.

Without taking her eyes off of the text in front of her, Aracelia rubbed at her tired eyes.

"My Lady, you need to take a break."

"Only a few pages more, Maricel," she answered absently, turning a page.

"You are all but asleep where you sit. Would it not be better to start fresh after a brief rest? Your fatigue could cause you to miss something."

With a sigh Aracelia leaned back in her chair. "You're right, as usual, Maricel. I confess the words are beginning to run together."

"Come, my Lady," Maricel said, helping Aracelia to stand. "I have a tray waiting in your chamber."

"Oh, Maricel. I don't know what I'd do without you."

"Probably fall asleep at your desk and wake up hungry and with a crick in your neck," Maricel said with a sniff.

Aracelia chuckled. They reached her chamber and Maricel let go of her arm. "If you be needing anything else ..."

"Just don't let me sleep too long," Aracelia said. "I have little time to waste."

"I make no promises," Maricel said from the doorway. "Mind you eat some of that," she said with a nod towards the tray, and closed the door behind her.

The tray was resting on a low table beside the bed. Aracelia took a seat on the bed, resisting the urge to fully relax until she'd had enough to eat from the tray to keep Maricel happy. She ate automatically, without really tasting what she was eating, her mind still on the books she'd left behind in the library.

Though the histories were dry reading, she thought she was getting closer to her goal. She hoped she was because time was growing short. By her calculations it would take a week, maybe more, for Jessica and her friends to make the journey from Wild Woods to the Shrine of Dorian by *estrada*. Her plan was to meet them there and there was only one way to do that – by using the Fae roads.

At one time the Fae roads were more than just conduits of magic. They were used for physical transportation as well. All the races had access to them, but as often happens with such things there came a point in history where a great conflict arose. The use of the Fae roads was abused, tainted, and finally forbidden. The access spells were forgotten.

Almost all. Aracelia remembered reading about the Fae roads when she was younger. There had to be a record of it somewhere. It took a great deal of power to step onto a Fae Road, that much she recalled. But she was not sure whether it was an incantation or force of will that would allow that first step.

With surprise she realized she'd finished the food Maricel

had left her. There was a silver goblet with a light, fruity wine in it. She finished that off as well and, without bothering to undress, stretched out on the bed.

"Just a few minutes," she murmured, eyes closed. "A few moments of rest and I'll get back to work."

She had not, however, counted on Maricel to lace her wine with conferil, an herb from her very own garden that was used to aid in sleep. The residual taste of it in her mouth was unmistakable when the sunlight streaming across her face the next day woke her.

Aracelia blinked the sleep away, somewhat disoriented from her long rest. Sitting up she frowned as she judged the time by angle of the sunlight streaming through the windows.

"Maricel!"

As though waiting for the summons, Maricel swept into the room bearing another tray. "If you're looking for me to apologize for dosing your wine, you might as well give it up. You needed the rest."

"The work I do is important– "

"I have no doubt it is," Maricel agreed, deftly switching the old tray with the new. "But what good will it do if you become run down, ill with fatigue? Who will help your granddaughter then?"

At Aracelia's age, few things surprised her. But this speech of Maricel's had her jaw dropping open. She shut it with a snap. "How did you know about her?"

Maricel looked at her steadily. "How long have I been your servant?"

"As long as I can remember. You're more family than servant."

"That's right. And I've learned a thing or two in all those years. Namely, how to keep my ears and eyes open and my mouth shut. I know more secrets about the royal family than you even know are secret."

Aracelia stared at her for a moment then slowly smiled. "I have no doubt. And what is your opinion on what I'm attempting to do?"

Maricel stopped fussing with the trays and stood quietly, hands folded together. "These are trying times we are living in. You can smell the rise of evil in the air. If I had a granddaughter steeped in magic, I would do everything in my power to help her. Rules be damned."

Tears pricked at Aracelia's eyes as she reached out and took Maricel's hand. "You are more than just a servant to me," she said. "You know that don't you?"

The other woman cracked a smile. "I know it well, but it's nice to hear all the same."

They looked at one another for another moment, then Maricel said briskly, "Well. Enough lazing about in bed. I'll draw you a bath, shall I? and lay out your travel clothes. I ken as soon as you find what you're looking for you'll be off."

"Thank you Maricel."

Chapter Forty-Two

I wonder if we're doing the right thing," Jessica mused as they sat around the evening fire. The Trembling Hills were two days behind them and they were camped in the relative shelter of an overhang in the rocky hills they were traversing. Everyone turned to look at her.

"Care to be more specific?" Howard asked.

"This whole journey to the shrine thing. I mean, we have no idea how far we have to go and it seems to be taking us pretty far out of our way. Maybe we should just head south."

"But Aracelia– " Ellen began.

"Aracelia thought we were in trouble with the dark elves. There's been no sign of any dark elves, not even before we hit that big grass plain of death. We don't even know for sure she wanted us to go to the shrine."

Dominic got up from where he was sitting on the other side of the fire and dropped down beside her.

"What's really going on?" he asked, putting his arm around her. Leaning back, he took a better look at her. "You've seen something, haven't you?"

"Not really," she said, squirming a bit under his scrutiny. "I just ... I just get this uneasy feeling every time I think about the shrine. I feel in my gut that something bad is going to happen when we get there."

"What kind of bad?" Ellen asked. "I mean, bad as in we're going out of our way for nothing, or bad as in we're all going to die?"

Jessica frowned. "That's just it, I don't know."

"Maybe it's just nerves, maybe you're just worried that we're getting closer to your dad and granddad."

"That doesn't make sense. If I was so worried about meeting them, why would I get the urge to speed things up by bypassing the shrine?"

"I don't know," Ellen said, throwing her hands up in exasperation. "You're the one with the hinky gut."

"Bottom line," Howard put in, "is what do you want to do about it?"

"What do you mean?"

"Well, do we keep going or do we change our direction?"

"I– " she shook her head slightly. "I'm not even sure it's anything, it's so nebulous. I guess we keep going to the shrine."

"Are you sure?" Dominic asked. He was a strong believer in portents, even when it was just a gut feeling.

She leaned closer to him. "Yes, I'm sure," she said with more conviction than she felt. "How much farther is it to the Sirani Sea?"

Kaelan shrugged. "Three days, four – should there be nothing to impede our progress."

"And will there be?" Ellen asked before Jessica could.

The elf looked at her, confused.

She ticked off on her fingers as she spoke. "We've escaped capture by dark elves, crossed a grassland filled with man-eating bugs, and survived a landscape that tried to toss us like a salad. I can't help but wonder what's next."

"There is naught but the small dangers every traveler would face," he said reassuringly.

"Small dangers," Howard put in. "You mean like running into some kind of magical creature or bandits, right?"

"Unless it's mating season for the water dragons of the Sirani Sea," Sebastian said thoughtfully.

"Water dragons!" the three non-natives chorused.

At Sebastian's grin, Howard punched him lightly in the arm. "Not funny."

Paranithel found Thackery in the parlor off the Great Hall, frowning over a sheaf of papers clenched in his fist. The room doubled as an office for the administration of the school.

"Is there a problem?"

"I had thought to close the school temporarily," Thackery said with a sigh, "But I have been receiving numerous requests to house the students beyond the school term."

"It is not surprising, when you consider the increasing trouble in the north."

Thackery glanced up at him. "I sense you have more to add."

Paranithel sat down in the chair on the other side of the desk. "I have been in touch with the network of wizards."

At one time Thackery would have scoffed at the so-called network of wizards, calling them doddering old men more interested in their glory days than working any real magic. But that was before.

"And what news from the network?" he asked finally.

Visibly, Paranithel relaxed in his chair. "The network is

spread thin. Every day there are new disappearances, and not just those with magical talent. Any creature with magic is at risk. There has been a steady stream of magical beings migrating to the east and south."

Thackery nodded. "It is hardly surprising."

Paranithel sat back in his chair and eyed the younger man soberly. "With every passing day Anakaron gains more strength – "

"Stolen strength."

"Aye, stolen, but he gains and we sit here doing nothing."

"What would you have us do? Raise an army and storm his lair?" There was an edge to his voice that hadn't been there before. "And what, pray, will we use for soldiers, the half-trained children under our care?"

"We cannot just sit here doing nothing while our enemy's power grows! Soon it will too late and he will grow too powerful to be stopped."

"There are other considerations that must be factored in," Thackery said quietly.

"I understand that you are afraid– "

"Of course I am afraid! Anyone with any sense would be afraid. We are talking about an evil like no other, one that took the woman I loved from me and would not think twice about taking my daughter should he learn of her existence."

"You– "

"I will not make any commitments until she reaches us and we can send her safely back to the earthly realm. Then I will gather what power I can, any with power who I can persuade to accompany me, and I will face Anakaron for the final time."

Paranithel opened his mouth, then shut it again. They were

quiet for several minutes before he broke the silence.

"Well, then," he said, getting to his feet. "We had best hope she arrives sooner rather than later."

With that he left Thackery staring moodily at the papers on his desk and made his way to his rooms in the south tower. He was winded by the time he climbed the spiral stone staircase and collapsed into the nearest chair to catch his breath.

As much as he was relieved that Thackery was finally taking the threat of Anakaron seriously he'd felt a frisson of fear at the look in the younger man's eye. He had a sinking feeling he knew what he was planning to do.

Thackery was powerful, more powerful than he was willing to acknowledge because he did not trust his power. Which meant he did not believe he would truly succeed in a direct confrontation.

This was why he would take others with him. He would make a good showing, let Anakaron fill with the knowledge of his success, and then use the anarchy spell.

The anarchy spell was something no right-thinking wizard would ever use. It could only be used once. It drew power while at the same time amplifying it until it burst free, consuming the caster, and everything within a league, in a fiery explosion.

There had to be a better way.

For all that Thackery looked down his nose at the precognitive arts, Paranithel knew they, too, had their place in the magical realm. Perhaps he was more open-minded about such things, or perhaps it was the fact he was descended from a long line of seers, but he could never understand how one could believe in magic and not the otherworldly talent of precognition.

With a shake of his head, he pushed up from the chair and

went over to the desk wedged between the wardrobe and the bookcase. There was already a fat, white candle sitting in a shallow dish on the desktop and with the snap of his fingers he lit it. Sitting down again he reached over to the bookcase, fingers closing over a carved wooden box. He placed the box on the desk in front of him and rested his finger-tips on it, remembering happier times.

It had been a gift from Aracelia, the box, her first gift to him. The only thing he'd treasured more was their daughter. Opening the box, he lifted out the silk wrapped deck of cards, her second gift, and carefully unwrapped them. He could feel their power as they were freed from the silk.

It was not a deck to be used lightly and he did not do so now. Every other method of divination had failed him – these cards, imbued with Fae magic, would not.

Chanting a spell of enhancement and protection he shuffled the cards and slowly laid them out face down in the moon and stars spread. Setting the remainder of the deck aside, he took a deep breath and let it out slowly, causing the candle's flame to dance.

One by one he began turning them over, letting the cards tell their story. The Journey, the Lake of Fear, the Flying Death, the Faery Queen, the Well of Sorrow. He turned the final card over and his breath came out in a hiss.

"Aracelia," he murmured. "What are you up to?"

Chapter Forty-Three

W e're close," Kaelan muttered. "I'm sure we're close. Perhaps just over that rise."

Jessica did not have the heart to remind him that he said the same thing the last three mornings running. She dropped back to ride beside Ellen.

"How are the supplies holding out?"

"Not good," Ellen admitted. Since she was the one doing most of the cooking, she was in charge of the supplies. "In fact, if it wasn't for the game Dominic and Sebastian are managing to find, and the foraging you and Kaelan are doing, we'd have been out two days ago."

"I was afraid that was the case."

"Maybe we'll get lucky," Ellen suggested. "If we don't find the Siren Sea maybe we'll find a village or something."

"Even the Darkwood Forest had the occasional inn," Jessica said.

"I guess that's the difference between 'travelling south' and 'fleeing for our lives'," Ellen said, grinning when Jessica turned to look at her. "Better accommodations."

"Well, there it is," Kaelan said, relief evident in his voice. Even he'd been wondering if they were ever going to reach the Sirani Sea.

The water stretched from one edge of the horizon to the other, with the shadow of hills or low mountains on the other side. The island with the Shrine of Dorian on it was a mere speck on the water.

"We might as well camp here tonight," Dominic said, dismounting. "The sun's too close to setting – there's no point stumbling around in the dark."

Jessica sat on her steed a moment longer than everyone else, staring at the sea from her higher vantage point. Why was Aracelia so set on them going there?

She was still pondering this when they were sitting around the campfire later. "This Shrine of Dorian," she asked. "What do you know about it?" The question was directed at Kaelan, Sebastian, and Dominic.

Dominic shrugged. "For my part, I just know it's a shrine on the Sirani Sea. The Cult of Dorian built it a few hundred years ago and then pretty much died out."

"Really?" Howard asked. "Why?"

"Most likely because the Sirani Sea is poisonous."

"Poisonous?" Jessica, Ellen, and Howard chorused.

"Now he tells us," Howard muttered.

"Didn't we mention that?" Sebastian said. "It's why there are no settlements anywhere near it."

"Then why was Aracelia so insistent we go there?" Jessica asked, voice edging from irritable to angry. The men looked at each other, somewhat at a loss.

"It must be the power of the Well," Kaelan said. All eyes focused on him. "The Well within the shrine is said to be one of the most powerful."

"But if the sea is poisonous, wouldn't the well– oh, not that kind of well," Ellen said.

"Yes, but surely there are Wells closer," Howard pointed out. "And Jessica's not supposed to use her power so it's not like she needs to juice it up."

"Maybe there's something extra special about this particular Well," Sebastian said.

Kaelan spread his hands wide. "I cannot say what was in the Lady Aracelia's mind."

"I have another question," Jessica said. "If the shrine is on an island in the sea, how are we supposed to get to it?"

"And the faithful will find the way," Sebastian intoned. He grinned at the look on the faces that turned towards him. "As I understand my religious instruction, the Followers of Dorian built a causeway."

"Huh. I guess that's better than trying to build a raft or something," Jessica said.

"Now I have an important question," Ellen said. "I get that we've been travelling more west than south, but once we've been to the shrine how much longer is it going to take us to get to Jessica's family in the south?" She looked around at her companions. "It's not that I haven't been enjoying the adventure and all, but my parents are probably already freaking out."

Kaelan and Sebastian looked at Dominic who looked anywhere but towards Ellen.

"Guys?"

Dominic scraped a hand through his hair and shot a quick glance at Jessica who quirked an eyebrow at him in return. "From what Jessica's told me of your world things move at a much faster pace than they do here." When the expression on her face began to slide towards alarm he quickly added, "But with the aid of the *estrada* it will shave weeks off the journey."

"Weeks?" she repeated weakly.

"It should take no more than two, maybe three months in all," Kaelan told her.

"Months? Are you freaking kidding me?" Ellen jumped to her feet, fists clenched and face pale. "I've already been away too long. If I'm gone for months they're going to have the Mounties out looking for me!"

Mounties? Kaelan mouthed to Dominic. Dominic shrugged.

"It'll be okay, Ell," Jessica told her, getting to her feet as well. She went over and gave her a hug. "If we can figure out how to get you home, I'm sure we can figure out a way to back up the time."

"Actually– " Howard began, but Jessica shot him a look and he shut up.

"I'm going to lose my job!" Ellen moaned.

"We'll figure something out," Jessica told her, drawing her back down to a seat again. "I promise."

As they were breaking camp the following morning, Jessica noticed Dominic staring intently towards the Sirani Sea.

"What is it," she asked.

"I'm not sure," he answered. "If I didn't know better, I'd say it was smoke from a fire."

"Maybe it's just mist coming off the water, or maybe a small waterspout or something." Jessica looked towards the sea, squinting her eyes in the early morning light. "No, I think you're right. I think there's someone down there."

They stood in silence for a moment.

"Do you think whoever's down there is the reason Aracelia sent us here?"

"I guess there's only one way to find out," Dominic said, turning away.

They made their way unhurriedly down the sloping grade, aiming for the tiny fire on the shore. Sometimes they lost sight of it as the land dipped and curved, but the white plume grew steadily larger. By the time the land leveled out again they could see it was a signal fire burning blue on a small altar between a tumbled pile of rock and the shore.

"Magic," Dominic said, a frown on his face as he concentrated. "It was built and is being maintained by magic."

"But who built it?" Jessica asked. "And why is it blue?"

"I don't know, but the magic is old."

"You can tell that?"

He flashed her a grin. "I'm a man of many talents, as you well know."

"I wonder..." Sebastian said thoughtfully. Howard gave him a poke in the ribs as his voice trailed off.

"You wonder what?" Howard asked.

"What? Oh. Sorry. I wonder if the fire is to mark the start of the causeway for those seeking the wisdom of Dorian."

"And that pile of rubble could have been a traveler's rest or had a guardian or guide living in it," Howard finished for him.

"Head's up, people," Ellen said suddenly. "We've got company."

Their attention turned to the causeway.

"I thought you said the cult of Dorian had died out?" Jessica said.

"As far as I know, they did," Dominic told her.

They stood in a loose group on the shore and continued to watch as the speck on the causeway drew steadily closer. It was obviously a person, a tall, slender person, and before long it had resolved itself into . . . "Lady Aracelia!"

Kaelan, with his keen elven eyesight was the first to recognize her.

"Aracelia," Howard echoed. "But how did she beat us here?"

Jessica held back a bit when the others moved forward to greet her. The last time she'd seen Aracelia had been as a friend, a good friend who'd started to tutor her in the rudiments of magic. She'd felt a closeness to the elf she couldn't explain. But now everything had changed with the knowledge that Aracelia was, in fact, her grandmother.

She studied her now as she drew closer. It was hardly surprising she hadn't connected the tall, stately elf with her mother. She'd only seen her mother once, in a ghostly realm, and though similar in figure and stature her mother was dark, where Aracelia was fair.

"Have you no greeting for me, granddaughter?" Aracelia said to her now.

Jessica stared at her mutely for a second, then without realizing she'd moved found herself enveloped in a fierce hug.

"You have no idea how I've longed to do that," Aracelia said, loosening her hold. "I feared you would not forgive me for keeping our true relationship a secret."

"How could I not forgive you?" Jessica said with a sniff, moved beyond words to see the tears pricking in her grandmother's eyes. "I've never had a grandmother before."

With a laugh Aracelia released her and turned to the others.

"It is good to see you all, my friends. I feared greatly for your safety knowing the dark elves were involved."

"How did you get here before us?" Ellen wanted to know. "Not that I'm not glad to see you."

"It is an old magic," she said evasively.

"Then how about this," Howard said. "Where do we go from here?"

"To the shrine," she told them.

They looked at the crumbling shrine out on the water, then at each other.

"Do not fear," Aracelia said with a smile. "I have not lost my mind. You'll just need to trust me."

Chapter Forty-Four

It was decided that plans and explanations would do better on full stomachs. There was no fuel to make a proper fire and Ellen refused to use the magical one, there was just something about a blue fire was very off-putting. But by finishing off the last of their rations, no one went hungry.

"Will the causeway hold under the weight of the *estrada*?" Ellen asked. "It looks a little... fragile."

"We will not be taking the *estrada* from this point forward," Aracelia told them. She waited until the hue and cry died down before adding, "I'm sorry, I do not mean to seem mysterious, but the best way to explain what I have in mind is to show you."

Though Dominic and Sebastian clearly had misgivings, they helped the others strip the gear from their mounts. They separated out the riding gear, piling it up in the rubble where Aracelia cast a protection spell to keep it safe until someone could collect them.

Ellen hugged Epona and the mare rested her chin on the human's shoulder. "I'll miss you," Ellen said tearfully. "You weren't just a mount, you were a friend."

"I'll bet she was a *Black Beauty* fan as a kid," Howard whispered loudly.

"Shut up, Howard," Ellen said briskly, taking one last swipe at her eyes. "And it was *The Black Stallion*, not *Black Beauty*. I still have all the books."

She took the pack Kaelan had been holding for her. They all watched as the *estrada* wheeled and galloped away.

"Everyone got everything?" Aracelia asked. At the assents she added, "Well then, let us pay our respects to the demi-god Dorian."

She led the way but the others paused at the edge of the sea, eyeing the causeway dubiously. It appeared to be made of stone and Jessica wondered out loud how many followers of Dorian had lost their lives in its building. The weathered stone was covered in dirt and moss, pitted here and there where the sea had eaten away at it.

"Are you sure this is safe?"

Aracelia shrugged. "It was perfectly solid when I crossed it, but it is slippery in places so watch your step."

"Wait a minute," Jessica said. "You still haven't told us why we need to get to the shrine in the first place. And how are we going to continue our journey without the mounts?" That same sense of uneasiness that she felt before was filling her now, like a sense of impending doom.

"I know it's asking a lot of you all, and I promise I will explain. But for now I ask for your trust, there is no time for debate." Apparently Aracelia was starting to feel the same sense of urgency.

She led the way and they slowly made their way across the causeway. They chose their steps carefully, making sure to stay away from the crumbling edge and the poisonous water lapping beyond. Kaelan stopped without warning, causing Ellen to slip slightly as she narrowly avoided bumping into him.

"What is it?" she asked, grabbing onto his arm for stability.

"I do not know," he said with a frown. He was watching a dark smudge undulating over the water in the distance. It appeared to be drawing closer.

"What is it?" Ellen asked again. "A storm?"

They others stopped to look too. Sebastian was the first to realize the danger. "That's no storm– " he started to say.

"Harpies!" Dominic shouted. "Everyone move!"

Disregarding the dangerous footing they raced towards the tiny island holding the shrine. They were only a few yards away when the harpies struck. With a rushing sound of wings the screaming hoard descended. The travelers didn't even take time to draw their weapons, focusing their efforts on reaching the shrine.

The shrine itself didn't offer much protection. The temple-like building was made of stone but the walls were crumbling and the roof had fallen in long ago. The harpies circled and dove, still shrieking.

Aracelia had begun chanting even before she reached the shrine. Within it the Well began to glow.

"Hurry," she told them. "Into the Well. And whatever you do, keep moving!"

If anyone had any misgivings about obeying her orders, they kept them to themselves. Jessica and Ellen went first, followed by Sebastian, then Kaelan and Dominic. Last to enter was Aracelia. They raced along a nebulous path, one that twisted and shook as though trying to throw them off. Then one by one the exited the Well into the blinding light of a desert sun.

Dominic and Kaelan drew their swords to deal with the handful of harpies that had come through with them. When

Aracelia exited the Well, the bright glow suffusing it snuffed out and she stumbled to her knees.

Jessica knelt down beside her, one hand on her shoulder. "Are you all right?"

Aracelia nodded, reaching up to pat her hand.

"What– what just happened?" Ellen asked, looking around in wonder.

"It was a Fae road, was it not?" Kaelan asked, shaken by the experience. "One of the forbidden magics."

"Yes," Aracelia said, still breathing heavily.

"Forbidden magics?" Ellen asked.

Kaelan looked at her, a troubled expression on his face. "In ancient times the Fae were able to access the Fae roads and thus travel between Wells. But the spell was deemed too dangerous and became forbidden."

"So ... where are we?" Ellen asked, looking around them.

"Somewhere in the southern lands would be my guess," Dominic said slowly.

"I have a better question," Sebastian said grimly. "Where's Howard?"

Jessica's head snapped up and she looked around.

"I am sorry, my friends," Aracelia said. With Jessica's help she got to her feet. "I tried to save him, but I could not. When last I saw him the harpies were carrying him away."

Jessica stared at her, appalled. "Carrying him away where, and why?"

"We have to go back!" Sebastian said. "We can't leave him behind."

Aracelia was already shaking her head. "We would be risking ourselves for naught. The harpies will be long gone by now."

"But– "

"I don't understand," Ellen said, "Why did the harpies attack? Were we trespassing on their territory or something?"

"No," Kaelan answered with a frown. "They are to be found in the mountains."

"So what set them off? And why did they take Howard? Harpies are female, right? Do they kidnap men to use for breeding or something?"

"I believe I can answer that question," said a new voice. The elderly man in a long dark robe and a conical hat had come up to them unnoticed.

"Paranithel," Aracelia said with genuine affection. "It is so good to see you my dear friend."

Paranithel, Jessica thought. This would be her long lost grandfather. His hair and beard were long and white, but his face had laugh lines that spoke of a happy person. He was tall and thin, but despite his obvious age he was not stooped.

"Oh my dear," he said, brilliant blue eyes focused on Jessica's face. He went over to her and took her hands in his. "You are so very much like your mother."

"Grandfather," Jessica whispered, tears pricking at her eyes as he folded her in his arms.

Ellen sniffled a little and rested her head on Kaelan's shoulder when he put his arm around her.

"Forgive me for interrupting such a tender moment," Sebastian said, not sounding sorry at all. "But you said you thought you knew why the harpies took Howard."

"Of course." Paranithel released Jessica, his own eyes suspiciously damp, but kept ahold of one hand. "He was wearing his half of your moonstone pendant, was he not?"

"How did you– "

"I think it gave him comfort."

"But why– "

"The harpies were sent by Anakaron, I am sure of it."

"Anakaron? But why Howard, why not someone more powerful, like Aracelia? Sorry," she said, turning to her grandmother, "But if he was looking to drain magical power..."

"It was not power he was after," Paranithel said, shaking his head. His hat slipped to one side. "Or at least not just power. By now Anakaron would have heard rumors there was a child, but not whether the child was male or female. He must believe Howard to be the son of Kiranthus and Farenalisia."

"He thinks Howard is me, because of the pedant?"

"I'm afraid so, my dear."

"Oh, this isn't good. This isn't good at all."

"No, I'm afraid it is not."

Chapter Forty-Five

Howard woke slowly. Various parts of his body ached, not the pleasant ache from working out but more like he'd been pummeled. And his throat was a little raw. At least whatever he was resting on was soft and comfortable; it made him reluctant to open his eyes and face reality.

A frown crossed his face. What had he been doing last night that left him in such rough shape anyway? It must have been some party. The last thing he remembered was ... His eyes snapped open as he sat up abruptly.

"Harpies!" One hand went to his throat – now he remembered why his throat hurt, from all the screaming while he was being carried away. Not one of his proudest moments, to be sure.

Since he was obviously not still being carried away by the harpies, he took a minute to look around. Where the devil was he?

The bed he was in was opulent, there was no other word for it. It was massive, with a carved, dark wood frame, a canopy, and heavy curtains tied back at the corners. And just how many birds had given their lives to fill this mattress? It was too soft to be anything else.

The bedding, curtains, and canopy were a dark forest green – the curtains made of velvet and the bedding something with a silkier feel to it. The fact that he could feel that silkiness all over made him suddenly realize he was naked – the only thing he was wearing was Jessica's pendent.

The lighting was from torches set around the perimeter of the room, and from the fireplace on the opposite side of the room which appeared to be made from stone. There was a plush looking rug on the floor, and tapestries on the walls but no windows that he could see.

There was a wash stand set up in one corner, and a table with a couple of wooden chairs in another. Two more chairs, these looking well padded, were grouped near the fireplace with a smaller table between them, a softly glowing oil lamp giving off a pale, yellow light.

His thinking was still a little muddled – could he have been unconscious long enough to reach the southlands? If so, he had to admit to being impressed with the accommodations. But where were his clothes, and where was Sebastian?

"Guess there's only one way to find out," he muttered.

But before he could do more than shift in the bed, a door he hadn't noticed opened. Two women entered, one with long blonde hair carrying a tray, and one with dark curly hair carrying a stack of folded material. Howard's eyes widened and he quickly pulled the blankets up to his chin.

"I will let his eminence know his guest is awake," said the dark-haired one, setting her load down on the larger table and slipping back through the door. The blond woman continued to the bed and looked at him with a serious expression.

"I am Nari, I am to attend to your injuries."

"Ah, nice to meet you, Nari. Where exactly am I?"

She shook her head. "I am here to tend to your injuries."

"It's just a couple of bruises, maybe a few scratches."

Ignoring him, Nari poured water from the pitcher into the washbasin and brought it over to the small table beside the bed.

"I'm fine, really."

But Howard's discomfort was no match for Nari's determination. Wrestling the covers away from him, she proceeded to do as she said, tend his injuries. Fortunately, his injuries weren't severe and the salve she used on his bruises was cool and soothing.

"Now I shall help you dress," she informed him.

"Oh, ah, that's all right," Howard assured her. "I've been dressing myself since I was a toddler. I'm really good at it."

Her eyes widened slightly. "The master has ordered me to dress you when you awaken. I dare not disobey."

Howard didn't know who this 'master' was, but he already didn't like him.

The ordeal of having someone help him dress, especially a female person, left Howard flushed with embarrassment. Had he not been so tired from his misadventure he might have done a better job of fending her off, but in the end she had her way before he was able to convince her to leave

He was sitting in one of the cushioned chairs near the fireplace, picking at the food on the tray, when the door opened again. This time it a man in robes so black they seemed to absorb light entered. He was tall and lean, and carried a twisted wooden staff that was topped with a dark red crystal. His face was pale, eyes dark, and he sported a neatly trimmed goatee.

He raised a hand as Howard began to struggle to his feet.

"Please, do not trouble to get up. You need to rest and recover fully."

"Ah, thank you. I– "

"I am glad to see you were not too badly damaged during your journey here."

"About that, I– "

"We have much to discuss, you and I," the man continued. "But for now you need do nothing more than enjoy the few luxuries my home has to offer."

"What's going on?" Howard asked. "Where am I? Where are my friends?"

"Do not distress yourself, your questions will be answered in due time."

"Are you the reason the harpies attacked us?"

"Later," the man said firmly. "For now, rest."

He turned to leave and Howard spoke up, "Who *are* you?"

The man gave a short bow. "My name is Anakaron. Welcome to my home."

He swept out the door, closing it softly behind him. Howard sat for a moment, a stunned look on his face. He was in serious trouble.

Chapter Forty-Six

It took some convincing before Jessica was persuaded to leave the vicinity of the Well. In her head she knew Howard wasn't just going to show up inside it, but her heart didn't want to believe he was gone.

"What's this dark wizard likely to do to Howard?" she asked.

Paranithel wished he was able to reassure her, but doubted she'd believe him. "I think it will depend a great deal on Howard himself."

"Howard's one of the smartest people I know, Jess," Ellen told her. "And you know how much he loves to role play – the second he figures out what's going on he'll dive into the role he needs to play."

"Provided he does not give himself away first," Sebastian added quietly.

Jessica looked over at him and realized he was suffering every bit as much as she was.

"Come," Paranithel said. "The castle is not far. Let us refresh ourselves and together, with Thackery, we will come up with a strategy to retrieve friend Howard."

Jessica sighed, and with one last look towards the Well, trailed along behind the others.

"I know that look," Aracelia said as she and Paranithel led the group towards the castle a short distance away. "There is something troubling you and I do not just mean the likelihood young Howard is in the hands of the blood mage."

Paranithel slanted her a glance. "You are too observant for my own good." They walked in silence for a bit before he sighed gustily.

"I fear that where his daughter is concerned Kiran– Thackery has a few unrealistic expectations."

"Such as?"

"If she had been raised here, instead of the earthly realm, she would be more...biddable, more willing to follow the advice of her father."

"In other words, to do as she's told and not question it," Aracelia said dryly.

"Exactly!" Paranithel said.

"I think you both forget she has elven blood in her," Aracelia pointed out. "And do you remember her mother as being the biddable sort?"

"Well, no."

"But I do agree that Jessica's spirit is going to come as a shock to her father. And he'd best remember that though untrained, her power is vast."

"That is exactly what I am afraid of," Paranithel admitted.

They passed through a barrier, much like the one that enclosed the elven enclaves.

"Nice work," Aracelia murmured.

Paranithel smiled at her. "We had a little help from the

southern elves."

"There are elves here in the south?" Ellen asked curiously.

Kaelan met her curiosity with his own. "Why would there not be?"

"I don't know. Somehow I always pictured elves in a forest setting. You know, like *Lord of the Rings*."

"Lord of the Rings?"

"Wait until we get Howard back," Jessica said. "He'll spend days explaining it to you."

Kaelan still looked somewhat confused, but shrugged it off. "I'll look forward to it. But to answer your question, there are elven enclaves in all the lands."

"There is a map in the castle," Paranithel put in. "It shows all of the magical sites – Wells, elven enclaves . . ."

"Each enclave is unique to its region," Aracelia added. "There are even enclaves under the seas."

She went on to describe some of the attributes and differences of the various enclaves. Jessica realized her grandmother was trying to distract her from her worry over Howard. It only partially worked.

A better distraction was her first view of the castle. While she hadn't expected it to look like the castle at Ghren, she did think it would be made of adobe or stucco with arches and domes. Instead, it was like something out of a fairy tale, with turrets and ramparts, and a delicate looking bridge spanning a courtyard, all made out of a creamy white stone.

"It's beautiful," Ellen exclaimed. "Does it have a name?"

Paranithel smiled faintly. "To most it's simply the Southern Magic Academy."

There were arrow slits in the walls surrounding it. Someone

must have been watching through them because as they neared the massive gates opened to greet them. They passed through another barrier as they crossed the threshold and the temperature dropped by several degrees.

The courtyard was paved with cobblestone. To one side of the castle proper was a stable yard, to the other was a series of gardens and trees sandwiched between the building and the wall.

"Just a little bit of the north," Paranithel said, gesturing towards them.

He led the group towards the double doors of the castle itself. At a gesture from his staff the doors opened wide.

"Welcome to our home," he told the weary group.

"Oh, Master Paranithel!" A slender, teen-aged boy in a brown robe hurried up to him. "There you are! Master Thackery has been looking for you!"

"And where is Master Thackery right now, Walfrid?"

"He's– "

"Paranithel!" The shout resonated in the great hall. "Where the devil are you hiding?"

"Ah. Never mind. If you would be so kind to show my guests to their rooms, I'll see to Thackery." He turned to the group. "In anticipation of your arrival I had rooms prepared. We can meet with Thackery after you've rested."

"Thank you," Aracelia said, shooting a glance at Jessica. "As usual, your wisdom is infallible."

"This way," Walfrid told them, gesturing.

Paranithel watched as the boy led them away, and with a resigned sigh went to deal with Thackery.

"Where have you been?" Thackery snapped when Paranithel

tracked him down to his office. "I have been looking for you all day."

"I had business to attend to," Paranithel said mildly.

"What business could possibly take precedence over our plans to move on Anakaron?"

"You'd best be seated for what I have to tell you."

Thackery eyed the older man. "What have you been up to?"

"I have just returned from the Well– "

"The Well? I thought we agreed that Well activities should cease on the chance that Anakaron is able to track Well usage."

"This was an exception, and it was not of my doing."

"You're talking in riddles, old man, and I have little patience for it."

Paran sighed, and took a seat himself. He was stalling, but he didn't know why. "What do you know of the Fae roads?"

"The Fae roads?" Thackery frowned as he returned to his seat. "Are they not the Fae name for the ley lines that connect the Wells on the magical plane?"

"In ancient times the Fae were able to travel the roads from Well to Well. I'm not sure why they chose to stop the practice, but the spells used for this purpose became forbidden knowledge."

"Being able to travel from Well to Well would have given the elves a great advantage."

"Yes. But it required a great deal of power and they were not able to tap into the Wells themselves to do so."

"This is all very interesting," Thackery said with what he believed to be great patience, "But what has this to do with why you were at the Well outside the castle?"

Paranithel sighed. "I do not know if one needed to be of the highest-ranking Fae or merely to have Fae blood in them to activate the Fae roads ..."

"The highest ranking – Aracelia. Do you mean to tell me Aracelia is here, and she used forbidden Fae magic to get here?"

"Not just Aracelia."

"Not just– Jessica! You're telling me that Jessica is here at last? Where? I must see her at once!"

"Hold!" Paranithel barked as Thackery pushed to his feet. "You have waited all this time to see her, you can wait until she is rested and more herself."

"But she is my daughter!"

"Yes, she is your daughter, and my granddaughter. But where we have known of her all her life, she has known of us for only a handful of weeks."

"But– " Thackery looked towards the door.

"There is another thing of importance I must tell you. Not all in her party made it safely to the south."

"What do you mean?"

Paranithel told him of the harpies' attack, and how Howard was carried off by them.

"Why would the harpies go out of their way– Anakaron!"

"That was our assumption as well. It is possible that he believed Howard to be your child, because of the moonstone pendant he was wearing."

Thackery remembered that pendant. It had been a favorite of Farenalyssia.

"Give Jessica time. Let her rest. She is here now, and safe. Let her come to terms with the loss of her friend."

Thackery took one last look at the door before his shoulders sagged in defeat. "You're right, of course. I would not wish to overwhelm her before we have even met."

Paranithel breathed a silent sigh of relief. He hadn't been sure Thackery would be reasonable. "Why don't I speak to the cook and arrange a feast for when they awaken. We can use the small parlor."

Chapter Forty-Seven

The tired group followed Walfrid up a broad curving staircase. Dominic kept a close eye on Jessica. He hadn't missed the way she started, hearing Thackery's voice, nor the way her tension eased when Paranithel sent them away. He couldn't blame her for her mixed feelings about meeting her father.

They turned to the right at the top of the stairs, following a short hallway to a longer one. Halfway down the long one they came to a set of double wooden doors and Walfrid threw them open with a flourish.

"Master Paranithel was unsure of how many of you there would be and suggested the guest suite would be most appropriate. There are three sleeping chambers along each of the two hallways, along with a bathing chamber. And as you see here, a large common room in the center."

Jessica and Ellen looked at each other. "Dibs on the bath," they said at the same time. They disappeared down the opposite corridors leading off the common room.

"There is food and drink as well," Walfrid said a little uncertainly.

"I'm sure we'll find everything we'll need," Aracelia said in amusement.

"If you desire aught else, you have only to ring." He indicated the bell pull by the door and then took his leave.

Dominic shook his head and sighed. "Well I, for one, am not waiting on the ladies to enjoy our repast. We could nigh on starve to death should we try."

Kaelan joined him at the table, but Sebastian claimed he wasn't hungry and Aracelia said she wished to unpack. They disappeared down opposite corridors.

The two men ate in companionable silence, and then picked up their packs and also chose opposite hallways – Kaelan following the one taken by Aracelia and Ellen, and Dominic the one taken by Jessica and Sebastian.

Two of the doors along the hall were closed. One, presumably the bathing chamber and the other the room Sebastian had chosen. Dominic poked his head in the remaining two rooms and without hesitation chose the larger of the two bedrooms.

It boasted a large, fieldstone fireplace with two well upholstered chairs facing it on either side. The large, wooden framed bed was high, and dark green velvet curtains were drawn back at the four corners. There was a tall wardrobe, a trunk at the foot of the bed, and a woven rug between the side of the bed and the east facing window.

He'd brought Jessica's packs in with his own, but wondered if she'd feel comfortable sharing a room with him, now that they'd reached their destination. He hoped she would, but if not there was still an empty room left.

Jessica, took longer than usual with her bath, and came out of the bathing chamber wearing a very becoming heavy, dark blue robe. Dominic was becoming concerned. While she and Ellen were bathing an invitation to dinner had arrived, in several hours. She only nodded in turn at the request.

She nibbled at the offerings of food, and made no protest when Dominic suggested they retire to their room. He closed the door firmly behind them and watched as Jessica wander aimlessly through the room.

"Are you all right?" There was no response as she moved over to the window to stare out. He had the feeling she wasn't seeing anything.

"Jessica?" He went over and put a hand on her shoulder.

"I'm sorry, what?" She turned to stare at him blankly.

"I asked if you were all right."

"I'm good, I'm fine." Her half-hearted smile belied her words.

He drew her over to the bed and sat down with her. "You do not have to meet with him – we can leave right now if that's your wish."

"You'd do that for me?"

He raised the hand he was holding to his lips. "You should know by now I would do anything for you."

"You sweet talker you." She leaned her head on his shoulder. "I guess since we came all this way I might as well stick around and meet the old man."

"After everything you've faced, meeting your father should be easy."

"And maybe he'll have some ideas on how we can rescue Howard."

Privately he doubted it. In fact, he strongly suspected that Thackery was going to want to keep Jessica well away from any kind of action.

"What can you tell me about him," Jessica asked.

"It seems like a lifetime ago I last saw him," he admitted. "And I think we have both changed a great deal. But the Thackery I knew had a kindness in him, and a great sadness as well."

"I wish I had something nicer to wear to meet him than my travelling clothes," she said wistfully.

As if in answer to her request there was a tap at their door.

"Enter," Dominic called.

Ellen poked her head though the door. "I have a present for Jessica from her grandmother." She came the rest of the way into the room and handed her the bundle she was carrying. "She thought you might like something a little fancier for when we go down to dinner."

Jessica's eyes lit up. "She's wonderful! Tell her thank you for me."

"If you would like some time alone together, I can go to the common room," Dominic said, half rising from his seat.

Ellen held up a hand to stop him. "Thanks anyway, but I think I'm going to take a nap. We've got plenty of time."

"Sounds like a good idea," Jessica said. "I'm clean, I'm fed, I could probably use a rest too."

"Okay, see you later." Ellen closed the door gently behind her.

"Did she seem kind of funny to you?"

"Funny how?" Dominic asked.

"I don't know, like there's something going on I don't know about."

"Maybe she's not taking her nap alone," he suggested.

Jessica looked at him askance. "You think so? Her and Kaelan?"

He shrugged. "I don't know who else it could be."

Jessica looked thoughtfully at the door. "Well. Way to go Ell." She slanted her gaze towards Dominic. "Maybe we should take a nap too."

He grinned at her. "Maybe. But I won't guarantee how much sleep you'll get."

A knock on the door woke Jessica from the best sleep she'd had in days. Dominic was already up and opened the door to a sober looking Sebastian.

"Aracelia says it's time to go down to dinner."

"You go ahead," Jessica told them. "I just need a couple of minutes to dress."

Dominic searched her eyes. "You don't need to do this. We can leave right now if you're not sure you want to meet him."

"No, it's all right. I'm sure." She got up and kissed his cheek. "Only a fool expects a woman to be ready on time."

His lips twitched into a grin, which is what she'd been trying for.

He kissed her forehead. "Don't be too long."

Since she'd had her bath earlier, all that was left was to dress in the clothes Aracelia had given her. The material was soft and flowing – an embroidered tunic, dark green on a slightly lighter green, over matching flowing trousers. The outfit was both comfortable and beautiful and she had a smile on her face as she joined Aracelia and Ellen in the common room.

Ellen was wearing a similar outfit, only hers was in a deep, dark red. Aracelia, however, was wearing a full-length dress of silver, clinging though not tight through the torso, falling away in sweeping folds to the floor.

"Grandmother, you look beautiful," Jessica exclaimed.

Aracelia smiled. "I do not know which pleases me more, the heartfelt compliment or that you called me grandmother."

A flush rose on Jessica's too pale cheeks.

"Well, I'd say we're all looking pretty fine," Ellen said to break the awkwardness.

"I heard the tale of your experience in formal court garb," Aracelia said, "And thought you both might be more comfortable in elven apparel."

"You're right about that," Jessica agreed.

"Ditto," Ellen said, taking one last look in the full-length mirror on its stand in the corner of the room.

"She means she agrees," Jessica said, seeing the look of confusion on Aracelia's face.

"Shall we ladies?" Ellen prompted.

Jessica took a deep breath and nodded. Aracelia touched her arm as she would have passed.

"You have nothing to fear from Thackery," she said gently. "What he has done was done of love for you, for the desire to protect you."

"I know," Jessica said with a sigh. "I may not agree with his methods, but I know he meant well."

"And remember," Ellen said cheerfully. "You've got all that awesome power just waiting to be unleashed. If he pisses you off you can just turn him into a toad or something."

Aracelia looked appalled at the thought, but Jessica just laughed.

"Okay, I think I'm ready. Let's go beard the lion in his den."

Chapter Forty-Eight

As the door to the private parlor opened, the man staring intensely into the fire started and turned quickly. When he saw only the three men on the threshold he visibly relaxed.

"The, ah, ladies will be along in a moment," Dominic said, a little uncertain of his welcome. He needn't have worried.

"Dominic!" A smile lit up Thackery's face. "I cannot tell you how good it is to see you."

The two men came together and embraced. "I had not thought to see you again," Dominic admitted, "But it is good to do so."

"I searched for you, you know," Thackery said, releasing him. "I was able to track you to the sea, but no further."

"Though I did not think so at the time, I was fortunate," Dominic told him. "The men Ewan hired could not stomach actually killing me."

He moved further into the room to clear the doorway.

"And Sebastian." To the bard's surprise, Thackery greeted him just as warmly. "There is not much I miss from Ghren, but your voice is one of them."

Sebastian smiled wanly. "I would not have become a bard had it not been for you."

"Nonsense. It was your destiny. And who is this?" he asked,

releasing Sebastian and focusing on the third member of their group.

"This is Kaelan, of the Darkwood Elven Realm. As fierce a warrior as he is a friend."

The pleasure of the introduction could be seen on the elf's face. "I'm honored to meet you," he said, with a slight bow.

"Would anyone like a drink?" Paranithel, who had been lurking at the opposite end of the room, asked, waving a decanter. "I'd like a drink." It was obvious he'd already had a few.

They were saved by having to answer as the ladies arrived at the parlor door, Aracelia leading the way. Thackery stood frozen by the fireplace.

"Thackery," Aracelia said. "It has been a long time since we last met in person."

She might as well have saved her breath for all the attention he paid her.

"Jesseminathus." The name came out on an exhaled breath as Thackery closed the distance between him and his daughter.

"I prefer Jessica," she murmured.

"Oh my dear," he said, folding her in his arms. "I have waited so long to meet you."

Jessica wasn't sure what she was feeling. This man was her father, yet he'd sent her away to be raised by strangers. Maybe it had been for her own good, but still....

"I don't know what to say," she said hesitantly. "It's nice to meet you just doesn't seem adequate somehow."

"I can feel your power," he murmured. "You fairly vibrate with it. Which is all the more reason to keep you safe from Anakaron," he added, letting go of her again.

"Well," Aracelia said, coming to Jessica's rescue. "She's safe enough here."

"As much as any of us are," Paranithel added dolefully.

A look of annoyance flashed across Thackery's face, but before he could snap at him, Aracelia spoke. "Perhaps some food is in order to soak up some of that wine."

"Of course," Thackery said stiffly. He went over to the bell pull by the door and gave it a tug.

The group ranged themselves around the table – Sebastian, Ellen, and Kaelan along one side, with Jessica taking a seat between Aracelia and Dominic along the other, and Thackery and Paranithel each taking an end.

Dinner had been waiting only on the summons, so no sooner had they sat down than it was being brought in. It was an unusually quiet affair, no one knowing quite what to say. Even the senior students who'd been drafted as servers, normally a chatty bunch, picked up on the tension in the room and were unusually quiet, though they memorized the scene before them to recount it accurately to the others.

Howard paced in his room. He'd been in trouble before, but never this deep and he'd always known how to get out of it again. This time he had no clue what he should do.

It didn't take a genius to deduce that Anakaron, and even the name sent a chill through him, thought he was Jessica. Well not Jessica precisely, but the child of Kiranthus and Farenalyssia. Probably because of the moonstone amulet he was wearing. He recalled Jessica telling him that it had been a gift from Aracelia to Jessica's mother. He fingered the medallion as he paced. God help him if Anakaron discovered the truth.

What happened to the others? Had they been taken by the harpies too? His one attempt to leave the room had been halted by the two armed guards outside of it.

"You are to remain inside," one of them told him.

"If there is anything you require, a servant will be sent to you," the other offered helpfully.

Howard declined the offer and thanked them politely before retreating back into his room.

He was just starting to feel the first pangs of hunger when the blonde servant returned, once again carrying a tray.

"I have sustenance for you, my lord," she said, eyes downcast.

"Ah, thank you," he said, moving to take the tray from her. She neatly avoided him and set the tray on the table.

Howard sat down and stared at the bounty before him, then frowned as he realized the woman was standing almost at attention, off to the side.

"Aren't you going to join me?"

Her wide-eyed gaze flew to his before she got a hold of herself and lowered it again. "No, my lord. The repast is for you alone."

"Seems like a lot of food for one person," he muttered. "And I'm no one's lord. Just Howard will do."

He sampled several of the dishes but he really didn't have much of an appetite.

"If the meal is not to your liking I can have whatever you wish prepared."

"Pepperoni pizza with mushrooms and jalapeño peppers?"

"I– " She looked faintly alarmed.

In fact, she looked a little scared and he had to wonder what the penalty was for failing to meet a guest's needs. Howard was a little ashamed of himself.

"I'm sorry," he said. "I was just joking about the pizza. The food was fine, I'm just not very hungry."

"Very well, my lord– "

"Howard," he corrected.

"Very well, my lord Howard. I'll remove the tray."

"Do you have to leave so soon?" he asked, feeling suddenly lonely.

Again her startled gaze met his for an instant before she dropped it again. "I am here to serve, my lord Howard."

Slowly she moved towards the bed and her hand went to the fastening of her dress.

Howard's eyes took on a saucer-like appearance. "What are you doing?"

She frowned, looking totally puzzled. "My lord?"

He glanced from her to the bed and then flushed red. "Oh, no. No, no, no. That's not what I meant at all when I said I wanted company."

"I do not understand."

"I'm not– that is– I don't– "

"If you do not find me pleasing another can be sent in my place."

"No! That's not– " Howard heaved a sigh. "You're fine, I'm just not – I think I'd rather be alone after all."

She shrugged. "As you wish, my lord Howard." Picking up the tray, she turned to leave. "If you have need of anything, simply inform one of the guards."

"I'll do that, thank you."

The door closed behind her and Howard collapsed into the chair with a groan. He was mortified at the thought she'd been so easily prepared to give herself to him. He needed to figure out a way to escape this place, and the sooner the better.

Chapter Forty-Nine

Thackery suppressed a sigh as the last of the dinner things were cleared away. If he'd ever spent a more uncomfortable meal, he couldn't remember it. And from the look of things, the others felt pretty much the same. Even the small talk was uncomfortable.

"For many years I had planned your homecoming," he said to Jessica, "And never had I imagined it would be so...so..."

"Extraordinary?" Aracelia suggested.

He frowned at her. "Perhaps a better word would be adventuresome."

"It's definitely been that," Jessica agreed.

"It pains me to have to admit this, but had I known the blood mage was on the rise I would never have risked bringing you here."

"Blood mage? Oh, you mean Anakaron."

"Yes, Anakaron." He toyed with the stem of his wine goblet.

"His is an old evil," Aracelia said. "And very cunning. We all missed the signs of his rising,"

"We have to do something about him," Jessica said.

"Yes," Thackery agreed. "I have given the matter a great deal of thought and I have been working on a plan."

Jessica was a little surprised. Somehow she hadn't thought it would be this easy. "That's great!" she said. "You probably know Anakaron better than anyone, so you'll know where he's hiding and how to get to him."

"It does not matter where he is –"

"You're not thinking of trying to draw him out instead, are you? That might be dangerous for Howard."

"Howard?"

Jessica was too busy forming her own plans to notice Thackery's surprise. "Unless you were thinking of drawing Anakaron out and the rest of us could rescue Howard."

"Jessica," Dominic said quietly, touching the back of her hand. "I think Thackery has something else in mind."

"Quite right, my boy," Thackery said gratefully.

"Oh." Jessica sat back in her seat. "Sorry if I jumped the gun. What's your plan?"

"First, with Aracelia's assistance, I will send you home. Then –"

"Whoa!" Jessica held up a hand. "Wait just a minute. I'm not going anywhere until we rescue Howard."

"This should be good," Ellen whispered to Sebastian. At his confused look she added, "It's like the rock meeting the hard place."

"I'm sorry, my dear. Paran told me of Howard's capture by Anakaron. I will be forever grateful to him for his part in bringing you to me, but a rescue is out of the question."

"Well you're obviously not asking the right question."

He looked a little confused. "I don't know what question you're talking about."

She huffed a breath. "The question right now is what you're going to do to help us rescue Howard."

"I have told you," he said with the patience one would use for a child, "A rescue is out of the question."

"Why?"

"Why?" he repeated.

"Why is rescuing Howard out of the question?"

"Because it is far too dangerous!" he sputtered.

"More dangerous than being taken by the witch guard?" she asked. "More dangerous than facing a horde of dark elves? More dangerous than man eating bugs or hills beset by earthquakes?"

"Yes!"

"Then at least we have some idea what we're up against."

"Are you addled?" He looked to the others for help but found none. "We cannot just go to Anakaron and demand Howard's release. And even if it were possible, I would not allow you to go anywhere near him."

Jessica slapped her hands on the table as she sprang to her feet. "Fine. If you won't help then we'll rescue him ourselves."

"I forbid it!" Thackery got to his feet as well.

"You forbid it? Who are you to forbid anything?"

"I am your father!"

"You may have fathered me," Jessica snarled. "But you're a far cry from a father to me. You had no hand in raising me. I've done pretty well without you so far."

"Well you have me now and I will not let you risk your life on some ill-conceived rescue!"

"Oh, yeah? Well just try and stop me!" She slammed out of the room before he could even respond.

After a moment of silence Dominic pushed back from the table. "I'll just – I'll just see that she doesn't get lost," he said, and followed her out.

Paranithel passed something to Aracelia under the table. She smiled and tucked it away. "It seems you were correct, my dear."

"What are you mumbling about," Thackery demanded.

"Ah, nothing really. Just a small wager."

"A wager?" Thackery's eyebrows rose. "A wager on what?"

"On who would lose their temper first," Aracelia said mildly. "You or Jessica."

"Ah," Ellen rose to her feet as Thackery flopped back down in his chair. "Dinner was lovely but I think I'll turn in now," she said. "Goodnight, everyone." She beat a hasty retreat to the door.

"I find myself fatigued as well," Kaelan said. "I take my leave and wish you a pleasant evening." He hurried after Ellen.

"I fear I take Jessica's side in this dispute," Sebastian said, and left without further speech.

"Well," Aracelia said, reaching for a carafe of wine. "You certainly have not lost your talent for clearing a room."

"I will require your assistance in sending Jesseminathus and her friend Ellen home."

"Jessica," Paranithel said.

"I beg your pardon?"

"She prefers to be called Jessica."

Thackery shot him a dark look. "I do not care what she is called, she needs to be sent home and as soon as possible."

"No," Aracelia said succinctly.

"No? No what?"

"No, I will not aid in your attempt to send her home against her wishes."

"She has been trying to get home since she first appeared in Ghren!"

"While that may have been true in the beginning," Aracelia

said calmly, "Things have changed. She has changed."

"It matters not. I am her father and– "

"No you are not."

"Have a care, it is your own daughter's reputation you are calling to question."

"Oh, there's no doubt you fathered Jessica, but she was correct – you had no hand in raising her. You are not her father, you are a stranger."

His mouth opened and then shut again.

"You need to take the time to get to know your daughter," Paranithel said gently, "And for her to get to know you."

"Perhaps, if things had been different. But you know as well as I the danger she is in. The safest course is to send her home, out of Anakaron's reach."

Aracelia finished her wine and rose gracefully to her feet. "The safest course is not always the wisest."

"What the devil is that supposed to mean?" he asked Paranithel as she left the room.

"It means, if you are to have any chance of a relationship with your daughter, you had best at least give a thought to the rescue of her friend Howard."

"The lad is probably already dead, drained dry like all the others."

Paran shook his head. "I do not think so. As long as Anakaron believes him to be yours, he is safe."

"I cannot risk my daughter's safety, no matter who Anakaron holds prisoner. You've felt her power, can you imagine what he would do with her?"

"I know," Paranithel said with a sigh. "But you under estimate the bond between your daughter and her friend."

"I understand how close they are, and the debt of gratitude we owe him, but to attempt to rescue him would be folly beyond belief."

"Then you had best come up with a better argument than "because I said so" before you speak with her again."

Chapter Fifty

When Dominic reached the suite, Jessica was pacing angrily in the common area.

"How can he think I'd want to poof back to earth at a time like this? Just who does he think he is?" she demanded.

"He thinks he's your father," Dominic said mildly. If he'd learned nothing during their time together, it was how to deal with her moods.

She whirled on him. "Are you taking his side?"

He raised his hands in defense. "Not at all, but he's had a lifetime of caring and worrying and concern for you. I think he just forgot that you're still new to all of this. I also think he sorely underestimates how much your friends mean to you."

"You've got that much right at least," she said, refusing to be mollified.

"I'm sure once he has time to think it through..." His voice trailed off. He remembered Thackery as being just as stubborn as his daughter. Once he had time to think things through he'd probably come up with a better plan to send Jessica back to the earthly realm than the direct approach.

"Once he thinks it through he'll what?" she asked.

He was saved from having to answer as Ellen entered the suite, followed by Kaelan and Sebastian.

"Are you okay?" Ellen asked, going directly to Jessica.

"No. I'm mad as hell."

Ellen led her over to one of the small sofas and sat down with her. "As first meetings go that could have gone better."

"You think?" Jessica asked, unwilling to let go of her mad.

"Perhaps," Kaelan said tentatively, "things will look better in the morning."

She shot him an angry look.

"In any case, he can do nothing about returning you to your former home without the Lady's assistance."

"Well thank God for that!"

"I think I can understand his feelings," Sebastian said. "As much as I fear for Howard's safety and wish for his return, it is far too risky for you to be part of any rescue attempt."

"I can't just sit around doing nothing," Jessica said, close to tears. "It's my fault he was taken – he wanted to give me back his half of the pendant but I told him to keep it."

"And had you been wearing it," Aracelia pointed out from the doorway, "you'd be Anakaron's prisoner in his stead."

Jessica sniffed back her tears. "Are you here to send me back?"

"I think we know each other better than that," Aracelia said. "I promise you I will do nothing without your consent. Indeed, I will make sure your father does not either."

"Thank you."

"Now, perhaps, as Kaelan has suggested, we would all benefit from a good night's sleep."

"I think you're right," Dominic agreed. "Perhaps in the morning we can start discussing plans."

There was a knock on Howard's door and it opened to admit the dark haired woman who'd been assigned to him. It embarrassed him that he couldn't remember her name.

"The master wishes the pleasure of your company," she said.

Well, it looked like he was about to find out what was in store for him.

"Of course," he told the woman. "Lead the way."

Swallowing his fear, he followed her out into the corridor.

Howard tried to observe as much as he could, thinking it might come in handy later. The corridor was long, and dimly lit with lit sconces every few feet. They passed several closed doors and twice the openings for other corridors, but always on the left. He wondered if the corridor went all the way around in a circle. If so, then sooner or later they'd have to pass the way out.

Unfortunately, before they came to such a point they turned, taking a path away from the outer edge. They passed no one, which Howard found rather odd. Where were the guards? The servants needed to keep everything clean? Didn't Anakaron have any minions?

The room he was led to differed very little from the room he'd been given, save for the furnishings. This one was a well appointed parlor – albeit a dark and sinister parlor worthy of bad a horror movie castle.

There was a large, stone fireplace at one end, with logs laid out for a fire. There were comfortable looking chairs on either side with a small round rug on the floor between them.

Anakaron, this time wearing a robe the color of oxygen rich blood, stood beside a narrow table against one wall.

"Welcome, my honored guest," he said.

The woman leading Howard left him at the entrance and faded back into the corridor.

"Might I offer you a drink?" He held up a carafe filled with a pale blue liquid.

"Ah, sure," Howard said, moving a few steps into the room. He figured it was safe enough, the wizard probably had far more inventive ways to kill him than poison.

Anakaron passed him a crystal goblet and gestured to the chairs. "Please."

Howard sat down and took a sip from his goblet and couldn't hold back a small sound of pleasure. It was probably the finest wine he'd ever tasted.

Anakaron smiled thinly over the rim of his own goblet. "One of the rare Elvish vintages."

Howard nodded in acknowledgment.

"I trust you are being well taken care of?"

"Yes, I have no complaints," Howard said carefully. "I wonder, however, if you could tell me what became of my travelling companions."

"I fear I cannot say for certain," Anakaron told him. "They seem to have disappeared from the Temple of Dorian."

"Disappeared?"

"Without a trace. Never fear though, I have people out searching for them even now."

Howard believed him, he looked too put out not to be telling the truth. But the real question, one he didn't have the nerve to ask, was what would he do with them when he found them.

"I am sure your grandmother filled you head full of my misdeeds," Anakaron said, "But there are two sides to every tale."

"Actually," Howard said, taking a sip of his wine, "She hardly mentioned you at all, save that there was a darkness to the northwest for which she felt you were responsible."

"How ...civilized of her. But surely your father– "

Anakaron seemed to be on a fishing expedition. Howard decided to take a chance with a half truth. "To be honest, I haven't actually met my father yet."

"Indeed?"

"He and another wizard, I think he's supposed to be my grandfather or something, sent me to a world without magic when I was a baby and only just recently brought me back. Something in the spell went awry and I ended up in the elven realm instead of wherever it was they meant to send me."

"This is most astonishing," Anakaron said. "And how do you feel about being sent hither and yon without so much as a by-your-leave?"

"Truthfully, I'm a little ticked," Howard replied, warming up to his role. "I mean, I had a pretty good life – I was happy where I was – and then all of a sudden, bam! I'm in some other world, surrounded by elves pointing spears at me. Spears, for crying out loud!"

"And you truly had no idea of your origins?"

"Not a clue. I was told my mother died when I was a baby. This is all I have of hers." He held the pendent up.

"This is most astonishing," Anakaron said. "So you would have no allegiance to these men you have been travelling to see."

He snorted. "Not bloody likely. I just want them to send me home again."

Anakaron thought it over for a moment. "This is most interesting indeed. And did the lady Aracelia say nothing of your magical origins?"

Howard thought fast. If the dark elves were working for Anakaron and had been following them, they might have seen him using magic. "She said something about my parents having magic and that I probably did too, but she said it could have skipped a generation." He strove to look a little disappointed, but then brightened up. "But I was able to break through the barrier around one of the elven realms, that was pretty cool. And I was getting pretty good at locating water, like a living dowsing rod."

"Elemental magic," the wizard murmured. "Did Aracelia test you?" he asked carefully.

"Test me?"

"For magical potential."

Howard shrugged. "Didn't seem to be much point if I was just going back to where I came from. Not much call for magic in the real world."

"Real world," Anakaron echoed. Howard could almost see the wheels turning. "Perhaps you would allow me the honor – a simple test, not the complicated ones the elves are prone to use."

"Sure, why not? I've got to admit you've got me a little curious."

"Excellent!" Anakaron rose.

"What, right now?"

"There is no purpose in waiting," Anakaron said blithely. "If you would care to accompany me..."

"Why not? Guess there's no time like the present."

Anakaron led Howard to a cavernous throne room. As they passed the threshold, torches around the perimeter flared to life. Howard had to admit, if only to himself, that it was pretty impressive. But not as impressive as the chamber itself.

The black walls were smooth and curved, like the inside of a dome. There was an altar set in the center, surrounded by concentric circles, geometric shapes, and symbols carved into the glass-like floor. Just beyond the altar was a dais topped by a throne. Howard wasn't sure if the throne was carved or pieced together, but he was pretty sure it was made of bone.

There was a long, twisted staff made of some dark material lying on the altar. The large red crystal topping it flared to life as Anakaron picked it up.

Howard startled back a step. "Neat trick," he said.

Anakaron smiled thinly. "There is nothing to fear, it will take but a moment to assess your skill."

Howard swallowed hard but held still as the wizard lightly touched the staff to his forehead. He felt an uncomfortable, tingling sensation for just an instant – like something sifting through his mind, his thoughts – and then it was gone. Howard pulled back sharply. "Wow! That was..." Evil. Pure evil. "Intense." A shiver went up his spine.

"You possess a strong talent for the Elemental Thought of magic," Anakaron told him, "And a quite minor one in alchemy, conjuring, and healing. Not what I would expect from the offspring of two such talented wizards."

"Aracelia said something about having been raised on a magicless world diluting my natural magic," Howard said, improvising. He shrugged. "I didn't really understand."

Anakaron eyed him for a moment, the red from the jewel reflecting in his eyes. At least Howard hoped it was just a reflection.

The light in the staff seemed to pulse. It was almost as though they were communicating. Howard was suddenly reminded of one of the old sword and sorcerery novels he used to read. There was one about a sword...if only he could remember the details.

"If your grandmother is correct," Anakaron said, "Perhaps with time and practice your powers might increase."

Again, Howard shrugged. "I don't know what to do with the power I've got," he said. "I haven't a clue what I'd do with more."

Anakaron smiled. "It would be my greatest pleasure, my young friend, to teach you."

Chapter Fifty-One

The next morning, at the Magical Academy, one of the students tapped hesitantly on the door to the visitor's suite. The guests had gathered in the common room, just finishing breaking their fast.

"Master Paranithel suggested you might enjoy a tour of the castle," he told them. "It should take until the mid-day meal, at which time you are requested to join Master Paranithel and Master Thackery in the dining hall."

There was a brief discussion while the student waited patiently. Aracelia begged off, saying she was still somewhat fatigued, but the others agreed. Jessica saw it as a delaying tactic – Thackery just didn't want to have to discuss Howard's rescue with her – but she found herself curious. She had her own plan forming, and it would be helpful to know the ins and outs of the academy.

"Are you troubled at the prospect of Jessica being sent to her own world?" Sebastian asked Dominic, halfway through the tour. They were lagging a few yards behind the others.

"What? No, why would you think that?"

"You have a pensive, dare I say troubled look about you."

"No, I'm more worried about what she's up to," Dominic replied with a nod towards Jessica.

Sebastian looked towards where she was busy having their guide explain something to her. "It appears she is interested in the organization of the library."

"Yes, it appears so. But I'm telling you she's up to something."

Throughout the rest of the tour Dominic kept an eye on Jessica. He watched as she poked into corners and charmed the students they happened across. She paid particular attention to the herb garden just outside the kitchen, asking many questions of the girl in charge of it.

He was no closer to figuring out what she was contemplating than before when they joined Thackery and Paranithel for the mid-day break.

"Did you build this castle," she asked Paranithel, "or was it already here when you decided to settle here?"

"Both," Paranithel answered, pleased at her interest. "The basic castle was here, we added the wall and towers after we'd settled here for a time."

"And once we were able to erect the barrier we were able to control the temperature within and added the trees," Thackery added.

"And the students?" Ellen asked, curious. "Did you settle here with the plan to create a school of magic?"

Thackery graced her with a smile. "We had discussed the possibility of opening a school, but we'd barely settled here when the students just started showing up."

"I recall how annoyed you were that they started arriving before we were ready for them," Paran said with a smirk.

"Yes," Thackery agreed. "But you have to admit we made good use of them to ready the school. They became our first students. All graduated now."

"This place is so big," Jessica said. "I'm surprised you're able to run it yourselves."

"We had other instructors, my dear," Paranithel said, "But when the troubles began to escalate we sent them to be with their families."

"And the students?" Ellen asked. "Didn't they want to return home too?"

"It was deemed safer for them to remain here,"

"Is that because this is a school for wizards and the parents think you're able to defend it against Anakaron, or is it because it's so far south they think it's out of his reach," Jessica asked sweetly.

Paran coughed into his sleeve, while Ellen quickly said, "I must say, the food here is far better than most schools I've had experience with. My compliments to the chef."

"There is no chef," Thackery said a little stiffly. "We have a cook whom the students take turns assisting."

"Cooking is a magic unto itself, wouldn't you say?" Aracelia observed, staving off another jab from Jessica.

"If that's true, then we have found a type of magic Jessica has little talent for," Dominic said with a cocky grin. He decided it was time to lighten the mood. Despite a glare from Jessica, he proceeded to tell the tale of one of her first attempts at creating a meal from magic and accidentally conjured a giant, flaming chicken instead.

"Actually," Ellen said when he was done, feeling an obligation to defend her friend, "Jessica's quite a good cook, at least on our world." Her eyes twinkled as she glanced at Dominic. "One of her former boyfriend's was studying to become a chef and they'd practice ... cooking together."

Conversation seemed to falter a bit after that, and before long the students were clearing away the empty plates. Thackery mumbled an excuse about having work to see to and left. Paranithel sighed, exchanging a meaningful glance with Aracelia.

"I have been thinking on young Howard," Aracelia said when they returned to their suite. Paranithel came with them.

"Being so new to his powers, is it possible he might have forgotten he has any?"

Jessica and Ellen looked at each other. Ellen shrugged.

"I doubt it," Jessica said. "The last few years magic moved from being an interest to an obsession with Howard. I can't imagine he'd forget having magical powers."

"But he might not be confident enough to try using them," Ellen said. "Remember what happened the first time you used yours? He might decide to err on the side of caution."

Tapping a finger thoughtfully on her chin, Aracelia said, "There might be a way to find out how Howard fares without alerting Anakaron."

They looked at her expectantly. Blinking, she looked up again with a rueful smile. "Sorry, I was just thinking. While I was unable to test Howard thoroughly, he did show the potential to become a master of the elements."

"Ah! That is excellent!" Paranithel chimed in.

"It is?" Jessica asked dubiously.

"For one, it will aid Anakaron's belief that Howard is the offspring of Kiranthus and Farenalyssia – it would be unlikely their child would have little or no magic."

"As well, being attuned to the elements it would take little effort to contact him using one of the elemental affinities."

"Elemental affinities?" Ellen asked before Jessica could.

"Creatures aligned with the elements," Paran told her. "Water sprites, sylphs, fire salamanders, earth entities ..."

"And you believe one of these creatures could be persuaded to carry a message to Howard?" Sebastian asked hopefully.

"Yes, I do."

"Anakaron has never had much use for what he terms the lesser magics – mind, healing, and elemental. His ego is such they seem inferior to him," Paranithel added

"Water seems inferior to rock, yet given time it can erode the rock away," Kaelan murmured.

"Exactly so."

"Okay, so how do we do this?" Jessica asked.

"I think for our purposes a pixie would be best," Aracelia decided. "Wind imps are more suited to carrying physical messages, but a pixie can speak mind to mind. They're quicker too. So first I will need to summon a pixie and persuade it to carry our message."

"As I recall, you're able to be quite persuasive when you set your mind to it," Paranithel said.

With an enigmatic smile, Aracelia seated herself at the table. Closing her eyes, hands folded neatly in her lap, her brow furrowed in concentration.

There was a puff of displaced air, then a shimmering spark darted about the room.

"Oh! It's beautiful," Jessica said.

If she strained, she could just barely make out the tiny winged being at the center of the spark, a shimmering creature with wings of gossamer.

"I thank thee for thy prompt answer to my call," Aracelia said formally. "I would beg a boon of thee."

The pixie did a circle of the room before hovering in front of the elf.

"One of our companions was taken by the harpies as we left the Shrine of Dorian. We believe he was delivered to Anakaron but we cannot be sure."

The creature shimmering and pulsed in front of Aracelia for a moment, then darted away to circle the ceiling. Returning once more to the elf, it grew brighter and pulsed frantically.

"Yes, he is in great danger from the dark one. If you could find out how he fares, and let him know his companions are safe, and that we search for a way to rescue him..."

The pixie spun in place, its color changing.

"I know it is a lot to ask of you..."

The pixie's glamour died down slightly and then brightened again.

"I intend to," Aracelia said with determination. "Thank you, I will."

The light winked out and the pixie disappeared.

"She says there are many wards and guards around Anakaron's lair but she believes she can pass through. She'll do her best to give our message to Howard and return to let us know how he fares."

"That was so cool," Jessica said. "Can anyone with magic talk to pixies?"

"Not quite. Unlike the wind imps, who can deliver physical messages, pixies can only communicate with those who have elemental magic."

"So theoretically, once we rescue Howard, Anakaron's been dealt with, and Jessica completes her training, she and Howard can send messages to each other with the pixies," Ellen said.

"Theoretically," Paranithel repeated, looking thoughtful.

Chapter Fifty-Two

Howard paced the confines of his room. Any way he looked at it, he was screwed six ways to Sunday. He didn't for one second believe Anakaron wanted to "help" him with his magic, especially not out of the goodness of his heart.

Flopping down on the chair near the fireplace, he stared broodingly into the fire. He needed to figure out a way to escape this place. With all her power Jessica could escape in a heartbeat. Maybe. Probably.

There was a puff of displaced air and to Howard's astonishment, a mote of bright light appeared.

Once he recovered from his surprise, Howard spoke. "Well hello there. What are you doing here?"

To his utter astonishment, she answered – in his head.

"She did? They're safe?"

The mote of light pulsed and flickered.

"You've no idea what a relief that is to hear."

There was a frown on his face as he concentrated on what the pixie was telling him.

"I can't stop them from trying, but they shouldn't take any foolish chances."

The light dipped and bobbed.

"Yes, I know their combined magics are formidable, but

Jessica needs to return to her own world until this is over."

The pixie went back to pulsing.

"I know how powerful she is, but she has next to no training. Anakaron would eat her alive."

There was a rattle at the door that had the pixie shooting towards the ceiling.

"You'd better get out of here while you can."

There was one last pulse of light.

"Yes, I'll remember. Thank you."

By the time the door opened, the pixie was gone. Howard breathed a sigh of relief as he realized it was just a servant with his evening meal and not Anakaron. She looked at him curiously and he wondered how much she'd overheard.

"You caught me," he said with a rueful smile.

"My Lord?"

"I was talking to myself – one of my bad habits."

"My lord Anakaron often does the same," she said, setting the tray on the table. "If you wish for anything else, just tell the guard at your door."

"Thank you," he said. He breathed a sigh of relief as she closed the door behind her.

Jessica paced back and forth in the common room of the suite.

"How fast does a pixie travel?" she asked.

"It's hard to say," Dominic said, trying to soothe her. "It depends on the age of the pixie, how far it has to travel –"

Before he could finish, the pixie was back.

"Thank God!" Jessica said.

Ignoring everyone else, it went straight to Aracelia to hover in front of her face.

"He is? Oh, that's good to hear." She turned to the others. "He's safe, at least for now."

The pixie pulsed to get her attention. "What? Oh. Yes, he would say that, I think so too." The light throbbed. "I understand. Thank you."

The pixie winked out of sight.

"What was all that about?" Jessica asked.

"Nothing really. She just wanted to reassure me that he's fine for now."

"Perhaps this would be an appropriate time to share what we have learned with your father," Paranithel suggested.

Jessica looked at him soberly. "Do you really think he's going to care?"

"He cares, my dear. He cares far more than you realize."

Jessica had her doubts but she was willing to give him a chance. She was, however, silent as Paranithel summoned Thackery to meet with them.

"Just how much talent does young Howard show for elemental magic," Thackery said, once they filled him in.

"Even untrained he shows potential to become a master of it."

"Hmm. That works in his favor. Anakaron has never believed in the merit of elemental magic."

He paced from one side of the sitting room to the other. "We might be able to use this to our advantage."

"You've been thinking of a plan?" Jessica asked.

He turned to her. "I told you I would think on it. Howard was invaluable in the aid he gave you when you first arrived, and he kept our secret although he was not happy doing so. We owe him at least the attempt of removing him from Anakaron's grasp."

"Thank you," Jessica said, tears pricking at her eyes.

"But I will only make the attempt if you return to your world to wait for him."

Her mouth opened in protest.

"On this point I will not be swayed. The conflict with Anakaron is not yours and fear for your safety will only distract me."

"Ever since I got to this world I've been saddled with all this magical power. Surely there's some way to use it and still stay safe."

"No."

"I don't have to go anywhere near Anakaron, I can just work behind the scenes."

"The moment you use any significant amount of power he'll be made aware of your presence. At the very least he will realize his mistake and Howard will be dead."

"You've been very fortunate thus far that your major workings have been in healing," Paranithel added gently. "Healing magic is hard to trace."

Jessica looked unhappily from one to the other. What they said made a kind of sense, but she didn't have to like it.

"I'll have to think about it," she said finally. Glancing at Dominic she added, "I have a couple of things to consider." Dominic was only one of them. The vision the water hag had was another.

Of course the water hag was looking at the big picture and if she was honest, Howard didn't really have an impact on that. At this point she saw no reason to tell Thackery about the hag's prophecy, it wasn't going to sway him. He seemed pretty stuck on sending her home, out of danger. The hag's vision would only make him more convinced he was right.

"I'll sleep on it," she said.

Thackery opened his mouth to protest, but Paranithel stopped him with a shake of his head. "That will be fine. We can discuss it further in the morning."

Jessica nodded, but was far from happy about it.

"If I go back to my world, will you go with me?" she asked Dominic when they were nestled in bed that night.

"Yes."

She angled around to get a better look at his face. "That's it? Just yes? I figured I'd have a fight on my hands to persuade you."

He smiled at her. "You should know me better than that by now."

She snuggled down again. "Yeah, I guess I should."

They were quiet for a while, each thinking their own thoughts, and then she spoke again.

"I wonder what Sebastian will do. I know he was planning to go back with Howard. Howard was really excited about showing him off."

"What do you think?"

"I think he'll stay here until Howard is rescued," she said with a sigh. "I guess it's a good thing one of us gets to."

"The advantage of having talent instead of magic."

"You've got that right."

Chapter Fifty-Three

Breakfast was a quiet affair. Jessica picked at her food, trying to ignore the glances of her table-mates. She sighed and gave up all pretense of eating.

"We might as well get this over with," she said, pushing back from the table. "Someone ring the bell and send for Thackery."

Kaelan was closest to the door and did as she requested.

"You're doing the right thing, Jess," Ellen told her. "Howard and I became close after you were gone – I know he wouldn't want you to risk yourself rescuing him."

"You're probably right, but it just makes me feel so helpless. And I hate feeling helpless."

"There is another thing to be considered," Kaelan said. "From what I've been told, your power nears that of the Lady Aracelia."

"With training, it will one day surpass mine," Aracelia said.

"Think what Anakaron would do with such power," Kaelan continued. "He would drain you dry, as he has the elves, and there would be no stopping him."

"I never thought of that," Jessica said. "I hate to admit you've got a point."

The discussion came to a halt as Thackery, followed by Paranithel, joined them.

Jessica stood. "I might as well cut right to the chase," she said.

"I'll agree to Ellen and I being sent back to the earth realm, but I have a couple of conditions."

Thackery raised an eye brow. "And those would be?"

"First, that Dominic be allowed to come with me."

He turned to look at Dominic. "Is this your wish as well?"

"Where Jessica goes, I go also."

"With the Lady Aracelia's permission, I would also accompany them," Kaelan said, watching Ellen for her reaction.

"Are you sure?" she asked, a hopeful look on her face. "There won't be any other elves there, and there's no magic."

"But you would be there, that's all the magic I would need."

Her answering smile was radiant.

"Aracelia?" Thackery asked.

She, too, was smiling. "This comes as no surprise to me. He has my blessing."

Thackery sighed. "And your other condition?"

"That once Howard's been rescued and Anakaron has been dealt with, I'm allowed to return and complete my training."

He was very still for a moment, then as though unable to help himself, he reached out to fold her in his arms.

"It would be my greatest pleasure," he told her.

"I'll make the arrangements," Paranithel said, stroking a hand down Jessica's hair before patting Thackery on the shoulder. "We should be ready to cast the portal spell tomorrow."

"Well," Jessica said, eyes suspiciously damp. "We'll have to have a special good bye dinner tonight. Would your cook allow me to make a special meal?"

"You wish to cook for us?" Thackery asked, a little taken aback.

"To show there's no hard feelings," Jessica said.

"Jessica is an amazing cook," Ellen said loyally.

"If that is your wish, I see no reason why not."

"Excellent! Now, I'm not as familiar with the foods and spices here as I'd like to be. Could I borrow a couple of your students to help me out?"

"Of course, anything you wish."

"Then if you'll excuse me, I'm going see what you have in stock and start planning the menu."

Thackery was not the only one who was surprised by Jessica's request.

"Did that seem far too easy to you?" Dominic asked Sebastian, taking him aside as the wizards and Aracelia left after Jessica.

"It did seem somewhat reminiscent of that time in Wodenville where she appeared to acquiesce and then drugged our wine."

"You don't think she'd try something that foolish again, do you?"

"I do not think so, but I believe I will forgo the wine at dinner this evening."

Dominic and Sebastian both kept an eye on Jessica throughout the day, but other than requesting the assistance of two of Thackery's students, nothing she did seemed amiss. Still, Dominic was unable to shake an uneasy feeling and turned to Ellen for her opinion.

"I don't know guys," she said when Dominic and Sebastian cornered her in garden. "I mean, yeah, I kind of expected her to push a little harder on being in on the whole rescue thing, but she's not stupid."

"No," Sebastian agreed. "She is not, but she is most cunning."

"Some would even call it sneaky," Dominic added. "Did she tell you about how she drugged us so she could confront Ewan alone?"

"Well, yeah. I did hear something about that. But her mother's ghost told her she had to do it alone. I don't see her mother's ghost flitting around anywhere, do you?"

They had to admit they hadn't.

"Then I don't think you have anything to worry about. Jessica does like to cook, and I think she's grateful for the chance to show off for her father."

"She didn't seem all that accomplished a cook when we travelled the Darkwood Forest," Dominic muttered.

Ellen held back a grin. "That was cooking over an open fire. Jessica never did like camping much, but turn her loose in a kitchen and she's a whiz. No pun intended."

The two men looked confused.

"You know whiz, wizard?" She sighed. "Never mind. But there's something else you're forgetting."

"And that is?" Dominic asked.

"She may be more powerful than anyone else in this castle, but she doesn't have a clue how to use it. What's she going to do, raise an army of flaming chickens?"

"I see your point," Dominic reluctantly agreed.

"You've been a good influence on her," she told him, patting his arm. "She's not as impulsive as she was, now she thinks things through."

"Perhaps you're right," he agreed with a sigh. "But I'm still not drinking any wine with supper."

The two students Jessica recruited were Jaffrey from the map room and Inan from the library, but the assignments she gave them had nothing to do with cooking. Having been told by Thackery himself to render any assistance his daughter requested, they thought nothing of her requests and gave no thought to mentioning it to anyone.

Things were coming together nicely, Jessica decided smugly as she headed towards the kitchen. It didn't bother her in the least that Dominic dropped into the kitchen several times during the course of the day, although she had to bite back a snicker when he had his knuckles rapped twice by the wooden spoon Dudley, the cook, wielded.

"It smells amazing in here," he told them.

"Thank you," Jessica said primly. "But if you keep coming in here we're going to put you to work washing dishes."

Dudley glowered at him and nodded in agreement.

Dominic beat a hasty retreat and she breathed a sigh of relief. So far so good. He hadn't once thought to ask where the students she'd drafted were. He seemed to be buying the whole, dinner as a thank you thing. She might just get away with this after all.

"I just can't shake the feeling she's up to something," Dominic muttered to Sebastian later. "I know it doesn't make sense– "

"But you would not have survived all you have if you did not listen to your instincts," Sebastian told him.

Dominic sighed and ran a hand through his hair. "Then why do I feel disloyal for even thinking so?"

Sebastian looked at him soberly. "Because you care so deeply."

With another sigh, Dominic sat down. "It is a dilemma, is it not?"

Jessica went over everything in her head. The dinner had been an impulse she'd almost come to regret when she found what she had to work with in the kitchen. Other than the Beef Wellington, she was pretty sure nothing about the dinner was far out of the ordinary, but the dessert – the dessert was spectacular, thanks to Dudley's kitchen magic that would keep it cold.

The map Jaffrey had found for her was perfect, and safely tucked away in her boot, as were the pages removed from the volume of forbidden elven magic, which she studied periodically when no one was around. It had taken only a slight magical nudge using mind magic to squash any reluctance on Inan's part to provide them for her.

Jessica fingered the amulet around her neck, the one that hid her true power. It was a good thing Dominic didn't know that ever since she'd spoken with the water hag, she been secretly been studying the combative magics section of the book she'd brought from Ghren. A book she had yet to return to Thackery.

Not only had she been surreptitiously studying Thackery's book, without Dominic knowing, she'd picked up a couple of others. It wasn't like she'd lied to him, exactly. She'd gone to the apothecary to replenish her supply of herbs and as she browsed the shop while waiting for her order to be filled just happened to look through her collection of spell books. She just never got around to telling Dominic about her additional purchase, that's all.

He had such a bee in his bonnet when it came to her doing magic. Even little things like lighting a fire – which she had totally mastered, thank you very much. But ever since meeting her mother in the space between worlds she was a big believer in fate, and she knew her fate was tied to this world and what was happening in it. What the water hag told her only confirmed it.

There was a reason she'd been gifted with so much power, and that reason was to face down Anakaron, she knew it right to the bottom of her soul. She may not have any experience, but she was armed with knowledge. And she had the one thing Anakaron craved above all else – power.

There was no way she was going home without Howard, and if the hag had foreseen that Jessica was the only one who could stop Anakaron, then that's what she was going to do.

Chapter Fifty-Four

Jessica gazed around the table, beaming with satisfaction. As far as she could tell, the meal had been an unqualified success.

"Let us raise our glasses to my daughter Jessica," Thackery said. "She is as talented as she is beautiful. I do not know when I have had such a delicious repast."

"If you liked dinner, you're going to love the dessert," she promised.

"Dessert too?" Paranithel asked.

"I've always thought dessert is the best part of the meal. I worked really hard on it – I'm really anxious to see what you think."

Standing, she rang the bell that summoned the students she'd drafted as servers.

"Is that what I think it is?" Ellen asked, practically salivating when the students brought in two large bowls.

"If you're thinking English Trifle, you're right," Jessica said with a grin. "I thought about doing cheesecake – I make an amazing cheesecake – but it's a little heavy after a big meal. Trifle is so light it doesn't matter how big the meal it follows there's always room for trifle."

"It's heaven in a bowl," Ellen told them.

Another student entered with a tray of small bowls and two bottles of wine.

"I hope you don't mind," Jessica said to Thackery, "I raided your wine cellar to find just the right wine to go with it."

No one else at the table noticed the look Dominic and Sebastian exchanged.

"It's perfectly all right, my dear," Thackery told her

The students cleared away the detritus from the rest of the meal, leaving the two bowls of trifle on the table. Paranithel told them, "Once you lads have finished with that lot of dishes you can take the rest of the evening off. The dessert dishes can wait until morning."

"Thank you, Master Paranithel!"

"Now, my dear," he said, turning to Jessica. "Perhaps you would care to serve this most interesting concoction."

"It would be my pleasure," Jessica said.

She started by pouring the wine in fresh glasses, then ladled out generous helpings of the trifle into bowls.

"What exactly is in this?" Kaelan asked, staring dubiously into the dish.

"Unfortunately, it's not totally authentic," Jessica admitted. "I used sponge cake instead of lady fingers– "

"Lady fingers?" he asked, looking a little horrified.

"It's a soft, bland cookie," she explained. "The trifle is layers of cake, whipped cream, and berries. Dig in, everyone."

The trifle was duly sampled and it was agreed it was indeed the best part of the meal. Jessica saw with satisfaction that everyone all but licked their bowls clean. And if her bowl had been all cake and whipped cream, well that was just server's prerogative.

"Something wrong with your wine?" she asked, smiling sweetly across the table at Dominic. "You haven't touched it."

He shrugged. "I guess I'm just not thirsty."

"And I do not wish to replace the taste of your most excellent dessert with the taste of mere wine," Sebastian said.

"You flatter me," she told him.

"When you return for your training," Paranithel said, "You will have to make this again."

"It would be my pleasure," Jessica told him.

He finished off his wine and yawned. "Pardon me," he said, flushing slightly. "All this food and wine has made me sleepy."

Ellen found herself yawning as well. "Sorry," she said. "Me too."

Kaelan was blinking, as though fighting sleep.

"I wonder what could have been in that wine?" Dominic murmured.

"Grapes?" Jessica said, taking a sip from her own glass.

His eyes narrowed at her as he felt the tiredness begin to seep through him. Beside him, Sebastian's eyes were already closed.

"I don't understand," Thackery said from his end of the table, fighting to keep his eyes open.

"I think I do," Aracelia said, looking at Jessica. "I just hope– "

Whatever she'd been about to say was cut off as her chin drooped downwards. Jessica stared around at the sleepers gathered around the table and sighed in relief. She hadn't been sure it would work, but if her calculations were correct, they'd be out until morning. She took another sip of the most excellent wine.

She wasn't stupid, she knew Dominic and Sebastian had been expecting her to drug the wine, as she had in Wodenville. But it hadn't been the wine, at least not the wine they were drinking. It had been the wine-soaked fruit she used in the trifle that had been drugged.

She got to her feet and looked around the table. "I'm sorry," she said softly. "But I have to do this."

Getting out of the castle and making her way to the Well was easy. It was late enough that the students were all asleep, not that any of them would have been able to stop her. With luck, by the time anyone checked Thackery's private parlor she'd be long gone. Hopefully.

The walk to the Well gave her time for second thoughts, but surprisingly she didn't have any. She thought of Dominic and his reaction when he woke up, and was glad she wasn't going to be there to see it. She hoped he'd be able to forgive her. If she survived.

The night was warm and a full moon lit the path to the Well, almost as though this was meant to be. Jessica might have enjoyed herself if there hadn't been so much at stake. She tried not to think of all the things that could go wrong with her plan but they were like a parade through her head.

Getting away from the others had been the easy part. And memorizing the spell to open the Fae Road wasn't hard, but the spell itself would depend on how much elfin magic she had in her. There was a very good chance she'd be dead in the water before she even started. But if she succeeded...

From what she understood from her readings, it took elven magic to open the road, but it was the power of the Well itself that allowed for travel, and the ability to keep the road steady took an incredible amount of personal power. But the best part was, because the spell was begun with elven magic, it was nigh unto undetectable.

She felt the pull of the Well. It was interesting that the desert wind covered and uncovered the surrounding rocks with sand but left the area around the Well scoured clean. Jessica hesitated at its outer edge. She looked up at the moon, then back the way she'd come.

"Now is not the time for second thoughts," she told herself. She didn't have a choice. Pulling her attention back to the Well, Jessica ran through the spell in her head.

Taking a deep breath, she started the incantation and stepped towards the Well. Jessica felt the pull of her elfin blood. Repeating the incantation, she focused on the destination Well and the tenuous line that connected them. Stepping into the Well, she began to walk the Fae Road.

Unseen forces plucked at her, trying to make her stumble or fall. Strength of will wasn't enough, she needed the aid of her power to keep the path steady. Each step was draining, each step was a struggle, but Jessica continued to put one foot in front of the other.

She didn't know whether minutes or hours had passed before she felt a thinning in the darkness around her. One more step and she was at the edge of the Well. Another step and she was outside of it. She had a brief glimpse of tall trees around the Well, and time for the hope she was in the right place before darkness claimed her and she fell.

Chapter Fifty-Five

Howard was in danger of wearing a rut in the floor from his pacing. He wasn't one to believe in premonitions, but he couldn't shake the feeling that something bad was in the offing.

He gave a snort of laughter. Of course there was something bad this whole situation was bad. Flopping down in the chair he stared at the fire. There had to be something pro-active he could do, maybe even find a way to escape, but how? Absently he rubbed his thumb across his fingers, then started when the spark he created turned into a flame.

"Aracelia said I was a natural when it came to elemental magics, how can I use that?"

What had he done so far? He'd used earth magic to talk the ironwood trees into gifting him with staffs, and he'd been able to find water using his water magic. And he'd never forget the rush of using wind to break through the barrier the dark elves had changed, even if he had needed to borrow some of Jessica's energy to do it. But how could any of this help now?

This time he felt the pixie's approach before she appeared before him.

"You're back," he said in surprise. "Do you have another message from Aracelia?"

The pixie darted closer, almost brushing his cheek, before putting some distance between them again.

"You see my potential and want to be friends?"

Howard couldn't have held back his grin if he'd wanted to. "I'm honored. I've never had a pixie for a friend before."

The pixie dipped and circled.

"Yes, this is a very bad place."

She pulsed, changing colors.

"I appreciate the offer, but I don't think– "

There was a burst of light.

"I'm sorry, I'm sorry," Howard said, holding up his hands. "But this is also a dangerous place and I wouldn't want you to get caught by Anakaron or his minions."

The pixie zipped around the room.

"Yes, you're very fast," he agreed. "But– " He held out his finger and was delighted when the mote of light settled on it. "You really think I'll be an elemental master wizard after I've been trained?"

The pixie spun on his finger tip.

"That's very flattering, but I'm not there yet." He sighed. "And my potential isn't exactly going to help Jessica."

The mote of light wafted upwards.

"She's my friend. There's nothing I can do to stop her from coming here, I just wish there was something I could do to help her."

Pulling away slightly, the pixie seemed to fade a bit. Suddenly, she burst into a rainbow of color, pulsing frantically.

"Other elementals as well? Dwarves? What do– Anakaron forced them to carve out this cavern for him?"

Howard's brow furrowed as the pixie continued to flash.

"Well yes, that would be helpful. Can you take a message to them for me? But how– what's an earth entity?"

As the pixie continued pulse and flash, Howard tried to make sense of what she was telling him.

"You really think there are other elemental entities that would be willing to help if I summoned them? Well, I guess it's better than nothing. I'll give it a try."

The pixie pulled back to hover in the corner of the room up near the ceiling, twinkling there like a star. Howard stood, looking for the best place to try summoning one of the earth entities. The pixie flashed at him.

"Oh, good idea."

Moving to the center of the room he sat down on the floor. Closing his eyes, he focused on the magic within, tapping into it to send out an invitation for any earth entity that might be nearby. He'd thought about summoning one, but felt he'd have better luck if he invited one instead. Leaving it with free will was friendlier somehow.

The call was the ghost of a whisper on the air. Unless a human was attuned to the elemental magics, they would not hear it. It was a subtle call, offering the satiation of curiosity, the possibility of friendship. The call begged a favor, promising no harm.

In a shorter time than he expected, Howard felt a response to his invitation. He opened his eyes in time to see a small swirl of dust gathering in front of him. His jaw nearly dropped open – he hadn't really expected it to work.

"Thank you for coming," he said to the vague shape the dust formed into. "I– yes, I'll get to the point. I have a friend outside of this place who will be trying to get in– "

He paused to listen – the earth entity spoke directly into his mind, just as the pixie had.

"Yes, I know she'd be better off staying away, but she's going to want to rescue me."

Another pause to listen.

"Yes, I understand you have little power to help her, but the dwarves might have better luck. All I ask is you take a message to them for me."

It was getting harder for Howard to remain patient with the entity's protests.

"I don't know exactly. Maybe they could show her a hidden way into this place. I know if I was forced to carve a huge complex using an existing catacomb as a base, I'd make sure I had an escape route or two. Jessica could use one of them to sneak in undetected."

The entity became so anxious that it almost turned corporeal.

"If she's going to face Anakaron, she's going to need all the help she can get."

The pixie, who'd stayed up in her corner all this time, swooped down to add her two cents worth.

"No," Howard said. "I wouldn't do that. I'm new to my power, but I would never try to bend another to my will with magic. All I ask is that you take a message to the dwarves. Simply ask them to help her if they can."

The two elemental beings held a conversation which did not include Howard. He gave a start when the pixie simply disappeared and turned his attention to the earth entity again.

"Thank you," he said.

The dust blew apart and wafted to the floor again. Howard stood up with a sigh. It wasn't much, and maybe nothing would come of it, but at least he'd tried. Now all he could do is wait.

Chapter Fifty-Six

Thackery was the first to awaken and when he did it was slowly. Why was his head at such an unnatural angle? It felt like he'd fallen asleep in a chair. He straightened up, biting off a groan at the stiffness, and opened his eyes.

The rest of the dinner party was starting to show signs of life as he looked at each of them in turn.

"How is it possible that we all had enough to drink that we fell unconscious at the table?"

"I didn't have that much to drink," Ellen said, wincing as she straightened up in her chair. "And I don't feel like I have a hangover."

"I don't understand," Dominic said, shaking his head to clear it. "Sebastian and I didn't touch the wine that came with the dessert, and Jessica drank the wine served with dinner."

"Jessica? What has Jessica to do with this," Thackery asked. "Where *is* Jessica?"

"Gone," Aracelia said, holding up a note. She read it to the rest of them: "Dear all. Sorry that it had to be this way but I didn't have time to convince you that I know what I'm doing. I've always been a big believer in destiny and this is mine. I'd tell you not to follow me, but I expect that advice will fall on deaf ears. But I'll remind you I've got a heck of a good start on you, and there are three Wells near Anakaron's lair and you have no idea which one I went to. See you on the flip side, Jessica."

There was dead silence for a moment then an explosion of sound.

"She's gone to face Anakaron?" Thackery said, face pale.

"She drugged us?" Kaelan said at the same time.

"I'll kill her," Dominic said grimly.

"But we didn't drink the wine," Sebastian said, a little bewildered. When the others looked at him, he said, "She drugged our wine to sneak away to confront Ewan. We thought if she was going to try something, it would be the wine."

"It was the trifle!" Ellen said suddenly. "The fruit in the trifle is soaked in liquor – I'd bet my katana she whatever she soaked the fruit in was drugged."

"But she ate the dessert as well," Kaelan pointed out.

"But did she eat the fruit? Or just the cake and whipped cream?"

"One could almost admire her ingenuity," Paranithel said. At Thackery's glare he shrugged. "I said almost."

Thackery stood, swayed in place, then sat down again. "What did she drug us with? This weakness is not normal."

"My guess would be bakalin root," Aracelia said. "The sap from the root is quite potent, and long lasting."

"This is intolerable!" Thackery fumed.

"We can do nothing until the drug wears off," Paranithel said. "It is not just our strength that has been affected, but our magic as well."

"Surely you know of an antidote," Thackery appealed to Aracelia.

She shook her head. "There is none that I know of. As

Paranithel said, we must let it run its course."

"And meanwhile Jessica is running headlong into trouble," Ellen said.

"If anything happens to her, I'll throttle her!" Dominic promised.

"You!" Thackery spat out, pointing at Aracelia. "It is because of your testing of her abilities that she believes she can do this thing."

One slender eyebrow rose in disbelief. "You seek to cast blame? You are responsible for bringing her to this world and keeping her in ignorance. And was it not you who insisted she come to you here in the south when she would have been protected in the elven realms?"

They glared at each other across the table.

"You know," Paranithel said thoughtfully, "She reminds me of another headstrong young woman." The two turned to stare at him. "She, too, would often take risks and she did not care to be told what to do. In fact, she would most often do the opposite."

"Who are you talking about?" Thackery demanded.

"Farenalyssia."

Thackery opened his mouth, then shut it again. His shoulders slumped.

"I can't believe how much thought Jessica put into her escape," Ellen said.

"Because she's underhanded and devious," Dominic muttered.

"But she's also smart, and she wouldn't go to all that trouble to drug us if she didn't have a plan for the rest of it."

"I agree," Kaelan said, surprising them all. "Perhaps it involves spells from the books she was studying."

"What books?" Ellen and Dominic asked in chorus.

"The books she carried with her on our journey. Several were small, but there was a large one she would study early in the mornings."

Dominic's lips tightened as he pushed back from the table. "I'll go check our room."

"Who were the students she drafted into helping her?" Aracelia asked. "Perhaps dinner was not all they helped her with."

Thackery stared at her for a second and then rose to head out the door.

"Well," Paranithel said. "Perhaps I should see about breaking our fast while we sort this out."

Aracelia shook her head in amusement as he left the room too. "It's comforting to know that some things never change."

Chapter Fifty-Seven

Jessica woke to a myriad of sensations. There was the all too familiar soreness that came from resting on the ground too long. The air around her was cooler than it had been and it had an earthy smell to it – she'd made it out of the southlands at least. But then she realized there was a blanket covering her. She hadn't brought a blanket with her.

As much as she'd like to, she couldn't just stay here forever, so she forced her eyes open. There was a fire right in front of her, which was a surprise. Somehow she didn't think she'd exited the Well and built a fire before collapsing. And where had the blanket come from?

Muscles protesting, she levered herself up to a sitting position and only then noticed the elf sitting on the other side of the fire.

"Hello," she said cautiously. She did a quick, internal inventory and was surprised to discover she didn't feel too bad.

"You are not an elf," he said, eyes full of suspicion. "How is it you were able to travel the Fae road?"

"Who wants to know?" she countered.

"It is a forbidden magic, and known only to elves."

"Yes, I know. Fortunately I had just enough elven blood to make it work."

He stared at her for a moment before telling her. "I am Orrin of the Darkwood Clan."

Darkwood Clan, that would make him one of her grandmother's people. "My name is Jessica. I take it you moved me out of the Well?"

He nodded mutely.

"Then thank you, Orrin." She looked around. "Just how far away did you move me?"

"It was necessary to move to a safe distance. The Well was showing signs of the taint – you're lucky to have made it through."

"What's the taint?"

"It is a ... wrongness in the Well." He sighed heavily. "When the Darkwood Realm lost contact with the Wildwinds Realm– "

"I was there, in Wildwinds, I mean," Jessica interrupted. "It was overrun by dark elves. We barely managed to break free. They somehow infected the barrier with something evil."

He looked at her sharply. "You were in Wildwinds? How did you get in? What were you doing there?"

"Whoa, time out here." she held up a hand. "I got in through the barrier, it was only just starting to feel wrong but by the time we left whatever they were doing to transform it was almost completed. And I was there to help a sick friend. Now what about you, I take it you were there too? Do you know what happened to the other elves there?"

"I was sent there to determine why they had stopped communicating. There has been no messengers or contact – no word using the scrying mirrors."

There was a pot boiling over the fire and he used a dipper to fill two flat, heavy clay bowls. He passed one to Jessica.

"It's nothing fancy," he told her, "Just a vegetable stew."

"Thank you," she said, a little surprised at his generosity. "So did you discover what was going on?"

"After a fashion. As soon as we crossed the barrier my squadron and I were attacked by dark elves. I managed to escape into the trees. I tried to gather as much information as I could to take back."

He paused for a bite of the stew. "I almost wish I hadn't. The dark elves were somehow able to sap the will of those dwelling in Wildwinds– "

"Elfsbane," Jessica told him. "We think they poisoned the water supply with it."

Orrin nodded. "It makes sense. It was just the one village left when I arrived. I didn't know what had been done to them, but it was obvious they intended to take them somewhere. I traded my uniform for a set of clothes I found in the village and joined the line, pretending to be one of them."

Jessica frowned. She had a bad feeling about this. "And where were they taken?"

"Here," he said. "Or more precisely, in there." He pointed off into the darkness. "Into the mountain of Carenkraka, where the dark lord Anakaron drained them of their magic."

They were quiet for a while, finishing their stew in silence.

"Did you intend to come to this place when you stepped on the Fae Road?" Orrin asked.

"If here is the closest Well to Anakaron, then yes."

"Why?"

"Anakaron has a friend of mine, I intend to rescue him."

Orrin was already shaking his head. "It is impossible."

"Difficult maybe," she said with more confidence than she

was feeling. "But not impossible. What about you? What are you going to do?"

"I must go back and report to my commander," he said. "But first I must gather my strength. There is a barrier around the mountain, much like that around Wildwinds. I was... damaged escaping. It's like there's a piece of the barrier inside me."

Jessica opened herself to her healing magic and focused on Orrin. She could see a dark film over his aura. It was an ugly, oily thing and when she broadened her focus she could see it overlaying the land, like a net, radiating from the mountain. There was something almost mesmerizing about it....

Giving herself a shake, she pulled her focus back to the elf. The darkness seemed to feed on his magic and it seemed to be tethered to something. Using the purity of her healing magic, Jessica carefully broke the tether. The slime coating him began to dissolve.

"What– what did you do?"

"You were right," she told him. "There was a piece of the barrier in you. It was feeding off your magic."

"What did you do to me?" he repeated, eyes wide with wonder.

"I guess you could say I cleansed your aura." She shrugged. "It's no big deal."

"Perhaps not to you, but for me ... I owe you my life."

"No, you don't. Seriously, it might have very well dissipated on its own once you were far enough from the barrier."

"No, it is you that does not understand," he said slowly. "I would have carried that darkness within me unknowing to my kin and infected them all. I overheard the dark elves saying something to that effect but I did not understand at the time –

that is how they gained access to Wildwinds."

"Oh," Jessica said. "Then I guess it's a good thing we ran into each other."

"It was fated," said a voice from the darkness.

Faster than Jessica would have given him credit for, Orrin was on his feet, sword at the ready. "Show yourself!" he demanded.

There was a rustling in the underbrush and a short, stout, bearded man pushed through, hands held up in a peaceful position.

"I've come to guide the rescuer," he said.

"That would be me," Jessica said, scrambling to her feet. "But I didn't realize anyone knew I was coming."

The dwarf looked her up and down. "Ye don't be looking like much use."

"And you don't look like much of a guide," she returned.

He stared hard at her for a moment. "The elemental wizard Howard sent me."

"I knew it! Howard always was a quick study." She turned to Orrin. "Thank you for pulling me from the Well and sharing your dinner with me. Maybe I'll see you in Darkwoods some day."

"Wait! You can't go alone, I'll go with you."

Jessica shook her head. "No, this is something I have to do alone. And you need to get back to the Darkwoods Realm to tell them everything you've discovered."

She started to follow the dwarf into the woods, then turned back. "But you could do me a favor?"

"Anything you wish of me."

"When you're far enough away that you're not in danger,

could you get a message to my grandmother? Just tell her I made it here safely and Howard is as good as rescued."

"I will see to it personally," he promised. "If I may have the name of your grandmother?"

"She's the Lady Aracelia, of Darkwood."

She was gone into the darkness before Orrin remembered to close his mouth again.

Chapter Fifty-Eight

I s he going to be all right by himself?" Jessica cast a backward glance and tripped over a root as her reward.

"The likes of him are always all right," the dwarf said with a sniff.

"So ... Howard sent you to help me. Is he okay?"

"I have not seen the elemental wizard myself. The request came through an earth entity."

"Elemental wizard," she said with a smile. "Howard would love being called that." She thought about it for a moment and then asked. "So if you never met Howard face to face, why are you helping?"

"There are many of us who have no love for the dark lord. Now it's best to be quiet."

"Sorry."

She followed meekly for another few minutes. "Just one last question," she said.

"What?" he asked in a snarky voice.

"What's your name?"

His breath left him in a sigh. "I be Rabblyn."

"Thank you, Rabblyn."

It was night when Jessica stepped onto the Fae Road and night when she woke up next to Orrin's fire. She wished she'd thought to ask the elf how long she'd been unconscious. But as much as she would have liked to wait for more light before stumbling around in the woods, it was probably safer to move around in the dark. Still, she was getting tired of tripping over rocks and roots that she couldn't see.

She could tell they were walking through some kind of forest, but not what kind of trees. They were dense enough that even if there was a moon it wouldn't shed any light through the canopy. Her dwarf friend must be able to see in the dark, which was a handy skill she wished she had.

They changed directions twice – Jessica couldn't have found her way back to the Well even if she wanted to. Once he had her hunker down beside him.

"Dark elf patrol," he'd whispered fiercely when she hesitated.

Without another word, Jessica dropped to the ground beside him, hardly daring to breathe until it was safe again. After that she tried to walk as lightly and noiselessly as possible.

She figured dawn was approaching – either that or her eyes were finally adjusting to the darkness because she was having an easier time making out shapes – when a turn in the path took them through a tumble of rocks. Jessica was grateful for whatever time she'd been sleeping beside Orrin's fire, otherwise she'd have been stumbling with fatigue by now.

While they picked their way through the rock her mind worked on the problem of what exactly she'd do once she found Howard. She'd been so single minded about getting to him she'd given no thought so far as to how she was going to get him out. Maybe, if she was lucky, Howard was working on a plan.

And what if she ran into Anakaron? Yes, the amulet was shielding her magical abilities, but he'd only have to have one look at her to know she was related to Aracelia. And she wanted Howard safe before she confronted the dark lord.

The closer they got to their destination, the more her head filled with second thoughts and misgivings. Maybe she'd been a little too caught up in pulling one over on the others to sneak away, and the fun in getting away with it. How crazy was she, thinking she could go against the dark lord and win? She didn't even know the first thing about magical fighting, just what she'd read in the spell books.

Holy Saint Christopher! What had she been thinking?

Rabblyn stopped so suddenly she almost ran over him.

"What is it?" she whispered.

"'Tis another dark elf patrol. It's not like them to be out with dawn so near," he whispered back. Taking two steps off the path they were following, he spat on his hand and then pressed it to the rock face beside them.

To Jessica's amazement, the rock shivered and then dissolved leaving a gaping hole.

"Quickly," he said. "Inside. Follow the tunnel staying always to the right. It will meet up with the corridor where Master Howard is being held. His is the fifth door on the left."

Jessica looked dubiously into the hole. "But what about you?"

"I will lead the patrol away. Now hurry."

"I don't think– "

He gave her a shove into the passageway and then sealed it up behind her.

"– we should split up," Jessica finished as she fell into the tunnel.

She jumped to her feet and immediately tested the wall, but it was solid rock again. Well, it looked like she was on her own from here on in.

From the glimpse she'd had when Rabblyn opened the tunnel, the passage was narrow. He said to keep to the right, so she rested her right hand on the rough-hewn wall and moved forward.

Jessica wished she dared to create a light, but she had no way of knowing what might be lurking in the dark, ready to report back to Anakaron. She was sure Rabblyn wouldn't have sealed her in if he didn't think it was safe, but she wasn't about to take any chances.

The tunnel was more or less straight, and she followed it for what seemed like a long time, but was probably only half an hour, before it forked. She took the right fork as she'd been instructed, and kept going. The tunnel split twice more and each time she took the right fork. Finally, she came to a dead end.

"What the hell?" she muttered, feeling around for another passage. This wasn't good, this wasn't good at all. She couldn't see anywhere to go.

Suddenly, she realized she was able to see. There was a faint outline in front of her, a ragged shape that was allowing a faint outline of light to shine through.

Running her fingers lightly along the stone, she traced the shape. She couldn't really tell what the shape was, but she could feel a difference in the rock inside, it was lighter somehow.

Wait, there! There was a raised piece just at the edge, like a catch or something. Jessica pressed it and the shape swung inwards, toward her. She held her breath, waiting for the sound of the footsteps from a patrol or an alarm or some other sound of discovery, but everything remained quiet.

Mentally crossing her fingers, she peered into the long hallway on the other side of the opening. After the darkness of the tunnel it seemed bright, but actually the torches lighting it were spaced pretty far apart. There was no one lurking about and from the staleness of the air she deduced it wasn't a well used passage.

Jessica stepped through and carefully sealed up the tunnel behind her. From this side it wasn't noticeable. She brushed her hand over the wall but couldn't feel it. This could be a problem if they were planning to leave by this route. She brushed her hand again, and this time she felt a slight indentation. Pressing it, she breathed a sigh of relief as it opened.

Of course, when she shut it the whole thing disappeared again. How was she ever going to find it again? The walls of the passage were smooth and unremarkable, and the hallway was so very long. She looked around the floor but there was nothing helpful there. Finally, she opened the secret passage again and felt around until she found a stone. She used it to mark the wall of the corridor, then left it on the floor under the nearest sconce.

Dusting her hands in satisfaction, Jessica looked both ways along the hallway. Rabblyn had told her to stay to the right in the tunnel, but he hadn't said anything about when she got to the hallway other that Howard's door was fifth on the left. So left or right?

In the end she went with her gut and started walking to the left. Unless her sense of direction was skewed, the outside of the mountain was on the right, making the rooms part of the interior wall not the exterior one. Now all she had to worry about was getting caught.

Jessica moved as quietly as she could down the long hallway, keeping alert for the slightest noise. Of course, she had no clue what she'd do if she actually ran into anyone, she'd been in such a hurry to leave she left her sword behind at the castle.

The hallway curved gently and she had no trouble counting the doors as she went. The fact that they were all on the left reinforced the idea that the right side was the mountain side.

She reached the fifth door without seeing another soul. It was almost too easy. Putting her ear to the door she listened but couldn't hear anything. There was no way of knowing if Howard was in there or not, nor what kind of shape he was in. There was only one way to find out.

Slowly and carefully she eased the door open. There was no cry of alarm so she cautiously peered inside.

As rooms went, this one was pretty spacious. It was well furnished too. She spotted Howard in one of the wing chairs near the fireplace. He was sound asleep, but looked to be unharmed.

It was just so good to see him. Jessica sniffed back a few tears, and then said in a loud voice, "Well I like this. Here I go risking life and limb to rescue you, and you're just nodding off in front of the fire without a care in the world."

He started awake and the look on his face was almost comical when he saw her. "Jessica?"

Springing to his feet, he wrapped his arms around her in a fierce hug.

"I should be angry to see you here, but I'm too happy." He held her at arm's length. "How did you get here? Where's everyone else?"

Avoiding his eyes, she said, "Long story, for now let's just get out of here."

"Wait," he said when she reached for the door. "What about the guards?"

"What guards?"

"There were two guards outside my door."

"Howard, I didn't see anyone, now let's go."

But Howard was frowning. "That doesn't make sense. Why would they just– "

"Let's just count our blessings and get moving," Jessica told him. She opened the door and looked around. "It's all clear."

Still worrying over the lack of guards, Howard followed close behind as Jessica led him back the way she'd come. With the floor being as clear as it was, it was easy to spot the rock she'd left under the sconce. He waited until the panel was closed behind them before speaking.

"Dwarves?"

"You should know, you sent him to help me. How did you get him to agree?"

"I didn't, exactly. I had an earth entity ask if they'd help – I wasn't actually sure they would."

"Well we owe them a debt of gratitude. Not only did a dwarf show me this place, but he led a dark elf patrol away."

"Speaking of dark," Howard said. "Do you think we could have a little light? I can't see my hand in front of my face."

"Let's move away from the panel first."

They felt their way several yards down the tunnel and then Jessica whispered an incantation. A small ball of light appeared, floating just in front of them.

"You've been practicing," Howard said.

"C'mon," Jessica said. "I'll feel better once we're out of this mountain."

She didn't understand the sense of urgency she was feeling, but she didn't question it either. It was pretty much a given something bad was going to happen, it was just a matter of when.

Telling Howard about how she was able to get away from the others, and about the Fae Road and how she was able to use it made the return journey seem to take less time. The light stopped in mid-air when they reached the end of the tunnel.

"Shit."

"What's the problem?" Howard asked.

"I don't know how to get us out of here."

"Well how did you get in?"

"Rabblyn, the dwarf, spat on his hand and touched the rock."

"Hmm." Howard thought about it for a moment. "Let me try."

"What, you're going to spit in your hand?"

"That's disgusting. No, dwarves are creatures of the earth and I have access to earth magic. Let me try."

Jessica stepped back to give him room. Howard laid his hand on the rock and concentrated on his elemental magic. While the rock didn't just simply shiver and dissolve as it had for Rabblyn it did crumble away.

It was bright enough outside there was no need of extra light. Jessica banished it with a snap of her fingers.

"Way to go Howie."

"Thanks. Now which way?"

They hurried down the path between rocks, stopping when they reached the forest.

"What's the matter?"

"I don't know which way to go," she admitted. "It was dark and we were in a hurry."

"I say let's just put the mountain behind us and hope for the best."

"I don't know, once we're under the canopy we won't be able to see the mountain. I don't want to end up going in circles."

Howard thought about it for a minute. "What about the Well? Are you able to sense it?"

"Good idea." Jessica closed her eyes to concentrate. "Yes, I– " She frowned.

"What is it?"

Opening her eyes, she said, "I can sense it, but there's something off about it."

"But you think you can open it like you did before?"

"Pretty sure."

"Then let's go. I'm getting the heebie-jeebies just standing out here."

There weren't really any other options so Jessica led the way through the woods. It was slow going, made slower by her having to stop to get a new sense of direction every so often. The trees began to thin slightly and they came across a circle of ash on the ground.

"Looks like someone was camping here," Howard said.

"Yes, it was an elf named Orrin."

"Orrin? What was he doing here?"

"He was a scout from the Darkwood enclave. The rest of his group were killed and he needed to find out what the dark elves were doing with the Wildwind elves. I hope he made it back," Jessica added.

They started walking again. After a short time they came to a clearing in the forest. It was perfectly round and in the center was the Well.

Howard took several steps towards it before realizing Jessica wasn't following him. "What's wrong?"

"Can't you sense it? There's something off about it."

Howard turned his attention back to the Well. Concentrating hard, he could feel it too, the darkness emanating from the Well.

"What is that?"

"Orrin called it the taint. Pretty apt description, it's like the Well is tainted with something evil."

"I think it's pretty obvious we're not going to be able to use it to connect to the Fae Road," Howard suggested. "What now?"

"Now you and your friend will return to my citadel," said a voice behind them. "You disappoint me, Howard. I thought we had an understanding."

"Sorry," Howard said. "I guess I should have left you a note telling you I changed my mind." He turned to face Anakaron. "I'm just not cut out for a life of evil."

"Take them," Anakaron ordered, and disappeared in a puff of smoke.

A dozen dark elves, bowstrings pulled taut, arrows nocked, surrounded them.

Jessica and Howard held up their hands in surrender.

"I should have known this was too easy," Howard said.

"We both should have, Howard."

Chapter Fifty-Nine

How soon can we leave?" Dominic asked.

He'd asked the same question several times already, and each time received the same answer – when the drug had worked its way out of their system.

They gathered again in the dining room where they'd awakened. All trace of last night's dessert had been removed and fresh food had been brought, but barely touched.

It had been decided that when the time came, Aracelia, Thackery, and Dominic would follow Jessica on the Fae Road. As Aracelia pointed out, the fewer that went, the easier the trip would be on her. While no one questioned Ellen and Kaelan's fighting prowess, they were lacking in magical skills. The same could be said for Sebastian. Paranithel had wanted to go, but Thackery persuaded him that he'd be needed here in case they failed. But nothing could dissuade Dominic from accompanying them.

"I wish there was some way we could see what was happening with them," Sebastian said.

"Aracelia," Ellen said, looking thoughtful. "We were able to hear what was going on with Jessica using the moonstone pendant as a link. If Howard's still wearing his half, couldn't you establish a link with that?"

Aracelia looked at her in surprise. "I'd forgotten that. Yes, I should be able to."

Closing her eyes, she chanted a quiet spell. Nothing happened. Frowning, she tried again.

"Maybe you're not doing the spell right," Ellen suggested when once again it failed to work.

Opening her eyes, Aracelia shot her a look. "It is a simple spell, and with the pendent being elven in nature, if anyone could connect with it, it should be me."

"What does this mean?" Sebastian asked. "Does this mean Howard's unconscious or... dead?"

"No, it means that I cannot reach the pendent at all. Something is blocking me. Someone bring me a mirror."

Thackery went to the door and yelled for one of the students to fetch a hand mirror. Being well acquainted with their master's temperament, the mirror appeared quickly.

Aracelia cleared a spot off the table and sat down. Placing the mirror in front of her, she passed her hand over it and muttered the incantation. There was no change to the mirror. She tried again and this time the surface of the mirror went dark.

Startled, she sat back. "It is the same that happened when I was speaking with Jessica at Wildwinds."

"Maybe it has something to do with the way the dark elves changed the barrier," Kaelan suggested.

"Does that mean the dark elves made a barrier around Anakaron's lair?" Ellen asked.

"I do not know."

"Is this going to be problem getting in to rescue Jessica?"

Dominic asked.

"I do not know." Aracelia passed her hand over the mirror again to break the spell.

"I am feeling myself again," Thackery said. "It's time to leave for the Well."

Though only three of them were taking the Fae Road, the whole group made the short journey to the Well, united in their worry and fear.

"If I knew an appropriate blessing..." Paranithel said.

"How about, 'good luck,'" Ellen said.

"Yes, we'll definitely need luck," Dominic muttered.

Aracelia stepped to the Well. "All right everyone," she said. "Be ready to move as soon as the road is open."

Paranithel had moved off to the side, staring at the Well. At one time he had made a study of the Wells and retained a special affinity to them. Something seemed a little off, but he couldn't put his finger on what. Aracelia started her spell and the "wrongness" grew. No one else appeared to notice because they were watching her.

"Stop, stop, stop!" he said, waving his hands in the air.

Her concentration broken, the spell collapsed and Aracelia rounded on Paranithel. "What did you do that for? Do you know how hard this spell is to set up?"

"Look at the Well," he said. "Use your mage sight."

Confused, she did as he asked. Her eyes widened. "What is that?"

"I don't know," he said. "But I do know this Well is not safe to use."

"No!" Thackery said. "We need to use this Well to get to Jessica."

"Look for yourself," Aracelia said. "It cannot even be used to replace our magical energy."

Thackery looked and saw the same darkness lacing the Well as they did. "Where is this coming from?"

"I would say it's coming from wherever Jessica went to," Aracelia said.

"What does this mean?" Dominic asked.

"It means that Jessica and Howard are on their own."

Chapter Sixty

As long as Howard and Jessica kept moving, the dark elves pretty much kept their distance, almost ignoring them.

"I'm sorry," Howard said quietly.

Jessica shot him a glance. "For what?"

"For everything. If I hadn't been so obsessed with magic, I would never have attempted that spell that sent you here and we wouldn't have ended up here, being led to our deaths."

"Wow, that's putting a lot on your shoulders," she said. "First of all, your spell just kind of exacerbated what was already going to happen. I mean, Thackery and Paranithel were already planning on bringing me here, you just ... helped."

"Well, yes, but– "

"And if I hadn't ended up in Ghren I might never have met Dominic, and I wouldn't have missed that for the world."

He glanced over at her. "It's the real thing with him, isn't it?"

"Yeah, I think so."

"I'm happy for you. I think you deserve someone like him in your life, even if it's only for a short time."

"Let me ask you something, Howard. Why did you use the magic Aracelia sent you to come here? Why didn't you use it to enhance a bunch of little spells, like she meant you to?"

"Because I needed to see for myself that you were all right.

And I thought maybe there might be some way I could help – that's what friends do."

"Exactly." She nodded. "And that's why I had to come rescue you. I knew I was taking a chance, but that's what friends do. Now, tell me about Anakaron."

Howard heaved a sigh. "There's not much to tell. He kind of reminds me of Sauron from Lord of the Rings – totally an evil wizard, but at the same time kind of suave and sophisticated."

"You're right, that's not much to go on. I mean, we already knew he was evil."

"He's got this creepy staff with a red crystal on top that he's pretty attached to. In fact, it reminds me of– "

He broke off what he was going to say as they entered the mountain through a set of enormous metal doors that clanged shut behind them.

"It reminds you of what?" Jessica said.

"No talking," the elf in charge told them. "You will be silent unless the dark lord wishes you to speak."

As they moved through what looked to be a natural entrance to the caves, Howard's thoughts stayed on what he'd been about to tell Jessica. Anakaron had appeared to be somewhat charming at first, but once he was near the staff he underwent a change of personality. Almost as if the staff had some kind of power over him.

It reminded him of a book series he'd read a long time ago. It was swords and sorcery cycle he'd been fond of, one involving an elf-like hero and a sword that had a taste for blood, literally. He couldn't remember the name of the book, but the sword had been almost like a parasite, driving the elf to the brink of madness. Almost the way Anakaron was mad....

The dark lord was sitting on his throne of bones when they were brought into his great hall. They were marched across the decorated floor and stood facing him with their backs to the altar.

"It seems I misjudged your intelligence," Anakaron said. "Did you really think you could leave without my noticing?"

Howard shrugged. "I figured it was worth a shot."

"You had help, of course. Won't you introduce me to your companion?"

Jessica stood with her head bowed, her hair half-hiding her face.

"She's just a friend, she's of no consequence."

"I'll be the judge of that. But you had other help as well." He snapped his fingers and a pair of dark elves dragged Rabblyn in between them. Jessica made an involuntary movement but Rabblyn gave a minute shake of his head.

"Perhaps I was wrong to dismiss your elemental powers as inconsequential, if you were able to persuade the mountain folk to aid you. My patrol found him lurking about."

"You've got me," Howard said. "Let the others go – they're no threat to you."

"I should have disposed of this vermin after they finished creating my cavern," Anakaron continued, as though Howard hadn't spoken. "It's a mistake that's easily remedied. But first I want to know where each and every tunnel you left behind is."

"I'll tell you nothing!" Rabblyn said defiantly.

Anakaron flicked his fingers and the elves holding him brought the dwarf closer. "I was hoping you'd say that."

His eyes reflected the glow from his staff as he rested his fingers on Rabbyn's head. The dwarf struggled in the dark elves' grip but they held him fast. Anakaron's staff glowed brighter. Both Jessica and Howard made a move to stop him, but dark elves held them back.

They were forced to watch in horror as the dwarf redoubled his struggles and began to shrivel. Rabblyn gave a single gasp before he became nothing more than a withered husk.

The glow in Anakaron's staff dimmed, as did his eyes. "There's not much magical energy to be had in a mere dwarf, and his life energy was hardly worth the trouble," he said. "But I was able to extract the information I needed."

He made a dismissive gesture and Jessica and Howard found themselves released. And in fact, the dark elves left the chamber as well.

"Aren't you afraid we'll attack you?" Howard asked.

Anakaron's lip curled. "I hardly think the pair of you will prove to be a match for me. But I will need to decide what to do with you."

The jewel on his staff pulsed slightly, as though it was talking to Anakaron. Howard was once again reminded of the parasitic sword. Anakaron frowned and focused on them again.

"How were you able to breach the barrier around my mountain," he demanded of Jessica. "There was no disturbance in its energy."

"I used the Fae Road."

"Impossible. You're no elf."

"No, but my grandmother is." Jessica raised her head and looked him straight in the eye.

"Impossible!"

"Oh, it's entirely possible," Jessica said with false bravado.

"But Howard is the son of Kiranthus and Farenalyssia. It is he who wears the moonstone amulet."

"Howard is wearing half the amulet. It came in two parts, mine was lost in the Darkwoods Realm."

Anakaron came down two steps, his attention focused on Jessica. "You have no more power than he, you cannot be their child."

"Get ready to run," Jessica whispered.

"No, I won't leave you alone."

Anakaron took another step towards them, his eyes beginning to glow red.

"Things aren't always as they seem," Jessica said, and removed the amulet Granny Warrick, the gypsy, had given her to hide her true power.

"Now!" she whispered fiercely to Howard, giving him a shove towards the exit.

The dark lord reeled backwards in shock. "So much power," he whispered. "Such raw, untrained power."

Howard took a few steps backwards towards the exit but Anakaron hardly noticed, his attention was focused on Jessica, obviously shaken by the revelation.

"This is … incredible."

Howard took another step towards the exit and this time Anakaron waved a hand in his direction freezing him in place.

"I feel there has been a great misunderstanding between us," Anakaron said smoothly, the jewel in his staff pulsing. "It would please me greatly if you would join me for dinner. Afterwards, if you still wish to leave, I shall be happy to provide you with supplies and mounts, as well as a guide."

"That's very generous of you," Jessica said cautiously, her eyes losing their focus.

"I do not know what your father has said of me, but I fear it can be nothing good, despite the fact we were at one time great friends. I would the chance to tell my side of the tale."

"It sounds reasonable enough," Jessica said to Howard. "Maybe we've judged him too harshly – it's only fair to hear his side of the story."

"I– I guess so," Howard stammered, completely mystified as to her change in attitude. He noticed the glassy look in her eyes and wonder about it. Was Anakaron controlling her somehow?

"Excellent!" Anakaron said, transforming into the perfect host. "While dinner is being prepared perhaps you would care to freshen up?"

"That's a great idea," Jessica said. "Thank you."

Anakaron rapped his staff on the floor and a pair of human servants hurried forward.

"Escort our guests to rooms so that they may refresh themselves."

The servants bowed and then turned to Jessica and Howard, indicating that they should follow them. Howard shot a glance towards Jessica, genuinely puzzled at her attitude. He kept expecting her to zap their escort so they could make a break for it, but she went into her assigned room without a word to him.

Howard was shown to a room closer to the central chamber, almost identical to the one he'd been using.

"A bath and a change of clothing will be brought to you," the servant told him, and left him to his own devices.

Howard waited a few heartbeats and then went to the door, opening it slightly. As he expected, there were dark elves posted as guards.

"Provide us with supplies and a guide my ass," he muttered as he eased the door shut again.

Unable to help himself, he began to pace. He couldn't understand what had gotten into Jessica. It was like she was under a spell or something.

"Of course!" he said out loud. "He's using magic to alter her thinking." Probably through the staff somehow.

Unconsciously he started playing with the moonstone pendant.

"Why didn't he try controlling me?" he wondered. "Maybe he figured I'd be easier to persuade. Or maybe ..."

He looked down at the pendent. "Maybe I had protection."

That had to be it. He'd never really thought about the pendent other than it being a link to Jessica. But it had originally been a gift from Aracelia to Farenalyssia. Why wouldn't she have meant it as a kind of protection for her daughter?

Maybe if Jessica was wearing the pendent it would break whatever hold Anakaron seemed to have over her. The only question was, how was he to get it to her?

Chapter Sixty-One

Howard hadn't thought things could get worse after waking to find himself in Anakaron's clutches, but he'd been wrong, so very wrong. He almost expected the blood mage to just zap him into oblivion for his deception and be done with it, and maybe he would have if it hadn't been for Jessica. Maybe the shock of it would be enough to break whatever spell he had her under.

Under other circumstances he might have enjoyed the suit of clothing he'd been given – black leather trousers (close fitting but not uncomfortably tight) with a white, baggy sleeved shirt made out of some silky material, with a black velvet jerkin worked with silver thread over top. He really wished Sebastian could see him in this outfit.

After a couple of hours left alone in a room similar to the one he'd been in before, a servant came to fetch him for dinner. He was led to a large room just off the chamber Anakaron used as his as his throne room-come-audience chamber. His nervousness eased as he spied another servant leading Jessica from the other direction.

She'd been given a new outfit too. The dress suited her well. It had a scoop neckline and clung to her arms and torso before flaring out into a floor-length skirt. The dark green was flattering on her and it looked to be made of the same material as his shirt. But where his shirt was plain, her dress was threaded through with intricate embroidery and subtle beadwork.

"Wow, you clean up good," she said, giving him an admiring look.

"You too," he said, trying to muster a grin, but it was half-hearted at best. "I never thought I see the day where you'd wear such a fancy dress without a gun to your head."

Frowning slightly, she looked down at herself and a momentary expression of confusion passed over her face. "I—well at least it's not a full court dress."

They were prevented from further conversation as the servants opened the doors for them. Though there was a fireplace big enough to roast a pig in and a long table set for three, Howard got the impression this room was not usually used as a dining room. There was nothing decorating the walls and the floor was the same stone as the rest of cavern. The three chairs at the table were, thankfully, upholstered.

Anakaron was waiting inside, standing at the head of the table.

"Please, be seated," he said, gesturing to the chairs on either side of his place at the table as though they were honored guests instead of his prisoners

"Might I say you make a resplendent couple," he continued. "And may I also add that you are as beautiful as your mother. I knew the green would suit you, just as red always suited her."

"You knew my mother?" Jessica asked, pausing in the act of sitting down.

"Of course. Your mother, father, and I went to the magical

collegium together, in Mythago."

"I have to say, you've aged much better than my father has," Jessica observed.

Howard was a little relieved that the comment about them being a couple slipped right by her. Maybe that was what was keeping him alive, Anakaron thought they were a couple. And it was likely magic keeping Anakaron young, magic stolen from others.

Anakaron merely smiled, nodding slightly to acknowledge the compliment. Taking his seat, he rang a bell to summon the servants with their dinner.

"Howard mentioned you come from a world without magic, both of you. That must have made it difficult for you."

"Not really," Jessica said, helping herself to the platters that were offered to her. "I had no idea I had any magic, so it wasn't something I missed. Howard's the one who was always fascinated by magic."

"Indeed." Anakaron's attention turned to Howard. "And if your world has no magic, pray how did you end up on this one?"

"It was a total fluke," Jessica said before Howard could form an answer. She waved her fork for emphasis. "Couldn't happen again in a million years."

"Well, not accidentally at any rate," Howard said, shooting a concerned glance her way. It was almost like she was drunk.

"Hmmm. We must discuss this further," Anakaron said. "But I think at another time."

While Jessica ate with a good appetite, Howard barely touched his food and Anakaron, he noted, ate not at all. He recalled the previous meal they shared and he didn't think the wizard had eaten anything then, either. Did he just not like to eat in front of other people, or did he get his nourishment from magical energy provided by his staff?

"I do not wish to be indelicate," Anakaron said to Jessica. "But how is it one of your power is so lacking in training?"

She frowned slightly as she thought about it. "I guess I just haven't had time. I've been pretty much on the move since I arrived in this world."

Her answer seemed a little evasive. Howard wondered if the spell Anakaron had her under was wearing off – he'd left the staff in the throne room.

"It would give me the greatest pleasure to instruct you," Anakaron offered.

Howard stiffened automatically at the way he said it.

"Really?"

"What about your father Jess?"

"I– " Jessica turned to look at Howard, plainly confused.

"You seem fatigued, Howard," Anakaron said, making a slight gesture with his hand. "Perhaps you need a rest."

Howard felt the slight brush of magic wash over him, but that was all. It seemed he was right, the moonstone pendant was protecting him. But he figured it was best to play along.

"I think you're right," he said, pretending to stifle a yawn. "If you'll excuse me, I think I'll go lie down."

"If you insist," Anakaron murmured.

"Are you all right?" Jessica asked, confusion turning to concern. "Do you want me to come with you?"

"I'm sure that's not necessary," Anakaron said, making a different gesture with his fingers.

"I'm fine," Howard told her. "I'll catch up with you later."

Quickly, he left the room before Anakaron could summon a

guard to escort him.

He hated leaving Jessica alone with Anakaron but it couldn't be helped. However, he found it interesting that Anakaron seemed unaware of the moonstone's protective properties. Now all he had to do was figure out how to get the moonstone to Jessica before it was too late.

Jessica was feeling a little confused as she followed Anakaron to the throne room. On the one hand it would be nice to finally have some proper training, but on the other hand she couldn't help feeling something was off. What was she doing here?

Without being conscious of it, her steps slowed so that Anakaron reached his throne while she was still only partway across the room. She looked at the symbols on the floor beneath her feet, there was something about them that make her feel uneasy. Anakaron was speaking to her, but she wasn't really paying attention, she was too busy trying to understand what was happening to her.

"Once your training has been completed there will be none who can stand before us. You will be my queen and together we will rule this world."

That caught her attention. Someone else once made her the offer to make her a queen... Jessica shook her head, trying to clear the cobwebs away. This was wrong. This was all so very wrong. Why was she even listening to him?

"I had not thought to share my throne with anyone, but your power is too pure to be wasted," Anakaron was saying. "Perhaps, in time, your power might even surpass my own."

"No," she said, the answer slipping out without her even

thinking about it. Something was influencing her thoughts – awareness was helping her fight it.

"Just think of it– "

"No," she said, a little stronger. The cloud her mind had been wrapped in began to dissipate. Her awareness of 'self' began to return.

Anakaron had begun to mount the steps to his throne but stopped and turned, a frown on his face.

"I do not understand. This is what you want," he said.

"No, it's not." She backed away a step. "I don't want to be like you. I could never be like you."

"How are we so different?" he asked, taking a step towards her. "We are both capable of wielding great magics."

"Yes, but I draw on the Wells for my source," she said, backing away another step, "while you steal yours from living creatures."

His eyes narrowed a fraction and Jessica was suddenly questioning herself again. Perhaps Anakaron was right, it wasn't as though he was outright killing for power, he was just taking the magical essence from–

"Stop that!" She waved a hand in front of her face, drawing a sigil in the air between them. It was a glyph of protection she'd learned from one of her books. The amazing thing was, it appeared to work.

Anakaron halted in his tracks, all pretense of friendliness gone. "I would rather have you as an ally, willingly. But make no mistake, in the end I will have you, and your power as well. The choice is yours."

"There's another choice," she said, refusing to back up any further. "How about I just kick your ass?"

Drawing on the knowledge of combative magic she'd learned

from her books, she let loose with a bolt of lightning that knocked him hard enough that he staggered back a step. There was a blaze of red as light from the staff resting against the throne flared, but before Anakaron could grab the staff she hit him again, and again.

Each bolt sent him back a step until he was close enough to the staff to grasp it. The stone flared again as he swung it around to point it at her.

Jessica dove out of the way as he flung a bolt of pure, red energy at her.

"You cannot hope to stand against me," he said. "You are raw and untrained."

Another bolt followed his words and Jessica rolled so that she was behind a pillar. Her own bolts were not as effective and she wracked her brain for something else she could use.

Another bolt took a chunk out of the pillar she was using for cover. She darted towards another one, muttering a spell. All at once there were five Jessicas, each going in a different direction.

"Child's play!" Anakaron shouted, and rapped his staff on the ground. The illusions vanished, but Jessica was safely behind a different pillar.

"Crap," she muttered. Maybe she should go with something she was a little more familiar with.

Stepping out from behind her pillar, she held both hands out in front of her as though in supplication. Anakaron paused just long enough for her to hit him with a stream of fire, so hot it was almost white. Unfortunately, she wasn't able to keep up the intensity long enough to do him any real damage and he was able to quench it again. She ducked back behind her pillar, breathing heavily.

"Even someone with your power cannot keep this up indefinitely. And there is no Well from which to draw more."

Maybe not, but Jessica didn't waste her breath replying to him. Another blast of red energy shook the pillar at her back. This was not good, this was not good at all. There was only one thing she had left to try and it was a spell she memorized, but hoped she wouldn't have to use. Basically, it was a suicide spell, but at least she'd have the satisfaction of taking him with her.

Chapter Sixty-Two

Howard paced in his room, almost frantic with worry. He'd hadn't closed his door all the way, but kept watch instead, and when Anakaron and Jessica went to the throne room he tried to follow but the heavy doors closed behind them. If there was another way in, then he couldn't find it.

If Anakaron convinced Jessica to join him, whether she was under a spell or not, they were all screwed. He had to get the moonstone to her, even if he died trying. Filled with resolve he pushed the table and chairs to the side and sat down cross legged in front of the fireplace.

"Okay, here goes nothing," he muttered, and closed his eyes.

At first he focused on his breathing, in and out, deep and slow. When he felt centered, he looked inside himself for that beautiful colored strand that was his magic.

The elemental magics were easy to find, they were twined around each other, brighter than all the rest. It was so amazing that he'd had that inside all these years and never known it.

Basking in the feel of the magic, he sent out a call – fire, water, wind, and earth – humbly asking for a boon. Howard had no idea how long he sat like that, but a breeze caressing his face brought him back to himself. Then he felt the warmth of a fire and his eyes snapped open.

There was a fire in the fireplace, where none had been before. A small, grey, moisture-laden cloud hovered to the right while a wind imp hovered on the left. Between Howard and the fire was an earth entity.

Howard decided he'd be awed later, for the moment he cut right to the chase. "Thank you for answering."

A face appeared in the fireplace. "The time foretold has come." It hissed and crackled as it spoke.

"I have to get into the throne room to give this to Jessica," he said, lifting the moonstone pendent up with one hand.

The wind imp darted towards the pendent. "It is too heavy for me to carry," she said in his head.

The fire hissed and snapped while the cloud rumbled for all the world like thunder. The imp darted over to them, flashing brightly.

"I am of no use," whispered the earth entity. "But wind blows a fire hot; rain cools quickly and metal cracks; the door will open." It sank between the cracks in the stone floor until it was gone.

"What does that even– "

Before Howard could finish his sentence, the other three were gone. Scrambling to his feet, he hurried out of the room and straight to the throne room. By the time he reached it, the locking mechanism was blackened. He tried the door and it opened easily.

Howard sidled into the room, keeping to the shadows. To his astonishment, it looked like his help wasn't needed after all – Jessica broke Anakaron's spell all on her own. But it also looked like she was in serious trouble.

Jessica was running out of options. Four out of the six stone pillars were cracked and crumbling, and she had used most of spells she'd memorized.

"You are weakening, I can feel it," Anakaron said. "Give up now and I will let you live."

"As a slave to you and your dark power? I don't think so." She hurled another magical bolt at him, but it barely fizzled against him.

"Jessica, look out!" Howard yelled as Anakaron's return energy bolt ricocheted off the wall and hit the pillar right above her head.

"Howard? Get out of here. You need to warn the others."

"Oh, I think not," Anakaron said, and aimed his next bolt at Howard.

It struck him right in the chest and he flew backwards into the wall.

The staff, he told her, mind to mind, just before he passed out. *His power's in his staff.*

Of course! Why hadn't she realized it? Jessica limped to the next pillar, ducking behind it just as Anakaron fired another energy bolt her way. Taking a deep breath, she readied her final spell.

"By the shade of Errol Flynn!" she yelled, using the battle cry she'd once used in Ghren. Stepping from behind the pillar, she aimed a series of magical darts at Anakaron's feet. And when he raised the staff to send another bolt her way, she targeted the glowing jewel that topped it.

"No!" Anakaron screamed. The jewel fractured, then burst apart into a thousand pieces.

He crumpled to the ground as a vortex opened up, the shards

from the crystal spinning in an ever-widening whirlwind. The shards themselves turned to dust as the wind grew and then streamed away. The silence left in the wind's wake was deafening.

Jessica stared around herself, not quite able to believe it was over. Slowly she made her way over to the rapidly aging man lying on the steps to the throne. All the years he'd stolen had been taken away from him again.

Jessica stared down at him dispassionately. Somehow he didn't seem nearly as frightening or powerful now. Still, she took an involuntary step backwards when his eyes opened.

"I beg a boon of thee," he whispered.

"A boon?"

Slowly, stiffly, he reached into his robe and pulled out a small object in a velvet pouch.

"I ask that you give this to thy father, in memory of the woman we both once loved."

Cautiously, wary of it being a trick, Jessica reached down to take it from him.

"What– "

But it was too late. Anakaron was dead. And with his last breath the room around them began to tremble. Whether it was the damage done to the pillars, or Anakaron's magic keeping the roof up, it didn't really matter. The roof was coming down now.

Jessica clutched the small pouch in her hand and hurried to where Howard was just stirring near the doorway.

She helped him up and started dragging him with her through the door.

"Jessica? What's going on?"

"Talk later, escape collapsing mountain now," she said,

dragging him forward.

The floor pitched beneath their feet as they careened their way out of the throne room and down the hallway. Fortunately, the route the dark elf guards had used taking them inside was fairly straightforward and they were able to retrace their steps. The rumbling grew louder and there was a crashing behind them. They were pelted by loose rock and barely made it outside before the whole tunnel collapsed behind them.

They didn't stop, just kept going until they were several yards further along the path. Only when it appeared the cave-in had stopped and the rest of the area was stable did they pause to look back the way they'd come. There was a great cloud of dust settling behind them, but all was quiet.

Jessica and Howard looked at each other. "Did you– did we– are we– "

Jessica grinned at the stunned look on Howard's face. "Holy Saint Christopher," she said. "We did it. We defeated the dark lord."

They laughed and hugged each other then laughed some more.

"You mean you did it. All I did was get myself kidnapped."

"Seriously Howard, I couldn't have done it without your help. If you hadn't told me to go for his staff he would have cheerfully sucked us both dry and then laid waste to the world."

Howard opened his mouth to argue and then shut it again. Instead, he looked back the way they'd come.

"How did you know about the staff, anyway?"

He looked a little sheepish as he admitted. "Well, there was this series of swords and sorcery books I once read, about an elf who wielded this sword that was kind of like a parasite.

Anakaron always seemed like a different person when he was holding the staff. And there were all those stories about wizards imbuing inanimate objects with their power." He shrugged. "I just put two and two together."

"You always were a math whiz," she said with a grin, nudging him with her shoulder.

They sat there, side by side, for a few moments longer, just enjoying being alive. Then Howard turned to her.

"So now what?"

"Now what, what?"

"What do we do now?"

"Oh." She slid down off the rock. "I guess we go back to the others and face the music. Or at least I'll have to face the music."

He slid down as well. "What do you mean, face the music? You saved the world."

They started to walk down the trail that led to the Well.

"Yeah, well, I kind of had to sneak away to get here."

"Jessica, what did you do?"

Howard was frowning when she finished her story. "I can't believe you did that."

"I can't believe they already haven't come after me," she admitted. "The drug should only have lasted a couple of hours after they woke up. What is it?"

Howard was looking around uneasily.

"I'm a little surprised we haven't run into any dark elves," he said. "They're supposed to guard this place, aren't they?"

"You're right," Jessica agreed. "Maybe they're not comfortable in the daylight – you know, being dark elves and all."

Howard glanced up at the sky. "All the more reason to get out of here as quickly as possible, the sun's starting to set."

Fortunately, the path they'd taken when they'd been returned to the mountain by the dark elves was more straightforward than the path the dwarf had taken Jessica on. It only took another hour or so before they reached the clearing where the Well was.

"I fear you are too late, my friends," a familiar voice told them. Orrin stepped into the clearing. His eyes widened as he spotted Jessica.

"What is it?"

"You– your power. I have never seen the like."

"Oh, crap." She turned to Howard. "I left the protection amulet behind."

"You can see her power?" Howard asked.

"It is like a beacon."

"I'm thinking that's probably not a good thing," Jessica said.

"No it is not," Orrin said gravely. "There are many who would covet such power. Even within the elven realms you would have to take care."

"I wonder why it's so apparent now when it wasn't before? I don't mean before I started using the protection amulet, I mean when I first got to this world. No one seemed to notice it when I was in Ghren."

"Maybe because you weren't using it before," Howard suggested.

"Aye," Orrin agreed. "The more magic is used, the more it grows."

"Well that's just great," Jessica muttered. Changing the subject, she asked, "What did you mean we're too late?"

"If you thought to use the Fae Road, it is too late. Look to the Well."

Jessica looked towards the Well. She didn't need her magical sight to see the black miasma overlaying the magical energy.

"Holy Saint Christopher, what is that?"

"The taint," Orrin said. "Even now it spreads to all other Wells."

"What's it going to do to the magic of this world?"

He looked at Howard soberly. "It warps the magic, whether light or dark. Without a clean source of magic to draw from, in time, all magical beings will cease to be."

"How can we stop this?" Jessica asked, mesmerized by the roiling darkness overlaying the Well.

Orrin shrugged. "I do not know. It was said when Anakaron first came to power the Well at Mythago was tainted. It had not progressed to the point where it was affecting the Fae Roads, but it still took an entire blessing of unicorns to cleanse it."

"It's true about unicorns?" Howard perked up with interest. "They're able to cleanse water with their horns?"

"Aye, although in this case it was cleansing the magic. And two of them died in the process."

"A cleansing..." Jessica mused. "Do you mean like the cleansing I did on you?" she asked Orrin.

He looked a little uncomfortable. "In a sense, it would be much the same thing. But even one of your great power could not hope to attempt such a thing."

"Jessica," Howard said, a warning note in his voice. "Don't even think about it. You need to wait until the others get here."

"It's going to be way too late by then," she said. "Don't forget, healing is my strongest magic."

"Jessica..."

"Don't worry, Howard. I've got this. If I could regenerate

Dominic's hands, I should be able to clear some black gunk from the Well."

She stepped towards the Well, reaching out with her healing magic.

Orrin hadn't exaggerated. The darkness overlying the Well was strong, and spreading along the Fae roads. But she knew if it wasn't stopped now, it would be too late for everyone.

"Jessica, you almost died healing Dominic."

She ignored him and stepped into the Well.

The wrongness of it stole her breath away. When she was able to breathe again the air burned her lungs. The taint filled her up, burning like acid, eroding her sense of self. But like a beacon, the green of her healing magic was before her. She grabbed onto it desperately, fighting the blackness that was like a sticky web being absorbed into her skin.

Jessica took a breath of clean air, then another. The taint had become a living thing and fought her. Time stood still as she used the green of her healing to burn away the black of the taint. She couldn't stop, couldn't pause, for every time she did the taint redoubled its efforts.

The healing magic faltered and the taint surged forward. Just as she had during Dominic's healing, Jessica began to pull magic from other sources – the earth, the trees, and most of all herself. Slowly the green healing magic began to overwhelm the black of the taint.

It was not enough to cleanse the Well, she followed the lines of the Fae roads. She swayed where she stood, mouth open in a soundless scream. Still, she chased down every drop of the taint until it was burned away by her healing. The darkness of oblivion beckoned and Jessica fell into it head first.

Chapter Sixty-Three

Howard took an involuntary step towards the Well but Orrin put a hand on his arm to hold him back.

"We cannot interfere."

"But we can't just– she doesn't know what she's doing."

"Perhaps not, but to interfere is too dangerous, not just for us but for her as well."

In his heart Howard knew that, but that didn't mean he had to like it.

"So what can we do?"

"We wait," the elf told him.

"I hate waiting," Howard muttered.

A black cloud rose up from the Well, enveloping Jessica from head to toe, obscuring her to their view. It billowed and roiled like the smoke from a tire fire. Howard would have expected it to give off a stench like burning rubber, but there was no smell, save for the earth and leaves of the surrounding forest.

Afterwards, he couldn't have said how long they stood there, helpless. It might have been hours, it might have been minutes.

"Am I crazy, or is the cloud thinning out?" Howard asked.

"I believe you are correct," Orrin said. "I would not have believed it possible."

The dark, oily smoke thinned enough that they could see a

figure standing at its heart, glowing with a faint green aura.

The smoke became more like a heavy fog, but the green glow in its center was beginning to dim.

"Her energy is almost depleted," Orrin said.

"Is she going to make it?"

"I do not know." The elf shook his head.

Only then were they aware of the creatures who had been steadily drawing closer to the clearing – dwarves and nymphs, water hags and trolls, and countless others Howard could not put a name to.

"Help her," Howard said. "Please."

There was not even a murmur from the creatures surrounding them, but several stepped forward to ring the Well. Though he did not have the sight to see it, Howard could feel the magical energy streaming from the creatures into the figure standing at the center of the Well.

There was a burst of green energy, flecked with gold. A white light flared up from the heart of the Well, burning away the last of the darkness.

When he managed to blink away the after burn, Howard stared into the Well. It took a moment to register what he was seeing, or rather what he wasn't seeing.

"She did it," Orrin said in a voice full of wonder. "She cleansed the Well."

"So where is she?" Howard asked.

"What?" The elf peered at the Well.

"Where did Jessica go?"

The other creatures had already left the clearing, but the water hag lingered. "Ssshehass gone where you cannot follow," she told him, her voice a sibilant whisper.

"What do you mean? Where has she gone?"

"Sssheisss in the ssspace between the worldssss."

"Well how do we get her back?" Howard asked frantically. He made a grab for the water hag's arm as she turned to leave but missed.

"You cannot," she told him. "Ssshe must find the way hersssself."

Howard stared at the empty space in the Well. This wasn't how it was supposed to end.

Jessica hurt. Every square inch of her from her hair to her toes and everything inside of her hurt. She'd have given anything to make the hurt go away, but she had nothing left.

There was a cool touch on her brow and suddenly the pain was gone. Her eyes blinked open and she found she was able to sit up. She blinked again – she knew this place, she'd been here before. The grass beneath her was lush and green. Butterflies flitted from flower to flower in the vast meadow. The sky was a haze of blue above her and a perfume laden breeze caressed her cheeks.

There was movement beside her and she turned, blinking again at the woman standing there. "Mother?"

"How do you feel?" Farenalyssia asked, helping her to her feet.

Jessica took stock of how she was feeling. "Empty," she said with a frown. "I feel totally empty."

Her mother nodded. "You spent every drop of your energy – magical and otherwise – to cleanse the Wells and the Fae Roads that connected them."

Jessica thought about that for a moment. She couldn't

understand why it didn't bother her more than it did.

"Did it work?" she asked finally.

The brilliant smile on her mother's face should have told her everything she needed to know, but Jessica needed to hear the words as well. Her mother, of course, understood this.

"Yes. You cleansed the source Well of the darkness and the cleansing followed the path to the others. The magic of the land is safe once more."

"I can't tell you how relieved I am to hear that," Jessica said. "For a minute there, while the taint was fighting my healing, I didn't think I was going to be able to finish before the magic ran out."

"Oh, but it did run out," Farena told her, taking her hand. "When I said you spent every drop of your energy, I did not lie."

"I don't understand."

"You would have failed had not magic been given freely to you by the creatures from whom Anakaron would have stolen it from. Creatures of both the dark and the light came to thy aid."

"Both dark and light?" Jessica asked. They began to walk through the meadow. "The light I can understand, but wouldn't the dark benefit from the magic of the Wells turning dark?"

Farena shook her head. "Not so. The taint was just that, a taint. A stain upon all magic, warping it whether it be light or dark."

"Well, I guess it was worth it then," Jessica said. At least she thought it was. The world was safe, it just sucked she wasn't going to be around to enjoy it.

"There's something I don't understand," she said. "If the magical creatures banding together are what helped me in the end, why didn't they band together in the first place to stop

Anakaron before it got so bad?"

Farena shook her head. "It is not in their nature for creatures of the light and dark to come together in harmony. Each would always feel their way is superior."

"Oh." Jessica thought that over a moment before asking, "So what happens now?"

"That is entirely up to you," her mother said with a smile.

"I don't understand," Jessica said. "Dead is dead, isn't it? Am I just going to hang around here with you for the rest of eternity?"

"Is that what you'd like?" Farena asked as they continued walking.

"No offense, as much as I'd like to get to know you better this place is just so...quiet I'd go stir crazy within a week." She frowned. "But I guess it beats moving on."

"Moving on?"

"You know, into the afterlife."

"Is that what you wish?"

"Well no. Not really."

They finished crossing the meadow and entered a glade. There were flowers growing in a riotous profusion of color beside a small pond. A weeping willow stood near the bank and a stone bench rested beside it, facing the water. Farena led Jessica over to it and they sat down.

"You remember this is the space between the worlds, my daughter, where everything is possible?"

Jessica nodded.

"Then you also know I have the power to send you back. Your life need not end here."

Jessica stared at her wordlessly.

"Tell me what is in your heart. If you could have a life of your choosing, what would it be?"

"Honestly? If I had the choice, I'd get one of those wagons like the ones the gypsies have and travel around with Dominic for the rest of our lives. Or at least until we decided it was time to settle down."

"And what of your magic?"

Here Jessica hesitated. "If it wasn't for magic I wouldn't be here, would I? And for the second time at that."

"It is a part of who you are."

"It just seems to be more trouble than it's worth."

"In the right hands, such powerful magic can do wondrous things."

"And in the wrong hands, it can do incredible evil," Jessica said, thinking of Anakaron.

She got up and walked over to the edge of the pond, staring into the water. Farena knew this was something her daughter needed to work out for herself and kept silent. Finally, Jessica turned back to her.

"Can you take the magic from me?"

Farena nodded. "Not all of it, it is too much a part of you for that, but enough that you would no longer have the ability to become a Master Sorcerer."

"Okay then," Jessica said. "You asked what I wished, so here it is. I wish for you to take as much of the magic from me as you can, and then send me back so I can live out my life with Dominic, if he still wants me."

"And where would you like the rest of your magic to go?"

"What do you mean?"

"The magic cannot be just loosed upon the world, it needs a vessel to contain it."

"A vessel?" Jessica asked. "Any kind of vessel?"

"A living one would be best, but yes, it can be contained within any vessel."

"What about a bunch of vessels?" she asked, thinking about the elves and other magical creatures Anakaron had drained, but kept alive so that he could drain them again once their magic was replenished naturally.

A smile broke out over her mother's face. "What did you have in mind?"

Chapter Sixty-Four

Howard was still trying to process what the water hag told him when he realized he and Orrin were alone in the clearing.

"What did she mean, Jessica is in the space between the worlds?"

"I do not know," Orrin answered.

"But she's alive, isn't she?"

"I do not know."

"Well what do you know?" Howard snapped.

"At this moment I feel that I know very little of anything."

Howard heaved a sigh and then walked around the perimeter of the Well. He didn't know what he was looking for, but he couldn't take just standing around doing nothing.

"So what do we do now?" he asked. "Just wait for Jessica to reappear? How do we know she's not just going to reappear someplace else?"

"I do– "

"– not know. Yeah, I get that."

Howard ran a hand through his hair in frustration. Maybe he should try a different tact with Orrin.

As he opened his mouth to say so, there was a shimmer within the Well. His mouth remained open as three figures coalesced inside the shimmer.

Orrin went down on one knee. "My Lady," he said.

"There is no need for formality, Orrin," she told him.

"Where's Jessica?" Dominic demanded.

Orrin rose to his feet and he and Howard looked at each other.

"She– she– disappeared," Howard said reluctantly.

"What do you mean, she disappeared?" Thackery, the third of the trio, asked.

"After she finished cleansing the Well, she just kind of ... vanished. One of the fairytale creatures– "

"A water hag," Orrin supplied.

"Right. There was this water hag who said she was some place called the space between the worlds."

There was a dead silence from the three travelers.

"Perhaps," Aracelia suggested, "We should make ourselves comfortable and you can start your tale from the beginning."

Thackery and Dominic made as if to protest, but she leveled a stare at them and they followed to the edge of the clearing where Orrin had made his camp, still within sight of the Well.

As the sun was beginning to lower in the sky, she sent Orrin off to fetch wood for a fire. A fallen log provided seating for herself and Thackery, while Dominic chose to pace back and forth.

"What is the space between the worlds?" Howard asked.

"Exactly as it sounds. It is a place between this world and the next," Aracelia told him.

"So kind of like limbo."

"She went to this place once before," Dominic said suddenly. "When she healed my hands, Granny Warrick said she had become lost on the Fae road and ended up in the space between the worlds. But it was only her spirit that was lost, she did not physically go there."

"Yes, that is usually what happens."

"Then what does it mean that her body is not here?" Thackery asked.

"I do not know," Aracelia admitted.

By the time the fire was built and they were seated around it, it was fully dark. Orrin began, telling of his experience with the dark elves, of trying to return to the elven realms, and meeting Jessica. Howard took up the thread of the tale, giving an abbreviated version of being taken by the harpies and then held prisoner by Anakaron, going into more detail over the arrival of Jessica and their attempt at escape. When he was finished he honestly couldn't tell whether his listeners were proud or appalled at everything Jessica had done.

"I find it astonishing that such disparate beings would work together to aid her in the cleansing of the Well," Thackery mused.

"I don't," Aracelia and Dominic said together. They looked at each other and Dominic gave a weak grin.

"Jessica has an uncanny ability of finding friends and allies wherever she ends up."

"And you do not realize the full extent of the pall Anakaron had cast over the land," Aracelia added.

"Anyway, Anakaron is gone – even if he'd been alive he'd be dead now, buried under his mountain. And the Wells have been cleansed of their taint. So anyone have any ideas on how to get Jessica back?" Howard asked.

"It is up to her," Aracelia told him. "There is nothing we can do but wait."

When it became apparent Orrin had nothing to contribute, he begged leave to return to the Darkwood Realm. Aracelia acquiesced, and gave him a message for the council. The rest of them settled in to await Jessica's return.

None of them slept easily that night but in the morning their vigil was rewarded by a glow from the Well.

"What is it?" Howard asked.

"I believe the Fae Road is being opened," Aracelia said, "But from where I do not know."

A form coalesced inside the glow, lying prone on the ground.

"Jessica!" The shout came from Dominic who beat the others to the Well. He scooped her up in his arms and held her close. "She's alive," he said, as if they doubted.

Aracelia laid a palm on Jessica's forehead and frowned. "Alive, but weak. I suggest we return to the southlands where we can care for her properly."

"Is it safe to take her back onto the Fae Road so soon?" Thackery asked with a frown.

"Safer than trying to care for her here," she said.

Dominic, still cradling Jessica in his arms, stepped aside so that Aracelia could work her spell. He didn't care where they were, he wasn't leaving Jessica alone ever again.

Jessica felt the familiar sensation of being awake, but kept her eyes closed and kept very still. She had only a vague recollection of talking with her mother again and wasn't sure just exactly where she was now. Furthermore, she wasn't in a rush to find out.

It was soft, whatever she was reclining on. She might be in a bed, but then again, the grass in the space between the worlds was super soft too. So were clouds, at least they looked soft.

It was warm, but she didn't think she was in the sun. And there didn't appear to be a breeze of any kind so she probably wasn't outdoors either.

A gentle snore came from somewhere on her left. She knew that snore – a smile spread across her face and she opened her eyes.

There he was, Dominic, slouched down in a chair beside her bed, sound asleep. He was going to have a terrible crick in his neck when he woke up. She was, in fact, on the verge of waking him when some inner sense had him opening his eyes.

"I do not relish the thought of spending the rest of my days waiting for you to awaken from a magic induced slumber," he said.

"This is only the third time," she protested.

"Even once is too many. My poor heart cannot take the strain."

"Your heart is as strong as an *estrada's*," she said with a grin, sitting up properly in bed.

He straightened in his chair, winced, and then came over and sat on the edge of the bed.

"Seriously Jess, you need to let your father train you properly so this kind of thing doesn't keep happening."

"You mean me fighting an evil wizard and saving the world?"

He scowled down at her. "You know what I mean."

"I do, and I'm sorry," she said.

Leaning over, he hugged her to him and then kissed her. "I'm glad you're all right," he said.

"Me too," she said as he released her again.

"But we need to have a serious talk about your penchant for running headlong into danger by yourself."

"I've got a better idea," she said, running her hand up his arm. "Why don't I give up my magic and we can travel around in a wagon like we did with the gypsies?"

Dominic pulled back to stare down at her. "I could not ask you to do that."

"You wouldn't be, I'd be doing it on my own. It makes sense, when you think about it. No more magic means no more danger."

"Would you not miss it, being so powerful?"

"You know how much I've struggled with it – it just seems to be more trouble than it's worth."

"I think," he said slowly, "If that is what you wish, then it matters not whether you have magic or not. It is you I love, not your power."

"Good answer," she said, grinning at him. "Because I've already gotten rid of it."

She went on to tell him about her time in the space between worlds and what her mother had offered her.

"And I'm not totally powerless," she said. "I haven't turned into a complete muggle, I can still light fires and heal people, but there's no danger of me trying to light a candle and setting a whole forest on fire."

"What's a muggle?" he asked,

And Jessica gave a laugh of sheer joy.

Chapter Sixty-Five

Later, much later, it was time to say goodbye. Aracelia had already gone, saying she hated goodbyes and saw no reason to prolong things. But first she gifted Howard, Ellen, and Jessica with elven scrying mirrors. Because it was elven magic it was self perpetuating, even in the mundane realm.

"Cool," Ellen said. "It's like an interdimensional cell phone." And then, of course had to explain what a cell phone was.

With the mirror, there was no need for Howard to stay in the magical realm for training in his elemental magic – he could do it remotely. As much as he enjoyed the magical realm, he missed home. And he couldn't wait to show Sebastian his world. So it was that he found himself standing with Sebastian, and Ellen and Kaelan, as Thackery opened the portal between worlds.

"Is this thing going to knock us unconscious?" Ellen asked. She had this vision of them ending up in a big passed out pile on the other side.

"The other time was like being swept into a vortex," he told her. "This will be more like stepping through a door. You should feel nothing but a temporary sense of displacement."

"I'm going to miss you," Jessica said, eyes pricking with tears as they hugged.

"Me too," Ellen said, sniffling. "But we can still talk with our mirrors. And how weird is that?"

Jessica laughed. "And any time you want to visit, just let me know and I'll arrange things with Thackery or Aracelia." She gave Ellen another hug and turned to Kaelan. "You're going to be blown away by the art over there," she said, hugging him next.

"It is very windy there?" he asked, puzzled. She just shook her head with a short laugh and moved on to Sebastian.

"I wish I could be there to see your face when you're introduced to rock 'n roll music," she told him. "And the symphony."

"I have a present for you," he said. He took a sack from a grinning Howard and handed it to her.

"What in the world?" She looked from one to the other, puzzled.

"Open it," Howard urged.

Shrugging, she did so. And began to laugh as she pulled out a pair of thigh high boots, identical to the ones she'd been wearing when she first appeared in Ghren.

"They're perfect, thank you," she told Sebastian, hugging him to her again. "Make sure he stays out of trouble, will you?" she whispered in his ear, nodding towards Howard.

"You can count on me, milady."

Finally, Jessica turned to Howard. "Oh, Howard. I don't know what I would have done without you."

"So you've finally forgiven me for sending you here in the first place?"

"You sent me on the biggest adventure of my life," she said, hugging him. "And I wouldn't have missed it for the world," she whispered in his ear.

Standing back, she was glad to see she wasn't the only one with damp eyes.

"Okay, enough of this," she said. "It's not like we're never going to see each other again. Don't forget, Dominic and I are coming for Christmas. So Howard, you'd better master that elemental magic of yours to make sure there's lots of snow."

"You got it, Jess," he said with a grin.

She stepped back and Thackery cast the spell that opened the portal. One by one her friends stepped through, and the portal shut behind them.

"Well, I guess that's that," Jessica said briskly to cover the fact her heart was breaking. She really was going to miss them all. A part of her would love to be there to see what Sebastian and Kaelan made of the mundane world, but she really needed to figure out her place in this one first.

"I don't know about anyone else," Dominic said, slipping his arm around her waist and turning her from the arch the portal had appeared in. "But I could use a drink."

"I think we all could," Thackery agreed. "But first, I have something for you in the courtyard."

He turned to lead the way before they could question him. They looked at each other and Dominic gave a shrug, but they followed behind without a word.

"Oh! It's beautiful!" Jessica exclaimed when Thackery opened the door to the courtyard. It was a brand new, beautifully carved, wagon such as the gypsies used in their caravans. It was a little larger than the one that had been burned by King Ewan's guardsmen, but it was painted bright yellow with red wheels.

"If you must travel about the land like a pair of vagabonds, you can at least do it in style," he said gruffly, his speech ending in an "oof" as Jessica hugged him.

"There is a pair of horses waiting in the stable to pull it," Paranithel added, coming around the side of the wagon where he'd been seeing to its supplies.

"I don't know what to say," Jessica said, hugging him as well.

"I do," Dominic said, grinning. "Thank you. I know how hard these wagons are to come by."

"It's fully supplied," Paran said when Jessica released him. "So you can start your travels whenever you wish."

"About that," Jessica said, darting a quick glance towards Dominic. He nodded and she went on. "How would you feel about us sticking around for a while, maybe getting to know you better?"

Thackery looked stunned. "I'd like that very much."

"Good." Jessica tucked her hand in his arm and led him back inside. "Now how about that drink?"

"Anything you wish, my dear."

"Anything?" she asked with a wicked smile. "Then how about changing your name back to Kiranthus?"

"My name?"

"Thackery just doesn't have the same ring as Kiranthus. And Kiranthus is who Farenalyssia fell in love with."

"Consider it done, my dear."

About the Author

Residing in Cobourg, Ontario, Carol has always had a love of reading and writing. She grew up reading Edgar Rice Burroughs and Robert E. Howard so it's no wonder her first love is fantasy, followed closely by science fiction.

She always believed she was meant to be a writer of short stories, however her stories tended to be rather long. They also tended to have a romantic thread running through them. Finally caving in to the inevitable, she embraced her genre and began writing novels of fantasy/science fiction adventure with a dash of romance thrown into the mix. She has never regretted it.

Today she writes a variety of prose: non-fiction, flash fiction, short stories, and novels – in a variety of genres: humour, horror, contemporary, romance, science fiction, and fantasy. She's also a prolific poet.

Visit Carol on her blog at: http://www.randomwriterlythoughts.blogspot.com She can also be found as Carol R. Ward on Facebook and Carol R. Ward on Twitter.

Other books by the author

The Moonstone Chronicles

Magical Misfire

Lucky Dog

Ardraci Elementals

An Elemental Wind

An Elemental Fire

An Elemental Water

An Elemental Earth

www.ingramcontent.com/pod-product-compliance
Lightning Source LLC
Chambersburg PA
CBHW031052260626
47172CB00001B/31